8 Pm

THE LAST GIRL

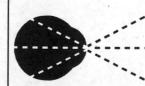

This Large Print Book carries the
Seal of Approval of N.A.V.H.

THE LAST GIRL

JANE CASEY

THORNDIKE PRESS
A part of Gale, Cengage Learning

GALE
CENGAGE Learning·

Detroit • New York • San Francisco • New Haven, Conn • Waterville, Maine • London

GALE
CENGAGE Learning®

LIBRARY OF CONGRESS CATALOGING-IN-PUBLICATION DATA

Casey, Jane (Jane E.)
   The last girl / by Jane Casey. — Large print edition.
      pages ; cm. — (Thorndike Press large print crime scene)
   ISBN-13: 978-1-4104-6109-4 (hardcover)
   ISBN-10: 1-4104-6109-2 (hardcover)
   1. Dysfunctional families—Fiction. 2. Family secrets—Fiction. 3. Murder—Investigation—Fiction. 4. London (England)—Fiction. 5. Large type books.
I. Title.
PR6103.A847L37 2013b
823'.92—dc23   2013016235

Published in 2013 by arrangement with St. Martin's Press, LLC.

Printed in the United States of America
1 2 3 4 5 6 7 17 16 15 14 13\

For Áine Holland

ACKNOWLEDGMENTS

This book is the product of much hard work by many talented people. I owe thanks to them all, but particularly the fiction team at Ebury: my editor Gillian Green, Caroline Newbury, Hannah Robinson, Louise Jones, Jake Lingwood, Fiona MacIntyre, Susan Pegg, Hannah Grogan and Martin Higgins, and everyone in the sales department. They are very dedicated and it's lovely to work with them. I am also indebted to Justine Taylor for her painstaking copyediting.

I am incredibly lucky that Simon Trewin is my literary agent and that he has such a wonderful assistant, Ariella Feiner. They are a great team, infinitely supportive and understanding. Just as important, they have a good line in jokes. I am also very grateful to their colleagues at United Agents, particularly Jessica Craig and Zoe Ross.

The Last Girl would never have been finished without the help and encouragement of my family, especially Frank and Alison Casey and

Kerry Holland. Philippa and Simon Charles, and Michael and Bridget Norman, provided unstinting hospitality for many weeks while I was writing. I am also very grateful to my extended family and friends for their help and enthusiasm; it makes all the difference.

Since one of the main characters in *The Last Girl* is a criminal barrister, part of the book is set in his chambers. I must emphasize that all of the characters are complete inventions, as is Three Unicorn Court, though the Temple certainly exists.

I find one of the hardest things about writing a novel is to think up characters' names. I am very pleased to have been allowed to borrow Caitriona Bennett's name for a key character in this book. I am also grateful to Áine Holland — to whom the book is dedicated — for the use of her first name as Maeve's middle name. I think it suits her.

Finally, I must thank Edward, Patrick and James for their very important contributions to the writing process — Edward for entertaining me, Patrick for turning up at the right moment, and James, as ever, for everything.

PROLOGUE

She'd been swimming for almost an hour. Her legs felt weak, her arms heavy every time she lifted them out of the water into the night air that still shivered with the heat of the day. She moved like a windup toy, mindlessly. Up and down. Up and down. Nothing could make her stop. Nothing could break her concentration. She was the water; she was made of water. She was not Lydia. She was gone.

Halfway through the next length something went wrong with her breathing; she inhaled water and stopped swimming, treading water while she coughed. It wasn't a big pool. It took just a few halfhearted strokes to reach the shallow end. She dragged herself up to the wall and leaned her elbows on the side, holding her head. She coughed again, feeling terrible. After a minute she risked a look around and saw that she was alone.

Fatigue hit her like a truck then. She had done too much. It had seemed important, though, not to give in. It had seemed like the sort of thing her father would appreciate. He'd nodded at her when she had climbed into the water. She'd been shivering although the pool was warm, slipping in quickly in case he mocked her for being a baby. He'd done his lengths, his arms crashing through the surface of the pool, his legs stirring up chaos behind him. For a man so lean he displaced a huge amount of water, as if it was only when he was submerged you could see the energy he threw off. She had kept to the side of the pool, barely causing a ripple herself, struggling to cope with the waves he created that splashed in her face. And when he'd pulled himself out, shaking off water like a dog, he hadn't spoken. He'd sat on the bench under the trees smoking an illicit cigarette, wrapped in a toweling robe, Mollie beside him with her head on her paws. Lydia hadn't known if he was watching her and hadn't cared to check. She just assumed he was. She had been busy, anyway. She had been count-ing. A hundred lengths, first, and then fifty more, and then ten more, and ten more, and three more after that. Two hundred was the target but she hadn't made it. She had failed.

In the lights that shone under the water, Lydia's skin looked dead. She stared at her wrinkled fingertips, at her bluish-white thighs that were foreshortened by the water, at the swell of her stomach under her long-sleeved

T-shirt, rounded and soft, quivering as she struggled to catch her breath. Disgusting.

She waded over to the steps, pulling herself up by the handrail. The water felt as if it was clinging to her, reluctant to let her go. She felt bowed down by tiredness, by the impossible weight of gravity. She had left a towel on the arm of a chair and wrapped it around her, shivering at the touch of the soft fabric where it met her skin. Leaving a trail of wet footprints across the stone patio, she opened the back door, turning the handle slowly and silently. The rule — her mother's rule — was that you showered and dried off outside in the pool house so that no one would track water through the kitchen and drip on the immaculate ivory carpets in the rest of the house. Lydia paused on the threshold, listening, staring into the dark room with wide eyes. She had no intention of taking off her swimming costume in the pool house, of being any more naked than she had to be on the long walk to the privacy of her bedroom.

Satisfied that she was alone, she padded through the kitchen, the marble floor cold against her feet. In the hall she moved more quickly, on tiptoe. The carpet felt wet already, she thought. Her father had probably done the same thing. He didn't have a lot of time for her mother's rules.

The sitting-room doors were almost closed, a thin strip of light striking across the hall.

Lydia hesitated before she passed through it, afraid that moving quickly would draw attention. Going slowly was too risky. There wasn't a sound from inside the room, but she knew her mother was there; she could feel the weight of her presence. It was safest not to look as she passed, not to try to see inside, but Lydia couldn't help a quick glance, glimpsing red. She was halfway up the stairs before it occurred to her to wonder what she had seen. What could possibly be so bright? The sitting room was white and black, icy perfection, and her mother only wore neutral colors. Laura, maybe.

Arrested by the thought of her sister, Lydia turned, her tiredness lifting slightly. She could just *look*.

She was as quick and graceful as a deer as she bounded back down the wide steps, as she padded to the door and put a hand on it to push it open a little further, holding her breath. No one could have heard her. No one would even know she was there.

Just a quick look.

They should have heard her when she started to scream, but no one in that room was capable of hearing anymore. No one in that room would ever hear anything again.

CHAPTER ONE

"The only thing I know about Wimbledon is the tennis." Derwent drummed his fingers on the steering wheel.

I stared at the map. "What do you need to know? It's an expensive place to live. Smart. Out of your price range. Not the sort of place we usually fetch up. Still two miles away at a rough estimate, and God knows how long that's going to take."

"Lights are changing, Kerrigan. I'm going to go on straight."

"No, don't do that." Straight ahead of us was a queue of cars that stretched to infinity, or at least the A3. I turned the map around, desperately searching for the right road. "Left. Turn left."

"I'm in the wrong lane." The car surged forward, going straight into the one-way system from hell. "Should have decided sooner."

"I don't know why you sound so smug. We're both going to be stuck in the same traffic."

"Yeah, but it's your fault. So I can enjoy myself by blaming you."

"It's not my fault that you broke your sat-nav." The ice in my voice did nothing to cool the temperature in the car; I could feel sweat trickling down my back and shifted in my seat. The windows were down but the air was stagnant, hot even though the sun had set hours earlier. August in London, and the weather was at its worst. "Since we're stationary, do you mind putting the air-conditioning on?"

"Waste of petrol. Someone's got to think of the environment." He stuck his head out of his window and sniffed enthusiastically. "Fresh air is better for you."

A hundred exhausts belched fumes in front of us. "This air is not fresh."

"Nor are my socks," Derwent admitted, sticking a finger down the side of his shoe and proving his point with a waft of sweaty-foot smell. My nose wrinkled and I turned my face away, not caring that he found it funny.

"Why is there so much traffic at this time of night anyway?"

"Need you ask? Roadworks. It goes down to one lane from three. We should never have come this way." Derwent inched forward although the car in front hadn't moved. "Almost midnight. What were you planning

14

to do this evening?"

I had hoped for an early night, but I knew better than to say anything that hinted at bed. The DI was as quick to go after innuendo as a terrier barreling down a rat hole. "Nothing much. You?"

"Nothing you want to hear about, I imagine." A sidelong glance. "Your loss."

"I doubt that." I knew very little of his private life, but that was precisely as much as I wanted to know about it. I just wished he felt the same way about me.

"What about your boyfriend?"

"What about him?"

"Is he at home?"

"He's working." *And that's all I'm saying, so move on.*

"You're probably pleased to have something to do. Gets you out of the house, doesn't it?"

Thank God. Work talk. "It sounds like an interesting case."

"It sounds like a domestic." Derwent rubbed a hand over the back of his neck and looked at it, then wiped it down his trouser leg. "I'm sweating like a pedo in a playground."

He was reliably, casually offensive, but every now and then he still managed to shock me. I had decided that he was an acquired taste, and that I could get to like him some day. Today was not that day.

"Look, if you don't take the next left we're

15

going to be here until midnight."

"It's one-way." He was leaning forward to see, hugging the steering wheel. I peered in the same direction, seeing the no-entry signs.

"Oh, bollocks."

"I could blue light it."

"Not a good idea," I said automatically. There were strict rules governing when we could travel on blues and twos. Getting to work was not an emergency.

Derwent looked at me sideways. His hair was ruffled and he'd caught the sun across the bridge of his nose. He looked all of eight years old. "Please?"

"Why are you asking me? You're the senior officer."

"That's right. I am." He sounded pleased at the reminder. "Well, off we go. Hit it, Kerrigan."

The siren hadn't finished its first whoop before Derwent had pulled out of our line of traffic, making for our illegal turn. We had two wheels on the pavement most of the way. I closed my eyes and muttered, more or less involuntarily, "Jesus, Mary and Joseph."

"Talk holy to me, Kerrigan. You know I love it when you pray."

"Just concentrate on what you're doing, okay?" The streets weren't empty enough for rally driving. Because of the weather, people were still out walking their dogs or jogging, in spite of how late it was. They really weren't

16

expecting to be confronted with an unmarked car bearing down on them from the wrong direction, even if we did have our blue lights flashing.

We were, however, making progress, and as Derwent pulled out onto the main road — causing a bus to slam on its brakes — he gave me a wide grin. "That's better, isn't it?"

"Better than sitting in a traffic jam," I allowed.

He shook his head. "You just can't say it, can you? 'I was wrong. You were right, Josh. I should always listen to you.' "

"You're right. I can't say that. Turn right after these traffic lights."

"Up the hill," Derwent checked.

"That's where we're going."

Up the hill. Up into the rarefied air of Wimbledon Village, the pretty, exclusive little enclave where expensive boutiques, delis, galleries and cafés catered to the tastes of the locals and their apparent desire to spend my annual salary on fripperies and cappuccinos. Up to where the houses were detached, set back from the road, and priced in multiple millions. It was leafy and lavish and a different world from where I lived, even though that was only a few miles away as the crow flew.

Derwent was paying scant attention to the road, leaning into my personal space. He whistled. "Look at that one."

"The house?" It was a white-painted mansion with yew lollipops on either side of the front door.

"The Aston Martin, Kerrigan. I couldn't give a fuck about the house."

"Think that's a footballer's gaff?"

"Could be. Someone with a few hundred grand to spend on one of their cars. I saw it on *Top Gear*. Beautiful, isn't it?" He had slowed to a crawl and was creeping along, hugging the curb as he stared at the car. A BMW overtook us with a blast from its horn and Derwent raised a hand to acknowledge it, hopelessly distracted.

"They'll call the police if you're not careful. Stop drooling."

"That car or a night with Angelina Jolie. I'm not even joking, I wouldn't stop to think about it."

"I wouldn't worry. You're not likely to have to choose any time soon."

"Angelina would understand," he said with conviction. "She'd appreciate it. She'd feel the same way." He flicked a look at me. "You don't get it, do you? It's just a car to you."

"It's a means of getting from A to B. It may not be quite as beautiful, but so is the one that we're sitting in currently. And I would like to get to B before the SOCOs and the boss have packed up and headed home."

"Ooh, the boss. Why didn't you say? We'd better hurry." Derwent took off with a wheel spin that left six feet of rubber on the road.

I ignored the sarcasm and the stunt driving and said nothing else except to direct him through the narrow tree-lined roads until we reached the white wooden barrier that cut off Endsleigh Drive from its neighbors.

"Cul-de-sac with no vehicular access except for residents. So whoever did it had to walk there."

"Unless it was one of the residents."

Derwent frowned. "Bit extreme for a neighborly dispute." He held his ID out of the window so the policeman guarding the barrier could see who we were.

"Six houses, all with gates. High hedges." I could only see the roofs of most of the houses. "No one will have seen anything. But they might have heard something. This place must be quiet usually."

"Not now."

"Nope." We drove through the barrier, past the group of spectators hanging around in shorts and T-shirts with the familiar mixture of shock and excitement on their faces. They stared into the car curiously and I stared back, making eye contact with a middle-aged man wearing an expensive watch and a dingy polo shirt, and a younger one whose face was half-hidden by a baseball cap. A couple of seconds and we had gone past them, and the patrol cars with their lights whirling, and the vans for the SOCOs' equipment, and the first

19

outriders of the media pack. I'd have been shocked if they hadn't been there — they made it to most crime scenes long before I did, no matter how quickly I responded, and this was the sort of case that would appeal to them. The very minor thrill of appearing on the television news had long since worn off for me, although it was the one thing that consoled my mother about my career choice. I ran a hand through my hair, despising myself for preening but aware that the heat and humidity had made the usual bad situation worse. I could just hear the message Mum would leave. *Did you ever think of brushing your hair before you left the house, Maeve? Surely you'd have had time to run a comb through it . . .*

Both sides of the road were fully parked up but Derwent refused to drive out again.

"It's not far. And you run marathons, so you can't be that lazy."

"I don't mind the walk. I mind people not knowing I'm a big-shot police inspector." He settled for blocking in a car that I recognized as belonging to the pathologist, Dr. Hanshaw.

"Glen's not going to be pleased."

"Glen is going to be here for a while. And I'm not exactly scared of him anyway." Derwent got out and stretched, revealing a damp patch that took up most of the back of his shirt so the material clung to his really quite impressive muscles. I plucked my top away from my skin, knowing that it would be translucent where it had been pressed against me. The heat was like a coat wrapped around me. I pulled a face, then bent down to look for the water bottle I'd stashed at my feet. It was too light when I picked it up. Empty, but for a few drops at the bottom.

I was still looking at it when Derwent leaned down. "Are you getting out or what?"

"Did you drink my water?"

"What?"

"I had half a bottle of water here. Did you drink it?"

"You must be hallucinating, Kerrigan. You finished it yourself."

"Bullshit."

"Really. I watched you."

I knew he was lying but I still hesitated, doubting my memory for a moment. He sounded so sure of himself — which was usually a dead giveaway that he wasn't telling the truth. As if to confirm it, his face twisted into a grin, at my expense.

"Come on. Time to go."

There had been a time when I was scared of Derwent, and I still wouldn't argue with him, but not because he intimidated me. He was a senior officer and I would never win. Plus, he liked it too much. I threw the bottle into the back of the car with extreme bad temper and slammed the car door as hard as

I could. Derwent led the way up the path, past two PCs who were suffering in their body armor. The stab vests were miserably uncomfortable in the heat, I recalled with sympathy, glad that I only had an equipment belt, and that was slung over my shoulder. It was one of the perks of being in CID. The fact that I didn't usually go out on arrest raids or anything that was expected to be violent meant that I hadn't had to wear body armor for a very long time. It was especially hard on the uniforms when there was almost no chance they would need the vests. Whatever violence had been done at number 4 Endsleigh Drive, the danger had been over for hours.

We stopped inside the canvas screens in front of the front door, shedding shoes and pulling on paper suits to avoid contaminating the crime scene. An extra layer was exactly what I didn't need and I wriggled crossly, already stifling.

"What do we know about the victims?"

"Mother and daughter. Vita and Laura Kennford. Mum's forty-nine, Laura's fifteen." Derwent recited the details from memory, without hesitation. He was a far better police officer than casual acquaintance with him might have suggested. The bluff misogyny was a large and unfortunate part of his personality, but he was also razor sharp and totally dedicated to his job.

"And they were stabbed?"

"You know as much as I do about that." He looked at me shrewdly. "You're not trying to spin this out, are you? Trying to find a reason to stay out here until the bodies are gone and the place has been tidied up?"

"Of course not. Why would I do that?"

"Because you don't trust yourself."

He wasn't completely wrong, which made it all the more annoying that he'd spotted what I was doing. I was getting used to dead bodies — I had seen enough of them since I'd started working on Godley's team — but I still couldn't quite take them in my stride. It wasn't the blood or the spilling intestines, the splattered brain matter or the smell of decay, though all of those things had the potential to turn more experienced officers than me pea-green. It was the violence that made me stop in my tracks. The desire to destroy another human being, the will to carry it through, the ruthlessness or thought-lessness we encountered every day. The waste. And all we could do was sling the kill-ers in prison, if we caught them. I'd never been a fan of the death penalty, but murdered children made me think depriving someone of their liberty was a pretty pathetic punish-ment.

Meanwhile, Derwent was waiting for an answer. I squared my shoulders. "I know you like to think of me as a shrinking violet, boss, but I'm just not."

"You're hard as nails, Kerrigan. We know that." He took my arm and steered me out of the tent and up to the front door. "Come on. Feel the fear and do it anyway."

Inside the house, I looked past the usual organized chaos of crime-scene technicians and police officers coming and going, searching for signs of what had taken place there. The hall was huge, double-height, with a very modern chandelier suspended in the middle — lozenges of textured glass stuck together at haphazard angles. Wide stairs swept up to an open gallery with rooms leading off it, but all the doors were closed. Bedrooms, I presumed, and bathrooms. Nothing to see from where I stood, anyway. There was no furniture in the hall at all, just a set of double doors on either side and a glass door at the back. The only color came from a tapestry that hung on the wall by the stairs, six feet by ten at a guess, and fiercely abstract in tones of gray and orange.

It was the only color, that is, apart from the red tracks that marked the cream carpet. Blood, still harshly bright in the glare from the chandelier, not yet darkened to brown. Fresh. There was a story there, a narrative that some specialist would unravel, but I couldn't help trying to fathom it. Footsteps coming from the right-hand side of the hall, fading as they got closer to the door at the back, spreading and blurring where water had mingled with blood. Coming back toward the front door, much fainter now. And then a set of smudges on the stairs, where someone or some people had run up two or three at a time, moving fast. A forensics officer was crouching five steps from the top, minutely examining something and then sealing it in a paper envelope. Her concentration was total as she peeled a sheet of sticky film off the carpet. Trace evidence. There'd be a lot of it.

Through the doors on the right I could hear the murmur of conversation and the crack of camera flashes. Derwent made a move toward them but stopped dead when someone said his name. We both turned to see Superintendent Godley coming through the doors on the other side of the hall, looking grim. He had had his silver hair cut since the last time I'd seen him, and a thin line of paler skin traced his hairline. He had just been on holidays, sailing in Croatia, and his tan made his teeth very white and his eyes extra blue. At that moment he was very far from smiling and his eyes were narrow with disapproval.

"You took your time."

"The traffic was terrible. We got here as soon as we could," I explained, cringing a little in spite of myself.

Derwent shrugged. "We're here now. What's going on?"

"Have you ever come across Philip Kennford?" Godley was speaking in a low voice.

"As in the barrister? The QC? That Kennford?"

"Got it in one."

Derwent whistled. "This is his house? Fuck me, there's money in getting criminals off the hook, isn't there?"

"Who is he?"

The inspector turned to look at me, unimpressed. "Don't tell me you've never come up against him, Kerrigan."

"I haven't been doing this for very long," I reminded him. "Only a few of my murders have gone to trial yet."

"But you must have heard of him."

"Vaguely," I said.

"Do you 'vaguely' recall the Catford strangler? That freak who was raping and murdering women in their own homes? He did for eight of them before he got arrested."

I ignored the fact that Derwent had dialed the sarcasm up to eleven. This one I did actually know. "Because his son got done for aggravated assault and the DNA showed he was related to the killer."

"Yeah, they'd got DNA from inside one of the victims and it was a near match to the son — close relation — so it was only a matter of going through the family and finding the guilty party. They only got DNA off one body, and only a trace of it at that because he used condoms most of the time — just

26

couldn't resist dipping into the last one he killed bareback, or he decided it was worth the risk. Maybe he thought he was in the clear because no one had ever come knocking on his door. Peter Harbold his name was, an accountant by profession, a pillar of the community — no one you'd ever have suspected. Twisted bastard, as we found out."

"Keep your voice down," Godley warned, glancing behind him. "Kennford's in there."

"I don't care if he hears what I think of his client," Derwent snapped. "I don't care if he hears what I think of the defense that got him off."

"He got off?" I hadn't remembered that.

"He did indeed. The DNA sample wasn't collected properly, according to Kennford. He found an expert to say it could have deteriorated before it was analyzed so it couldn't be relied upon. And Harbold had been very careful about covering his tracks so everything else was circumstantial. No confession, no difficulty in handling cross-examination, no criminal record. The jury wouldn't convict, even after a majority direction. Split down the middle. Cretins on one side, decent people on the other. The prosecution wanted a retrial but the judge said no go. No chance of winning unless there was new evidence, and there wasn't."

"Are you that sure they were wrong?" I asked, genuinely curious. I knew that Derwent didn't have a lot of time for the jury system but he sounded particularly vehement.

"I knew the officer in the case. Mate of mine. He wasn't in any doubt about it. Couldn't shake Harbold in interview. The guy had an answer for everything. He was prepared, my mate said. Just too smooth to be right."

I nodded. I had done interviews like that too. Innocent people got flustered. They tended to ramble, to answer at great length, trying to be as helpful as they could. Innocent people were nervous, generally. It was the guilty ones who took it in their stride.

"You can't blame Kennford for doing his job," Godley said. "And in this case, he's a victim."

"Or a suspect."

"If you like, Josh. But you should probably speak to him before you make up your mind about that."

"Fair enough. Let's have a crack at him."

"Crime scenes first." Godley led us across the hall. "I want you to get a look at them so you know what to ask."

"Scenes? So they weren't killed in the same place?" I asked.

"No, Vita and Laura died in here." Godley pushed open the door. "But they weren't the only ones who were attacked."

I wasn't really paying attention to the

superintendent anymore. I was fully occupied by scanning the room, seeing the before and after, order and disorder, life and death. The pristine chill that I'd noticed in the hall was here again, the pale colors and lack of ornament, except for the art on the walls. It was a large room and minimally furnished — a couple of designer chairs that looked more like sculpture than seats, black lacquered tables on either side of the fireplace, chrome and glass lamps. Modern, expensive, to my eye overdesigned — and now disturbed. Two huge rectangular sofas faced one another at right angles to the fireplace, but one of them was pushed out of alignment and its cushions were scattered over the floor. A body lay in front of it, on carpet that was saturated with blood. She was on her back, her head tilted to stare blindly at the fireplace, which was itself painted with arterial spray. One leg was thrown negligently onto the sofa so her legs were splayed, but her clothes didn't look as if they had been disturbed. She was lying as she had fallen, as if maybe she had been curled up on the sofa and had toppled off during the attack. The angle of her head was so extreme that I couldn't see her face, but from the skinny jeans and camisole top, I thought it was the younger victim. Laura. Laura, who had evidently had her throat cut, right down to the bone. Laura, whose killer had only just stopped short of decapitating her. Laura, whose hair was matted with blood, whose clothes were soaked, who had died horribly. Laura, who had been fifteen. I swallowed and looked away, searching for the other victim.

She was at the other end of the room, at the center of chaos. Vita had made it further than her daughter, probably trying to escape through the French windows that led to the garden. The curtain pole had come down on one side, the heavy silk material pooling under the body. I walked toward her, leaning to see. I had only spotted one injury on Laura's body but Vita's was a different story: multiple slashes and stab wounds that Dr. Hanshaw was busy annotating. As far as I could judge, Vita had been slim with bobbed fair hair. Her trousers and top had once been pure white, linen and silk respectively. One of her shoes lay on its side by my feet and I bent over to look at it. A caramel-colored suede loafer with a gold snaffle. Somehow I wasn't surprised to see it was made by Gucci.

"Blood." Derwent's nose was wrinkled. "Like a butcher's shop."

I had been trying to ignore the smell, breathing shallowly through my mouth. It was exceptionally strong, and somehow worse for being fresh. The room was saturated. There was a trail leading from Laura's body to where Vita lay, in scattered droplets and in small pools. A table lay on its side, the lamp that had been on it shining an oval at the opposite wall where a constellation of blood spatter gleamed. The base of the lamp had broken and porcelain shards littered the floor. Vita had fought hard for her life, and lost.

Derwent had wandered off and was now prowling around the room, whistling tunelessly and inspecting the fittings, generally acting as if he was there to look at the house with a view to buying it. Godley beckoned to Hanshaw and Kev Cox, one of our regular crime scene managers. "Talk us through what happened. Josh, come here. I want you to listen to this too."

I had to hide a smile at Derwent being called to heel like a badly behaved dog. I didn't hide it quickly enough.

"Why don't you ask Kerrigan what she thinks?" There was a glint in Derwent's eye as he strolled back toward us. "See what she makes of it."

"I'm not sure that's fair." Godley's voice was mild.

"What do they call it — a teachable moment? This is a chance to show Kerrigan what she doesn't know, isn't it? And Kev and Glen here can show her how important it is that she listens to them rather than jumping to her own conclusions."

"I may not be very experienced, but I know better than to ignore expert opinion." I turned to Godley. "Look, I don't want to waste anyone's time —"

"I don't mind." Kev was one of the sweet-est people I'd ever met. Of course he didn't mind. Hanshaw, on the other hand . . .

"If you want to test your DC's analytical skills, feel free." The pathologist folded his arms. "This should be good."

And suddenly, they were all looking at me. I swallowed, fighting panic. I was still dry-mouthed from dehydration and my head throbbed, a tension headache that was only getting worse. I made myself concentrate. *Show no fear.* "Okay. I should point out I've only just come in, and I haven't looked at the bodies closely."

"Understood." Godley had an encouraging expression on his face. I didn't dare look at Derwent.

"Well, what happened in here was quick. Neither of the victims had time to leave the room, and there are two exits so they had their choice of escape routes. That could mean there were two killers, but I'm not sure it's beyond one person to have done this."

"Who was first?" Godley asked.

"Laura. She didn't have time to get up off the sofa before she was attacked. I think the killer stood behind her to cut her throat." I looked over at the sofa, thinking. "Vita was standing up behind the other sofa when Laura was attacked."

"How do you work that out?" Derwent's

tone was seriously skeptical.

"She ran toward her daughter. That chair is knocked forward — it would have been in her way. If it had been the killer who knocked it over when he was going to attack Vita, it would have been lying on its back." I walked forward to stand at Laura's feet. "Vita stood here and fought with the killer. She must have been aware that Laura was beyond help once she got close enough to see the damage that had been done to her. She would have known her life was in danger too. There's blood here that's cast off from the knife. That suggests multiple movements with a bloody blade, but it looks to me as if Laura was dealt with in a single cut. And whatever he used, it must have been very sharp."

"Two slashes, in fact," Hanshaw said. "But you're right, the cutting edge was extremely sharp, and both strokes were decisive."

"Vita ran when she could get away from the killer. She lost one shoe here, the other over by the window. She must have been quite badly injured at this point because she was losing a lot of blood and I'm guessing she held on to the curtains for support." I considered it again. "Or maybe she was trying to hold them in front of her to block the blade."

"There are slashes in the material." Kev was nodding happily.

"Those doors must be locked or she'd have

got through them. I bet Philip Kennford is obsessive about home security — he knows too much about criminals not to be. There's a keypad for an alarm system in the hall by the door, and the gate at the bottom of the drive is an electric one with an intercom. I'd say the key for those doors is kept somewhere inaccessible, and they're never left unlocked." I turned to Kev. "Was there any damage to the front door? Or any other windows or doors?"

"No signs of a break-in. The back door into the kitchen was open, but the other daughter was out in the garden, swimming. She'd have seen anyone who used that door."

"The other daughter?" Derwent asked.

"Laura's twin," Godley explained. "Her name's Lydia."

"What was she doing swimming in the middle of the night?"

"You can ask her." Godley changed his mind as he said it. "Actually, no, you can't. She's in no state to be confronted by someone like you."

"I don't know what you mean." Derwent was grinning. He positively reveled in his reputation. He'd certainly earned it.

"Well, if there wasn't a break-in that just leaves two possibilities, doesn't it?" I said. "Either the killer was let into the house —"

"Or he was here already," Derwent finished for me.

"That's all I've got." I looked at Godley. "What did I miss?"

"What happened before the killer attacked them. And what happened afterward."

"I haven't been around the rest of the house yet."

"I know. I'm not asking you to guess." He raised his eyebrows at the others. "How did she do?"

"Very well. For a police officer." Hanshaw was always more vinegar than honey. Kev was nodding too, though, and Godley smiled at me. I felt a warm glow that had nothing to do with the weather. At least I did until I caught Derwent's eye and was reminded that the inspector didn't like junior officers to be too clever. I quelled my instinct to look modest and gave him the same look back, my best attempt at cold steel. *So you thought you'd found a way to embarrass me, did you? Too bad I'm sharper than you thought I was. Next time, try harder. Or better yet, don't try at all.*

Godley got back to business. "Right. Give us the details, Glen. What did the killer use?"

"The blade was large. Something like a machete or a professional kitchen knife. Not serrated. All Vita's injuries are consistent with cutting, so the killer didn't get too close to her and I don't have much hope for DNA traces under her nails. She has defense wounds to both hands and wrists — severed

35

tendons in a couple of places. Three or four of her injuries would have been enough to do for her and I don't yet know which was the decisive one. She bled out into her chest cavity, which is why she had time to fight before she died."

"Who are we looking for?"

"The killer wasn't playing about. You're looking for someone strong and probably tall. Right-handed. Violent, as you might have noticed yourselves. The first victim's throat is cut to the spine. I don't see that very often. But there's no sexual component, unless you think the killer has a thing for cutting. He or she treated both of them differently, which may be significant, but then again it may not. Victim one was despatched efficiently and quickly. Victim two fought, which may account for her more numerous injuries."

"Or the killer might have wanted to take his time with Vita. Anything else?"

"Not until after the PMs. I'll do them tomorrow morning, first thing."

"I'll be there." Godley always tried to attend the postmortems. I preferred to read the reports afterward. It was much less distracting to read the cold, clinical description of what had happened to the victims than to see their internal organs in full, lurid detail.

"I'm happy for the bodies to be moved now." Hanshaw was already gathering his belongings.

"The lads have finished in here until the bodies come out. Then I'll send them in again, make sure we haven't missed anything underneath either of these poor ladies."

I hadn't realized until Kev said it that the SOCOs had finished up while we'd been talking, slipping out of the room like paper-clad ghosts. He edged toward the door himself.

"If we're done here, I'm just going to check how they're getting on upstairs."

"Good stuff, Kev. Let us know when you're finished." Godley waited until they had left the room and we were alone with the bodies. "So?"

"Laura didn't stand up," I said quietly. "She didn't even know she was in danger. She knew her killer or she wasn't scared."

"You know him," Derwent threw at Godley. "What do you think of Philip Kennford?"

"I think he would make a good suspect. If he didn't have an alibi."

"Which is?"

"The first officers who responded found him lying unconscious in his bedroom — he was out cold. He's the other person who was attacked. If you can work out how he beat himself up, you can put him at the top of the list of suspects." Godley shrugged. "Until then, he's in the clear."

Derwent frowned, thinking. He opened his mouth but whatever he was going to say was destined to remain unsaid, because out in the hall Glen Hanshaw was throwing an epic tantrum.

"Some bastard's blocked me in. Would the person driving the blue Honda please move their fucking car? I'm warning you, you've got five seconds before I ram it out of my way."

"Whoops." The expression on Derwent's face could only have been described as naughty.

Godley raised his eyebrows. "Was that you?"

"There was nowhere else." He sauntered toward the door, pulling his keys out of his pocket. "Better face the music, I suppose. How long have I got left?"

"You're into extra time. I'd hurry if I were you. Glen knows a hundred ways to kill a man without leaving a mark."

"Do I look worried?" Derwent let the door swing closed behind him, but not before I heard him say in an ultra-innocent voice, "Sorry, is there some sort of problem?"

"I've never heard Glen sound like that before." Godley sounded amused.

"I've never even heard him swear."

"Josh does have a talent for bringing out the profane in people."

"That's an understatement."

Godley looked at me quickly. "You don't mind him, do you?"

"I'm used to him. I sort of don't want to be there when he meets Philip Kennford, though. I don't think he's going to be terribly sympathetic."

"That's why I keep him around. I'm hoping he can shake Kennford into telling me the truth. I have a feeling I'm being spun a line and I can't think why." Godley shook his head. "Something about this just doesn't seem right to me."

I looked past him at the teenage girl's body stiffening into its awkward pose. I didn't say it, but it seemed to me patently obvious that there was nothing right about that at all.

CHAPTER TWO

"I'd have thought you'd be too busy to stay." Derwent was standing with his hands in his pockets, a scowl on his face.

"I have time." Godley checked his watch. "Well, enough to speak to Kennford and his daughter."

"I can handle it." The scowl had deepened, if anything. "It's not like you to want the limelight, boss."

I winced in spite of myself. The media presence had trebled, if not quadrupled, since we'd been in the house. I had heard them shouting questions at everyone who came and went. I had been unwise enough to return to the car for my notebook. It was now bathed in bright light from the cameras, and my trip had provided at least thirty seconds of footage for the rolling news programs to use over and over again, for the sake of having something to illustrate the human interest story of the night. It was summer. Nothing much was happening in the rest of the world. A forensic officer arriving after us had told me the Kennford murders were the lead on every bulletin, even though they couldn't know what had happened inside the house. Not when we weren't clear on it ourselves.

"Come off it. Attention from the media is certainly not why I'm still here. I'll be leaving as soon as I can." He checked his watch again. "It's my name on the policy log, Josh. I need to see what direction this investigation is taking before I leave you to it. And besides, I know Kennford."

"Not well."

"To say hello to." Godley sighed. "If it was me, I'd want the SIO to take enough of an interest to meet the survivors. It's the least I can do."

Godley was the senior investigating officer, the man at the top, and he took his role seriously — as Derwent knew very well — no matter how many murder files he was currently handling. I stared at the inspector meaningfully. *Just drop it. It's not going to happen.*

"Let me interview the girl."

"I told you, you aren't the right person for that." Godley leaned against the kitchen door, edging it open. "We'll make it quick."

He held the door open and I darted through it without meeting Derwent's glare; it wasn't my fault and I wasn't going to allow myself to feel guilty. On edge, perhaps . . . There would be retribution. I could count on that.

She was sitting at the kitchen table, a slab of white oak that could have accommodated ten people easily. A female officer was sitting beside her with a box of tissues on her knee. The inevitable cup of tea stood in front of the girl, steam rising from it. It didn't look as if it had been touched. Her hair hung down in front of her face in narrow rats' tails and I recalled that she had been swimming even as I noticed the faint tang of chlorine in the air. She hadn't showered since she'd been in the pool, I thought, but she was dressed, in jeans and a long-sleeved top that hung off her tiny frame. I knew she was fifteen, but she looked no older than twelve.

"Hello, Lydia." Godley pulled out a chair on the other side of the table and sat down. "I'm Superintendent Godley. I'm leading the investigation."

There was no response.

"This is Detective Constable Kerrigan."

I sat down too, lacing my fingers in front of me on the table. I had pinned a pleasant smile to my face, a smile that was completely unnecessary because, despite Godley's best efforts to get her to respond, Lydia didn't so much as look up.

After a few unproductive minutes, Godley turned to the uniformed officer and motioned to her to join us on the other side of the room, out of Lydia's hearing. The officer was in her forties but glamorous with it, made up to the nines and with carefully dyed blonde hair. She wore a wedding ring, and I was willing to bet she was a mother herself and that was how she'd been given the job of minding the girl. "Is she all right?"

"Out of it," she said quietly. "The doctor had to give her something to calm her down. She hasn't said anything since."

Godley nodded. "No point in trying to interview her now, then. Did she say anything to you before she was medicated? Did she notice anything?"

The officer shook her head. "She said not. She was swimming. Had her head underwater. Not surprising she didn't know anything or see anyone."

"It was worth a try. If she had seen something we'd need to know about it." He looked across at her, his lips compressed. "It's frustrating, though. I'd love to know what she thinks about her mother and her sister, and how they died."

"I imagine she's trying not to think about it," I pointed out. There was something about the girl that made me feel she needed someone to stand up for her, to protect her. She was completely still, except for an occasional shudder that passed through her entire body. I couldn't imagine what it must have felt like to find her mother like that, and her sister. I couldn't imagine how she would live with the memory, once the sedatives wore off. She might have been uninjured, but that didn't mean she was unharmed.

"Shame the doctor couldn't hold off a bit longer, though."

It wasn't like Godley to be so hard-edged and I knew the expression of shock on the uniformed officer's face mirrored my own. It was a sign of the stress he was under, but that didn't make it any more pleasant.

"Well, you didn't see her earlier. She was completely hysterical. Screaming." The officer shuddered. "You wouldn't have got any sense out of her. I only just got her to shake her head when I asked if she'd seen or heard anything, and I had to ask about a million times."

Months of practice at Derwent-soothing came to my assistance. "It doesn't matter. We'll talk to her again. Besides, we've still got Philip Kennford to interview."

Godley laughed without humor. "I hope you're not pinning your hopes on that."

"He'll want to help us, won't he?"

"I wouldn't count on it." Godley looked down at me but I had a feeling he wasn't seeing me. "There are people who find lying as natural as breathing."

"And Philip Kennford is one of them," I said.

"Philip Kennford is the biggest liar of them all."

■ ■ ■ ■

Philip Kennford looked remarkably composed for a man who had recently lost his
wife and daughter and who was still dealing
with the aftereffects of being knocked unconscious. He had been waiting for us to get
around to interviewing him for a couple of
hours, but he didn't seem to be irritated by
the delay. The bandage on his forehead
couldn't spoil the patrician elegance of his
looks: a strong nose, piercing blue eyes and
thick gray-and-black hair that he wore slightly
longer than I expected, curling over his collar. A square jaw offset the full mouth,
undercutting any suggestion of weakness. He
was look-twice handsome, I thought, and
seemed younger than his forty-five years. At
one time he would have been seriously
athletic, and he still evidently kept himself in
shape. His polo shirt and jeans were pristine,
although his feet were bare. I wondered if it
was habit or a sign of being more distressed
than he at first appeared.

He sat in a wing-backed leather armchair
that was easily the most traditional thing I'd
seen in his house so far, leaning into it as if
he was too exhausted to think about standing. He had crossed his legs and the upper
foot swung like a pendulum in an unhurried
rhythm. One hand held a cigarette that sent a

thin blue plume of smoke into the already stuffy study, while the other rested on the head of a black-and-white dog, a collie. It was leaning against him and didn't move from its post as we trooped in and arranged ourselves in a semicircle in front of him. The dog craned its head to look at us, showing a good deal of white around its eye as it did so. I liked dogs but collies tended toward the unpredictable, which was another way of saying most of them were borderline psychotic, and I would no more have attempted to pat its head than I would have put my hand in a fire.

While Godley was doing polite preamble and introductions, I took the opportunity to stare around the room. It looked to me as if it was meant for a different house altogether, one that was closer to the traditional English country estate than the twenty-first-century minimalist chic we'd seen up until then. The walls were lined with books, mostly leather-bound hardbacks, and a giant mahogany desk dominated the space. Over the fireplace hung a deeply sentimental Victorian oil painting depicting a ragged boy in the hands of two uniformed policemen while his mother sobbed in the background. The bread he had stolen lay on the ground in front of him, while a meager cottage behind the little group suggested extreme poverty. It was called *Taken in Charge,* I saw, leaning in to read the little gold nameplate, and I seriously doubted the same person would have liked this and the acid-bright geometric abstraction of tapestry that hung in the hall. This was Kennford's territory. His wife had been allowed to do what she liked up to the door of his study; after that it was his taste that mattered.

"That looks painful." Godley was standing closer to Kennford than me and had bent down to look at his feet. Craning to see what he had noticed, I realized there was an untidy collection of cuts on the soles of Kennford's feet. His skin looked reddish and bruised around the cuts. All at once the lack of footwear made sense.

"They're unlikely to be fatal. There was glass on the floor of my bedroom and I didn't realize in time." Kennford's voice was mellow and deep, but to my surprise he didn't have the public-school vowels that were usual at the top end of the bar. He had a fine Yorkshire accent, and I warmed to him immediately for no good reason except that I liked the sound of it and I respected anyone who hadn't lost the accent they were brought up with.

"Bad luck," Derwent said.

"Not the worst I've had lately." He smiled very slightly to take the sting out of the words. "I can prove how it happened, if you're concerned. The paramedics were there when I did it. I got to my feet and staggered through it before they could stop me. They can be my witnesses."

"To be honest, you'd have to have pretty bad aim to cut your foot while you were slashing your daughter's throat and stabbing your wife to death."

Godley and I swung round as one to glare at Derwent. Kennford raised one eyebrow but otherwise didn't react at all.

"Mr. Kennford, we wanted to interview you now but we'll try not to keep you for very long." The superintendent was sounding very solicitous, trying to make up for his inspector's tact-free remark. "I'm sorry we can't give you more time to yourself, but you know better than anyone how important it is to get the ball rolling with a murder investigation."

"Of course. You must ask me anything you need to know, though I'm not sure I can be of much assistance." He frowned a little, stubbing out his cigarette in an ashtray that was already getting full. "I would ask you to make yourselves comfortable, but I'm afraid I don't have enough chairs for all of you. I don't usually have visitors in here."

A matching armchair stood on the other side of the fireplace but Kennford's was the only one that looked as if it got any regular use.

"We don't mind standing," Godley said, just as Derwent made a move toward the other armchair. A rising growl came from the dog's direction. That or the note of warning in the superintendent's voice was enough to make him stop short. He made a big show of leaning forward to read the spines of the nearest books, as if that had been his intention all along. It wasn't what you could call a convincing performance.

"The obvious question is the first one to ask. Do you have any enemies, Mr. Kennford? Ever received any death threats?"

"Yes." He let the word stand for a moment before he gave a wry smile. "But none of my enemies would go to these lengths."

"We're still going to need names, Mr. Kennford."

"I'll draw up a list. Not now. I'll need to check contact details and so forth, so I'll do it tomorrow in chambers." He shifted in his chair. "I'm not trying to tell you your business but you'll be wasting your time following them up. They're not murderous, most of them. And certainly none would target Vita and Laura if they had the chance to deal with me."

"You were attacked," Derwent pointed out.

"Not seriously. A knock on the head." He gestured to the back of his skull, to what I assumed was a bruise, but the damage was invisible because of his thick hair. "I'd just come out of the shower and I was toweling myself off. So much for natural instincts — I had no idea anyone was in my room. Then,

49

whack. Something hit me and I fell forward. The last thing I remember is the realization that I was going to hit the mirror. And I did."

"Which is where you got the injury on your forehead."

"Indeed. When I woke up, I was staring into the eyes of a very pretty paramedic named Aileen while lying stark naked in a pool of my own blood and a whole lot of glass."

It struck me as odd that he could comment on the paramedic's looks while his wife's body was being loaded into a mortuary van outside, but then maybe he hadn't understood what the noises from the hall meant. Then again, maybe he was just that sort of man.

"Did you hear anything strange before that?" Godley asked.

"Nothing. But I was in the shower."

"The dog didn't bark?" It was the kind of dog that went into paroxysms of rage at its own shadow. I couldn't believe it would have sat in silence while members of its family were murdered.

"If she did, I didn't hear her." He looked down at her silky head, pulling an ear. "She's not a guard dog, you know. She's a pet."

"Collies aren't generally placid."

"I didn't say she was." I caught a glint of steel in the last answer, the edge that made him a top brief. Another smile to rob the words of offense. "She hasn't read any Conan

Doyle. She didn't know it would be suspicious if she didn't bark."

"What did you do before your shower? It might help if you could talk us through your evening."

"I had dinner with Vita — salad and cold salmon. Neither of us was hungry, probably because of the heat. Vita had a glass of wine but I had water because I needed to do some work and I wanted a clear head. The girls were doing their own thing — they rarely eat with us. After that I went out for a swim. Lydia came out later and swam lengths for a while. That's where she was when it happened, I suppose. I came in from the garden at about nine and she was still in the water. I'd stayed outside for a bit after swimming, enjoying the night air. And smoking. I suppose I'd better admit that now." Another wry smile as he picked up his lighter and flipped the lid on his pack of cigarettes, tapping one out. "Vita disapproved so I hid out there. I kidded myself that she didn't know about it, but of course she did. Turning a blind eye is the secret of a happy marriage, isn't it?"

Derwent jumped on the opening. "Did she have to do that a lot? Turn a blind eye, I mean?"

Kennford shook his head very slightly as he lit his cigarette. He blew out smoke and said, "You know, I don't think we've started off on the right foot, Mr. Derwent."

51

"And I don't think you've given me an answer."

"Josh." Godley was glaring. *Save it for the next interview when we might be trying to make him sweat* . . . "Did you notice anything strange while you were outside?"

"No, but you can't see much of the house from where I was sitting." He anticipated the next question. "And I wouldn't have heard the doorbell either."

"Do you think that's how the killer gained access?"

"That's what I've been assuming. There was no damage to the front door, was there? Or the windows?"

"None that we've found. Would your wife have answered the door at that time of night if she wasn't expecting a visitor?"

"We have a video entry system. She could have checked who she was letting in before she opened the door."

"Does it record?" Derwent was practically quivering with excitement.

"That would make your job easier, wouldn't it? No, it's a real-time camera. Just shows who's there at that time, and not very clearly. They have to stand in exactly the right place or you just see their elbow, which isn't much help. I never bothered with it. I can't stand things that don't work properly."

"Did Vita usually check it?"

"I didn't watch her answer the door, Mr.

Godley." He sounded irritated. Not a man who liked to say "I don't know," I thought.

"Did you see anything that struck you as unusual when you came in from the garden?"

"Nothing. But I didn't put the lights on in the kitchen or the hall. I just went straight upstairs."

"In the dark?"

"I knew the way. And it's not as if there was much to bump into." He raised his eyebrows, inviting us to laugh with him, though none of us took him up on it. It seemed I was right about his taste being very different from his wife's.

"Did you see Vita or Laura when you came in?"

"No. In fact, I thought Laura was out. She had gone around to a friend's house and I'd expected her to be there all evening."

"Which friend?"

"I don't know. Vita knew."

And you didn't listen when she told you about it.

"Didn't you hear voices from the sitting room?" Derwent asked.

"I didn't stop to listen. I wouldn't have expected to. As far as I knew, Vita was in there on her own."

"What was she doing with her evening?"

"I haven't the faintest idea."

"Reading? Watching telly? Phoning her friends? Embroidery? Surfing the Internet?"

There was obvious irritation in Kennford's voice when he answered. "There's very little point in naming pastimes to see if any of them ring a bell. I didn't ask her how she planned to occupy herself and she didn't tell me."

"Didn't you care?"

"I respected her privacy." He looked at Derwent's left hand. "You're not married, are you? I wouldn't expect you to understand, but sometimes you need to give each other space to breathe. Too much interest in each other's lives can be smothering."

"Sounds like someone's been reading the Relate handbook."

"Let's move on," Godley said hastily. "Did you see anyone strange hanging around in the last few weeks? Anyone you didn't recognize? Anything that made you suspicious?"

"I've been racking my brains, but no."

"You've got a very serious alarm system," I said. "Did you use it when you were in the house?"

"Not when the door to the garden was open. When we were upstairs at night, yes. But the alarm is based on the perimeter being secure, so we couldn't have ground-floor windows or doors open when it was on. In this heat we never bothered with it."

"Were you worried about anyone in particular?" Godley asked. "Was that why you had the alarm put in?"

"My wife had it installed. I assumed it was to reduce the cost of our insurance, but I never asked. We had to pay through the nose because of all the art she bought."

"I noticed you have quite an impressive collection."

"If you like that sort of thing." He sounded bored. "I didn't pay too much attention to what she wanted to hang on the walls. She knew her stuff, though. She ran a gallery before we were married."

"Successfully?" Derwent demanded.

"Yes, if you mean that it was a very successful way of losing money."

"So you made her give it up."

For his next birthday I was definitely going to buy Derwent a copy of *Charm for Beginners.*

"I never made Vita do anything. She sold the gallery when she found out she was pregnant with the twins. She only ever wanted to be a housewife, it transpired, and the twins were a very good reason to avoid going back to work."

"Would you have preferred her to work?" Godley asked.

"It would have given her an interest outside the family."

"Even if it cost you money?" Derwent again.

"It never cost me a penny, mainly because I don't have two coins to rub together." He laughed. "Don't be fooled by the big house

55

and the fact I'm a QC. I'm still a criminal barrister, when all's said and done, and no one gets rich off legal aid, especially not when they're paying income tax at the level I do. My first wife takes whatever I manage to keep from the taxman. The money is all Vita's. Or it was, I suppose."

"And now it's yours." Derwent sounded exceedingly smug as he pointed it out.

"Indeed. And what a perfect motive for murder. But you need to come up with a reason why I would have killed my daughter as well." For the first time I picked up on a thread of raw emotion that roughened his voice. "And then you have to explain why I didn't go the whole hog and kill the other one too. It's not as if I didn't know where she was."

"Leave it with me."

Before Kennford could snap back, Godley leaped in with, "You know we have to look at all the angles, even the ones that are unlikely."

"And I know that husbands kill wives. They even kill their kids too, sometimes. But I didn't." He rolled his cigarette against the edge of the ashtray, moulding the ash into a cone. "You said Laura had her throat cut. Didn't you?"

Derwent looked across at Godley for permission to speak, and got a nod. "She had a serious injury to her neck."

"Did she suffer?"

"I'm not a pathologist."

"Don't treat me like a fool. I'm not a civilian and I don't need to be lied to. You've seen plenty of murders. You know what happened in there." He pointed in the direction of the sitting room, his hand shaking very slightly. "I'm asking because you're enough of a bastard to tell me the truth. Did she suffer?"

"It was probably too quick. She wouldn't have known what was happening until it was over."

"Did Vita see it?"

"Yes."

"I can't imagine how she must have felt." He said it more to himself than to us, muttering it into his chest.

"She tried to fight."

"She was good at that. Never backed away from an argument."

But she had tried to run when she knew she was doomed to lose. And she had certainly suffered, something her husband didn't seem to care about. It made me slightly uneasy that he didn't ask about how she had died.

"When will you be finished here?" He stubbed out his cigarette though there was a good inch of white paper left. "We'll need to get someone in to clear the room out, I suppose, and clear up the mess upstairs. I don't know where to start. Vita would have sorted all that out."

"We're going to need to keep the house as it is for a while, Mr. Kennford. In fact, I was just going to ask if you had somewhere else to stay."

"Oh. Right." He looked down at the dog. "I'll make a couple of calls. I rent a flat in town, but animals aren't allowed. I've got a friend with rooms in the Temple, the lucky sod. He's got a house in France where he goes for the summer. If I can make arrangements to stay in his rooms, Mollie can come with me because tenants' dogs are allowed. And Lydia would be all right there. I think there's a sofa she can use."

He certainly had his priorities straight, I thought. Poor Lydia was one step down from the dog — maybe two. That wasn't what was bothering Godley, though.

"Is there anywhere else Lydia can stay? Someone you trust? A friend, or a relative?"

"She won't mind roughing it for a few days."

"I'd prefer it if she was somewhere else."

"Not with me, you mean." His eyebrows drew together and his mouth narrowed, his face transforming into something positively unsettling as his anger showed in it. He pointed at Derwent. "You're just like him, aren't you? You've made up your mind already."

"That's not true. But two members of your family died in this house, and you were at-

58

tacked. Lydia is the only one who wasn't harmed, at least physically. She could be a very important witness. If you're together, you'll discuss what's happened. You won't be able to help it. When she's ready to talk to us, I want to hear what she thinks, not what you've suggested."

"I don't believe you."

"You should." Godley changed tack, his voice softening. "Look, I have a daughter around the same age. I know you want to protect her, but the best place for Lydia is a proper home, not a borrowed flat where she doesn't even have a bed. Is there anyone she could stay with?"

"Vita's sister lives in Twickenham."

"Does she get on well with Lydia?"

"I haven't a clue. Renee is a mystery to me, but she seems perfectly pleasant."

"You sound as if she's a stranger," I said. "Twickenham's not far from here, is it? Don't you see her often?"

"I don't. Vita might have. I don't really have much to do with the in-laws, I'm afraid." He didn't sound too guilty about it. I paused to marvel at a world where it was possible not to see close relations who lived nearby. My mother kept track of every up and down in the lives of even quite distant members of the family, no matter what part of the globe they had made their home, and I was expected to do the same. Family was family even if only by marriage; what happened to them *mattered*. But Philip Kennford didn't seem to subscribe to the same point of view.

"Does Renee have a family?" Godley asked.

"Boys. Older than Lydia and Laura. Crispin is twenty, I think. Tobias is two years younger."

At least she would have some maternal instincts we could appeal to. Godley appeared to be thinking along the same lines. "Do you think she would be willing to look after Lydia?"

"I imagine so. If she has nowhere else to go."

It was hardly a ringing endorsement, but it was better than nothing.

"I'll have Lydia taken round there once your sister-in-law agrees to have her. We'll need to break the news to Renee about what's happened. Would you like to call her or would you prefer me to send a family liaison officer around?"

"Renee might take it better if it comes from someone who's on the spot. Someone neutral, I mean." And Kennford would happily take advantage of anything that meant he didn't have to talk to her. He limped to his desk and wrote her address on a slip of paper. We would be going there the following day to interview Lydia if that was where she ended up staying. I rather hoped I'd get a chance to

60

ask Renee what she thought of her brother-in-law.

Godley took the paper from him. "Fine. We'll get it organized."

"Where is Lydia, anyway?" Kennford looked around as if he expected her to materialize in the room. It was late in the day for him to be worried about his surviving daughter, I thought, but Godley was too professional to show a trace of disapproval.

"She's resting. I have an officer with her in case she needs reassurance, but she's under sedation at the moment anyway."

"Went to pieces, I imagine." Kennford sounded scathing.

"She walked in on the corpses of her twin sister and her mother lying in their own blood. She thought you were dead too. She didn't know if the killer was still in the house and she was deeply traumatized but she held it together for long enough to call 999 and let our lads in. I think she's entitled to a handful of tranquilizers and a lot of sympathy." Derwent wasn't usually soft-hearted but when he leaped to your defense, he did it in style. I could have given him a round of applause.

"Lydia is not a strong person, DI Derwent. Laura got all the backbone when they were in the womb. She was worth ten of her sister." He shook his head. "You don't know Lydia.

With respect, I do. I'm not surprised she's in a state."

Kennford didn't actually sound respectful, but he stopped short of sneering the words, which was more than could be said for Derwent when he repeated them.

"With respect, I'm not surprised either. But I can understand it and empathize. Maybe you should have a go at that. Given that she's still alive and everything, you might want to try being a father to her."

"Are we finished?" Kennford snapped.

"I am." Derwent headed for the door, stopping halfway and wheeling around. "There was one thing that was bothering me. Why do you need a flat in London if you live in SW19?"

"During big trials I don't like to come home. It's distracting. I function better if I can close myself off from the world and concentrate. I can stay at work until midnight if I like, grab some cereal for dinner, get up at five and keep going. You can see how that lifestyle doesn't really fit in with family life."

"Oh. So it's not a shag pad, then."

"I beg your pardon?"

"I think you heard." He shrugged. "Just going by your reputation, Mr. Kennford. I'm sure it's all very innocent and aboveboard. You know how people love to talk."

"I do. And I know it's not worth listening to gossip."

"Listening isn't the same as believing. I make up my own mind about that. But I do like to know what people are saying."

Kennford got up, pushing the dog out of his way, but rather than confronting Derwent he squared up to Godley. The two men were about the same height but I thought the boss edged it on looks. "I can't say I'm filled with confidence, Superintendent. I happen to know your team's being kept busy at the moment — what is it, ten gang murders in the last month?"

"Eleven."

"So you have your work cut out for you, don't you? And you're not going to put your top people on a couple of murders like this, even though it's an interesting story and it will get into all the papers. You just can't spare them. This can't be your priority and that's why you've chosen Inspector Obvious and his bimbo sidekick to go through the motions."

I caught Derwent's eye. We really hadn't made a good first impression.

"They are very able officers, experienced in handling difficult cases, and I have total faith in them. I can assure you they will receive ample support from their colleagues, and from me. I can further assure you that I am capable of running this investigation at the same time as the other investigations on my team's workload. That's why I do the job I do. And it would help a lot if you'd let my officers do their job, and answer their questions honestly, no matter how personal they may be. You know better than to think it's for no reason, Mr. Kennford, so stop pissing about."

I had been right about the strain beginning to tell on Godley; nine times out of ten he would have ignored a jibe like Kennford's, and I couldn't recall the last time he'd lost his temper with a grieving partner. Not that Kennford was distraught — far from it. In fact, he seemed to be pleased to have got a reaction.

"I'm not surprised that this is the approach you're taking, but it's still disappointing. Just promise me you won't let your investigation be sidetracked by chasing after rumors and spite that have nothing to do with the death of my wife and child."

"You have my word. We will find whoever did this and bring them to justice." Godley waited for a beat. "Whoever they are."

"Even me?" Kennford gave a humorless laugh. "Point taken. But you won't be knocking on my door, I assure you. Now if you don't mind wrapping this up, I've got a thumping headache and I've got to sort out somewhere to stay. Then I have to pack, if I'm allowed to take things out of my bedroom. I think it's time to draw this delightful conversation to a close."

"I agree." Godley looked slightly awkward. "We'll have to have someone with you when you pack, just so we know what's left the house."

"Afraid I'll smuggle the knife out in my suitcase?"

"I have to avoid any suggestion that the crime scenes were compromised, Mr. Kennford. You understand how important it is to preserve the evidence as much as we can — so we don't have to answer any difficult questions when the case comes to trial."

"The sort of thing I'd make into grounds for immediate acquittal, you mean?" He rubbed his eyes, looking exhausted. "You do whatever you need to. I'm not going to kick up a fuss about any of it. I'll follow your lead, if that's what you want."

"That will help," Godley said evenly. "Answering our questions will also be useful."

"That's what I've been doing."

"One last one, then. You must have been thinking about this, so it should be easy to answer. Who do you think murdered your wife and your daughter?"

"I don't know. I can't think of anyone." Kennford held Godley's gaze as he replied. He sounded completely sincere. "If I had any suspicions about anyone, you would be the first to know."

I couldn't have said why, but I didn't believe a word of it.

CHAPTER THREE

"Just as a matter of interest, what would it take to get you to be sympathetic?"

"What do you mean?"

"I suppose it's not as if his entire family was wiped out. Just most of it. So if they'd all been killed, or maybe if the house had burned down too . . . or — no, this would definitely do it — if they'd stabbed the dog. Then Kennford might have got a 'Sorry for your loss.' "

Derwent spread his hands wide, mock-apologetic. "What can I say? I have no time for people who make their living off getting criminals out of trouble. And I can't stand people who play favorites with their kids. Twins too. How much worse would you feel if it was your twin who was the chosen one and you were out in the cold?"

"Seems like it hit a nerve. Remind me, do you have any siblings?"

"None I still speak to." He walked away and I didn't have to be particularly intuitive to know he didn't want to say anything more about it. He was reflected almost perfectly in the black marble tiles of the kitchen floor. I didn't think it was the right time to point out he was leaving smudgy footprints all over it.

"Look at this. How much do you think it set them back?"

"The kitchen? Tens of thousands, I should think."

"I mean the whole thing."

"Millions. No expense spared." I played with the folding door that ran across the back of the room. It slid back into position with a nudge, the engineering flawless. "Do you buy his line about not earning anything from his work?"

"Everything's relative, isn't it? He'd probably think what we earn is pocket money."

"We're not overpaid though, are we?"

"That's because they know we're stupid enough to do this job for nothing."

"Is that how you feel about it?"

He looked around quickly. "Isn't that how you feel?"

"More or less," I admitted. "But I wouldn't have thought you were in love with the job."

"I don't know about being in love. But I'm good at it, and there's always something important to do. Something that matters. I don't know how people do jobs that just make money. I couldn't bring myself to care about working in a bank or an insurance company."

"You'd get fired before your probation period was up for being rude to the customers."

"Fuck, yes. I'd be dead meat."

He was opening and closing drawers and cupboards, looking for nothing in particular. I knew better than to ask what he was doing. The SOCOs had gone through the cutlery and checked the murder weapon wasn't sitting in a drawer or the dishwasher; it had happened before. They were gone now, as were Kennford and his daughter, in separate cars. Godley had gone too, about half an hour before, with instructions to us to be in the office at eight for a team briefing about the case. He wasn't going home, despite the late hour. Kennford had been right about the gang murders: they were Godley's main headache. While it was nice to know he thought we could handle the Kennford case, I was uneasily aware that Derwent and I were on our own in more senses than one.

The house was ours for as long as we wanted to snoop around and Derwent was taking his time about it. I checked my watch surreptitiously. It was getting on for two. No chance of slipping off to call Rob. At least he understood about late nights; he had worked enough murder inquiries in his time. And he did long enough hours on his new job on the Flying Squad. I barely saw him most of the time.

68

Derwent peered into the fridge. "They don't eat much, do they? A bit of lettuce, some tomatoes, leftover salmon and a packet of smoked mackerel." He pulled a face. "Where's the real food?"

"What — cheese and steak and potatoes? You sound like my dad. It's not a proper meal unless there's meat and potatoes on the plate."

"What about the vegetables?"

"Those he can take or leave."

"Old school."

"You don't know the half of it." And I wasn't going to start telling him. I had a feeling Derwent's interest in my family extended only to what he could mock.

"I'd be the same about my greens if I didn't have to watch what I eat."

"Worried about your spare tire?"

"I don't have a fucking spare tire." He fingered his stomach. "I run, remember? It's part of my training to keep an eye on my nutritional intake."

"Right. It's just that I've heard your metabolism changes as you reach middle age. That's why I thought you might be on a diet."

I left him fizzing with inarticulate rage and slid out into the garden. It was landscaped with immaculately trimmed shrubs and tall trees that blocked the neighbors' view. No flowers. Not much space besides the pool, which was ice-blue and well maintained.

Lights shone under the water, answering a question I hadn't voiced about how Kennford and his daughter were able to swim late into the night. I skirted the pool and crossed the grass to a wooden bench under a beech tree. It took me a few minutes to scan the ground with my Maglite but I found the spot where Kennford hid his cigarette butts behind a piece of sculpture that reminded me of a melted snail shell. It didn't prove he'd been there earlier that evening, but at least I'd confirmed he was telling the truth about something. I sat on the bench and checked the view of the house. The kitchen stuck out, blocking the line of sight to the sitting-room windows. Even if the attack had taken place while he was outside, he wouldn't have seen anything.

"Having a rest?" Derwent was silhouetted against the light from the kitchen. I crossed the garden toward him.

"Seeing what Mr. Kennford could see from here."

"And?"

"He couldn't."

"Let's put one tick in the truth column, then. What's next?"

"Follow his route into the house, I suppose."

He stood back. "Lead on."

I was glad I got to go first. It meant I was able to pick a path that avoided the worst of the bloody footprints. The SOCOs had measured and photographed them so there was no pressing reason to tread carefully, but I was superstitious about it. Death had walked through those hallways not long before and I wasn't all that keen to match him stride for stride. If Derwent noticed, he didn't say anything about it. He might even have felt the same way, but there was no point in asking him. He'd never admit it.

The footprints had all but disappeared by the time we reached the upper hallway, absorbed by the thick carpet pile, but there were still traces. Enough that you could see the killer had gone to each room in turn.

"He didn't know the house," I said softly. "He didn't know which room to try."

"We don't know what he was looking for. He didn't kill Kennford when he had the chance, did he? God knows, I'd have had a crack at it if I'd had the time and the tools to hand."

"Maybe he didn't have time. Maybe he was worried about Lydia interrupting him."

"Doing what? A spot of burglary? Kennford said there was nothing missing as far as he could see." Derwent pulled open the nearest door and looked in, flicking on the light. "It all looks neat."

"Especially for a teenager's room." I moved past him to stand beside the bed. There was nothing on the walls except for a full-length mirror and none of the usual clutter of make-up, clothes and jewelry that I would have expected. The desk by the window was strictly for books and papers with an Apple laptop in the center, a top-of-the-range Mac-Book Pro. The room felt sparse, somehow, and not quite permanent — as if the person who slept there was only using the space for a day or two. "Do you think this is Laura's or Lydia's?"

"Lydia's." Derwent was checking the books on the desk and turned one around to show me her name inside the front cover, written in tiny, neat letters.

I bent to look under the bed. "She seems like a cheery soul. Maybe she just keeps the fun hidden." There was a stack of fashion magazines under the bed and I hooked them out to flick through the pages, looking for nothing in particular and finding just that.

"Working hard to get Daddy's approval. No frivolity here. Just hard work and exercise. She's fifteen, for God's sake. She should be trying to get served in pubs and staying out late."

"And he'd probably respect that more."

"That's what I've heard."

"So you said earlier." I shook my head at him. "That was just trouble-making."

"Shake the tree — see what falls out. Sometimes you get the coconut. Sometimes you get the monkey."

"And sometimes you get damn all."

"True." He opened a door to reveal a bathroom. "Oh, perfect. Of course the teenager needs an en-suite room."

Every surface in the bathroom bristled with bottles and cosmetics, and the cabinet on the wall hung open. It didn't seem in keeping with the sterile order in the room behind me.

"There's another door on the other side. Maybe it's shared with her sister."

I was right, as it turned out, and Laura's room more than made up for the lack of mess in the other bedroom. Clothes spilled out of her wardrobe and chest of drawers so doors and drawers couldn't shut, and more were piled high on her chair. It was the first place I'd seen photographs — formal, framed ones on the top of the bookcase, candid shots tucked into the corners of the mirror, family and friends framed in montages on the wall, a selection marching across the windowsill, clipped to tiny wire stalks. Most of the pictures had Laura herself in them — fair hair like her mother, blue eyes like her father, extraordinary prettiness that she had made the most of with makeup, but she was equally stunning without. She looked popular and outgoing, the sun to her twin sister's shadow. Lydia appeared in a few but only just, often with her head half-turned away or her hair hanging down around her face.

"Identical," Derwent observed, looking over

my shoulder. "But only one of them got the looks, even so."

"It's all about attitude, isn't it? Maybe Lydia has the brains."

"You'd hope she got something."

Laura had a profusion of electronic equipment — music decks, a Bang & Olufsen iPod dock, an iPad and a laptop that was open on her bed, on standby.

"If you wanted to burgle somewhere, you'd start here," Derwent commented. "Lots of disposable consumer goods." He poked the computer and it whirred, then came on. "Log-out screen for her Gmail account. Shame she hadn't left herself connected. We could have had a snoop."

"Do you think this was about her?"

"I'm not ruling anything out at this stage and nor should you."

I acknowledged the sense in that, but I couldn't imagine a teenage girl inspiring the kind of murderous hatred that had ended her life. I picked up a big digital camera that was wedged onto the bedside table. It was a massive, expensive Canon with a professional lens. It took me a second or two to work out how to turn it on so I could review the images on the memory card.

"Bloody hell."

"What's up?"

"Laura had a boyfriend."

"So?"

"Laura had sex with her boyfriend."

"How can you tell?" Derwent was rummaging through her chest of drawers. He held up a packet. "Because she was on the pill?"

"Because she took extremely detailed pictures of herself engaging in sexual acts." I handed the camera to him. "There are forty-two pictures on that memory card and you can't see his face in any of them."

He scrolled through at top speed, a look of distaste on his face. He was pretty far from being a prude but he had a real problem with underage sex, even if it was consensual. Something in his past, I presumed, but I'd never got very far with finding out what.

"Do you think he's the same age?"

"Give or take a couple of years." The boy's body was pale and lean, not heavily muscled, almost hairless. Laura had focused more on herself, or allowed him to. The images were close-ups mostly, both sharp and graphic. I felt we had intruded on something she had a right to keep private, and hated that it was our job.

Derwent put the camera down on the bed and sighed. "Big job to do here going through her belongings. Any sign of a phone?"

I shook my head. "It could have been downstairs, I suppose."

"Didn't see it there either." He looked around, visibly flagging at the thought of starting to go through Laura's room at that

75

late hour. I wasn't exactly disappointed that the next words out of his mouth were "Where next?"

The next one turned out to be a guest room, bland and luxurious in equal measure, with a bathroom off it.

"Bigger than my flat." Derwent didn't sound impressed. "Where do you think Vita got her money?"

"Not the gallery, from what Kennford said. Family, I suppose."

"Daddy worked hard so you don't have to."

"You can't criticize her for inheriting money, if that's where it came from. What was she supposed to do? Hand it back?"

"It's not the having that bothers me. It's how she threw it around. Look at this place. It's halfway between a museum of modern art and a show home. Whatever happened to living modestly? You can't tell me they needed all this crap."

"They could afford it and they liked it. They were entitled to live here undisturbed and enjoy their money."

"They might as well have been sitting in a shop window counting their cash. It's just stupid to draw attention to yourself, especially if you are loaded. And especially, you'd have thought, if you routinely work with big-time criminals."

We filed out into the hallway. The next room was where Kennford had been attacked; we had visited it earlier with Godley. It had as much character as a five-star hotel room. An Eames recliner stood by the window and a Damien Hirst spot painting hung over the bed, both shorthand for "I have money and taste but no imagination." The mirror on the wall had been wide and full-length, positioned just where Kennford would have seen himself coming out of the bathroom. Derwent moved soundlessly on the thick carpet, sliding around the corner of the bathroom wall to lie in wait within arm's reach of me. He mimed hitting my head.

"Could you see me?"

"Hard to tell." Almost none of the mirror glass had survived in the frame. "Depends on whether the lights were on in here. And if he was looking."

"He was probably staring at himself. The body beautiful."

"Think he's vain?"

"Don't you?" Derwent had found a wardrobe and stood back to reveal a row of immaculate dark suits. "All handmade. Shoes too. Shirts and jumpers on this side, on the shelves."

"Where are Vita's clothes?"

"Not in here. But didn't you hear him say this was his room? Maybe Vita sleeps elsewhere."

Looking around, I had to agree. There was something masculine about it, and something that suggested only one person used the room. The headboard of the bed was upholstered in gray velvet, probably the perfect fabric to show wear and tear. There was a scuffed area on the left side of the bed: the right was pristine. A biography of Marx lay on the bedside table on the left, along with some loose change. The other table was empty. I went into the bathroom.

"No women's cosmetics in here. Quite a bit of stuff for men, though."

"See? Vain." Derwent poked around, not finding what he was looking for. "He must have it somewhere else."

"Dare I ask?"

"Viagra."

"Surely not."

"Magic little blue pill. Essential accessory for the pork swordsman. Especially at his age."

"He's not old."

"Probably starting to give a bit, though. Not quite as firm as he used to be. Not able to keep going as long."

"I'm not having this conversation," I said flatly, heading out to the hall followed by Derwent's laughter. "Anyway, he probably keeps it in his shag pad, as you so elegantly put it."

"Not much reason to have it in this house." He sauntered out after me, looking over my shoulder as I opened the next door, which led to the largest of the bedrooms. Gray walls, cream carpet, a geometric patterned throw on the bed. More of the same aseptic neatness and puritan style, but enough personal items on the dressing table and by the bed for me to be fairly sure it was Vita's room. "Separate bedrooms don't exactly say hot sex, do they?"

"Maybe he snores. Maybe he can't keep his hands off her and she had to banish him to another room to get some rest."

"Speaking from experience, Kerrigan?"

"Don't try to make this about me. I'm thinking about Vita." Vita, who had no mirrors in her room at all. At least, none on show. There had to be one somewhere. She was too much of a perfectionist not to have a way of checking how she looked, even if she needed to prepare herself for it. I opened the wardrobe door and found a full-length one inside the door, along with rows of ironed and folded clothes in neutral colors, slate gray to ice white via every possible shade of beige. "Disciplined, wasn't she?"

"And into exercise." Derwent had stepped onto the running machine that lurked in one corner of the room and was poking buttons. "This is bigger than the one at my gym."

"Don't break it."

"You sound like my mum." The belt began to move and Derwent straddled it, watching the screen. The machine was quieter than I

79

would have expected. "She has it set to a six-mile run. Fast too. Incline and everything, so she must have been fit. I can't see the point of it, though. Plenty of hills around here."

"Control. She could measure her progress. Count the calories."

Derwent hit the stop button and the machine whirred to silence. "So she did her exercising in here, in private. Away from the family. What else did she do?"

"Groomed herself." I was looking through the collection of pots and lotions on the dressing table. "Crème de la Mer doesn't come cheap. Nor does Shiseido. Nothing but the best for Vita."

"Trying to keep Mother Nature at bay. She was older than Kennford and he had a wandering eye." Derwent opened one of the pots and sniffed suspiciously at the contents. "Worth slapping a bit of goo on now and then. If she wanted to keep him, that is."

"It seems she did." I shook my head. "I can't really see what he brought to the marriage. No money, according to him. He wasn't even here when he was working."

"And that would be most of the time. He's in demand. Chances are he uses his flat during the weeks." He lay on the floor to peer under the bed. "What's this?"

I knelt beside him as he stretched to retrieve a wooden box, rectangular, about eighteen inches by twelve. "Jewelry?"

"I bet they have a safe." He flipped the lid up. Three silver objects sat in the box, cradled in purple silk. Derwent lifted one out, a long curved shape covered with apparently random bumps. "Sculpture."

"Not quite." I was having trouble stopping myself from laughing. I reached out and pressed a button on the base and it hummed into life. Derwent held it for a second, uncomprehending, and then dropped it with a shudder.

"Don't tell me that's some sort of dildo."

"That's exactly what it is. These are high-end sex toys."

Derwent stripped off his gloves and took a fresh pair out of his pocket, pulling a disgusted face. "You could have warned me."

"I wasn't sure. I'm not exactly in the market for things like that. They cost a fortune. And I don't need that sort of thing, obviously," I added, heading off an off-color remark before he could begin to form it.

He pointed suspiciously at a pebble-shaped one. "How does that work?"

"No idea."

"That one looks like a whisk. Where do you think it's supposed to go?"

"Wherever you fancy, I should think. Isn't that the point?"

"Perverted," Derwent announced.

"That's a bit harsh." There were ribbon tabs at either end of the purple silk tray. I lifted it out and discovered a collection of books, DVDs and some more toys. "*Fanny Hill.* The Marquis de Sade. *At Her Master's Pleasure.* This one seems to be all about spanking."

Derwent had picked up a book with a vast Viking on the cover, holding a scantily dressed redhead who seemed to have swooned. " 'Drogo forced her thighs apart with one cruel knee, his desire for her unstoppable, his manhood as hard as the iron hilt of his sword. She fought to free herself even as she ached for him to ravage her. As he plunged his whole length into her, violating her most secret places, she shuddered with ecstasy, her body betraying her at the moment of her greatest shame.' Fucking hell. Drogo needs arresting."

"You'd never get a conviction. Look at what she's wearing. She was asking for it."

"I will never understand women. How could you get excited about being raped?"

"Well, it's not all women, is it? And it's a fantasy. Not everyone wants to live out their fantasies."

"What if Vita did and Kennford wasn't into it?"

"Well, that would explain the sex toys."

"Nothing to say she was using them on her own." He moved on to the DVDs. "*Anal Attraction IV.* Well, that is the standout from the series. Everyone knows the first three are a bit samey."

"Do you think she had someone on the side?"

"Safe assumption, if you believe the rumors about Kennford. I doubt he'd have the energy to violate her with his iron manhood after spending all week shagging. And it looks as if Vita wasn't undersexed. So what if she found someone who was happy to play the rapist? Someone who liked it rough, who liked to slap her around?"

"And what if this mythical person got carried away and decided to murder her and her daughter?" I shook my head. "I'm not seeing it. Why kill Laura? If he was excited by the thought of killing Vita, you'd think it would have happened while they were having sex, not in the living room on a Sunday evening. And then the attack on Kennford. That's not in keeping with a sex murder."

"Halfhearted too. All that violence downstairs and a tap on the head for him." Derwent sat back on his heels. "Try this. Vita has a secret lover. Laura finds out, wants to know what the attraction is, and starts shagging him secretly. Kennford discovers them together. Laura spills the beans on her mother's relationship. Kennford goes mental, kills her, kills his wife, bashes his head against the mirror in his room to give himself an alibi and waits for the one in the swimming pool to come into the house and discover the bodies."

"If you found your underage daughter in bed with a strange man, why would you wait for him to leave before you started to lash out? We should have another body. Your theoretical lover would be the obvious place to start."

"Maybe Kennford's a coward and he was too scared to tackle him. Or maybe he had enough self-control to wait until he could execute his plan."

"To kill his favorite child because she slept with her mother's lover, and to kill his wife because she had a lover in the first place, even though he is notoriously unfaithful himself?"

"No one said it had to be logical."

"Doesn't fit with the planning," I pointed out. "You're suggesting that he was blinded with rage and jealousy. He had to set this up, if it was him. He had to wait for the right moment."

"Okay. So maybe the motive is wrong. Maybe he wanted to kill Vita and he wasn't expecting Laura to be there."

"Why did he want to kill Vita?"

"Because she'd had enough. She was going to kick him out and find someone else, someone who would appreciate her many millions and ravish her five nights a week. If they got divorced, you can bet his lifestyle would take a bit of a knock."

I looked around the room, at the wardrobe

doors hanging open, the box spilling its secrets on the floor, the many expensive ways Vita had attempted to stave off the effects of aging. "All of this says that she wasn't happy. She had high standards for herself and she was anxious to keep her husband. But she wasn't satisfied. You could be right. Maybe she felt she'd done all she could and he still wouldn't give her what she needed."

Before Derwent could answer, my phone rang. "Bit late for a call, isn't it?"

"It's Rob." I headed for the hall, the phone still ringing in my hand. At least being out of the room gave me the illusion of privacy. I leaned against the wall and answered it. As always, the sound of his voice was enough to make me smile.

"Still at work?"

"Yeah, but hopefully not for long."

"Wish I could say the same. Listen, I'm going to be out until breakfast. We're set up on these ramraiders and it looks like they're planning something tonight."

"You sound happy about it."

"You know me. Always at my best when I'm stuck in the back of a van, weeing into a bottle."

In the background, someone made a comment I couldn't quite hear and Rob laughed, covering the phone to reply.

"That's fine." I said it quite loudly. *Hey, you're the one who rang me . . . The least you could do is pay attention.* "As I said, I'm still working. And I've got to be in the office by eight, so I might not see you in the morning."

I waited for him to ask me what I was doing, and where, but instead he said, "Well, I suppose I'll see you when I see you."

"As usual."

"It's a bit like that, isn't it? Talk to you later, mate."

"Bye." I disconnected and looked at the phone. *Mate?* I hadn't expected "I love you" or "darling," but *mate?*

When Derwent spoke, he was standing so close behind me that I jumped a mile. "If you don't mind me saying so, it sounds as if you and Vita had a fair bit in common."

"I do mind, and you're completely wrong," I snapped.

"Not getting what you want, are you? Here. This might help. I won't tell anyone." He handed me a book. *Justine,* by the Marquis de Sade. The pages were soft and the spine ridged with much reading and rereading. It looked as if it was one of Vita's favorites.

"In six hours, we have to be at a conference with the boss. I don't have time to indulge your little jokes." I slapped the book against his chest and he grabbed on to it automatically. "Now, if we're finished, I'd like to go home. If we're not, I suggest we get on with it."

Derwent looked thoughtful and I recalled with a sinking feeling that every now and then he liked to remind me that he was a senior officer. Moreover, he took great pleasure in putting me in my place. And he could manage on very little sleep.

"We still haven't found that phone, have we?" He checked his watch and sighed. "Oh dear. Looks as if we're going to be here for a while."

"Do you really think we need to find it now?"

"No." He patted my shoulder. "I think *you* need to find it. Let me know how you get on."

CHAPTER FOUR

"And Kennford wasn't able to give you a list of people who wished him harm." The speaker was Una Burt, Godley's latest DCI, and the first woman who had held that position. Proof that women didn't need good looks to get onto Godley's team, she had the long face and square features of a particularly plain horse, if that horse was short-sighted enough to need thick glasses. She was also exceptionally good at her job, tremendously serious and a massive pain in Derwent's arse. I didn't know her well enough to like her but I admired her, not least for being deaf to the comments that were made about her. The mildest one I'd heard was, "Someone told me Burt was born a female but you'd never know by looking." She was too bright not to notice the sneers but she had perfected the expression of someone whose mind is on higher things. And maybe it was; she came with an impeccable track record from her previous job on another murder squad. There had been murmurs when Godley told us she was joining the team, both from within and outside the squad. He was getting a reputation for being a poacher, which was starting to piss off people. Bringing in new talent from outside made it harder for anyone in the team to move up the ladder, and DCI Burt was nothing if not talented. As for why she wanted to work with him, there was no great mystery about it. He was the best the Met had to offer. She'd have been mad to turn him down.

One person who absolutely wished she'd done that was sitting beside me, shifting irritably in his chair. Spoiling for a fight, I recognized, and was glad I had managed to keep my temper through the long hours of searching through Kennford's house and the mordant drive back through building traffic that had left me just enough time to shower and change before heading out again. I had also had time to notice that Rob wasn't home, that he hadn't been home, and that the milk had gone off. Domestic bliss it wasn't. And not what I had signed up for when I moved in with him, I reflected on my way to the station, where a hot, overcrowded train left me short-tempered and crumpled. The meeting room was airless too and I struggled to keep a yawn in, my jaw creaking with the effort. I'd never fallen asleep in a conference yet, but there was always a first time for everything. Dog tired was no way to start a murder investigation and I would have given a lot to curl up for a snooze somewhere peaceful, like under the table.

"He didn't want to talk to us about his enemies and we weren't really in a position to twist his arm. We're seeing him today at his chambers. Either we'll get it out of him there or we'll find someone willing to tell us what he doesn't want us to know." Derwent was aiming for bored but his tone actually came out as sulky. He rocked back so his chair teetered on two legs.

"But I'm interested in why he wouldn't tell you straightaway." DCI Burt twirled a pen through her fingers, spinning it from one end of her hand to the other and back again. She was looking down at the notes in front of her, not at Derwent, who was now probing the inside of his cheek with his tongue. "Most grieving relatives cooperate. Unless they have something to hide."

"Remember, Kennford is a lawyer," Godley pointed out. "It's second nature with them to watch what they say."

"I would have thought he would want to rule out a few avenues of investigation for us."

"And I would have thought anyone who was targeting him would have made a better job of smashing his head in." Derwent snorted. "God knows it's big enough. Never met anyone so arrogant."

"Takes one to know one." The comment was made in an undertone but Derwent still heard it. He glowered at Harry Maitland, who looked not remotely abashed. Colin Vale moved his chair away from Maitland a little.

"You can't rule him out, obviously, but I agree, the killer could have done a better job of dealing with Kennford." She tapped the end of her pen on her pad. "Unless they were under pressure and ran out of time. Maybe they realized the other daughter was still alive and made a run for it before she discovered them."

"She's not what you'd call intimidating," Godley said. "If the killer could handle her twin and her mother at the same time, I don't think Lydia would have posed too big a problem. It bothered me a lot that Kennford wasn't stabbed, especially given that we didn't find the knife in the house. The killer should have been able to use it on him and I don't know why he didn't. It makes me wonder if we have two attackers."

"Or one. Philip Kennford himself." No one around the table looked particularly shocked, I thought, as Derwent outlined the theory we'd discussed in the small hours, Kennford staging an attack on himself by head-butting the mirror in his room. "He could have broken the glass first to limit the amount of damage he did to himself. I didn't see a bruise on the back of his head — did you?"

"His hair is too thick." Godley made a note. "We can ask the paramedics what they made of him when they examined him. Colin, can you track them down?"

Colin nodded morosely, which meant nothing. He always looked morose. It probably wasn't a coincidence that he always got the worst jobs, the grinding routine bits of investigation that had to be done but rarely threw up interesting results. It was a shame for him that he was good at that sort of work, painstaking and diligent in a way that Derwent, say, was not.

"We still need to get that list from Kennford, though." Godley checked the clock on the wall. "I've got the PMs on Vita and Laura this morning."

"We'll be there too." Derwent was speaking for me as well, I realized with a sinking feeling. I would give a lot to miss the autopsies.

"Good. Let's arrange to see Kennford this afternoon at his chambers. I want to be there. I want to show him we're taking it seriously."

And make up for losing his temper the night before. He was also aware of the need to keep his DI under control, I guessed. Derwent was rocking on his chair, smirking. "I'm going to make Kennford wish he'd never picked a fight with me."

"I think Kennford isn't telling us everything he knows, but I don't think we should make the mistake of concentrating on him and him alone." Everyone around the table turned to look at me with varying degrees of interest. "We've got two victims who might equally have been the real targets. We don't even know if it was one of them or both of them. Maybe Laura was collateral damage and Vita was the one who was meant to die, or maybe it was the other way round. Either way, we need to know as much as we can about them."

"Did you find anything useful last night?" Godley asked.

"Define useful." Derwent yawned widely before going on and I felt my jaw creak in sympathy. "We found that Laura had been making amateur porn with an unidentified male, and that her mother had a keen interest in the professional kind. She had quite a collection."

"Any diaries? Letters?"

"No, but it is the twenty-first century, boss. We were looking for phones and e-mails."

I didn't wait to see if Godley was amused or annoyed by Derwent's smart-arse remark, hurrying in with, "Without success. Laura must have had a phone but I couldn't find it, and I turned the place upside down. I really don't think it's in the house. Vita's was in her handbag, switched off. No idea what the PIN is — we tried all the obvious ones but no luck. We need to get it unlocked so we can track down her friends, find out if they knew anything about her personal life."

"Computers?"

"Vita didn't seem to have one, but we'll check that with Kennford. He has a laptop — we let him take it away with him as he needed it for work. And he's not a suspect, officially."

"Yet," Derwent interjected.

"Both girls had laptops too. We've got Laura's and I've sent it for analysis."

"Laura had every gizmo going," Derwent said. "Her room looked like the stockroom at a branch of Comet. But there wasn't anything that takes us much further, on first examination. Mind you, we haven't got into her emails yet."

"That's something I want to ask Lydia about this morning," I said. "She might know her sister's password. She might also know where Laura was supposed to be last night. Kennford said he was expecting her to be out. I'd like to know where, with whom, and why she changed her plans."

"Teenagers are unreliable by nature," Maitland said. "I should know, I've got two of them. Never tell you half the things they get up to and never get around to doing most of what they plan to."

"It's a change in their routine," I countered. "Something different. Something unexpected. So far it's the only strange thing we

can be sure of, and even though there's nothing to say it's connected, I still think we
should find out where she was meant to be."

"With the boyfriend, maybe." Derwent
clicked his fingers. "But she broke up with
him instead and went home, so he killed her,
and her mum for good measure. Case
closed."

It was a good thing I was used to sarcasm
from that quarter. "I'm not suggesting it's as
straightforward as that. It's just an anomaly.
Anything out of the ordinary should be investigated."

"It's worth finding out more," Godley said.
"Do we know who the boyfriend is?"

"He's Mr. Faceless McAnonymous in the
pictures and I bet Kennford didn't have a
clue he existed." Derwent scrawled something
in his notebook. "We'll have to ask Lydia who
her sister was banging."

Alarm bells were going off in my mind. If
Derwent took that line with her we could
forget finding out anything at all. "I'm not
going to ask her that straight out. She's not
likely to tell me, even if she knows."

"How would she not know? They were
twins."

"Doesn't mean they were close." I looked
at Godley instead of Derwent, hoping he
would referee. "When we went and searched
their rooms, Laura's was a mess, but it gave
you the feeling she enjoyed life. She certainly

had everything any teenager could want in the way of gadgets and toys. Lydia's was like a nun's cell. I don't know how much they had in common apart from DNA and shared womb space, but they definitely led different lives."

The superintendent nodded. "She sounds shy, from what her dad said. Josh, you should take a backseat for that interview. Actually, don't go. I don't want you scaring the girl out of talking. Maeve has a better chance of gaining her trust if she goes on her own."

"So you're keeping me out of it again." Derwent's chair thudded down on the carpet. "It's a pretty important interview and you want to send Kerrigan alone?"

"She's more than capable."

I tried to look more than capable. Una Burt was frowning at me but not with disapproval; more as if she'd never really noticed me before. Maitland had crossed his arms across his barrel chest and was grinning, all set to enjoy the show. Colin looked bored, but then he was generally uninterested in human interaction.

"She's not sufficiently experienced and she's far from infallible," Derwent insisted.

"I don't have any doubt about her abilities."

"Well, I do. And she'll miss the postmortems."

"I imagine we will cope without her."

96

I could feel my face burning. It was bad enough to be criticized in front of senior members of the team. The fact that Derwent and Godley were actually fighting about me was mortifying.

Godley put the cap on his pen with an air of finality. "You'll get your chance to be useful later, Josh, when we're dealing with Kennford."

"I don't like her going on her own. It's too important to run the risk of fucking it up."

"Drop it, Josh. I've made my decision."

Derwent opened his mouth to keep arguing but I got in first. "There is another option. Someone else could come with me."

"Who?" Derwent demanded.

"I thought Liv Bowen would be a good person. She's not intimidating and she's a good listener."

"You don't need anyone else to hold your hand." Godley sounded dismissive. I wondered how much of his faith in me was real and how much was generated by his determination not to back down in the face of Derwent's skepticism.

"It's not for hand holding. You know how useful it can be to have two officers instead of one when you're interviewing someone who's likely to get emotional. I don't want to get caught up in feeling sorry for her. I'm going to need time to think about what I ask her, but she still has to feel we really care about her and her grief. It's just less intense if there are two of you there to respond. I'll have time to stand back a bit."

"And she can make sure you ask everything you should," Derwent added.

"It's not like she has one chance to talk to the girl, Josh. If we need to go back and re-interview her, we will." Godley turned to me. "For the record, I don't think you need her to come with you, but I can see your point. One-to-one interviews are never easy, especially when you're dealing with a vulnerable person."

"We need to talk about what you want to find out from her," Una Burt said. "What's the main thing?"

"What was going on with her sister," I suggested.

"I'm more interested in her parents' relationship problems," Derwent said. "Divorce is a decent motive for Kennford."

Godley looked amused. "Still barking up that tree, Josh? See what you can find out, Maeve, but don't push her too far. She might not want to reveal family secrets at this stage, and her mother is dead, remember. I don't expect her to say anything negative about their marriage, or her mother, until she gets used to the idea that she's gone."

"We obviously need to know what she saw last night," Maitland said. "If anything."

"And why she's not dead. That automatically makes her a suspect in my book."

Godley's mouth twitched. "Brutal as ever, Josh. And still you're surprised I don't want you going along to meet her. But you're right, we need to know if she was left out deliberately or if she was just out of the way at the right time."

"Or whether she was supposed to die in Laura's place." Una looked around the table, blinking behind her thick glasses.

"I'm not following." It must have cost Derwent quite a lot to admit that, I thought. He certainly said it through gritted teeth.

"They were identical, weren't they? And Laura wasn't supposed to be there." She shrugged. "We can't be sure Lydia wasn't the target all along."

Derwent was on my heels as we left the room after the meeting, leaning in close so no one else could hear him.

"Well done. Thanks for getting rid of me."

"It wasn't deliberate."

"Bullshit. I know payback when I see it. You were pissed off about having to search the house properly last night and you got your revenge by making me look like a tit in front of everyone."

"If you looked like a tit in front of everyone it was nothing to do with me." I turned around to face him, keeping my voice low and my expression pleasant. "I'm not like you. I don't bother with holding grudges. And if I'd been pissed off about the search last night I'd have said so at the time."

"The famous Kerrigan temper." He leaned against the wall, always just that little bit too close to me for comfort. "I'm still waiting to see it."

And that's exactly why I'll never lose it in front of you. "I'm sorry if you're disappointed about not interviewing Lydia but it was Superintendent Godley who made that call. And I agreed with you, for what it's worth. I shouldn't be seeing her on my own."

"Yeah, much more fun if your rug-muncher mate comes along for the ride."

"Talking about me?" Liv turned around in her chair. Either Derwent hadn't noticed her sitting near us or he hadn't cared.

"Must be. You're the only dyke on the team. As far as we know." He turned his head, tracking DCI Burt as she walked through the room with her head down, lost in her thoughts.

"May I ask why I came up in conversation?" Liv sounded interested rather than offended; she had heard enough remarks about her sexuality to take a bit of slang in her stride, even if it was stridently homophobic. Also, she was one of the most self-possessed people I'd ever known. It would take a lot more than Derwent calling her names to make her lose her cool, I imagined.

100

Something — Una Burt, maybe — had made the inspector lose interest in our conversation. He stood upright and stretched.

"Get back to the office by twelve, Kerrigan. We'll go over to Kennford's chambers together."

"Can't wait." I watched him walk away, pursuing his own agenda as usual.

"He seems cheery."

"Even more than usual." I rubbed my eyes. "We didn't get much sleep last night."

"Oh yeah?" Liv managed to get a world of meaning into just two words.

"Because of work, obviously. Have you heard about the mother and daughter who got stabbed in Wimbledon?"

"Philip Kennford's family? Of course. It was all over the news."

"They weren't named."

She shrugged. "It's common knowledge. More than a few people are delighted to pass on the news that Philip Kennford's involved. Not a popular fellow."

"Derwent and I spent the night going through the house and found a whole lot of nothing. If you're free, can you give me a hand with questioning a witness?"

"Here?"

"In Twickenham. She's at her aunt's house. It's the other daughter — I didn't think it was a good idea to bring her in. And Godley didn't think it was a good idea to let Derwent loose on someone who's bound to be feeling a bit vulnerable."

"Whereas I'm notoriously sensitive, being a woman." Liv pushed back from her desk and stood up, straightening her immaculate white shirt. "Anything that gets me out of the office is fine by me. This place smells of armpits."

"That's man smell," DC Ben Dornton said in an ultramasculine voice from his desk opposite where Liv had been sitting. "No wonder you don't like it."

"That's I-can't-be-bothered-with-deodorant-even-though-this-room-isn't-air-conditioned smell," I said. "Not raw testosterone, or whatever you think it is."

He braced his hands on the top of his head, airing out his underarms. "Breathe deep, ladies. Fresh sweat is a known aphrodisiac and there's no need to thank me."

"I'm not convinced," Liv said, holding her nose.

"You'll miss it when you're gone."

"Gone where?" Like a gopher on the prairie, Peter Belcott popped up from behind his computer. Afflicted with rampant small-man syndrome, he was easily my least favorite colleague and I didn't bother to answer him, or even look at him. I liked to pretend he wasn't there, not least because I knew it annoyed the crap out of him.

"Out for an interview on Maeve's new case." Liv was logging out of her computer.

102

"Oh, right. You've found something more interesting to do than the gangland shootings. Fair enough. What's so important about a load of drug dealers being murdered? In fact, why don't you take the rest of the day off? I'm sure we'll manage without you."

"The boss approved it," I said tiredly. "And given that most of the team is currently working on the shootings, I doubt it will make a huge difference if Liv isn't here for one morning."

It was fatal to attract Belcott's attention. "Yeah, and I noticed you managed to get yourself onto this new case somehow. I've been watching for a while, Kerrigan. You're always the boss's first choice. Why would that be?"

"Because I'm good at my job."

"We're all good. That's why we're here. What I want to know is why you're his favorite."

I laughed. "Belcott, you're paranoid."

"I've been keeping track." His face had flushed red, which didn't suit him. "You get special treatment. Just makes me wonder if it has something to do with the boss's marriage being on the skids. Stands to reason he's gone over the side with someone."

"What are you talking about?" I asked, genuinely confused.

"I'm talking about Godley shagging around. Seems to me you're a likely suspect. There's no other explanation for why you keep getting preferential treatment."

Dornton looked over his shoulder at Godley's office, where the blinds were drawn and the door was closed. "Keep your voices down, for fuck's sake. He can probably hear every word you're saying."

"I don't care." Belcott sounded defiant, something that was calculated to bring out the worst in me.

"I do care, actually. I resent what you're suggesting and it's not the first time you've made a comment like that, based on nothing except that you seem to be convinced you're entitled to everything you ever wanted and the fact that you're jogging along as a middle-of-the-road DC must be someone else's fault."

Struggling to speak, Belcott took a second to reply. *"Bitch."*

"Yeah, I've heard that before. It doesn't surprise me you couldn't come up with anything original." I jabbed a finger at him. "If I hear you've been saying that about me to anyone, I'm going to report you for harassment. I'm going to make your life a misery. And I don't know where you're getting your ideas about Godley's private life, but I'm willing to bet you're way off."

"You would say that."

"I'd say it because it's true."

"Oh, fuck off, Princess Perfect." Belcott

turned on his heel and walked out.

I turned back to Dornton. "What was he trying to imply about Godley's marriage?"

"The boss has been sleeping here, in his office. Because of the shootings, he says. Better to be on the spot in case there's another one."

"That's no reason for a conspiracy theory. It definitely doesn't mean he has to have been having an affair. I don't know anything about Godley's private life, but I do know they've just been away on holiday. That's not what you do if you're on the point of breaking up, is it?"

"Keeping it together for the sake of the kid," Dornton said wisely.

"The kid is sixteen. I think she could cope."

Liv was brushing her long ponytail. "You have to admit it's a bit weird that he's camping out here. He doesn't live that far away."

Changing sides easily, Dornton said, "Not the point. Think about the disruption. Coming and going at all hours. And he's trying to keep his family out of it, isn't he?"

"He has good reason," I said with a shudder. "He's right in the middle of a fight to the death between two of the most unpleasant criminals I've ever come across. John Skinner hasn't had any qualms about targeting Godley's family before, and now he's got a life sentence without parole he has less to lose."

"He's got nothing. Nothing at all. And

Godley was the one who put him back inside for good, so he must hate him." Dornton shook his head. "Makes you wonder why he's bothered with fighting a turf war against Ken Goldsworthy again."

"Because Goldsworthy is up for it," Liv suggested. "He can tell he's close to winning and Skinner can't back down. Last time, Goldsworthy didn't have a hope in hell of coming out on top and that's why he ended up having to make do with a corner of Hertfordshire while Skinner got most of London. But Skinner was in Spain then, not cooling his heels in prison."

"The last time I saw Ken Goldsworthy he was charming the pants off Mrs. Skinner," I reminded Liv. "Literally. I bet that's the sort of thing that would motivate Skinner to keep fighting, and doing it across our patch makes it Godley's problem, so there's an added incentive."

"It's pride. And force of habit." DS Maitland had been tuned in to the entire conversation. Now he leaned across Liv to nick a pen off her desk. "You know and I know that Skinner should give up now and enjoy his retirement at Her Majesty's pleasure, all the comforts of home supplied as and when required. But he never knew when he was beaten before, so he's not going to walk away from a fight if he still has one dog to bark for him."

"And that's about all he's got, as I understand it," I said.

"Yeah. He lost a few of his best and brightest when he was looking for his daughter." His daughter, who had led him to act so recklessly that he had essentially walked into custody after years on the run. His daughter, who had turned up dead in spite of everything he'd sacrificed for her. "Recruitment isn't so easy when you're stuck in prison. It's not as if he has a lot to offer. Come and work for me and I can guarantee you a quick death and no share of the profits because there aren't any."

"But if he wins —"

Maitland shrugged. "Then he gets the lot. And he's not in a position to enjoy it, so whoever's been on his side is quids in. Hence the new agreement."

"New agreement?" I looked to Liv for an explanation.

"The latest we're hearing is that he's gone in with some immigrants. We don't know much except that they're supposedly Eastern Europeans, which could mean anything from the Baltics to Afghanistan. The word is, they carried out the last killing — the two lads who were dumped behind the ice rink in Streatham. They're not on our radar so far so I can't tell you any more than that."

"And luckily for us they're not on Ken Goldsworthy's radar either, so we've had a couple of nights off. Not that it'll last." Dornton finished off with a cavernous yawn.

"You don't seem too bothered," I said, amused.

"I just can't get that worked up about a load of drug dealers and scumbags killing each other. I know the tabloids are screaming for us to do something, but I don't see them making any useful suggestions."

"It's all window dressing, isn't it?" Liv said. "Godley needs us to look busy so the Chief Constable will leave him alone. We can chase around from crime scene to crime scene, but the truth is we're always too late to do anything useful. By the time we find whoever did the last murder, they're usually bleeding out on a pavement somewhere in Peckham or Tooting."

"Rough justice, but it works." Dornton shrugged. "You might as well go off and do something more useful with your time, Liv."

"While 'London descends into chaos.' " I turned around the newspaper that was lying on Liv's desk so Dornton could read the headline. He snorted in disgust.

"Give it a rest. There are thirty or forty possible targets for Skinner and his boys — more for Goldsworthy, probably, now that these foreign lads are in on it. Someone else is going to die, and soon, but there's fuck all we can do about it."

Liv nodded. "All we need is for John Skinner and Ken Goldsworthy to agree their territories and the killing will stop."

"It sounds so simple when you put it that way. I can't imagine why we haven't done it already." Godley walked past us without waiting for Liv to respond, which was probably a good thing as she looked too mortified to speak.

"That's the sort of thing that usually happens to me," I said once he was well out of earshot.

"Well, it's true." She grinned at me, recovering fast. "Good thing he didn't come along a bit earlier, isn't it?"

"Like when Belcott was accusing me of sleeping with him? He is the only person on this team who could put two and two together and come up with sixty-nine."

"There's more of it about than you'd think." Dornton caught my eye and ducked down behind his computer, muttering something about having work to do.

"Well, if you hear anyone else saying it, Ben, you know what to tell them. Besides, it's not as if the Kennford case is fun. If it was up to Derwent, we'd be working on the gang shootings."

"Really?"

"Really. He used to be on Godley's task force dealing with organized crime. He's got the background and the experience but for some reason he's not involved. He feels he's been sidelined in favor of DCI Burt, and it kills him that he's lost out to a woman."

"Is that his problem?" Liv asked, fascinated.

"I'd say it's one of the many."

"Did he tell you all that?" Dornton's eyebrows were hovering around his hairline.

"No." I smiled condescendingly at him. "But a woman knows."

"So that's why you're top of the boss's list. Feminine intuition."

"That's right. It's just our natural advantage. Don't worry. One day you men will start being given the same opportunities we enjoy. Until then, I'm afraid you're just going to have to work harder than us to get the recognition you deserve."

"Very funny, Kerrigan."

"I've never been more serious."

"You could try and make yourself look a bit better too. Smarter. Do something with your hair," Liv suggested. "And tidy your desk."

"Good idea. A few fresh flowers would make a world of difference. Little masculine touches add a lot to the workplace."

Dornton glowered at me. "I hope you're better at being detectives than comedians. Go and do your interview, for God's sake, and leave me alone."

"Back soon," Liv trilled. "Try not to miss me when I'm gone."

"I'll be counting the minutes."

I headed for the door, the smile on my face fading as I started to focus on what I was about to do, on the fact that I was responsible for running an interview that could make all the difference in tracing the killer of two people, one still a child. When it came down to it, office politics didn't matter. All that mattered was getting a result, and if I didn't, I'd only have myself to blame.

It was no consolation to know there'd be a queue of people ready to do the same.

CHAPTER FIVE

Whatever else they had in common, Vita and her sister both had an eye for expensive real estate. Renee Fairfax's home was far more traditional than the house I had searched the night before: a detached, white-painted Georgian property with extensive gardens that ended in a particularly pretty bit of the Thames. Polished antique furniture, silver knickknacks and gilt-framed pictures gleamed in the rooms I could see from the hall. That was where Liv and I had been left to wait for the housekeeper to find Renee herself. I felt most definitely out of place and couldn't tell if Liv felt the same way.

She had been scanning her surroundings with interest. "What do you think Mr. Fairfax does for a living?"

"Something that brings in big money to afford a place like this. It makes the Endsleigh Drive house look basic."

"Not too shabby, is it?" Liv ran her toe over the fringe of the Oriental carpet. "I feel like

I'm on a film set."

"I know what you mean." Even the flowers were perfect, great vases full of red roses that stood on two matching half-moon tables on either side of the hall. I wandered over to one to inhale their sweet scent, noticing in passing that there were two tiny drops of water on the table. I wiped them away before they could leave a mark on the varnish. When I turned to go back to Liv, she raised her eyebrows.

"You look perplexed."

"I am, I suppose. These flowers are fresh. They were put here this morning."

"So?"

"So what kind of person cares about having fresh flowers on display in her home less than twenty-four hours after her sister's brutal murder?"

"Maybe it was the housekeeper's idea. I can't really believe they have servants. I thought that kind of thing went out in Victorian times."

"Not if you're very, very rich."

"And these people definitely are. Where do you think the money comes from?"

"Inherited, I'm sorry to say." Unobserved by me, a tall red-haired woman had emerged from the shadows at the back of the hall. Renee, I presumed. She was lean to the point of emaciation, her white cotton shirt and narrow pink jeans hanging off her frame. I tried to remember what I'd just been saying about her and her family, and whether it had actually been offensive or just speculative.

She advanced toward us, moving into the light. She was nothing like her sister in appearance, but striking in her own way. A long necklace of jade beads and gold links was looped twice around her neck and hung inside her collar, the green startlingly dark against paper-white skin. Her shoulder-length auburn hair was blow-dried to perfection and she had elegantly arched eyebrows over cold green eyes. It was the classic redhead coloring and I thought it was all natural, even to the darker brows and lashes. She had been unlucky to get the delicate complexion that traditionally came with red hair — unlucky because it showed her age cruelly. Wrinkles fanned out from her eyes and curved around her narrow mouth. Her forehead was smooth and shiny, like soap, and I recognized the signs of an expensive Botox habit. Her voice had a metallic quality, which contributed to the impression I had formed, more or less immediately, that she was pure steel.

"I'm DC Maeve Kerrigan. This is DC Liv Bowen." Renee folded her arms as I introduced myself so I abandoned any attempt at shaking her hand. "We're investigating the deaths of your sister and your niece."

I was deliberately brutal in how I phrased it to see if I would get a reaction of any kind, which I did not.

"I gathered that. I'm afraid I'm not sure how I can help." She was too composed. It was either a way of disguising her grief or she simply didn't feel any.

"I'd just like to ask you a couple of questions, if I may."

"Such as?"

No point in starting small. "Do you know of anyone who might have wanted to kill your sister?"

"Certainly not." She seemed to find the very idea an insult. "This entire situation is completely grotesque."

That was one way of putting it. "It must be very shocking."

"Naturally. It's been extremely traumatic." Renee did not look particularly traumatized. However, she was hugging herself as if she was cold, which was surely impossible on such a hot day.

"Did you see much of your sister? Speak to her often?"

"We spoke. Not daily. A normal amount." She shook her hair back. "We were on good terms."

It was a fairly formal way of putting it, but I let it go for the moment. The truth about how people related to one another tended to come out, whether they wanted to hide it or not.

"Would you have known if anything was

worrying her?" Liv asked. "If she was frightened, for instance?"

"I imagine she would have said something if she was *frightened,* though I can't imagine what would have made her feel that way. As for anything worrying her — well, she had plenty of things to be concerned about."

"Such as?"

"Family issues. Mothers always worry about their children. Some wives worry about their husbands. Vita had good reason."

"What do you mean, Mrs. Fairfax?"

"I mean that Philip was not a good husband and teenage girls are not straightforward. Vita found it hard to deal with the three of them. And when Philip should have been backing her up, he was always away, *working.*" She sounded deeply scathing.

"He does seem to be a busy man."

"Busy playing around. He is consistently unfaithful."

It fitted in with what Derwent had said about him. "Is that a recent development?"

She shook her head. "He's always been the same. He married her for her money, as I always told her. Having got his hands on it, he had no further use for her. I hope he's on your list of suspects because I wouldn't trust him in the slightest."

"Did he ever threaten her, do you know? Any violent incidents?"

"No." She sounded regretful.

"Would you have known about it if there were any incidents of that sort?" Liv asked. "Very often victims of domestic violence hide it, even from those who are close to them."

"The only thing he ever threatened her with was leaving her."

"And she didn't jump at the chance? He doesn't sound like the sort of person you'd want to stick around."

"She believed in marriage," Renee said coldly. "She believed in her vows, even if he didn't. And she wasn't cut out to be a single mother. She managed to persuade him to stay."

"Did you think that was a good idea?"

"She'd made her bed." Zero warmth; zero understanding.

"Did she have any enemies?"

Renee laughed. "She wasn't a character in a soap opera."

"Ordinary people have enemies too, Mrs. Fairfax."

"Not people like Vita."

"Sometimes," I insisted. "Wealth and privilege don't exempt you from other people's envy. Quite the opposite."

"I'll have to try to remember that," Renee drawled, and I felt myself blush. I very much disliked being made to feel inferior because of my accent or my job or the fact that I was clearly impressed by my surroundings. Class was still an issue and only those who never needed to worry about it in the first place thought it wasn't. I had to make a special effort to keep myself from sounding nettled.

"Can you think of anything that might help us find your sister and niece's killer?"

"Hard work?" She arched an eyebrow, then shook her head, becoming almost human before my eyes. "I'm sorry. I couldn't resist being flippant. I just don't think there's anything I can suggest. I'm at a loss."

"I understand." To be charitable, she was probably in shock. And she had apologized. I was prepared to be magnanimous, if not friendly.

"Can you tell us about Vita's wealth? How much was she worth?"

"I don't know to the nearest pound. A considerable amount, though. The money came from banking, originally. My grandfather had his own. He made a fortune in the Far East in rubber and mining interests."

"Ethical?" Liv asked with a raised eyebrow.

"It was the thirties. No one cared about that kind of thing then." And it didn't look as if Renee cared much now. "He was one of the richest men in the world at the time, but after the war, his investments had lost a lot of value. My generation inherited the last of it — a few million."

"Each, presumably," I said.

"Of course. But that's all there is. It was up to each of us to find a way of using the money to start a business and make it a success."

"So Vita set up an art gallery. According to Mr. Kennford, it lost money."

"Too risky. She was gambling with her inheritance."

"And that's not your approach."

"I'm an investor in the past. I deal in antiques. I know the market and my buyers know I only acquire the very best pieces, so the risks are small."

"And the profits?" Liv asked.

"I set the prices; I decide the profit. And I run my own interior design business too, so I can always find a home for what I buy. I'm risk-averse."

"But Vita didn't mind taking a chance."

"She could be impulsive." Renee's mouth was drawn tight with disapproval. "She never learned to look before she leaped."

"Is there anything else you think we should know?"

She shook her head and I looked at Liv to check whether she had anything else to ask. I got a no.

"In that case, perhaps we should speak to Lydia now."

Back to the steel. "I don't understand why you need to bother her today."

"We weren't able to get an account from her last night because she was under sedation, but that makes it all the more important we get to hear what happened and what she saw as soon as we can."

"Well, she won't talk about it with me. Won't talk about anything. The girl's practically mute."

They were bony shoulders to cry on, I thought. Renee Fairfax wasn't overflowing with sympathy and kindliness. I wouldn't have confided in her either, but diplomacy suggested I should find a tactful way of putting it.

"It's sometimes easier to talk to someone you don't know rather than a family member. Lydia won't want to upset you by talking about what happened to her mother and sister, especially if you were close to them." I paused to let Renee tell us about her relationship with her sister, but the narrow mouth remained firmly closed. "We never met Vita or Laura so we're neutral. She doesn't have to protect us from what she saw."

"We're trained to talk to young people in difficult situations," Liv added, using her most dove-like tone of voice, a low murmur that was infinitely soothing. I tried to imagine Derwent doing the same, and failed. On the other hand, his brand of macho tough talk might have made Renee go weak at the knees. It had its own strange appeal, I could imagine, if you weren't used to being treated that way. Maybe Godley had been wrong to stop Derwent from coming with me. So far, Liv and I weren't having much luck.

"I still think you should leave her alone. It can't help to go over it now, while she's still getting used to the idea they're gone. I can get in touch with you when she does feel able to discuss it."

"That's just not possible, I'm afraid. We need her to think about what she saw while it's still fresh in her mind. And we are looking for a very violent murderer, so we don't have the luxury of waiting until Lydia feels ready to talk to us." I waited to see what Renee Fairfax would come up with in reply. A shrug, it turned out.

"I can't be there while you talk to her, if it's going to take a while. I'm far too busy — I've got a meeting in half an hour. So if you need her to have a guardian-thingy —"

"That's up to you. If you need to work and she wants to speak to us in the presence of an appropriate adult, we'll have to find one. But that shouldn't be a problem." I sounded more confident than I felt. I needed to get this interview done and head back to the office before Derwent lost patience entirely and threw me off the case, which I had little doubt he would if I gave him the excuse. I definitely didn't need a delay while we scratched about for a court-appointed social worker to sit down with us and hold Lydia's hand.

The gamble worked. Renee's shoulders dropped a half-inch. "Oh, well. If you must.

She's in the garden. I sent her out to get some fresh air after breakfast."

Because breathing deeply would make up for half her family being savagely murdered. "That's fine. We can speak to her there." I looked past her, to where French windows gleamed greenly at the back of a drawing room. "Is this the best way to get out there?"

Renee might have been on the ropes but she had a punch or two left in her. "The best way for *you* to find her" — the emphasis was subtle, but definitely there — "is to go back outside and follow the path around the house. She's down by the river in the teahouse." A long hand fluttered vaguely. "You can't miss it. It's painted Chartwell green."

I had no idea what that looked like but I was damned if I was going to admit that to Renee. I nodded confidently and headed for the front door before she could come up with any other reasons why the interview couldn't go ahead.

Liv hung back for a moment. "And are you coming with us?"

"I'll meet you there."

What Renee actually meant, it transpired, was that she would cut through the house and take a shortcut to the teahouse, a small, pretty wooden pavilion on the edge of the water, open-sided to take advantage of the breeze from the river, painted a muted shade of blue-green. By the time Liv and I had trekked around the house and hacked through the shrubbery to find it, Renee had been able to talk to Lydia alone for a couple of minutes. Preparing her, I assumed, but the body language was strained. The older woman was leaning over her niece, her arms still tightly folded, her head poked forward like a hunting bird. She was turned away from us so I couldn't see her face to make a guess as to what she had been saying, but I doubted it was anything I would consider helpful. Lydia's head was bent over a sketch-pad. She was shading a drawing, a delicate sketch of some peonies that nodded in a water glass on the table in front of her. Her expression was stubborn. She was as pale as she had been the night before, and on a day when the temperature was comfortably in the high twenties by mid-morning, she was wearing a black long-sleeved top that hung down over her hands and swamped her tiny frame. She wore jeans, loose rather than fitted, and heavy boots. I had lost touch with teenage fashion but I was pretty sure grunge was still out. If anything, most young girls seemed to wear as little as possible, especially in the middle of a heat wave. I wondered with a vague sense of disquiet what Lydia had to hide, then chided myself for jumping to conclusions. There was nothing to say a fifteen-year-old had to dress like a stripper just because most of them seemed to.

Renee turned at the sound of our feet on the steps and announced, fairly unnecessarily, "Here they are now."

Lydia didn't look up. Nor did she respond in any way to our greetings, concentrating instead on her drawing. I sat down opposite her, on a bench that ran around the inside of the teahouse, and Liv sat beside me. Renee perched on the railing and took out a pack of Sobranies. Her hand shook a little as she fitted the black-and-gold cigarette between her bloodless lips, and I waited for her to light it with a dainty silver lighter before I began.

"Thank you for talking to us today, Lydia. I know this must be hard for you, so we'll try to keep it short."

No response.

"We met last night. I'm DC Kerrigan. This is DC Bowen. If it's easier, you can call us Maeve and Liv." Again, there was no answer.

"That's a lovely drawing. You're very talented."

Slowly and deliberately, she turned over the page of her sketchpad to hide the flowers she had drawn. In their place, she began to draw a random pattern of jagged angles and dark squares, filling the white space with practiced ease.

"I didn't see any art in your bedroom."

That got me a glare for a second. *You were in my room, looking through my stuff.*

"Your room was bare compared to Laura's." She flinched and leaned her head on one hand, pressing her ear against her palm to block me out. "Would you say you had a lot in common?"

"You're obsessed with people's relationships," Renee commented, her voice husky. Smoke was drifting in Lydia's direction and she fanned it away from her. "That's all they asked me, Lydia. Whether your mother and I got on."

"Our job is all about people," I said simply. "What they were like. How they got on with others. Who loved them. Who hated them."

"Why should you care?" Lydia was looking at me again, this time holding my gaze. She spoke quietly but there was a challenge in her tone, something that reminded me of her father.

"Because finding out how people lived can tell us why they died."

"Do you think what happened is Laura's fault? Or Mum's?" Her eyes were suddenly full of unshed tears.

"The only person who is responsible for what happened is the person who brought about their deaths. Neither of them is to blame, and I really do mean that." I leaned forward. "But Lydia, to find out who killed them we have to find out why they died, so we need to know what was going on in their lives. We don't yet know what happened last

125

night and we need your help to work it out."

"I can't tell you anything."

"You can tell us what you saw and what you heard." She was shaking her head already. "You might not think you saw anything useful, but you were there and we weren't. Just tell us what happened yesterday."

"Start at breakfast and keep going," Liv suggested.

Lydia almost smiled. "We didn't eat breakfast together."

"What happened instead?"

"Dad got up early. So did I. He fried sausages and Mum gave him a bollocking when she came down for leaving the dirty pan on the cooker."

"What were you doing while he was cooking?"

"I went out for a run."

"Before breakfast?" I pulled a face. "I couldn't do that."

"It's not that bad once you get going." She was fidgeting with her sleeves, pulling them down over her hands. "I like to go out early."

"Before it gets too hot."

"Yeah. And it's good when there aren't too many people around."

"You're quite into sports, aren't you? Running in the morning, swimming in the evening. When I was your age I just lay around the house all day watching TV." It was a casual comment but Lydia reacted to

126

Liv's remark as if she'd been slapped. She tucked her chin into her chest, physically withdrawing from the conversation. I shot Liv a warning glare. Lydia's tiny frame, the clothes that effectively disguised her body, the exceptional neatness of her room and her obsessive exercising made me wary of commenting on her appearance or her routine. She was certainly a perfectionist, maybe something more than that, and my instinct was to leave the subject well alone or risk losing her trust completely.

"Right, you came back from your run and your dad was in trouble with your mum. What time was that?"

"Half eight, I think? I don't wear a watch."

"Where was Laura?"

A half smile. "She was in bed. She didn't get up until lunchtime."

"Was that her usual habit?"

"On a Sunday. She was out on Saturday night — she didn't get in until after three."

"Where did she go?" I was curious; she was too young for pubs and clubs.

"To see friends."

"Can you give me their names and addresses?"

In a soft voice, she listed five names, all girls. "I'm not sure of the addresses but they all live in Wimbledon or Kingston. They're in school with us."

"Don't worry. I can get their addresses from

127

the school." I tapped my pen on my notebook. "What about boys? Did Laura have a boyfriend?"

"No."

"Really?"

"Yes." Lydia blinked at me, all innocence. "We're not allowed have boyfriends. Not until we're seventeen."

I couldn't tell if she was lying deliberately or if she genuinely didn't know what her sister had been up to. I grinned. "That sounds like a parent's rule to me. And those are the kind of rules that get broken, usually. It's easy enough to mislead your parents if you want to, isn't it?"

A vehement shake of her head. "We wouldn't have gone behind their backs."

"Are you sure?" In the car, I had brought Liv up to speed on the images we'd found on Laura's camera. She knew as well as I did that we weren't getting the full story. "Is it possible that Laura was seeing someone that you didn't even know about?"

Lydia looked stubborn. "No way. She wasn't seeing anyone."

"But she was staying out late. With friends, you said. You don't know if she was really there, do you? She might have been meeting a boyfriend."

"She wasn't."

"Lydia's told you Laura didn't have a boyfriend. Stop bullying her."

I had almost forgotten Renee was there. "I'm sorry, Mrs. Fairfax." To Lydia, I said, "We're not trying to bully you. We just want to be absolutely sure we know the truth about Laura's love life. It could be significant."

"There's nothing to know." Lydia was pulling at her sleeves again, worrying at a loose thread.

"I'm afraid that's not the case."

"Why are you so sure she had a boyfriend?" Renee demanded.

I looked at Lydia warily. If she really believed what she'd been telling us, it was time to shatter some illusions. "We found things in Laura's room that lead us to believe she was in a relationship."

"What sort of things?"

I hesitated. "The contraceptive pill. Condoms."

"That doesn't mean anything," Renee snapped. "Teenagers get prescribed the pill for all sorts of reasons. And they're given condoms for free. Aren't you, Lyd? My boys always had hundreds of them in their rooms, not that they had much of a chance to use them. Wishful thinking was what it was."

Lydia had gone scarlet and was staring across the lawn, clearly wishing she was somewhere else, somewhere a million miles from our conversation.

"There were other things, Mrs. Fairfax. I don't need to go into detail, but we are absolutely sure that Laura had been engaging in sexual acts with one or possibly more partners. We are obviously very keen to trace anyone who was involved with her, which is why I keep asking Lydia if she can identify anyone who might have been . . . close to Laura." It was a nice euphemism. Derwent's version would have been something like, "Anyone who was stuck in her up to his nuts."

"I didn't know." Lydia's voice was so quiet I had to strain to hear her. "I promise, I didn't know."

"We can talk to her friends," Liv said, "so don't worry. We will find whoever it was."

"She was so young." Renee sounded stunned. "Things have changed, haven't they?"

"I think young people have always done more of that sort of thing than adults want to believe," I said. "It's just that you can prove it now that everyone has a digital camera and access to the Internet."

"Vita would have been mortified. She thought Laura was an angel."

"She was underage, but as I said, it's not that unusual. If it was consensual and her partner was also underage, I don't think it would be seen as particularly controversial by the standards of today."

"What standards?" Renee made a noise that was very like a snort. "Of course, she got it from her father. He has the morals of an alley cat. The hypocrisy of banning boyfriends when he's famous for his floozies. I mean: you're going to go one way or the other, aren't you? It's no wonder —" She broke off abruptly.

"No wonder?" I prompted.

"No wonder she thought it was acceptable."

I was absolutely sure that wasn't what Renee had been planning to say, but with Kennford's daughter sitting between us I could imagine why she'd come to a shuddering halt.

"Speaking of the Internet, do you know Laura's password for her e-mail account?"

"She changed it all the time," Lydia said.

"What sort of thing did she usually use?"

"Completely random stuff. She collected eight-letter words. It made her laugh to have something weird that no one could ever guess."

More good news. "Did she have a list of them?" I asked, slightly desperately.

"Yes. On her phone."

Elation to despair in two short sentences. "About that — we can't find her phone. It didn't seem to be in the house."

"She always had it."

"Not last night. We found her bag in the living room —" I flashed on an image of Kev Cox delving through it with gloved hands. It had been on the sofa near her when her throat was cut and had come in for a good share of the arterial spray. Brown leather saturated with blood turned a vile shade of purple. Glad that they couldn't read my mind, I finished off lamely with, "— and the phone wasn't there."

"She usually kept it in her back pocket if it wasn't in her bag."

"She'd been sitting on the sofa. Would she have taken it out of her pocket to be more comfortable?"

A shrug. "I suppose."

"It's important we find it, Lydia. Do you know the number?" We could trace it using cell-site analysis, triangulating it by the nearest transmission stations.

"I have it written down somewhere."

"It's probably in your phone," Liv said. "I never remember anyone's number anymore because I just use my mobile all the time."

"I don't have one."

"Really? You must be the only teenager in Britain who doesn't."

"I don't like them."

"Your friends must find it annoying when they want to get hold of you."

She looked down again and didn't answer. Maybe Lydia wasn't the sort of person who had a lot of friends.

I looked down at my list of questions and blew out a lungful of air. To say we weren't making progress was an understatement. No boyfriend. No phone. Very little information we hadn't had already.

Lydia must have read the expression on my face. "I'm sorry. I'm not much use."

"No, you're being very helpful. You can only tell us what you know."

"I suppose so." She didn't sound convinced.

"Let's go back to yesterday," I suggested.

"I spent the morning reading in my room. I don't know what Mum did. Dad went into chambers to pick up a brief."

"And then?"

"Laura got up. She cooked lunch and I helped — pasta and pesto, garlic bread. But it was much too hot for a heavy meal." Lydia smiled a little, remembering. "No one finished it."

"Did Laura like cooking?"

"She loved it. She liked to make people happy."

"After that?"

"I tidied up. Mum went off and made some phone calls. Laura watched TV and I went back to my room. Dad was working in his study."

Happy families. "Was that usual at weekends? You didn't do anything together?"

"Sometimes." She screwed up her face, trying to think. "Mainly we'd go shopping with Mum or on our own. Dad usually works. And in term-time, we have homework."

"Okay. You're doing really well. What happened after you watched TV?"

"Laura got ready to go out. Mum and Dad had dinner." She shifted a little in her chair. "I wasn't hungry. I stayed in my room until later, when I came down to swim."

I leaned forward a little, unable to stop myself. "Where was Laura going?"

"To see her best friend. Millie Carberry," Lydia added, seeing me scanning the list she'd already given me. I put a star against Millie's name.

"For any particular reason?"

"Laura said they were going to the cinema together. Millie is obsessed with Robert Pattinson so she wanted to see his new film."

"But they didn't go. Or at least Laura didn't."

Lydia was twisting her right hand around the opposite forearm, over and over. "No. She didn't."

"Who knew she was supposed to be out last night?" Liv asked.

"I don't know. She probably put it on her Facebook page."

"And I bet she's popular." I had a sinking feeling. It was getting to be familiar.

"She's got hundreds of friends."

"Okay, well, who would have known she wasn't out?"

"I have no idea. It must have been a last-minute thing. I didn't see her before I went out to the pool. I suppose I just assumed she'd gone out." Lydia was pale now, paler

134

than the drawing paper in front of her. A thin sheen of perspiration shone on her forehead and her upper lip. The temperature had climbed steadily while we'd been talking. The breeze from the water seemed to have dropped. I lifted my hair off the back of my neck for a second.

"I think we're in for a record-breaking day if it keeps up like this."

"I can't stand this weather," Renee said violently. "I wish it would rain."

Lydia closed her eyes.

"Are you okay, Lydia? Do you need a glass of water?"

"I'm fine." Her eyelids fluttered, then opened. I thought she looked dazed. It was time to start thinking about winding up the interview. She twisted her hand around her arm again, her knuckles white as she squeezed.

"I'm sorry to keep asking about Laura's plans for last night. It's just that we need to work out if she was the killer's target or not."

"You mean if we were all supposed to die or if it was just Mum or Laura." Her lips were bloodless.

"That is sort of what I mean."

"They hurt Dad. They killed Mum and Laura. They left me alone. Don't you think that's strange?"

"Not strange. Interesting. It might be significant. It might not."

"I've been wondering about it." Her eyes were closed again. "I've been thinking about whether it should have been me in there. I keep seeing her. And the blood."

"It might help you to talk to someone about what you saw. A counselor. The FLO can arrange that."

"FLO?" Renee inquired.

"Sorry. Family Liaison Officer."

"Oh, him. I sent him away. Horrible little man." She shuddered.

"I think they're used to that." Time to be diplomatic again. "I would give him a call. He might be able to help."

Beside me, Liv gave a smothered exclamation. I looked and moved in the same moment, jumping forward just in time to stop Lydia from hitting her head on the floor as she slumped out of her seat. I was peripherally aware of Renee sliding off the railing and stepping forward, reaching out, but all of my attention was focused on her niece. Before she could touch her, Liv grabbed her arm.

"Wait."

Lydia's eyes were closed but I could see her chest moving and her pulse was rapid under my fingers.

"She'll need an ambulance."

"I'll call them." Liv was staring down at her. "What's that?"

She was looking at a red smear on Lydia's bony wrist, where her sleeve had slipped back. Gingerly, I lifted the material away from the girl's skin. It stuck for a second, then pulled free. I pushed it back to her elbow, revealing a long, deep cut on her forearm seeping blood along its length. I stared at it for a second before registering that my fingertips were wet.

"Jesus, her sleeve is saturated. She's been bleeding the whole time we've been talking."

Renee looked at me accusingly. "But she wasn't injured. You said she wasn't injured."

"I didn't know. No one did. She didn't tell anyone."

And if she'd been telling us the truth about what had happened the previous night, she shouldn't have been hurt at all.

CHAPTER SIX

Renee was happy for me to go in the ambulance with Lydia, happy to stay at home while Lydia waited with us for treatment at A & E, and happy for her to be transferred to a ward for twenty-four hours' observation without feeling that she needed to come to the hospital herself. Renee was happy as long as she didn't have to put herself out, in fact. I didn't particularly mind — it was a lot easier to deal with the hospital staff without having a relative there, as they were prepared to talk to me in Renee's absence.

"Self-inflicted. This morning, probably." The doctor was young, tired, very thin and distracted by paperwork. He was leaning on the reception desk where Liv and I had cornered him.

"Are you sure? It couldn't have happened last night?" I had to stop myself from grabbing the file he was looking at just to make sure I had his full attention.

"Probably not. Looks more recent than

that." He shrugged. "You could try asking her."

"She's been out cold since we found out about it," Liv said.

"Pretending, maybe. I'd say she just doesn't want to talk to you. She's been speaking to the nurses and she was awake when I saw her, even if she wasn't very chatty." He didn't look up and I couldn't tell if he was being rude deliberately or if he was just distracted and too busy to be diplomatic.

"Well, that would make sense too." I was aiming for conciliatory. "I get that you can't be certain about when it happened, but why are you sure she did it to herself? You don't seem to have any doubts about it."

"Not really, no."

"It's just that we need to be sure it's not a defense wound or something she did in a fight." I leaned in closer. "It's a serious case. Murder. I need to know if she's a suspect or not."

"I can't help you there. All I can say is that the scarring on her arms and legs suggests she has a long-standing history of self-harm. Going back years, probably. If she has been involved in something like a murder, it might have brought about an incident of self-harm. Stress can do that."

"Sorry, she gets upset about her mother and sister being murdered so she tries to slit her wrists — is that what you're saying?" Liv was looking nonplussed.

"She wouldn't have intended to cause herself any serious or lasting harm. Self-harmers generally report a psychological release in cutting or burning themselves, as if the physical pain counteracts their mental anguish. It's common in sufferers of depression. And teenage girls."

"And sufferers from eating disorders?"

"Them too. It all goes hand in hand." He shrugged. "She looks like she was pretty dedicated to it, to be honest. I'd be surprised if this is her first time to be hospitalized, looking at some of the scarring."

"But you don't think she wanted to end up here?" I said. "It's not a cry for help?"

"I'd be more inclined to think she wanted to keep it a secret. She probably went too far without meaning to." He snapped the file shut and opened the next one on the pile. "She fainted because of blood loss. The cut isn't actually that bad, even though it's deep. At least it's clean."

"What do you think she used? A knife?"

"No. Something like a razor blade. Probably just from an ordinary disposable razor. They're easy enough to break apart."

I thought of Vita's injuries, and Laura's neck wound. They were definitely not razor cuts.

"It was deep, though," Liv objected.

"Nothing to stop you from cutting deeper

if you can stand it, even with a standard razor blade." He looked up from his file. "They say it makes you euphoric. You don't feel the pain. You don't feel anything at all."

"Hence the attraction of it."

"Exactly." He looked at me approvingly. I was fairly sure we were about the same age, but he had the condescending medical manner down pat. "It's her way of dealing with her emotions. Other people drink or take drugs. She cuts herself. Not as unusual as you might think."

"If you say so."

"It's not too bad an injury. I'm just keeping her in because I think she could do with a bit of being looked after, and there's no way to be sure how much blood she actually lost so we might as well play it safe." He looked up again. "Did you say her mother and sister were killed yesterday?"

"In Wimbledon."

"Shit. I heard about that. That's her, is it?" He shrugged. "Not actually a surprise that she's not in the best of moods."

"You can see why we're concerned to know how and when it happened."

"I can. But I've said what I think. You'll have to ask her for her version."

"Can we talk to her now?"

He leaned back to see her cubicle. The curtains were still closed. "If you've got time before she's transferred to the ward. She's going to the pediatric unit and I'd prefer to let her have a rest undisturbed once she gets there."

Liv set off toward the cubicle but I hung back. "Do you think she'll do it again?"

"Probably. Sometime."

"Should we be concerned for her safety, though? Should her father? I've got to know whether she needs to be sectioned for her own good."

"I wouldn't do that."

"You think giving her space is a better approach."

"Not necessarily. But I wouldn't put my worst enemy in a secure psychiatric unit. However bad things are out in the real world, it's got to be better than that." With a muttered goodbye he strode away, his chinos cinched in painfully tightly around a narrow waist. He lived on his nerves, I thought, and seemed to be naturally inclined to be snappy, but his heart was in the right place. I would pass on what he'd said to Renee, and Philip Kennford, and let them decide what was best for Lydia. I was just glad it wasn't my decision.

Inside the cubicle, Lydia was curled up on her side, her head buried in the pillow, her bandaged arm stretched out beside her. Liv was standing by the bed and shook her head at me as I came in. *No luck.*

I shook Lydia's shoulder, not in the mood

to take no for an answer. "We know you've been awake and talking, Lydia, so just give us five minutes and we'll leave you alone. I promise."

Ten long seconds ticked by before she rolled onto her back and stared up at the ceiling, still mute.

"The doctor says you did it to yourself. Is that right?"

A nod.

"When? Last night?"

"No." I could barely hear her say it.

"Before the murders?"

"No."

"When, then?"

"This morning."

"Before breakfast?"

A nod.

"Why, Lydia?"

I wasn't really surprised not to get an answer.

"The doctor said he thought you'd done it before."

Her face was immobile, like a mask.

"Did your mother know you did this kind of thing to yourself?"

A flicker of pain passed over her face before it returned to the mask. She looked more like her sister, strangely, despite the lack of animation — far more beautiful than I had thought her before.

"What about your father? What should I

143

tell him?"

Again, her face changed, but this time it wasn't grief, or pain, or the hard-edged composure I'd seen earlier. This time it was something closer to anger. Something that might have been hatred. And if I'd thought I was misreading it, what she said next would have confirmed it for me.

"He won't care." The three words were distinct, unmistakable, and her voice was suddenly stronger. Her eyes met mine and I felt a definite chill at what I saw in them. "Tell him what you like. He won't care at all."

By dint of driving as if I was the lead car in a high-speed pursuit and then running the half mile from where I got parked, despite the heat and my heels, I made it back to the office in time to meet Derwent and Godley on the front steps, heading out. Both of them were grim-faced, but that wasn't unusual after a morning with Glen Hanshaw.

"You missed the show." Derwent didn't look impressed.

"I was stuck at the hospital." Which he had known, since I'd phoned. I wasn't capable of being in two places at once, and even if I'd had a choice I'd have been happier to sit around on waiting-room chairs drinking bad tea for endless hours than watch the autopsies.

"How was the girl?" Godley asked.

"Damaged." I didn't have the breath for anything more.

"Tell us about it in the car."

"Did you find out anything useful?" Derwent sounded truculent, still nursing the chip on his shoulder about being left out.

"Depends what you mean." I really needed to do something about my fitness levels; I was still struggling to breathe normally. "Nothing more about the murders."

"So we still have no idea who killed them?"

"None whatsoever."

"Fucking marvelous."

I couldn't have put it better myself. "Did you find out anything at the postmortems?"

"They both died of blood loss arising from multiple injuries inflicted with a bladed object or objects."

"Did you find out anything we didn't know already?"

"He confirmed Laura wasn't a virgin, but we had plenty of evidence of that from what we'd seen on her camera. She had a bruise on her cheek that was a bit older than her other injuries — a day, maybe. Nothing to say how she got it." Derwent shook his head. "Better hope Kennford's had a change of heart about how helpful he's prepared to be. At the moment, we've got nothing."

Philip Kennford's chambers were in Unicorn Court, a narrow paved yard in the Inner

Temple, just off the Strand. I always felt as if I'd stepped back in time when I went to the Temple. As an outsider, it didn't seem to me as if the warren of courtyards, cobbled roads and walled gardens had changed much since the nineteenth century, except for the cars that were parked everywhere. A lot of it dated from much earlier than that, which accounted for the spellbound tourists wandering around, cameras at the ready. According to the panel above the archway Unicorn Court had been built in 1732 and was made up of six narrow buildings, wavering red-brick structures that each housed a separate set of chambers.

"Kennford is at this one," Godley said, stopping outside the third. A board on the wall proclaimed it to be the chambers of Timothy Kent QC and Pelham Griggs QC, with the barristers who worked there listed below. "They're a top defense set. They mostly do crime but they've a sideline in human rights. I don't expect you'll have worked with anyone here, but you might have come across them in court." Translation: this is the other side's territory. "Josh, you're still on your best behavior. I want to give him a chance to cooperate. Pissing him off at this stage is not going to help anyone."

"Whatever you say."

We trooped in and up the narrow staircase to the first floor, where there was an extremely modern reception desk with an equally up-to-date receptionist sitting behind it. She showed us into a small, stuffy meeting room that was dominated by a dusty fireplace big enough to accommodate a roasting ox. Four leather armchairs were placed around a coffee table; it was all very comfortable and civilized and far removed from the more unpleasant realities of criminal law. The narrow window overlooked one of the Temple's secret gardens, a stamp-sized square of lawn surrounded by white-flowered shrubbery and climbing plants. I opened the window, letting in the smell of new-mown grass and a breeze that was marginally cooler than the air in the room.

"Give me a key to that garden, a deck chair, a cold beer and a radio tuned to the Test Match and I'd be happy." Derwent had come to stand beside me, peering down at the lawn below.

"I don't see the point in cricket."

"Why doesn't that surprise me?"

"It goes on for too long. It's just not exciting."

Derwent reeled back, clutching his chest theatrically. "How can you say that? It's pure poetry."

"Yeah, well, I wouldn't listen to poetry for four or five days either."

A knock on the door made me jump and I turned to see a silver-haired man, long-limbed but with a distinct paunch. He had a high color in his cheeks and generally looked as if he knew his way around a pint. "Welcome to Three Unicorn. I'm Alan Reynolds, chief clerk."

Which meant that he basically ran the place, as I understood it. The clerks handled work coming in and bills going out — the business side of things. There were no secrets in the clerks' room. They knew far more about their barristers than the barristers might realize, or like to admit. The position of chief clerk in a big set of chambers was a powerful one, and they were paid accordingly. For all that it was losing the battle with his gut, Reynolds' pin-striped suit looked as if it had cost serious money, and his shoes were handmade.

Godley had jumped to his feet and was shaking hands with Reynolds. "Chief Superintendent Godley." He introduced us and I just managed not to wince after experiencing the brief but powerful pressure of the clerk's grip. His clothes gave off a waft of cigar smoke as he moved. Someone who liked the finer things in life, I thought.

"I'm sure you know why we're here," Godley said once the formalities were out of the way.

"Mr. Kennford will be with you shortly." Reynolds sank into one of the armchairs and crossed his legs at the ankle. "It's a bad business, this."

"Very upsetting," Godley agreed. "How is Mr. Kennford today?"

"Same as ever, you'd think. But he's not the sort to show how he feels. He's at the Old Bailey next week for a murder and that's his main focus at the moment."

"You'd have thought he'd have better things to think about," Derwent said.

"I offered to take a few things out of his diary. Give him time to come to terms with what's happened. But he's a professional." Reynolds sounded approving rather than censorious. "He's had these cases for months. He doesn't want to back out now, and if he wants to work, I'm not going to stop him."

"I don't know if I'd want him defending me in the circumstances. His mind can't be on his job."

Reynolds bristled, which was doubtless what Derwent had intended. "You'd want him because he's the best there is. Simple as that. I've had solicitors on the phone all morning to check he can still do their briefs, panicking in case he might return them."

"He sounds popular."

"Very well respected."

"And liked?"

Reynolds hesitated. "He's got his admirers. There's a few who don't like him, but that's personalities clashing, not work."

"Does he always win?" I asked.

"No. No one does. You can be the best

149

advocate in the room and be unable to get the jury to agree with you if they choose not to."

"But he's successful."

"Very. I could have him on his feet every day of the year if I gave him every brief that came in with his name on it. He's old-fashioned, though. Likes to prepare cases. He actually reads the papers, which is more than I can say for some QCs."

Derwent was looking out the window again. Without turning around, he said, "Mr. Kennford told us he'd had death threats as a result of his job. Who would they be from?"

"I couldn't say," Reynolds said levelly.

"Presumably you knew about them."

"Some of them."

"So you can tell us who threatened him."

"Some of them, we never found out who it was. He did some work in Northern Ireland on a tribunal to investigate the British army's involvement in paramilitary hit squads. He was counsel for the army. That didn't make him too many friends on the Republican side. We had bomb scares here — had to evacuate the building. It all turned out to be rubbish but you've got to take it seriously, don't you?"

"The Irish are capable of anything," Derwent said gravely, without looking in my direction. He had been in the army and had done tours in the Six Counties, I knew, but he never talked to me about it, and he certainly gave no hint of it to Reynolds.

The chief clerk wagged a finger. "I'm not saying anything against the Irish. But if someone rings you up and tells you there's a load of Semtex hidden in the building, you've got to listen. Especially if they sound like a Paddy."

I probably spoke more sharply than I needed to. "Right. So we'll put all Republican terror groups on the list." *Or maybe just anyone with an Irish accent.* "Who else?"

"There was one gentleman." Reynolds spoke slowly, reluctant to give us the details. "It was a rape. A minor. He was a teacher and the alleged victim was one of his students. He was acquitted on appeal, but unfortunately he blamed Mr. Kennford for his original conviction."

"What was his name?" Godley asked.

"Christopher Blacker."

The boss caught my eye. *You can look into that one.* "Did it amount to anything?"

"It never became a police matter."

That didn't mean much. It wouldn't have been good for Kennford's reputation — or that of his chambers — if word got out that a dissatisfied client was gunning for him. I could imagine them deciding to handle it themselves, whatever had happened.

"Anyone else we should know about?"

"The father of a young lady who was

murdered some years ago. Her boyfriend was tried and acquitted, and the father felt he shouldn't have got off. Understandably, you know. He thought that Mr. Kennford owed him an apology. Vandalized his car. Now that did end up in court, but he pleaded guilty and got a suspended sentence for criminal damage, which was fair enough given the circumstances. Mr. Kennford was very understanding of his position and made a statement asking for leniency. So that ended up being all right."

Except for the dead girl and her grieving father. "Do you have his name?"

"Gerard Harman. The daughter's name was Clara. Mr. Kennford's client was Mr. Harry Stokes."

"Did they ever catch anyone?" Derwent asked casually.

"For her murder? Not as far as I know."

In other words, they'd had the right man in the first place, in spite of the fact he'd been acquitted.

"That was a good day's work, then, wasn't it?" You couldn't miss the sarcasm in Derwent's tone and Reynolds didn't. Nor did he get upset.

"That's the system."

"Oh, yeah, you don't make the rules."

"That's right. And Mr. Stokes was entitled to be defended to the best of Mr. Kennford's abilities."

"That's what I don't understand. Why would Kennford spend his time and energy defending a piece of shit like that?"

"Because he's good at it, and it needs doing."

"Sewer maintenance needs doing too, but I don't see him queuing up to volunteer."

"I don't think he'd be much use in a sewer," Reynolds said mildly. "But he knows his way around the Central Criminal Court."

"It's worth looking into Mr. Harman's whereabouts." Godley was tapping his pen on his notebook. "Kennford's daughter was killed. If he blamed Kennford for his daughter's killer being let off, maybe he wanted him to see what it was like to lose a child."

"What about his wife?" Derwent asked.

"Accidental. She walked in on the murder."

"It's possible." Derwent didn't sound convinced. "We should check him out, though."

Reynolds sat forward in his chair, preparing to stand up. "That's all I can think of at the moment. Mr. Kennford might be able to come up with some more."

As if on cue the door swung open to reveal Philip Kennford, tieless and with rolled-up shirtsleeves. His hair was ruffled as if he had been running his hands through it, but he didn't look distraught — more as if he had been interrupted at work and was keen to get back to it.

"Apologies for keeping you waiting. Alan, what are you doing in here?"

"Offering the police any assistance I could, that's all, sir." Reynolds grinned at his star QC. Calling him "sir" was convention, not respect, but I thought he genuinely liked Kennford.

"Going through my worst failures, you mean. I thought I could hear the rattle of skeletons tumbling out of cupboards."

"Hardly."

"Who did you mention? Blacker?"

"And Harman."

"That poor old sod." Kennford winced. "One of those times you wish you could leave the law out of it."

"As with Mr. Blacker?" Godley inquired.

"One dissatisfied client is not worth involving the energies of the Met. As I'm sure you'd be the first to agree, Inspector." Kennford raised his eyebrows at Derwent. I had the uncomfortable feeling that he was issuing a challenge, even though so far Derwent hadn't said a word, hostile or otherwise. He had definitely made an impression the previous night. Perhaps mindful of Godley's warning, Derwent didn't respond directly.

"How are you today, Mr. Kennford?"

"I feel okay. Bit of a headache. Nothing serious."

"I'm glad to hear it." Derwent paused for a moment. "I actually meant to ask how you are coping with your very recent bereavement." He leaned on *very recent,* not needing to add "you heartless git" but clearly implying it.

"I'm trying not to think about it."

"Really? I'd have thought it would be the main thing on your mind. In your shoes I'd be trying to work out who had it in for me, or my family. I'd be wondering if I'd missed a chance to save them. I don't think I'd be able to concentrate on work."

"Do I really need to point out that we're quite different in temperament? As I said last night, I am prepared to leave you to find out who did this. It's not my job to investigate crimes. It *is* my job to prepare trials and be an advocate for my clients, so that's what I'm doing. It takes my mind off the horrible experiences I've endured in the last day or so, and it makes me feel less helpless in the face of an apparently random act of violence, because if I allowed myself to think about it properly, I have to tell you, I don't think I could be responsible for my actions."

Kennford's voice had been rising as he delivered his speech, his accent thickening, and he finished by thumping his fist on the back of the chair nearest him, as if he had no other vent for his emotions. Reynolds looked down at his hands, embarrassed by the barrister's loss of control. A quick look around the room confirmed that Godley, Derwent

155

and I were maintaining the same studiedly neutral expression. What they were thinking, I didn't know, but I was admiring Kennford's ability to pull a big scene out of the bag when required. Heartless workaholic? No, just too devastated to confront the reality of his loss. How horrible of us to suggest anything else. A jury would have loved it, but Philip Kennford was playing to a tough crowd.

Reynolds brushed some imaginary fluff off his knee. "Would you like me to stay, Mr. Kennford?"

"To make sure I don't say anything stupid?" Kennford shook his head. "No, Alan. You've got better things to do."

The chief clerk stood and nodded to Godley. "If I can do anything to help, just ask."

"Appreciated." He waited until Reynolds had left the room. "Do sit down, Mr. Kennford."

Rather to my surprise, Kennford took over the armchair the chief clerk had vacated. Maybe he was going to cooperate after all.

"If you haven't been thinking about the crimes, I take it you don't have any more suggestions for our list of suspects."

"No, I don't. I've told you what I can, and Alan has given you some more names, though I think you'll be wasting your time if you chase after someone like poor old Harman."

"He did make threats against you, though."

"The usual kind." Seeing that that wasn't

enough, Kennford drawled, "He promised me exposure, disgrace, ruin, a visitation from the Four Horsemen of the Apocalypse and the seven plagues of Egypt. You name it."

"Did he carry out any of his threats at the time?"

"No. Or if he did, I wasn't aware of them."

"Is that everyone you can think of?"

Kennford nodded.

"We've been concentrating on people who don't like you, but is there anyone that you consider to be an enemy?"

"I don't have a quarrel with anyone. There are those who have a problem with me, but I have better things to think about than wrongs that were done to me."

I couldn't help butting in. "You said your ex-wife took your entire income."

"So she does. That was the decision of the courts when we divorced. I couldn't really argue too much since she'd been with me through law school and my first few years at the Bar, and I'd been playing away with a very wealthy woman. Vita," he added for clarity. "She wasn't in good health and the judge thought she needed the money more than I did."

"Are you on good terms with your first wife?"

"Of course not," Kennford snapped. "There's a reason we divorced."

"I thought you split up because you were

157

being unfaithful to her," I said blandly.

"We split up because she hadn't the sense to turn a blind eye."

Unlike Vita. We all thought it; no one actually said it.

"When was the last time you spoke to her?"

He rubbed his eyes. "Last year. I pay her once a quarter rather than monthly because my earnings aren't consistent month to month — I get paid for cases I did years ago, sometimes. I was late with her money and she rang up to know where it was. It was a short conversation."

"Pleasant?" I asked, deadpan.

Kennford laughed. "I like your sense of humor."

Appreciating women came naturally to him — he could no more help flirting with me than he could stop himself from breathing. For a moment I felt myself being drawn in by his charm in spite of myself, but then the words "bimbo sidekick" popped into my mind.

"And what's your ex-wife's name?"

"Miranda Wentworth. She went back to her maiden name when we got divorced." A grin. "Actually, my name was the one thing she didn't keep."

Attuned to other people's reactions to him, he must have noticed the lack of a response because he switched his focus to Godley.

"Look, I appreciate the in-depth focus on

me and I don't mind answering your questions, but I can't see this getting us anywhere. Miranda's not a killer. She's extremely bitter about how our marriage ended but she wouldn't take it out on the girls, and I don't know why she would have waited twenty years to attack Vita. As far as I know, she's not in the best of health, so she wouldn't have been able to attack them, and she certainly wouldn't have had the height to hit me over the head or the strength to push me into the mirror."

"That does seem impossible," Derwent agreed.

Kennford was on to him straightaway. "Back to thinking I did it myself?"

"It's always a possibility until we're sure you didn't."

"And with that in mind, I'm going to need to take your mobile phone," Godley said.

"My God, so you really are including me on the list of suspects." Kennford gave a strained laugh. "You just base your investigation on probabilities, don't you? There's a certain inevitability to it. If it's a domestic murder, of course the husband must have done it, regardless of who he is or how he acts. But I suppose you can't understand what I'm doing here today, instead of sitting in a dark room drinking cheap whiskey and letting my beard grow, or whatever it is you think I should be doing."

"We don't expect everyone to react the same way to a death in the family," Godley said calmly. "You aren't a suspect because we think you aren't upset enough."

"Why, then?" Kennford's jaw was tight with anger.

"You are a suspect because you don't seem interested in helping us to find the people who murdered your wife and daughter. Over the course of two interviews, you have told us as little as possible about your life. Your clerk gave us more information in a brief conversation than you have so far." Godley began to lay out the facts, showing him the cards we were holding. I watched Kennford, curious to see if it was a winning hand. "You are a suspect because you have a weak alibi and a possible motive for wanting your wife dead because your marriage was on shaky ground. You were in the house. You had the opportunity to kill her, and the means to dispose of the murder weapon before staging your own attack. Laura wasn't supposed to be there so we can discount the fact that you don't have a motive for her death."

"I would tear that to shreds if we were in court. All you have are suppositions and implications. Where's the evidence?"

"That will come — if our suppositions and implications are right." Godley shrugged. "If they're not, you don't have anything to worry about because there won't be any evidence

160

for us to find. Either way, I need your phone."

Kennford took out a battered iPhone and weighed it in his hand. "This is my lifeline, you know. I've got to be able to keep in touch with the clerks and my solicitors. I haven't had to queue up to use a public phone at court since I was a pupil. And I need to check my e-mail."

"No BlackBerry?"

"I do it all on this. I have enough to manage without having a million and one gadgets to carry around."

"What about a personal mobile phone?" Derwent asked.

"For the legions of women who send me messages? So I can keep that line of communication secret?"

"You said it."

Kennford shook his head. "I couldn't be bothered."

"Didn't you care if your wife found out about your girlfriends?" I couldn't help asking.

Instead of being offended, he favored me with a sheepish grin. "Rumors of my philandering exaggerate the truth. I'm not going to try to mislead you. There *have* been other women, but not anything like as many as people suggest. It's something that happens, and it's not a big deal."

Derwent whistled the first line of "I'm Just

161

a Girl Who Can't Say No." Kennford ignored it.

"If Vita found out about any of them, she didn't discuss it with me. She knew that our marriage wasn't under threat. I wouldn't have left her for anyone, and I always made that clear to the women I slept with."

"Very laudable," I said sarcastically.

"I can understand that you need your phone. We'll do our best to get it back to you quickly." Godley waited until Kennford put the phone down on the coffee table, then leaned over and switched it off. "As you can see, that's turned off. It won't be on again until it's being technically examined."

"So you can't fit me up by writing your own messages. I know the drill." Kennford stood up and began to pace the room. "What about the possibility that this was a burglary attempt that went very badly wrong? Have you considered that?"

"It just doesn't seem to fit with the facts," Derwent drawled.

"Yes, it does," Kennford insisted. "The offenders got into the house, confronted Vita and Laura, tried to bully Vita into telling them where the safe was, not that we have one, and inadvertently killed Laura. Then they panicked and killed Vita to hide what they'd done. I know criminals and most of them aren't that bright. They're like foxes in a henhouse when their plans go wrong."

162

Derwent shook his head. "We were at the postmortems this morning, mate, and there was nothing accidental about your daughter's injuries. The damage to her neck wasn't a shaving cut."

The color had gone from Kennford's face. "Already? They did them already?"

"The quicker we have information from the pathologist about how a victim died, the better it is for the investigation," Godley explained.

"I suppose it is." He still sounded stunned. "My poor little Laura."

"What about your poor little Lydia?" I sounded sharp, but I couldn't help it. "I spent the morning with her."

"How enthralling for you."

"It had its moments. Would you like to know where Lydia is now?"

"In Twickenham?"

"In hospital."

That got his attention. "Why? What happened?"

"She collapsed. She had an untreated injury that caused significant blood loss."

"An injury? From last night?"

"No. Not from then. From this morning." I hesitated, not sure if it was better to approach the subject delicately or straight out. The direct approach seemed easiest. "It seems it was self-inflicted. Did you know she self-harmed?"

He sat down in his chair again and leaned his head against the back of it, his eyes closed. In irritation, it transpired. "Oh, fucking spare me. She had to find some way of getting attention, didn't she?"

"Mr. Kennford, Lydia's arms were covered in scars. I saw them. The injury that caused her to faint was particularly deep, but it was far from the first. The doctor she saw in A and E told me she had probably been cutting herself for years. Have you ever had her referred for psychiatric assessment?"

"We didn't need that to know she's a few sandwiches short of a picnic, but she's had plenty of attention over the years."

"While we were waiting for the ambulance to come Mrs. Fairfax told me Lydia was diagnosed with an eating disorder a few years ago."

"Diagnosed, treated at vast expense, released. Not cured, you'll notice. It was described as being under control. That's if you believe she had a real problem."

"I take it you didn't think that."

Kennford looked bored. "She needed to lose weight. She went on a diet, which was effective. Her mother panicked and took her to a specialist who was more than happy to diagnose her with anorexia nervosa. Vita was secretly delighted, of course. At her tennis club it's a fashionable ailment for a child to have."

"It's a life-threatening disorder," I said hotly. "And the cut on Lydia's arm —"

"I'm afraid I'm not interested. She did it to herself, so it merits neither sympathy nor attention."

"Don't you think she's been looking for your approval?" I couldn't believe how unmoved he was, how unsympathetic.

"She's been looking in all the wrong places, if that's the case."

"Laura was your favorite, wasn't she?" Derwent's voice was harsh. He was staring out of the window again and didn't bother to turn around. "Did Vita feel the same way?"

"Laura was a more attractive and rewarding child. We both felt that way. Vita was probably better at hiding her feelings from the girls. I didn't see the point in pretending."

"Maybe if you had seen the point in it, she wouldn't be lying in hospital right now." I shook my head. "You really are a cold person, aren't you? A normal father would have dropped everything to go and be with his child when she needed him."

"Does she need me? She's got doctors and nurses to look after her physically. Mentally too, I suppose. God, if she ends up in another loony bin she's going to have trouble when it comes to university applications. She can forget medicine as a career. She'll fail the psychological profile in a half second."

"What about her emotional needs? What about the fact that you're all she has left of a family?"

"Lydia learned a long time ago that Daddy was a busy person who wasn't always available for sports days and school plays. She came to terms with it, as did Laura. Vita was always there for both of them. Just because Vita's gone, I can't change the way I live my life." He turned to Godley. "You have all of these pathetic reasons why I would have wanted Vita dead. You haven't thought about why I needed her to be around. I would never have killed my wife — she was too bloody useful. And if that shocks you, Miss Prim" — he turned back to me — "you're not going to like this. When I met Vita, I wasn't even attracted to her. She was overweight, she had bad skin and her eyesight was terrible. I did like her money, and the fact that she worshipped me." He said it in a completely matter-of-fact way, as if it was entirely reasonable. "I didn't know why she was so keen on me. Then she got pregnant with the twins and I realized what she'd been after all along. What could I do but go along with it? The babies were going to need a father." *And you could get your hands on all the lovely money at the same time,* I filled in silently. "Vita really put in the effort. She knew she had to sort out her appearance, so she lost weight and got her eyes and skin lasered. She also knew

I wasn't going to be the most hands-on dad in the world. She saw where Miranda had gone wrong and she wasn't going to make the same mistakes, so she devoted herself to making my life easier and keeping the twins happy. She never asked me for anything. She strove to be the perfect wife, and as far as I was concerned, she succeeded."

"This is very moving stuff," Derwent commented. "But you're not getting paid by the hour here."

"I'm getting to the point. I had nothing to gain from Vita dying. The only thing I've got out of it is a headache. I can't leave Lydia with her aunt indefinitely, more's the pity, and she's clearly not able to look after herself. So now I need to find someone to keep an eye on her or I won't be able to do my job. Really, at her age, she should be able to be more independent."

"Laura was independent, wasn't she?" Derwent said softly. "That's how she was able to have a boyfriend."

"Neither of the girls had boyfriends."

"That's what Lydia told me," I said. "But Laura did."

"She wasn't a virgin, Mr. Kennford. In fact, she was a very experienced young lady, based on the pictures we found of her. Up to all sorts of things." Derwent was enjoying this.

The color had gone from Kennford's face again, but this time it was anger, not shock

167

that had bleached his skin.

"What the fuck are you talking about?"

"Sex. All kinds of sex. All kinds of positions. It was an education for me, looking through the pictures, let me tell you. I think I could probably qualify as a gynecologist now." Derwent settled himself against the window ledge. "Amazing to think she had done so much when she was only fifteen."

"I'll *kill* you." I don't think Kennford was aware of what he'd said. His hands were bunched into fists, shaking slightly as the adrenaline coursed through him.

"I'm just telling you what you didn't notice. Any idea who the boyfriend was? Or boyfriends, I suppose. Just because we only have pictures of one doesn't mean that there weren't a few. Taking after your good self, perhaps." Derwent laughed. "We used to call them 'ceiling inspectors' when I was in school. You know, flat on their backs most of the time, staring up at the ceiling while they were getting pounded by someone or other. They probably just call them sluts now."

"Don't talk about her that way." Kennford stepped toward Derwent, closing the distance between them.

"It's a touchy subject," Derwent agreed. "Hard to think about your own child like that. Especially if you'd fooled yourself that she was innocent."

"Josh." Godley spoke quietly, without the

168

edge that would have called Derwent off. It was his way of staying on Kennford's side while letting his DI do the dirty work. Which, as it happened, Derwent was more than happy to do.

"Must be a bit of a shock. But, according to you, sex isn't a big deal, is it? It's just something that happens." He waited a second. *It's all in the timing, Maeve.* "Happened to her a lot, evidently."

Kennford lunged, aiming a punch at Derwent's face. He sidestepped it and caught Kennford's fist as it shot past him, using the momentum to twist him around and push his hand up between his shoulder blades. I squeaked and jumped out of their path as they reeled around the room. The last time I'd got caught up in one of Derwent's little scraps, I'd ended up needing to go to hospital. It wasn't something I was keen to repeat. Derwent rammed Kennford against the wall, leaning in close to speak into his ear.

"Watch the window, mate. I don't want to fall out, do you?"

Kennford responded with a string of expletives that were barely comprehensible. "Bastard" was a word that recurred.

Derwent kept him pressed up against the wall. "Calm down. I don't want to arrest you for assault on a police officer, but I will."

"You wouldn't get it to court," Kennford choked out, kicking back.

169

"You reckon?" Derwent gave him a shake, like a terrier with a rat. "You need to get your priorities straight, Mr. Kennford. You keep giving us just enough, or what you think is just enough. You haven't been honest with us. Maybe you don't remember what that's like. Let me explain. Whatever you're trying to hide, we will find out what it is. We're only interested in catching the person who did this to your family, but it makes me very curious indeed that you don't seem to feel the same way." Another shake. "Don't underestimate us just because you've spent your career tying coppers in knots. Don't think we're idiots. And don't think you're going to get away with lying to me because I will not stop until I find out what it is you're lying about, and why, and you will regret it, Mr. Kennford. You'll wish you'd never started this, and it will be too late." He stepped back, taking some of the pressure off so Kennford could breathe. "Talk to us now and we'll forget this ever happened."

Kennford struggled free, turning round to face Derwent, his face flooded red from anger and embarrassment. The door to the room was open again, I realized, and fully occupied. In the foreground there were two young men who had to be junior clerks, and the receptionist. Behind them, in dark suits, there were more than a few barristers, male and female. All had the same expression on their faces: horror mixed with glee. A genuine fight involving a senior member of chambers: I was surprised no one had thought of selling tickets. Kennford glared at them, straightening his shirt where it had pulled to one side, then turned back to Derwent.

"I don't appreciate the threats. I don't know what you're talking about. I've answered your questions. If you're not happy with the answers, you need to think about whether you're asking the right ones."

"Everything's always someone else's fault, isn't it?" Derwent shook his head. "You've spent too much time with criminals, Mr. Kennford."

"What happened to my family isn't my fault," he said hotly.

A mild commotion outside the room turned out to be the chief clerk elbowing his way through the crowd outside the door. "Is everything all right, Mr. Kennford?"

The interruption gave Kennford a crucial couple of seconds to recover his temper, and an approximation of his earlier easy manner.

"Fine, Alan. Inspector Derwent was just trying to get a reaction out of me. And succeeded," he said, with a thin smile. "For which I apologize."

"No need to apologize to me. I've had worse." Derwent stuck his hands in his pockets. He looked remarkably pleased with himself.

"Somehow, that doesn't surprise me." Kennford turned to Godley. "Can I assume this interview is now over?"

"I think we're done for the moment."

"In that case —" He pivoted on the spot and punched Derwent, catching him full on the jaw and sending him sprawling on the floor, unable to get his hands free in time to break his fall. "That's for insulting my daughter."

It wasn't often that Derwent got what was coming to him but when it happened, by God it was fun to watch.

CHAPTER SEVEN

I got back to the flat in the late afternoon and spent a couple of minutes opening every window in the place, trying to get some air into it. I finished up in the bedroom where I kicked off my shoes and took off my limp, creased suit, changing into shorts and a vest top. I leaned out of the window as I tied my hair up, letting the air cool the back of my neck. That side of the flat overlooked the street and, in the distance, Battersea Park, the tops of the trees just higher than the rooftops around it. The park looked like an oasis of cool green shade but in reality it was brown. The grass had crumbled to dust and the trees were so dehydrated they were shedding leaves and twigs. Even the water in the lake had been low the last time I had been there. The ducks had looked suicidal.

Below me the street was quiet for once, the heat having driven everyone inside. Those who were out walked slowly, heads down. It was humid as well as hot, the air heavy with the promise of a thunderstorm, and I scanned the sky for clouds, longing for rain. London was not designed for extended periods of hot weather, as the melting tarmac in the roads could attest. The national obsession with the weather was in full cry, with an aerial shot of "St. James's Dustbowl" on the front of the *Evening Standard.*

"What else do you expect in summer?" Derwent had growled, folding the paper and flinging it to one side in disgust. "What else do you want?"

I hadn't answered. I wanted the salt tang of the Atlantic complete with rain squalls that swept in across the sand to drench everyone and everything. I wanted icy waves, mist-shrouded mountains and occasional, glorious sunshine. I wanted the west of Ireland where I had spent my childhood summers, blue-kneed and jumper-clad in August. I wanted the endless days, the sun impossibly late in slipping below the waves, the sky still bright in good weather until eleven or after it. London was a long way south and east from where I felt at home in summer. And at that moment, London was distinctly lacking in amenities such as fresh air and cool breezes. Then again, if I lived in the west of Ireland I'd probably be sick of rain before too long.

With a sigh, I took myself away from the glare of baking rooftops. I wanted a drink and the kitchen was the coolest place in the flat. Standing barefoot on the tiles, I kept the fridge door open as I drank a liter bottle of water, almost at a comfortable temperature for the first time that day.

"Ghetto air-conditioning. Very classy."

I jumped, spilling the last drops down my top. "Hello, stranger."

Rob was standing in the doorway, leaning against it. Not for effect, I thought. He looked exhausted, his eyes squinting with tiredness. It was so long since I'd seen him properly I noticed immediately that he'd lost weight, his jeans sitting low on his hips.

"Is there any more water?"

"Loads." I threw him a bottle but kept my position at the fridge. I'd move when I had to and not before.

He drank half of it in one long swallow, then set it down on the table so he could get on with unbuckling his belt.

"Hey, whoa there." I wagged a reproving finger. "I don't see you for weeks and then as soon as we're in the same room you expect us to get right down to it. I'm sorry, you're going to have to buy me dinner first."

"Get your mind out of the gutter, Kerrigan." His trainers and socks went first. He shucked off his jeans, emptied the pockets and stripped out the belt, then wadded them straight into the washing machine. "It's far too hot for that kind of thing. Not that you aren't looking lovely today, may I say."

"Oh, sure. I'm always at my best when I'm underslept. Especially when I've been lightly poached for eight hours."

Rob was looking at my legs, most of which were on display. "Going for a run?"

"Hardly. This is the officially the least clothing I can wear and still qualify as dressed."

"When will this fucking weather break?"

"It's supposed to get hotter midweek. No sign of it changing until the weekend."

His T-shirt followed the jeans. "What a pisser. If you think it's hot out, you need to experience the back of the van. It's a mobile sauna."

I ran my hand over his back as he bent to put his socks in the machine, feeling his ribs. "No wonder you're looking skinny."

"Less of that, if you don't mind. This is my fighting weight." He ducked sideways, away from me. "Don't come near me. I stink."

"Mm. I quite like it." I smiled to myself, remembering Dornton and his man smell. It definitely depended on the man. Him, I could resist quite easily. Rob, not so much, even in his current state of scruffiness. "When was the last time you had a shower, anyway?" I reached out and rubbed the bristles on his chin. "Or shaved?"

"Shower was yesterday morning. Shave? Not sure." He grinned at me, his teeth looking very white in contrast with his dark stubble. "What about if I grow a beard?"

"What about if you don't?"

"Oh, come on. It would make life so much easier."

"For you, maybe, but stubble rash is not a good look."

"If I ever got the chance to inflict it on you." He said it lightly but there was an underlying truth to it. Not my fault, and not his, but not good for either of us. I leaned my head on my arm, watching him move around the kitchen.

"It's nice to see you. Why are you at home?"

"That surveillance didn't work out."

"How come?"

He picked up the bottle and drank the remainder of his water before replying. "Let's not talk about work now. At least, let's not talk about my work. Why are you here? Bit early for you to knock off, isn't it?"

"Early start. Late night last night. And we've hit a bit of a dead end." I shrugged. "Godley had other things to do, and none of my interviews are until tomorrow, so even Derwent couldn't think of a reason to keep me at work."

"Godley's other things including a shooting in Camberwell."

"You heard."

"Talk of the Met." Rob's forehead wrinkled. "I'm not being rude, but isn't it time he sorted that out? It's too many bodies, Maeve. It makes us look bad."

"I think he would if he could."

"Makes me wish I'd never left the team."

"Because DS Langton would have brought peace to the drug dealers of South London and the Home Counties?"

"Because DS Langton enjoys locking up murderers," he said calmly. "And I'd like to know more about what's going on."

"I'm not involved either, you know. I know about as much as you do."

"Useless." He tweaked my ponytail. The height of romance. And I'd worried that moving in together would change things between us.

I let the fridge door close. "I'm going to set a good example and have a shower. It's the only way I'm going to cool down."

"Good idea." He stood where I had been and opened the door again. "This is the opposite of good for the environment and we'll probably end up in the sixth circle of some sort of ecological hell but I can't think of anything better to do."

"I'd climb in and close the door if I thought I'd fit." I peeled my top over my head. "Back in a bit."

I'd been in the shower for about two minutes when the door opened a crack.

"I thought of something better to do. Budge up."

"This shower was not built for two." I made room for him all the same.

"Jesus, that's cold."

"It's not that bad," I protested. "It's tepid. You're just hot."

"Yeah, baby. You said it." He was busy with the soap, scrubbing the accumulated sweat and dirt off. I pressed myself against the wall to leave him enough room, the tiles cold on my back. He rinsed away the lather at top speed, finishing by dousing his head. Emerging from under the water he shook it, sending droplets flying everywhere. I put my arm up to protect my face.

"What are you, a dog or something?"

"Oh, sorry. I wouldn't want you getting wet."

"This is my shower. You're just here on sufferance. I can kick you out if you don't behave yourself."

"Define behave," he said, in the voice that made me literally weak at the knees, as he took a step closer to me. I tried to act as if I hadn't noticed.

"Hogging the shower is not allowed. Splashing is not allowed."

"Is this allowed?" His hands moved as he spoke, sliding on my skin. I clung to him wordlessly.

"What about this?"

"Rob." It was all I could manage.

He kissed my neck slowly, working up to my mouth. Instead of kissing me properly, though, he stopped. "I'm very worried you'll get stubble rash."

"I really don't care." I rubbed my cheek against his, feeling the coarse grain of his beard. I actually liked it.

"I don't want you ripping yourself to shreds."

"I can cope." I kissed him to prove it, pressing myself against his body. I was almost the same height as him, matching him physically. The feel of him was familiar and yet there was a strangeness too, a distance between us that hadn't been there before. I pulled back to look at him.

"What?"

"Nothing. Just . . ."

"It's been a while." As usual, on my wavelength. It was spooky at times how closely he could track what I was thinking. He grinned down at me. "Don't worry. I think I can still remember how."

"Can you remember the last time we tried to have sex in the shower?"

He winced. "Remember it? I'm still seeing a chiropractor."

"I'm sorry. Tall people are a liability on wet tiles."

"Tall people also talk too much." He flicked the shower off before lifting me up and I wrapped my legs around him, clinging to him as he carried me to the bed. The tiny part of my mind that was still engaged with practical matters decided not to make a fuss about the

180

fact that we were both dripping water. It didn't matter about getting the sheets wet. It was hot. They would dry.

And that was the last coherent thought I had for a while. When I looked back on it, I only remembered images: the late afternoon sunlight slanting into the room, turning it gold. The white curtains at the window billowing as a stray breeze caught them. Rob's eyes, very blue. The line of his jaw. His eyelashes, long and dark when he closed his eyes. His hands. His body over mine.

And one other thing: the tone in his voice that I'd never heard before when he said, as if the words were wrung out of him against his will, "Oh, Maeve. I love you. I love you."

I held on to him and didn't know what to say, except the obvious reply. And I did feel that way.

But I didn't say it back.

He fell asleep almost as soon as he had rolled off me, a deep sleep that I didn't want to disturb. I lay beside him and stared up at the ceiling, the light moving across it and changing as the sun slid down toward the horizon. I kept one hand on him, feeling his heart beating slowly as he slept. He was cool to the touch and at peace, his face tranquil. Tired as I was, my mind wouldn't let me rest. I was turning it over and over, confusion beating elation every time. Why say it now? Was there a reason for it that I had missed? We had been together for eight months, on and off, and while I'd never doubted his feelings for me, I hadn't needed him to say it out loud.

And now he had.

And the only times I'd ever heard that phrase before had been to make up for something the other person had done, whether I knew it at the time or not. I trusted Rob — I thought I trusted him, anyway — but I couldn't work out why he'd said it, and like that, and now, when things were probably shakier between us than they'd ever been. It made me — I paused for a second, checking I was right about it — terrified.

I lay without moving, afraid to disturb him, and waited to feel better. And waited. And waited.

And time passed.

"What time is it?" He came awake in a moment, sitting up on one elbow, instantly alert.

"Getting on for eight."

He rubbed his hand over his face. "Sorry."

"No need to apologize to me. You were shattered."

"Still, not very gentlemanly of me."

I reached up and pulled him down so I could kiss him. "I do value your manners but that's not the only reason I keep you around."

"Good to know." His stomach growled. "On the one hand, I would like nothing better than to stay here for the rest of my life. On the other, I need to eat something."

"What sort of something?"

"Not a burger or a pizza. I've had it with fast food."

"You may have noticed during your time at the fridge that there's practically no food in the flat. I haven't been shopping," I said apologetically.

"Not much have I." He kissed me again. "I know it's backward, but you did say I had to buy you dinner."

"I was only joking. You don't have to."

"I'd like to." He looked at me for a long moment and I wondered with a thrill of fear if he was going to mention what he'd said earlier. "It would do us good to get out, I think. Talk, for once."

About what? It was ridiculous to be so nervous. "Fine by me," I said brightly. "Do you want to get ready first?"

He looked dubious. "How long will you be?"

"Not long," I lied.

"Right." He threw back the sheet and swung his legs off the bed. "I'll book a table at Torino's for nine o'clock."

I checked my watch again. "That actually doesn't give me much time."

"I actually know." He leaned back and kissed my shoulder. "Better hurry up."

In fact, I was ready forty-five minutes later,

183

a near record considering I'd washed my hair and prettied myself up too. I wore a yellow cotton dress with a full skirt, an item of clothing completely unlike something a murder detective would wear. It was a dress that deserved high-heeled sandals so I dug them out, resigned to sacrificing comfort for fashion. Only women would think it was a fair trade-off, I thought, pivoting to see myself in the mirror. The fact was, the right shoes made all the difference, and Torino's wasn't far to walk. Or stagger.

Rob was reading when I went to tell him I was ready. He had managed to fit in a shave as well as changing into a clean shirt and jeans. Generally, he looked a lot more like himself. He glanced at me, then did a double-take. "Wow." He stood up and crossed the room, putting one hand behind my neck to draw me close enough for a kiss. "I meant what I said earlier, by the way."

"What do you mean?" My voice was sharp.

"You look beautiful today." He frowned a little. "What did you think I meant?"

"Nothing." I checked my straps weren't showing, acting casual. "Ready?"

"Half an hour ago."

"Well then, what's keeping us?"

"Not much, I suppose." He still looked puzzled.

I chattered about nothing all the way to Torino's, a small Italian restaurant in Battersea Square. That was a grand name for a triangle of pavement beside a surprisingly busy road, but on a warm summer night it was filled with tables from the nearby cafés and restaurants, and tiny fairy lights strung across the square gave it a magical feel. Rob had managed to book a table outside. I sat down opposite him and smiled, feeling relaxed for the first time. What did it matter that he had said he loved me at that particular time, in that particular way? Or that I hadn't said the same in return? He knew me well enough to know I was wary of commitment, pathologically afraid of feeling too much for someone else and getting hurt. Trust was the issue, not love, and I couldn't explain even to myself why I found it so hard to trust men — except that I saw good reasons every day to avoid making that mistake. Even Rob, who seemed to be a cut above the rest — certainly better than my last boyfriend before him — made me edgy. Especially when he surprised me. But why did I have to analyze every word for signs of impending doom? We were together, and that was all that mattered.

"What would you like to drink?"

"Lots," I said, disappearing into the menu, and when I resurfaced it was to the pop of a champagne cork. "What's this?"

"I just felt like it."

"Really?"

He nodded. "Drink it while it's cold."

185

There was something tremendously uplifting about drinking champagne for no particular reason, especially on an empty stomach. I got the giggles halfway through the first course, and Rob didn't help by speculating about the couples dining around us.

"They've had a row. This is a make-up or break-up dinner, and I think — yes, it's going to be a break-up." The blonde three tables over dabbed at her eyes, smearing mascara. Her dining companion was staring at his food, obviously wishing he was somewhere more private. His ears were scarlet. "Oh, there she goes . . ."

The blonde was threading an unsteady path between the tables.

"Maybe she's just going to the loo."

He shook his head. "She threw her napkin down on her plate. She's not coming back."

The man she had been with summoned the waiter.

"Ordering dessert for both of them," I suggested.

"Getting the bill."

"Damn," I said softly, watching the waiter print it out. "You're good at this."

"People are people." He leaned toward me, dropping his voice as he indicated the next table to us. "They haven't had sex yet but he's pretty sure tonight's the night." An ultraposh boy in a pink polo shirt was pouring wine for his date, who was all tousled hair

186

and lip gloss. "She's not going to let him near her, but she'll send out all the signs that it's going to happen. He has at least two more dinners left in him before he gives up hope."

"What makes you say that, you cynic?"

"He's scrawny, he has no chin whatsoever, his signet ring is the real deal and he's wearing a pink shirt without irony. He must be rich. She, on the other hand, is not only well off but a bit of a looker under the makeup and hair. She can do better. In fact, she's probably only with him to meet his mates."

"What about them?" I indicated an older couple who were drinking coffee, holding hands across the table.

"Married. But to other people. Tonight is their one chance to be together."

"How sweet."

"Is it?" He shook his head. "They're hurting the ones they're supposed to love the most."

"Only if they find out, surely."

"Whether they find out or not, it's still wrong." His mood had changed and I wasn't really surprised that the next thing he said was, "How's work?"

"You asked me that already."

"You said you'd hit a dead end."

I told him what had happened that day with Lydia, and at the end of her father's interview. "Funnily enough, Kennford didn't hang around to see if Derwent was all right."

Rob grunted. "I would have wanted to put a couple of miles between me and him too."

"He took it well, actually. He made a big deal out of how it hadn't been a fair fight and Kennford had taken him by surprise."

"Oh, because it would never have happened if he'd been on his guard."

"No, he's far too good at fighting for that."

"I would have loved to see him go down." Rob sounded almost dreamy as he imagined it.

"It made my day — that and Godley telling Derwent he wasn't allowed to arrest Kennford for assaulting him because it was his fault in the first place. Even better, the commotion attracted the attention of anyone who was in chambers, so on my way out I bumped into a barrister I'd met before. I didn't know he was at Kennford's set, but he's been there since he qualified, apparently."

"What's his name?"

"Kit Harries."

"I know him. Good bloke."

"He's one of the only ones who does any meaningful prosecution work there. He said there's not much competition for it so he gets his pick of what comes in. He's being monitored for Treasury Counsel."

"Ooh, fancy."

"I hope he gets it." Treasury Counsel prosecuted the majority of serious crimes — murders, terrorism, the big stuff. Kit, who was fair and round-faced and misleadingly young in appearance, seemed an unlikely choice for them. But he was good at his job, I'd found, and I'd liked him a lot. "Anyway, I couldn't really talk to him while the senior clerk was watching, but he mentioned he was going to be at the Old Bailey tomorrow. I thought I'd drift along and see if he had any inside information on Kennford."

"Good thinking."

"Thank you." I trawled through my salad, picked up a baby new potato on the end of my fork and examined it critically. "You know, my mother would say this wasn't fit for human consumption."

"How come?"

"According to her, potatoes this small are pig food. She hasn't really accepted that they're considered a delicacy now."

"And given that we're talking about your mother, I imagine she never will. Eat up, piggy. But make sure you leave room for dessert."

"I'm not sure I can manage it. Coffee, though."

"Keep you awake."

"It would have a job." I yawned. "Sorry. I'm not bored. Just tired."

"Didn't you sleep earlier?"

I shook my head.

"Now I feel even more of a heel for passing out."

"You needed it." I hesitated before I went any further. Something warned me to tread carefully. "Is everything okay at work?"

"Fine." One word, no detail. I plowed on.

"It's just that you seemed so worn out. I haven't seen you like that — ever, actually. And I've seen you busy before, you know."

"It's a different kind of work. Lots of watching and waiting. It's all right when it works out, but when it all goes to shit you don't have the satisfaction of knowing you've got the bad guys. And we didn't, today."

"Bad intel?"

"Bad op." He shrugged. "You know how it is. Sitting in the backseat, you can see how it should be done. When you're the one calling the shots, things aren't always so clear."

"Your boss got it wrong?"

"Basically. Picked the wrong moment to try to arrest the wrong people. We blew our cover and got nothing."

I sipped my champagne. "What's her name again?"

"DI Deborah Ormond." There was nothing to read into his tone, which was matter of fact.

"Is she nice?"

"She's okay."

"She's supposed to be good."

"Not today." He put his knife and fork together. "I've forgotten, did you want dessert?"

"No." I wasn't going to be put off. "Are you enjoying it, Rob?"

"What, work? It's fine."

"Are you sorry you left the team?" I had to know, even though it was basically my fault he'd gone. I was the one who'd revealed, without meaning to, that we were a couple. And we'd both known the rule: relationships were not allowed in Godley's team.

Rob knew what I was getting at. His eyes were steady as he reached across the table and took my hand. "I'm not sorry about us. Not even a little bit. The new job will be okay once I've settled in."

So it wasn't okay now despite what he'd said. I smiled anyway, or tried to, and joined in the discussion with the waiter about which dessert involved the most calorific intake. After Rob had absorbed something involving near-lethal levels of chocolate and I'd had an espresso that put a stop to the yawns for the time being, we walked back to the flat. We didn't say much on the way, but Rob's arm was around my shoulders and we walked in step with one another, in harmony.

Over the remainder of the meal I had talked myself out of being worried. There were bound to be problems with settling in to a new team, plus Rob had to get used to being a DS and all the extra responsibility that involved. He was working long, irregular hours, living off crap food and dealing with different levels of stress and frustration than he was used to. Of course he was a bit ill at ease. And he knew I would blame myself if he wasn't happy. He was too fair — and too nice — to let me torture myself about it. That was enough to make him cagey about work. I couldn't force him to talk. I just had to be there for him, I decided, and avoid adding to his problems by pitching a fit about never seeing him, and him not trusting me, and anything else my paranoid mind suggested.

Rob's flat was on the third floor so we'd been able to leave the windows open. Even so, the air was like soup when we got back and a mosquito was whining in our bedroom.

"Do you think it'll rain?"

"It should." Just as Rob answered me there was a low growl of thunder. "Too far away."

"Miles," I agreed. "Do you think we can leave the window open, then?"

"If we don't we'll die."

I got ready for bed while Rob stalked the mosquito, hunting it around the room with single-minded determination. It had been doing a fine job of lying low but made the mistake of flying past him and he caught it in his hand.

"Ha. Look at that." The insect was a black smudge on his palm.

"My hero."

He lay down and turned out the light. "At least I caught something today."

I was halfway to dozing already. "Well done."

He laughed and leaned his cheek on the top of my head for a second. "Go to sleep."

"You too."

"Any second now."

But I was aware he was still awake as I fell asleep. And at four, when the rain finally came, he was at the window by the time I woke up enough to remember it was open.

"Are you all right?" I asked, fuzzy with sleep.

"Never better."

"Come back to bed."

"I will. Go back to sleep."

I did, and maybe Rob did come back to bed for a while, but when I woke up in the morning I was on my own. The flat was quiet. He had already left.

CHAPTER EIGHT

At the Old Bailey I did my own version of a stakeout, loitering outside the robing room for an hour until I saw a familiar round face emerging. He was rigged out in full court regalia, his gown billowing as he walked, but his horsehair wig was squashed on top of the stack of pages and books he was carrying. Like most younger barristers he only put it on at the last minute rather than parading around in it. I couldn't imagine having to wear a wig to do my job, let alone the Batman cape, but it lent him a certain dignity that Kit desperately needed. He had to be in his late thirties but his face had all the hard edge of a particularly sweet-natured choirboy.

"Mr. Harries."

"DC Kerrigan." He grinned. "Why am I not surprised you've turned up here?"

"I just thought we could have a coffee, if you had time. It was a little bit hectic at your chambers yesterday and I'd really appreciate a quiet word."

"You want the dirt on Philip."

"That's a very negative way to put it. If there's no dirt, there's nothing to tell me." I grinned. "Mind you, if there *is* dirt, I'd like to hear it from someone I trust."

"And that's me, is it?" He laughed. "Flattery will get you a long way, Maeve, but I don't think it would be very loyal of me to tell you all about Philip's private life."

"Loyalty is something you earn, not an entitlement."

"Who's to say Philip hasn't earned it?"

"Has he?"

Kit shook his head, looking amused.

"This is all making me even more suspicious," I pointed out. "If there wasn't anything to tell me, you'd have said so."

"Expertly done. If I don't tell you what I know, I'll be making things worse for him, but if I do tell you, I'll be breaking his confidence."

"Did he ask you to keep secrets for him?"

"Not specifically." He blew out a lungful of air. "You know, nothing I know is a secret really, but I can imagine he wouldn't want me to talk to you about any of it."

"That's sort of why I need you. If he was prepared to be more forthcoming, I'd feel a whole lot better about him. As it is, I have my concerns."

"I doubt they're justified," Kit said instantly. "He's not the most ethical of men when it comes to relationships, but that isn't a crime."

"It might help me to understand why his wife and daughter ended up dead, all the same."

"I still can't believe it." Kit went silent for a second, his eyes cast down as he considered whether or not he could trust me. The good humor had gone, and with it the impression he gave of being a lightweight; for once I could see the agile mind at work. By the time he looked up again, though, the mischievous expression was back. "If I did talk to you, it would have to be conditional on complete confidentiality. If he found out I'd been talking about him, I might end up like your colleague."

"Oh, he deserved it. It's been a long time coming." He was coming round to the idea, but he wasn't there yet. I would give it one more shot, I decided. "Look, I'm not asking you to give evidence against him. I just want to know the truth about him, because at the moment I'm going on rumor, prejudice and gut instinct. That's just not good enough, so I need your help."

Kit looked over his shoulder, checking to see if anyone was close enough to hear us. He nodded to an older barrister who stumped past us, staring at me with open curiosity. I had deliberately cornered him in a very public part of the court building. Pretty much everyone who passed us knew who he was, and could guess what I was. And I wasn't going anywhere until I got a definitive answer, yes or no.

"Fine. I can't talk to you now — I've got a bail app in a murder in ten minutes and then I've got to talk to the CPS about another case. But I should be free around half past eleven."

"Do you want to meet in the canteen?"

"I'd only meet you there if I wanted the world to know about it." He thought for a second. "Do you know the New Bridge Café? It's around the corner from Blackfriars station, by the bridge, unsurprisingly."

"I can find it."

"I'll meet you there."

With that he was gone. I had an hour and a half to kill, so I went for a wander through the City. It wasn't my sort of place — too many people making too much money for doing nothing more than shuffling paper. The Square Mile was crowded with businessmen and tourists and in spite of the ancient monuments and churches dotted about the place I couldn't get any sense of the history of the area. There were just too many glossy office buildings jammed into too small a space.

It was another scorcher of a day and instinctively I headed for the water, crossing the river on the Millennium footbridge. The Thames oozed below my feet, the water level low. It smelt of brine and something unwhole-some reeking from the mud at its edges. From the center of the bridge I watched the shadows moving under the surface of the water, nameless things passing through the heart of London on their silent journey to the sea. It wasn't unusual for the river police to find bodies in the river — accidental drownings or suicides or murder victims. And every time I heard of one, I couldn't help thinking of the bodies and body parts they missed, the ones that slid down the vast estu-ary and into the North Sea without anyone knowing they'd been there at all.

A girl laughed near me and I jumped, brought back to myself. I had been staring at the water for too long, drawn further and further over the edge as I lost myself in dark thoughts. Dizzy, I leaned back from the rail-ing, looking up at the flawless sky, then back at the water. There wasn't a breath of air, even in the middle of the river, and the sun was cruelly hot on my head. Light sparkled on the surface of the Thames, glinting on the ripples that spread out from the small boats that motored up and down it. To my left, a group of teenagers were posing for pictures, the dome of St. Paul's behind them. To my right, a family had stopped to watch the boats. The youngest in the group, a boy of perhaps two, kicked his heels against his pushchair in delight. They were looking at a different city, a different world. I couldn't see it that way any longer, if I ever had. Soberly, I slid out of my suit jacket and kept walking.

On the South Bank I followed the path to the Tate Modern where the Turbine Hall was dark and blessedly cool, home to a temporary exhibition of sculpture that I couldn't quite bring myself to like. I wandered around some of the galleries wondering what made modern art good or bad. Vita had known, or thought she knew, but her husband and sister had both been scathing about her ability to spot talent. There was a room of tapestries that reminded me of the one in the Kennfords' hall, the colors jarring to me, the textures strange. Kennford had been off hand about his wife's art collection. He would probably sell it once he was able to take possession of his house again. Would he redecorate to suit his own more traditional taste? Would he bother? I suspected, meanly perhaps, that it depended on how the next Mrs. Kennford felt about it. She was probably lined up already, solving his housekeeping and child-care problems in one fell swoop.

There was no getting away from it: I might have cheered him on when he tackled Derwent, but I wasn't a fan of Philip Kennford. I couldn't say for sure if he was a murderer, but the more I saw of him, and the more I heard about him, the more certain I felt that he was just not a good person.

"He's not a bad person."

It was practically the first thing Kit Harries said to me when he'd negotiated his path through the crowded café to the table I had found at the back. The Bridge Café was a greasy spoon, I'd been delighted to discover, full of builders and scaffolders eating their third breakfast of the day. I'd ordered tea, which came in a thick white mug, already milked. It was the color of teak and tasted like there were at least twelve teabags in the pot. I was turning into my mother, I mused, ordering tea on a hot day, but there was something refreshing about it — probably the overdose levels of caffeine and tannin.

Having made his pronouncement, Kit stowed his bag beside our table and sat down. He had changed out of his bands into an ordinary collar and tie, but he still looked out of place in the down-to-earth environment of the Bridge. The elderly Italian waitress looked ecstatic when he appeared, though, and from the greeting he got I guessed he was a regular.

"Your usual, darling?"

"Why not, Maria. Why not."

His usual was a bacon sandwich on white bread, oozing ketchup, and a tea to match mine. It arrived in minutes and he laid into it as if he hadn't seen food for a month.

"No one else from chambers would come here." It was as if he'd read my mind. Between him and Rob, it looked as if I needed to work on my poker face. "This is strictly for the proles."

I had to resist the urge to shush him, ducking my head down and taking a sip of tea instead. His voice was particularly carrying, an asset given his profession but not ideal in his current surroundings. I had already got a very expressive look from a workman at the table behind Kit before he returned to reading his paper.

Cheerfully unself-conscious, Kit carried on, clear as a bell. "They don't know what they're missing. This place is a gem. So much more character than the chain coffee shops, and the food is better too."

"I like it," I said truthfully. It hadn't been redecorated since the early sixties, at a guess. The walls were pale green and hung with faded color photographs of the Italian Riviera. If the ceiling lights were chipped and the tabletops stained, that didn't take away from the character of the place, and it was perfectly clean. "How did you find it?"

"I collect caffs, the bleaker the better. And this happens to be halfway between chambers and the Old Bailey, so it's perfect." He leaned on the table. "Look, I don't mind talking about PK, but it's all strictly informal. You didn't hear any of this from me."

"Kit who?" I grinned at him.

"Exactly." He hesitated. "What sort of thing do you want to know?"

"I'm not looking for evidence. I just want to get a better idea of who he is and what he does." I lowered my voice. "Between you and me, my inspector is convinced he's the greatest shagger that ever walked the earth and everything he does is motivated by his cock. My impression of him is that he's a cold, uncaring individual who should never have been allowed to breed. He seems to be a good lawyer, from what I can gather. And he doesn't seem to be altogether keen on helping us to find out what happened to his family."

"He doesn't trust the police. That's the first thing."

"Why not?"

"He did a couple of cases where the defense was police brutality, and won. If it was true, the coppers involved were thoroughly nasty pieces of work. If it wasn't, every officer in the Met should be gunning for him for ruining their reputations."

"He's not popular," I admitted, thinking of Derwent's instant reaction to the news that we were in his house. "But he's not thick. He must know that Godley isn't like that. And he's a victim, isn't he?"

"Just because he's paranoid doesn't mean you aren't out to get him." Ketchup squirted out of the back of Kit's sandwich and splattered on the plate, bright red droplets that he dabbed with a piece of bread. I was blindsided by the memory of the white carpet in Kennford's house and looked away, glad I hadn't ordered food. Kit's forehead crinkled. "Sorry. I don't mean to be rude about your boss, or you. He's just wary."

"Oh, I don't mind about Kennford's opinion of us. What do you know about his private life?"

"Now there's a subject we could spend hours discussing. Do you want to know what I know or what I've heard?"

"Both, obviously."

"He's not the sort who likes to be tied down to one woman. He's got a flat in Clerkenwell — did you know about that?"

I nodded.

"He probably has a different girl there every night of the week. Keeps them from getting too serious, he says. Mind you, that only works if they're prepared to share. If not . . ." Kit whistled meaningfully.

"Bitch fights in Middle Temple Lane?"

"And worse. The trouble is, they all know about each other. He's lazy about going to look for new talent. Currently, there are at least four junior members of chambers who can tell you all about Kennford's sexual prowess."

"How junior?"

"One pupil. The rest were qualified."

I raised my eyebrows, surprised. "Isn't that against the rules? Sleeping with a pupil?"

"Massively." Kit shrugged. "Alan turned a blind eye and the heads of chambers aren't very hands-on. I haven't seen Pelham Griggs this year."

"So what happened?"

"Her pupil master took him aside and had a word. Kennford didn't care. He said she was old enough to know what she was doing and that she hadn't seemed to have any complaints. She was older that the usual pupil, thank God. She'd already been a teacher for a few years, then decided on a career change." Kit folded the last bit of bread into his cheek and chewed for a moment. "Not the first time he's done it, either. There's a barrister at Lincoln's Inn, Jodie Finlay. Stunning looks, very bright, very hardworking. Specializes in sex crimes these days and does very well at it too, when we all know it's not an easy gig. Kennford slept with her when she was a pupil at Three Unicorn, about fifteen years ago. She *was* young, straight out of college, and no money whatsoever — she's from the arse end of Cornwall and got where she is on scholarships. Kennford wanted her as soon as he saw her and spent a fortune on persuading her to sleep with him. He bombarded her with presents and kept taking her out to dinner until she felt obliged to give something back. That was how he described it to me, by the way — he wasn't under any illusions about how she felt about him. It gave him a thrill to coax her into bed when she had turned him down so many times. He's that sort of person — can't resist a challenge. And Jodie was a challenge, because even though she was young and impoverished, she was still a feisty one. If you ask me, the whole thing was a power struggle and Kennford declared himself the winner once he'd slept with her, more or less against her will."

The cook tossed something into a frying pan that made a noise like a million angry snakes. Suddenly the café seemed a few degrees hotter. My hair was damp against my skin and I shifted in my chair, struggling to concentrate.

"Hold on, he didn't rape her, did he?"

"Good Lord, no. Nothing like that." Kit looked shocked at the very idea. "He put her under so much pressure she didn't feel she could say no, but he didn't force her. It was still her choice to do it, but she made it clear it was a one-off."

"I imagine she regretted it."

"Instantly, I should think. The first thing he did was tell everyone he knew that he'd managed to sleep with her, and that it hadn't been worth the effort."

"Not very gentlemanly."

"He didn't like being turned down," Kit said simply. "Bad for his reputation. She should have been begging for a repeat performance, Kennford felt, but she wasn't having it. Anyway, she'd have walked into tenancy with us but she didn't apply for it. She got the hell out and went to another set."

"How do you know all this? Presumably it was before your time."

"The bar's a small world and I've heard both sides." He waved at the elderly waitress to get another mug of tea for himself. I was nursing mine. It seemed to get stronger as I got closer to the bottom, and the sides of the mug were stained dark brown. I could only hope my teeth weren't the same color. I asked her for water instead. It came lukewarm, in a short, stubby glass rimed with scratch marks. I drank it in one go.

"The first time I was up against her in court, Kennford came and found me so he could tell me not to be intimidated by her. He told me to remember she'd acted like a whore."

"Charming."

"Very much not and I didn't find it particularly helpful. She won, which was right and proper. I got to know her a couple of years later, when we were doing a big trial in Sheffield, both defending. One night we ended up having a few drinks and she gave me her version of what happened. She's never forgiven him for any of it, but I think the real problem was that she couldn't forgive herself." Kit looked embarrassed. "Bit of amateur psychology there for you."

"It seems like a fair assumption." I shook my head. "Honestly, Kennford sounds vile."

"In matters of the heart, absolutely. He's unscrupulous and undiscriminating. If someone takes his fancy, he goes after them, regardless of who they are or whether he's committed elsewhere."

"Or whether they're young and vulnerable."

"That just piques his interest. That and the unattainable woman. The world is full of aggrieved husbands who found out the hard way that Kennford couldn't be trusted with their wives."

"How aggrieved? Angry enough to want to get revenge on him?"

"I can't imagine any of them wanting to kill his wife and daughter, if that's what you're getting at. Much more likely to have wanted to sleep with one or both of them, I'd have said, for the full eye-for-an-eye effect."

"Did Vita sleep around? Was that how she coped?"

"I have no idea. I didn't know her — I saw her once at a memorial service for an ex-head of chambers, but that was all. Kennford never brought her to chambers functions. The potential for scene-making was epic. He said she wasn't interested in his work, and maybe she wasn't." Kit shrugged. "She didn't seem that interesting to me. She had to be a bit of a doormat to put up with his behavior. It's not as if she didn't know."

"How do you work that out?"

"Well, she was told on a couple of occasions. Once by someone I know, a very stroppy redhead who wanted to get back at Kennford for bringing their relationship to a close, so she called Vita and told her about the affair. She said she couldn't live with the deception, although she'd managed perfectly well for the previous three months while they were actually shagging." Kit's upper-class drawl was perfectly suited to making bitchy comments. I quickly glanced around — I wasn't the only one in the café who was hanging on every word.

"I take it she didn't get anywhere."

"Vita said she wasn't interested in hearing about it and put down the phone. There may have been repercussions, but I never heard about them."

"You said a couple of occasions. Who else talked to her about it?"

"A Lithuanian lunatic." Kit shuddered. "Even Philip would admit she was a mistake. He'd been defending her on money-laundering charges — part of a much bigger gang trial, so she was just an added extra. He got her off at half-time for lack of evidence. She was a stunner — amazing figure and the face of an angel." Kit shook his head. "He still should have kept his distance."

"But he didn't."

"No. He started up a relationship with her. Totally unprofessional but then he wasn't in the trial anymore, and neither was she, so he wasn't working for her. He can always justify these things, even if they're morally unjustifiable."

"But you said it was a mistake. Did he get in trouble for it?"

"With her, he did. She was determined to get him to leave Vita. She wanted to go straight and an English barrister seemed like a good means of supporting herself. That's PK's version," Kit added.

"Her version was different?"

"True love. And he'd promised her the moon and stars too. She moved into his flat and wouldn't move out again, so he got some heavies he knew to pack up her things and evict her with maximum force. That would have been fine if she hadn't had her own army of hooligans at her beck and call. They broke in and trashed the place — caused thousands of pounds worth of damage. Kennford might have managed to cover it up, but he had to ask Vita for the money to fix it. She went to inspect the flat and bumped into Niele — that's the girl's name — on the doorstep. Niele lost no time in telling her what had happened. And this is the kind of luck Kennford has." Kit shook his head, unwillingly admiring. "Vita made it quite clear to Niele that she wasn't going to split them up, and that she didn't care to know the details of the affair. She got rid of Niele for him when he didn't think he was ever going to be able to shake her loose. He said he wished he'd thought of sending Vita round instead of the heavies because she'd have done a better job."

"I don't get it. Why would Vita do his dirty work for him?"

"To protect her family. She was the typical mother tiger, apparently. I mean, that's why Kennford lost touch with his first daughter."

I blinked. "His what?"

"The first one. From his first marriage. Savannah." Kit leaned back. "Can it be possible you didn't know about her?"

"He never said. He told us about his first wife — Miranda, isn't it? I assumed they didn't have any children."

"Just the one. But what a one to have."

"What does that mean?" I asked, intrigued.

"Savannah as in Savannah Wentworth. The model. Supermodel, I should say, although that word's debased currency these days. She's always in the newspapers and celebrity magazines. 'Steal Savannah's Style' — that kind of thing."

"I don't really read celebrity magazines," I said apologetically.

"I read my girlfriend's and I'm not ashamed." He grinned. "Anyway, even if you haven't heard her name, you'll recognize her face. She was all over every second bus in London last Christmas, advertising some high-end perfume or makeup."

Last Christmas I had been pretty thoroughly preoccupied with hunting a vicious serial killer. What was being advertised on the buses had been fairly low on my list of things to notice. "It doesn't ring a bell for me, but that doesn't mean much."

"You will recognize her when you see her," Kit insisted. "She's always on the covers of magazines."

"One of the twins had a load of fashion magazines in her room," I recalled. "It was the one who seemed less interested in fashion. Maybe she had them because she wanted to find out more about her halfsister."

"If she did that was probably the only way she had to do it. He hasn't been in touch with Savannah for a while, he told me. I'm involved with a charity that helps AIDS orphans. I wanted to see if we could persuade Savannah to donate a dinner date for a charity auction. Not via him, was the answer."

"That's a bit cold."

"What was cold was moving out when she was nine or ten and not really seeing her from then until she made it big as a model. He got pretty excited by the glamour. He used to go to Paris to watch her do the big fashion shows there. Then Vita got jealous so she put a stop to it."

"Jealous? Because it brought him back into contact with his first wife?"

"No, nothing like that. Believe me, Philip didn't regret leaving Miranda for a moment. She was pretty high maintenance, even before she got sick. One of those people who's never happy, no matter what you do for her. Philip wasn't the best husband in the world as he'd be the first to admit, but he didn't make the mistake of marrying someone like that again. He wanted someone who would put him first and Vita was more than happy to oblige. No, Vita wasn't jealous for herself. It was all about the twins being neglected while he went gallivanting around the world."

"She was worried about the twins being overshadowed."

"They weren't model material, either of them. They looked a bit strange when they were younger — one was fat and the other one was scrawny and they both looked more like their mother than Philip. Besides, they were far too short." He twisted in his seat so he could address the builder at the table behind. "Excuse me, my friend, but can I borrow your paper for a second?" I was sure he would say no, but as if he was hypnotized, the man closed his newspaper and handed it over to Kit, who beamed. "You're a gentle-man."

"What are you doing?" I hissed.

Kit was thumbing through the paper. "Looking for the showbiz section. She's always in it. Ah, here we are." He tapped the page as he turned it around so I could see. "That's Savannah."

The picture was in color, but smudgy as newsprint often is. It was a paparazzo picture of a tall, very slender young woman with dark hair and piercing blue eyes. Her mouth was open, as if she had been talking to the photographer and was caught mid-word, but even in a candid shot she was utterly beauti-ful, with high cheekbones and delicate fea-tures. She was also exceptionally like her father.

"She's the image of him."

"Exactly. And he's an egotist. Seeing her triumph because of her looks was a mixed pleasure for him. On the one hand, he thinks she should be making more use of her brains, because by all accounts she was very bright — certainly clever enough to go to university. On the other hand, he loves the fact that she gets paid a fortune for looking pretty. And, incidentally, for looking just like him."

"He does think highly of himself, doesn't he?"

"Number one fan." Kit smiled wryly. "It's not that uncommon at the bar."

"It's not that uncommon in the Met." I was thinking of Derwent.

"He told me once that Savannah was his favorite child, and his one regret about leaving her mother was that he had to leave her behind too. He didn't think he'd done very well by her."

"Somehow that doesn't surprise me." He hadn't done that great a job on Laura and Lydia, it seemed to me, and he'd technically been around for their entire childhood. "Do you think Vita was the reason he fell out with Savannah the second time round?"

"She might have been. But I think there was something else too. You'd have to ask Philip. Or Savannah."

I had been reading the caption for the photo, which listed the designer clothes Savannah was wearing, down to her handbag and earrings. "It says here she's just back from a modeling trip to South Africa."

"Nice work if you can get it."

"I wonder if she was in the country on Sunday." I said it to myself, not really intending Kit to answer. He looked shocked.

"You can't think she was involved."

"Why not?"

"She's too . . ."

"Pretty? Glamorous? Thin? Come on, Kit, you know better than that. I'll have to get her to come in for an interview. I'll probably need to put guards on the door to stop my colleagues from bursting in to have a look at her." I folded the paper and handed it back to Kit, who slid it across the table to the builder with a loud "Thank you."

"Thank you too," I said when he turned back to me. "This has been very helpful."

"Really? I hope so." He rubbed his face. "I hope I haven't said anything that might get Philip into trouble. He's really not evil, even if he's not the best dad in the world."

"Or husband. Or lover." I grinned at Kit's discomfort. "I'm not going to arrest him for being a bit of a shit, don't worry."

"You know, thinking about Philip like this, he strikes me as a tragic figure. Almost Shakespearean."

"I don't see it."

"Well, his favorite daughter doesn't speak to him. His second-favorite daughter is dead. His marriages seem to have been pretty awful in their own way, and his romantic life is one catastrophe after another."

"He brings it on himself."

"No doubt. The best tragic heroes do." Kit pushed back his chair and got up. "I'm going to ask him if he wants to go for a drink later. Make up for betraying him to you, not that I'll tell him what I've done."

"The main thing you gave away was the fact that he has another daughter, and arguably he should have told us that himself."

"Maybe he thought you knew."

Or maybe he didn't want us to know. I said goodbye to Kit and watched him lug his bag out of the café. From what he'd told me, it was pretty clear Philip Kennford had a ruthless streak a mile wide. It made me wonder if his first daughter had inherited more than just his looks.

CHAPTER NINE

It was always well worth interviewing ex-wives, in my experience. They had intimate knowledge of the person you were interested in, and generally no loyalty to them whatsoever. The only reason to be wary was if they were so shriveled with bitterness that you couldn't trust what they were telling you was the truth. It helped that I was prepared to believe the worst of Philip Kennford, because Miranda Wentworth was equally prepared to dish the dirt.

"Philip's trouble is that he always thinks he knows best. He can't imagine that he might be wrong, and he doesn't put anyone else's needs ahead of his own, even those of his children. He comes first, always. That and his inability to keep his fly done up make him a very unreliable husband."

"You found him so," I said.

"Oh, yes. Desperately unreliable. And Vita did too. I hope he hasn't been trying to sell you a version of their marriage where it was all roses and champagne because that was far from the case, let me tell you."

Beside me, Derwent stirred. "Sorry, Miss Wentworth — *Ms.* Wentworth, I mean." He'd been corrected twice already and her china-doll blue eyes had just flashed with irritation again. He was finding it hard, I knew, to come to terms with the knowledge that the luscious Savannah Wentworth was Philip Kennford's daughter, and that he had managed to avoid telling us about her existence despite our best efforts at interrogation. Derwent's pride was hurt and his interest was piqued; he was quite a fan of Savannah, he had confided in me earlier when I told him what I had found out.

Aware he had lost ground, he tried again. "Sorry to interrupt, but how could you possibly know the state of your ex-husband's marriage? From what he told us about your current relationship, he wouldn't be inclined to confide in you, would he?"

"Not him. He never did when we were together, so why would he when we'd split up?"

"That's sort of what I was wondering."

"It was Vita who told me about it herself."

"Vita did?" I couldn't hide the surprise in my voice. "Why would she talk to you about it, Ms. Wentworth?"

"Because I'm one of the only women on the planet who doesn't represent a threat to her. Philip wouldn't touch me now — he

218

doesn't like going back over what he would consider to be dead ground." She smoothed the blankct that was spread over her knees. "He's not attracted to failure or weakness or ill health. I represent all three."

It was multiple sclerosis, she had explained to us within minutes of our arrival at her Hampstead flat to find her sitting in an armchair, unable to get up. She had become ill around the time her marriage broke down, and I had the impression she blamed Philip Kennford for her poor health. "The stress didn't help, according to my specialist," she had said as her caregiver put a tray down on the table in front of her. "It encouraged the illness to progress more quickly than it might have at the beginning. But there have been some times of remission since then, so I imagine it all evens out. Tea?"

She wasn't the sort of woman you could pity — too strong-willed for that, and too defiant. I had watched her struggle to manage the heavy teapot, not daring to offer to help, and thought even less of the man who had left her for a rich woman after she had been diagnosed with a progressive illness.

"It just seems strange to me that Vita would talk to you — and that you'd talk to her. I'd have thought she would be the last person you'd want to know."

"Because she stole my husband?" Miranda blinked at me, all innocence. "But there was a certain fascination in it, don't you see? I got to see the scales fall from her eyes. She worshipped him — absolutely adored him in every way. It's not a good basis for a marriage."

"And you had a ringside seat," Derwent said. "Must have been satisfying."

"It was, in a way. But it was sad too. She was very much in love with him and she came to me in a state of desperation to ask for my help. I mean, she had to be desperate, didn't she? She said she didn't have anyone else to turn to. She couldn't admit to anyone else that he was being unfaithful to her. She didn't have any friends, and whoever she'd confided in hadn't been very sympathetic or helpful. They just told her to get on with it and pretend she hadn't noticed. Which was essentially what I said too, but more diplomatically."

"What did she want you to do?"

"Tell her what I did wrong so she could avoid it." Miranda dimpled with a smile that made her extremely attractive; you could see how a daughter of Philip Kennford and this woman was well placed to win the genetic lottery. "She told me she'd pay me for my advice. Treat me like a counselor rather than a friend, or someone she knew. I told her straightaway I didn't want to be friends with her and she accepted that."

"What else did you tell her?"

"To tidy herself up. She was a mess." She said it without heat, stating a fact. "She'd had the twins by then and she was very overweight. She didn't have time to exercise, she told me, and I just laughed. 'Make time.' That was what I said."

"Is Mr. Kennford that shallow?"

"Of course." The blue eyes widened as they met mine. "Darling, all men are. That's why you have to look after yourself. Pay attention to grooming, even though most of them wouldn't notice a nice manicure or an expensive haircut. They'd notice the opposite quickly enough, let me tell you."

Miranda herself practiced what she preached, her hair a shoulder-length brown bob without a hint of gray, her mouth painted coral and still plump. Her nails were varnished shell pink, a color that matched her cashmere cardigan. She was slim, her legs narrow under the blanket on her lap, but looking at old photographs of her which were on display around the room, it wasn't solely the frailty of ill health. She had always been slim. The room where we sat was small, but nicely furnished with antiques and art. It looked both expensive and tasteful, though I couldn't guess if it was her supermodel daughter who paid for it, or if Philip Kennford's remuneration to her covered it all. She didn't work, we had established at an early stage. She never had. She had married Kenn-

221

ford when she left school, his child bride.

"So you advised her on her appearance."

"I told her to spend her money on herself, not on paying people to share their common sense. A regular facial, massages, proper cosmetics that she knew how to apply. The poor thing had tried but she looked like a clown, all red lipstick and smudged nail varnish." Miranda looked down at her own hands complacently. "I could only lead by example, but I think it helped that I was careful of my appearance. I also told her to get involved in the local community. Join the tennis club and meet the wives. Make contacts so Philip could circulate among people he thought were worthy of his attention. He's a terrible snob. I used to have little dinner parties so he could entertain important people, not being rich enough to make friends with their wives myself. People can be so judgmental if they think you're a social climber," she added without any apparent irony.

"Do you think Vita tried to live up to you?" I asked.

"Of course. Philip and I had been together for a long time. I had been able to make him happy until she came along."

"So she should have felt superior to you, arguably."

Miranda laughed. "Far from it. She persuaded him to sleep with her — which was never difficult with Philip — had the luck to get pregnant, and with twins to make doubly sure he'd be interested, and had enough sense to tell him she had sufficient money to make all his dreams come true. She kept building her little walls around him with whatever bricks and mortar she could find, but he still wasn't committed to her."

"He obviously wasn't committed to you and your daughter either," I said.

"We both got over the hurt that caused us." She blinked at me, daring me to challenge her. The skin around her eyes was soft and unlined, possibly because she rarely allowed her face to move. Possibly it was expensive plastic surgery. I had a feeling that if I got a look at her dressing table she would have a collection of creams and lotions to rival Vita's own.

"So you advised Vita on her appearance. What else?"

"I told her to leave him alone — let him do what he liked. She was running a risk that someone wealthier than her would come along and seduce him, but I never made the mistake of trying to control him and it gave us more than a decade of marriage."

"You think money would have been the motivation?" Derwent asked.

"It was in my case." The coral mouth tightened, then relaxed. "I'm not saying I was perfect, you understand, but I knew what Philip wanted." She ticked them off on her fingers. "Freedom. Decent food ready when he wanted to eat it. No domestic worries whatsoever. A wife he could show off when he wanted. And preferably one with the skills of a highly trained whore so he could have the same pleasures at home as when he played away."

I jumped, surprised in spite of myself at what she was suggesting. Derwent laughed.

"Was that the secret? Being a bit filthy now and then?"

She looked exceptionally demure. "It never hurt to try. Of course, poor Vita wasn't very interested in sex. Love, yes, but sex wasn't her thing, she told me. I told her, you'd better make it your thing. Read up on it. Learn about it. Practice. Treat it as a project, like losing weight or learning to play tennis."

"I suppose that explains the box," Derwent said to me in an undertone. "Homework."

"What else did you tell her to do?" I sounded stunned, even to myself.

"Learn to have a thick skin. Learn to take whatever she was offered and pretend to like it. Get rid of anyone who seemed a genuine threat, whatever the reason. She had money so she had power." Miranda shrugged. "It wasn't an equal struggle when Philip met her. If it had come down to a straightforward comparison of the two of us, I'd have won in every category. Even Philip admitted that to me. The only place where she was ahead was

224

the size of her bank balance."

"You didn't have family money."

"Me? No. And I wasn't earning anything. Money was always important to Philip. I couldn't compete with that, and I knew it." She shrugged. "Some people are born to privilege. They take what they can get, no matter who it belongs to. Vita was one of those. She'd never known what it was to want something and not be able to have it, so the thought of losing Philip was especially hard. I was used to not getting what I wanted. And of course, by the time he walked out I was glad to see him go. He wasn't the man I'd fallen in love with." She amended it instantly. "Maybe it was more that I hadn't realized what he was like in the first place. Anyway, I didn't want to hold on to him if he wanted to leave. But I wasn't going to make it easy for him. I fought him in court and got as much out of him as I could. I deserved it."

"I just don't know why you'd help her," I said. "I'd want to tell her all the wrong things to do and watch her marriage fail too."

"It wasn't in my interests." Miranda leaned back in her chair. "Oh, my first instinct was to tell her to get out of my house and never come back. I thought it was a cheeky thing to ask, in the circumstances. But then I looked at it from another perspective. If he stayed with her, she paid for everything. He was able to give me a lot more money than he would

225

have been if he'd been supporting his new family. I didn't have to worry about anything. If he left her, he might have gone back to court and got a different judge to agree to cut my payments."

"That would have been a disaster, I take it," Derwent said.

"Absolutely. I was having private treatment for the MS — I didn't see why I should have to slum it on the NHS when Philip could afford to pay for the best medical care. Savannah had expensive hobbies and I didn't want her to have to give them up just because her father had walked out."

"So Vita's money must have helped too."

"Everything helped." She narrowed her eyes. "You might not understand but I wasn't too proud to take it."

"Were you still in touch with her, Ms. Wentworth?"

She shook her head. "I hadn't spoken to her for years. Hadn't wanted to, either. She'd got what she needed from me. Vita wasn't the sort of person to keep in touch once I'd outlived my usefulness, and I didn't care to hear about her family life anyway. We parted without regret."

"So you don't know how things were between them at the time of her death." Derwent sounded disappointed.

"No. I can only guess. Philip won't have changed; he has never known how to be a

226

good husband. Vita just learned how to be a perfect wife instead."

"What sort of father is he? How was his relationship with Savannah when she was growing up?" I asked.

"What relationship?" She gave a little laugh. "He didn't stay in touch with her after he left — not properly. I reminded him about her birthday. I even bought her the bloody presents sometimes, and faked his writing on a card. There was nothing I could do to pretend he was there when he wasn't, though. He'd promise to take her out for the day and then never turn up, and I would have to ring Vita, and ring chambers, and try to find out if his phone was off because he was in court or because he'd switched it off to be out of range. Savannah got used to being disappointed."

"They don't speak now, do they?"

"Not at the moment." She looked guarded, and I realized she wasn't prepared to talk about Savannah. It made sense when her daughter was so famous that every tiny new fact about her had the power to make headlines around the world.

"The reason we ask, Ms. Wentworth, is because Philip didn't mention Savannah to us when he was talking about his family."

She raised her eyebrows. "Did you ask?"

"No," I admitted. "It didn't occur to us to ask specifically."

"Savannah has never been proud enough of him to want to boast that they're related, I'm delighted to say. She's quite happy to be an example of what you can achieve, despite being brought up by a single mother."

In the lap of luxury, I felt like saying, but on second thought it probably hadn't been easy given Miranda's health, and the fact that she came across as both cool and calculating rather than cozily maternal. I hoped the expensive hobbies had taken her away from the wintry focus of her mother from time to time. "Poor little rich girl" seemed like the appropriate phrase.

"So Savannah turned her back on her father in much the same way as he ignored her," I suggested.

"Yes." Miranda allowed herself a tiny frown. "Well, except that they did become closer when Savannah was starting to make real headway as a model. Philip traveled to watch her walk in the major European fashion shows. He loved the attention she got, and of course it turned Savannah's head completely that he was prepared to make the effort to come and support her even though no one knew or cared who he was. Until Vita put a stop to it."

"That must have annoyed you."

"Hardly. I didn't care if Philip never saw Savannah again. It annoyed me that she was so quick to forgive him. As for Vita, it made me proud of her," she said levelly. "She'd listened to what I taught her. Remove the threat. Demand that the focus is on you and your family. Never let him forget you or your daughters."

There was a framed photograph of Savannah on an end table, a black-and-white one that was obviously from a professional shoot. I wondered if it was her mother's choice to have such a recognizable but impersonal reminder of her daughter, or if it was Savannah's own preference.

"You must be very proud of her," I ventured.

"Yes." Again, something dragged the word out, a reluctance I couldn't quite understand. Something unsaid. "She's very successful. Of course, she was always bright. She could have been anything she wanted to be. Used her mind more."

"Hard to turn down that kind of lifestyle, though," Derwent said dreamily. "Travel. Money. Glamour."

"Yes. It does seem idyllic from the outside."

"But not from the inside?" I asked.

"You'd have to ask Savannah."

"We're trying to get hold of her, actually. She's a hard person to track down."

"When you do see her, tell her her mother sends her regards." Her voice had a brittle edge to it.

"You don't get to see her much, I take it,"

Derwent said.

"Not enough." The smile this time was a wavering one and I thought I had made the mistake of underestimating the strength of the woman's feelings for her daughter, simply because of her poise. "There's no amount of time that would be enough. I've missed her since she moved out a few years ago. Missed her every day." As if aware that she was revealing more of her true feelings than usual, she forced another smile. "It was ironic that Vita came to me for help, really. It was the first thing I said to her when she got in touch. I have never, never understood Philip. Nor have I understood the decisions he's made. I've always thought he must have sincere regrets about what he left behind when he left us, but he's never shown them to me. Then again, maybe he doesn't know what regret is like." The smile hadn't moved, and there was something chilling about it, something fundamentally unsympathetic. It was pleasure that justice had been done at last.

"Maybe he will know better now."

We left Miranda Wentworth to her perfect, barren little world, in my case with a sense of tremendous relief. Derwent seemed determined to have been charmed.

"Lovely woman. You can see Savannah takes after her."

"She looks just like her dad."

"That's jealousy talking, Kerrigan. You shouldn't think you can compete. You don't need to." He patted my knee. "No one cares about what you look like."

"You're not just barking up the wrong tree — you're in the wrong forest." I glared at him. "It is a simple fact that Savannah looks like her dad. Same build. Same features. Same everything. She's obviously a very attractive woman, but she gets her looks from her father."

"Shame Miranda didn't marry again. Probably couldn't think about that with a young daughter to bring up and her health troubles."

"Don't forget, she'd have lost out on the lovely alimony too."

"Money isn't everything, Kerrigan."

"It is to these people. I don't understand the attraction of it. It didn't make any of them happy, it seems to me. Kennford seems to have hated the house, given how he furnished his study and the fact that he doesn't stay there if he can avoid it. He wasn't in a good marriage. Mind you, I don't think he walked out on a better one."

"Where are we going now?" Derwent levered himself up in the driver's seat, trying to loosen his trousers. "I've spent so much time cooking my balls in this fucking car this week, my little swimmers are probably poached."

"I don't want to talk about your sperm count." I shook my head. "Did I need to say

231

that out loud? Why would you think I wanted to know about your balls?"

"So you can sympathize." He was still braced against the back of the seat, legs straight. "It can't be good for me to have my circulation cut off like this."

"Poor you."

"Try it with more feeling."

"That's all you're getting." I fanned myself with the map. "God, it's hot."

"Getting hotter," he agreed.

"Well, we need to go back to Wimbledon, I'm afraid."

Derwent groaned. "Mind you, it's high ground. It might be cooler over there."

"Dream on."

"Who are we talking to?"

"Millie Carberry."

"Who?"

"Lydia gave me her name. She said she's in school with them and was one of Laura's best friends. She was supposed to be with Millie when she died. I thought she might be able to tell us something about the mystery boyfriend."

"She's a teenage girl. They take an attitude to a vow of silence that puts the Mafia to shame."

"You don't know that. She might be in the mood to be helpful."

Skeptical was not the word for the look I got in return.

■ ■ ■

Derwent had his predictable moments. I
could tell, for instance, that when we arrived
at Millie Carberry's extremely nice detached
house in Wimbledon Village to find her still
in bed at half past two in the afternoon, he
was gearing up for a lecture on the Youth of
Today and their shortcomings. I could also
tell he was itching to swipe the beanie hat off
the youth who opened the door to us, sleepy-
eyed and yawning, and turned out to be
Millie's brother, Seth. He was wearing shorts
and a T-shirt, but I thought he had probably
just got out of bed himself; his clothes looked
rumpled and soft with sweat. The other thing
that occurred to me was that he might have
been stoned. He was very far from being with
it. I sniffed unobtrusively but couldn't smell
anything underneath the Jo Malone Red
Roses room spray that filled the air.

"Who are you again?"

"Detectives with the Metropolitan Police."
Derwent was not inclined to run through our
names more than once — that had tested his
patience enough.

"And you want to talk to my sister."

"We had made an arrangement to speak to
her. I spoke to your mother this morning," I
said. "She told me Millie would be happy to
speak to us."

"In Mum's world." Seth yawned. "She must have forgotten to say."

"Is she here?"

"She's at work."

"What does she do?" Derwent asked.

"She's a banker." He held up his hands as if to ward off our disgust. "Don't blame me. I just live off the proceeds."

"It explains the nice house."

"If you like this sort of shit. It's the Laura Ashley catalog Autumn/Winter 2010. That's page sixty-four." He pointed in through the door to the sitting room.

"Very funny. Can you get Millie for us?" Derwent's very limited patience had just run out.

He wandered over to the foot of the stairs. "Mills! Get up!"

There was a muffled response from overhead.

"It's the fuzz. You're wanted."

A thump, running feet and a scared face looking through the banisters.

"Millie Carberry?" I asked.

"Oh my God. What time is it?" She pushed back her hair from her face, a heavy tumble of fair curls. "I slept in."

"You're up now." Derwent was actually tapping his foot, I was amused to see. "Come and talk to us."

"I need to brush my teeth." She wriggled. "Can I have a shower?"

"You've got five minutes. Then we're coming to talk to you whether you're ready or not."

She ran, presumably for the bathroom, and Derwent and I turned to find that her brother had disappeared. With a shrug to me, the inspector led the way to a very glamorous kitchen, all marble worktops and chandeliers. We sat at the kitchen table for five minutes, then five minutes more, listening to muffled thumps from upstairs that seemed to suggest something was happening.

"What do you want to do?" I asked, as there was still no sign of her.

"Wait."

"You're the one who gave her an ultimatum. You should follow up on it."

"I hate teenagers." He didn't move.

When she finally appeared in the kitchen, Millie was wearing tracksuit bottoms and a very skimpy T-shirt. She kept tugging at the hem to keep it from riding up over her stomach. She was slightly plump, her cheeks rounded with baby fat. Her hair was bundled up in a very untidy knot at the back of her head, trailing tendrils around her face, which had undoubtedly taken at least ten of the twenty minutes we had waited to make it look so artless.

"I'm really sorry. I completely slept in. Mum did say you were coming. Can I make you a cup of tea?"

Millie's expensive education showed in her voice and her manners. Her brother sounded equally posh but had shaken off the politeness quickly enough.

"No thanks," I answered for Derwent.

"Do you know why we wanted to talk to you, Millie?"

She was filling the kettle anyway, her movements jerky with nerves. "I presume it's to do with Laura?"

"Correct."

"I can't believe it. What an awful thing to happen." She looked at us across the enormous breakfast bar, her eyes huge. "I don't know anything about it."

"That's fine, Millie. We just want to ask you some questions about Laura and how she was behaving before she died."

"Oh, okay. If I can help."

"Come and sit down," Derwent commanded. "You're miles away over there."

She padded over and sat on the very edge of a chair, seconds away from fleeing.

"What was Laura like, Millie? Can you give us some idea of her personality?"

"Oh. Well, she was fun. Very sweet. Thoughtful." She looked earnestly from Derwent to me and back again.

"Anything more to add?"

She pulled her feet up onto the chair. "Not really."

"We gather she had a bit of a rebellious

streak," I said gently.

"I don't know . . ."

"Did you know she had a boyfriend?" Derwent said, cutting to the chase.

"No. She wasn't allowed one. Her parents wouldn't let her."

"She still had one, though."

Millie looked confused. "She never said. I mean, I didn't know."

"You were her best friend, though. Lydia told us that. You must have known."

She shook her head vehemently. "I promise you, not at all. I didn't have a clue."

"You must have noticed her sneaking off to meet him," I suggested.

"No. Not a thing." She looked wounded. "I thought she was studying."

"Were you supposed to see her on Sunday night?"

"Sunday? When she died? No."

"Lydia told us a different story. She said you had an arrangement to go to the cinema. A Robert Pattinson film."

Millie blushed, presumably at the mention of the actor's name. She answered readily enough. "That was Saturday and she canceled."

"Lydia said it was Sunday."

"She must have been wrong."

"Laura had told everyone she was going to be out with you — and you had no idea? Aren't you friends with her on Facebook?"

"I'm not allowed to use it. Dad doesn't like it."

"That's practically child abuse these days, isn't it?" Derwent sounded skeptical.

"He read an article in the *Daily Telegraph* about identity theft that freaked him out." Millie rolled her eyes. "Anyway, it's blocked on my home computer but I use it at school, so it's not too much of a problem. It's just that I miss out in the school holidays. I have to go to the library to use the Internet, and all the computers are sticky, and it smells of wee." She grinned cheekily and Derwent smothered a laugh in a very unconvincing cough.

"But you're sure, it was definitely Saturday you were supposed to go out?" I checked.

"Yes, but she canceled."

"Did she do that a lot?"

"Yeah." Millie squeezed her knees to her chest. "I mean, I didn't mind, but she liked to change arrangements when it suited her."

"That would fit with using you for an alibi so she could meet her boyfriend," Derwent pointed out.

"Oh my God. You're so right." She put one foot down and kicked at the table.

"What's the matter, Millie?" There was obviously something she wanted to say. I glanced at Derwent, who leaned forward.

"The best thing you can do for Laura now — the only thing you can do to help her — is to tell us the truth, Millie. What's wrong? What do you think we should know?"

When she eventually replied, her voice was pitched at a nearly inaudible level. "The thing is, I know Lydia said I was Laura's best friend, and it was probably true, but she wasn't easy to get to know. I've got other friends who I'd say were closer. But she kind of didn't, so I can see what Lydia means."

"So we shouldn't be surprised she had secrets from you, is that it?" I asked. "And that you didn't mind it?"

"I'm not surprised, that's all I can say." She bit her lip. "Laura kept things to herself. She wasn't big on sharing. I know things weren't that happy at home, but she never really told me what was happening. Maybe she was afraid I'd spread it around school, but I never said a word to anyone. She didn't trust me."

"But she trusted you more than anyone else."

"I suppose." Millie blinked at us. "I just don't think that means very much at all."

CHAPTER TEN

It had been three years since Christopher Blacker was cleared — belatedly and on appeal — of raping one of his students, but it might as well have been three days. Nothing had faded in him — not the burning sense of outrage at the unfair treatment he'd received, not the anger at the poor representation that had sent him to prison for a year until his appeal was heard. And not the fear that brightened his eyes as he opened the door of his flat just wide enough to let us in. It was understandable. A conviction for statutory rape — even one that had been found to be unsafe on appeal — was a heavy burden to carry.

The flat was a dingy space overlooking a busy road in Acton, little more than a single square room with a narrow hallway and tiny bathroom. It wasn't quite a studio; one corner of the main room had been partitioned off to make a tiny bedroom. I glanced in as I passed, seeing a single bed and a row of hooks on the wall instead of a wardrobe. A cardboard box in the corner functioned as both bedside table and as storage for more clothes — underwear and T-shirts, by the look of the piles I could see. It reminded me of nothing more than a prison cell.

The rest of the flat wasn't much better. The carpet was old and thin, threadbare in places, patterned in red and black. A makeshift kitchen in the corner had a sink, a half-sized fridge and a hot plate but no oven. There was room for a two-seater sofa, which Derwent sprawled himself across without asking permission. Blacker sat down at the table by the window, his back to the light. I wondered if that was accidental or on purpose, a habit he had learned to hide what he was feeling from police officers. It didn't matter much anyway; the net curtains that hung at the window were dark gray with dirt and let in very little daylight. Derwent turned on a lamp that stood beside him, which marginally improved the situation.

"It's pitch dark in here. How do you manage to read that lot?" He nodded at the shelves that lined one wall. They were loaded with paperbacks. I skim-read the spines and saw that most of them were secondhand, old editions of classic nonfiction books that were dog-eared and faded.

"I manage." He unbent a little. "The wonder of electricity helps."

"Stick the main light on, Maeve," Derwent commanded. Blacker didn't protest so I flicked the switch. The bulb wasn't particularly strong but the extra light was enough to see my notebook, and the damp that was puckering the paper around the window. I looked at Blacker with interest. My first impression of him had been colored by the stress that was making his thin frame vibrate, but now I saw that he was attractive, or would have been if he hadn't been so gaunt. He had dark, curly hair that was long enough to cover his collar, heavy straight eyebrows over toffee-colored eyes and a sensitive mouth. He wore jeans and a white shirt with the sleeves rolled up, revealing thin forearms covered in black hair. His hands were long, with elegant, tapering fingers.

"May I sit here?" I indicated the other chair at the table.

"Yes, of course." Blacker leaned across and began to gather up the papers and books that were stacked up in front of me, his movements jerky and hurried. A cereal bowl lurked under the last pile of loose pages and I handed it to him without looking too closely at the contents. "Sorry. I use this table for work and eating. Sometimes at the same time."

"It's fine." I put my notebook down on the table, wishing I could give it a good scrub first. There was a constellation of old crumbs by my elbow and I could hear more crunching under my notebook when I leaned on it.

"It's not usually this messy in here. I work from home sometimes so I have to keep it neat." The words tumbled out of him at top speed. "It's just that I don't have any students at the moment."

"Students?" Derwent's tone was challenging and I shot him a warning look. We needed Blacker to trust us, not to clam up. He wasn't officially a suspect; we didn't have any grounds to arrest him if he refused to talk to us. He was well within his rights to kick us out, in fact, and I had expected him to refuse to see us right up to the point where he'd beckoned us in.

"I still teach. But not in a school. I couldn't go back after what happened." He clamped his hands together between his knees. "Legally, I could have. I tried. I just couldn't bring myself to do it."

"Too traumatized?" Derwent drawled.

"You can joke about it if you like." Blacker's voice sounded strained. "Probably seems funny to you. But I got flashbacks. Panic attacks. Couldn't breathe, let alone teach."

"Just from being in a school?" I asked gently.

He nodded. "I don't do well with large groups of people anymore. I didn't fit in, in the staff room — I thought everyone was judging me. It was worse in the classroom.

243

Every time someone whispered, I panicked. I thought they knew what had happened."

"Did they?"

"It was a different school. Different part of London. And I wasn't using the same name, with the head teacher's permission, so they couldn't have found out by searching the Internet." He swallowed. "It was just paranoia, really, but that didn't make it any easier to cope. I ended up leaving. Walked out one day. The kids weren't bad, but they could tell I wasn't able to deal with discipline problems, and things just got worse and worse. It was like being bullied, every class. Thank God they never found out about the court case. They just turned on me because they were bored and I was an easy target."

"What did they do?"

"Talked. Shouted things when my back was turned. Passed notes. Wrote things on the whiteboard before I got into the room. Two of the boys who sat on opposite sides of the room brought in a rugby ball once. They spent the class throwing it back and forth, over their classmates' heads. I pretended I hadn't noticed. I couldn't deal with a fight."

"What were you trying to teach them?" I asked.

"Math and physics." He grinned, showing white, even teeth. His face was so thin that the effect was more death's head than Hollywood, but once it might have been the latter.

"You know, math and physics aren't exactly crowd-pleasing subjects at the best of times. They're also not that popular to teach, which was why I was able to get that job in the first place. I had experience and a good reference from my old school, so the head was willing to overlook what she called 'teething problems.' " He pulled a face at the phrase; I guessed it had been the understatement of the century. "I used to love my job but I didn't miss it when I left. I wasn't sorry, even though I ended up being signed off work for months because I had a breakdown. The good old welfare state came to the rescue, with not quite enough to live on for not quite as long as I needed it."

"At least you had something coming in." Derwent didn't sound terribly moved.

"I had a bit, but it was a struggle to make ends meet. Not like now. Now I'm doing really well for myself." He smiled at the expression on my face. "It might not look like much to you, but this place even has a bathroom I don't have to share. It's all mine."

"Going up in the world." Derwent leaned forward, his eyes narrowed in concentration. Hunting. "Tell me more about the students you teach here."

"Worried for their safety? Afraid I might be molesting them?" Blacker was looking wary, a pulse jumping in his throat. "You're all the same, aren't you? Give a dog a bad name."

245

"It's a reasonable question."

"It's a question you'd ask if you were concerned about their safety," Blacker said harshly. "It's something you'd be curious about if you thought I was guilty."

"It's habit," I said. "DI Derwent likes to know everything about everyone."

Blacker gave me a look that showed what he thought of that particular line: not much. But it had taken his mind of Derwent for a moment, long enough for him to recover his temper. He fixed his eyes on the wall just above Derwent's head. "I teach students here, but I've got rules. The first one, and the most important, is no girls, ever. No students here on their own — they come in twos, or I go to see them at their house with a parent in the same room with us at all times. If one of them doesn't turn up when they're supposed to be here, I go to the library or one of the local coffee shops with the other one. We stay in public at all times. I make it clear from the start I'm not prepared to be alone with them."

"Doesn't that raise people's suspicions?"

"Mostly they're glad I've said it first. They don't want to look paranoid, but they're protective of their kids. Rightly so. There are plenty of weirdos out there."

"And plenty of students in need of extra tuition?"

"I usually have about six boys to teach — more coming up to the GCSEs and A levels, obviously, but I also do special tutoring for the Oxbridge entrance exams. I advertise locally, but most of my business is generated by personal recommendations. I am a very good teacher and I don't hate tutoring, especially when the boys get good results. I make enough money to survive. What else do you want to know?"

"Got a girlfriend?"

"Not at the moment."

"Since you went to court?"

"There have been women. Casually. Nothing serious." He ran his hands through his hair, frustrated. "Women, Inspector. Not girls."

"She was pretty." Derwent's comment was something of a non sequitur, but neither Blacker nor I had any trouble with following his train of thought.

"Isobel Sairey was fourteen at the time we were supposed to be having an affair. I haven't been attracted to a fourteen-year-old since I was fifteen or thereabouts. She was a pretty girl — she probably still is. But I didn't see her that way. She was just one of my students. If I thought about her at all before she made her allegations, it was just to wonder whether she'd understood the answer when she asked me a question."

"You must have been aware that your presence in a girls' school could cause trouble. A nice-looking fellow like you, and young, and all those teenage girls with their hormones raging out of control."

"I was a member of staff. I wasn't there to act as a focus for their emotional confusion, or whatever you're suggesting."

"That was what happened though, wasn't it?"

"I couldn't control what the girls thought or how they expressed it." Blacker seemed to have shrunk into himself. His voice was fainter, as if he was losing his hold on the conversation.

"You couldn't help it."

"I don't think I could have, no." The brown eyes were fixed on Derwent's. *Look, I have nothing to hide.* "I never talked about my private life. I never asked any of the girls about theirs — I didn't even ask if they'd had a nice weekend, mainly because I didn't care about the answer. I kept it about the work. I was pleasant to them when they behaved in class and did their homework, but I would never have been someone they would have wanted to confide in. I left that kind of thing to my female colleagues and counted myself lucky that I didn't have to think about it."

"But you should have been thinking about it."

"Yeah, in retrospect I was naive. I don't have any sisters. I went to a boys' school. I did have girlfriends, then and later, but I probably didn't realize how highly strung teenage girls can be. I'd just never been around them enough to know what they were like." He leaned back in his chair. "If you're expecting me to be bitter about what Isobel Sairey did to me, you're going to be disappointed. She was young and confused, and she didn't understand the consequences of her actions. I made peace with that a long time ago. When she's older, she'll realize what she did, if she doesn't already. I wouldn't want to have that hanging over me."

"You don't blame her for the fact you had to give up your job?" I said, surprised.

"Not directly. She was completely innocent. There was nothing malicious in what she said or did. She got out of her depth very quickly and I think she would have liked to stop everything long before it got to court, but once she was in the system the legal process had to carry on, regardless of what she would have liked. Believe it or not, I felt sorry for her at times."

"But not all the time."

"No. Sometimes I wanted to kill her." He gave me another grin and I saw the easy and unconscious charm that had led a student to fall head over heels in love with him. "Not literally, obviously."

"Obviously. You wouldn't be human if you weren't angry with her."

"I'll admit, I didn't think too fondly of her when I couldn't pay my mortgage and my

249

flat was repossessed. And when I was convicted I really wasn't thinking too much about her well-being. I was far more concerned with my own. Then, to compound the country-and-western doom and gloom, my girlfriend dumped me while I was inside."

I couldn't help being amused. "Did your dog pine for you and die?"

"I didn't have a dog. Shame, really. Otherwise I might have got the full set."

"But you, in your Christ-like wisdom, forgave her for her sins," Derwent drawled.

"I am a Christian. So what?"

Derwent chuckled. "I should have known. Did you catch it in prison?"

"I was already a practicing Christian. God was part of my life. He became more important while I was inside, but it wasn't a new thing for me." He didn't sound awkward or embarrassed when he talked about it — more matter-of-fact. For most people I met, talking about religion made them far more uncomfortable than talking about sex.

I wouldn't have put it as crudely as Derwent, but I was slightly surprised that a young man like Christopher Blacker, with his experiences, had a faith strong enough to stand up to Derwent's scorn. I looked around the room again, trying to see any clues. No crosses on the wall, no theological books in the bookcase, except for C. S. Lewis's *Screwtape Letters* and it was shelved with the

Narnia books so I was inclined to give myself a pass for having missed it.

"I can't say I've had the same blessing. I'm an atheist myself," Derwent said. *And proud of it,* I filled in silently. "I may be wrong, but I thought the whole thing was about forgiveness."

"That's a big part of it."

Derwent let me ask the obvious question. "So why weren't you able to forgive Philip Kennford for what he did or didn't do on your behalf during the trial?"

"I'm a practicing Christian. I didn't say I was a good one."

"All this and a stand-up comedian too."

Blacker sighed, losing interest in humor. "Look, the trial was a classic he-said, she-said thing. I had the truth on my side and not much more. I had character references and as much in the way of alibis as I could scrape together, but Isobel was too vague about the details for me to be able to contradict her directly. And character references mean fuck all in a room full of people who've already decided you're a predator who took advantage of a teenage girl. Not to mention the tabloids. *Je*-sus. They had me convicted long before the jury got around to it."

"From what I've read, the prosecution case was mainly based on her allegations," I said, knowing that Derwent hadn't bothered to look at the papers properly. "There wasn't a lot of evidence to corroborate what she said."

"That worked against me, unfortunately. It seemed straightforward to me — if there was no evidence it was because what she was saying wasn't true. It hadn't happened so there were no witnesses; there was no paper trail. The prosecutor made it look as if I'd been too clever to leave anything they could trace — no text messages, no e-mails, nothing that could be recovered and produced in court. It didn't seem to occur to the jury that I'd never sent her any texts or e-mails and that was why there weren't any for them to see."

"So it came down to her telling stories. That should have been easier to contradict."

"You'd think so, but it wasn't. The prosecutor struggled with it, but not as much as I did. We both had our hands tied because she was so hazy in her evidence. You couldn't prove what had happened either way. She said something had happened. I said it hadn't. One of us had to be lying."

"And your barrister didn't push her to be more specific in her account, so you'd have a chance to prove you weren't there at the times she suggested you were?"

"Kennford sat on his arse and let her spin a fairy tale. He didn't seem to think it was his place to intervene."

"There are limits to what they're allowed to do," I said. "It's not like American law shows where the witness gets interrupted every two seconds by the defense lawyers objecting to something or other."

"I know that. I do have some experience of the legal system in this country now." He rubbed his face again. "He had an opportunity to take her on when he cross-examined her. He could have taken her through her evidence and shown the places where it just didn't add up. But he didn't bother."

"Did you ask him about it?"

"Of course. As soon as we left court for the next break, we met in an interview room nearby and he told me I had to trust him. He said I had to let him do his job and wait to be released. He said if he put Isobel under any pressure, she'd snap, and he'd look like an asshole in front of the jury. 'We need them on our side, Mr. Blacker. We need them to think we're honorable, decent men. Gentlemen, if you like. And being tough on Miss Sairey isn't going to help our cause.' Bullshit." The word exploded from him, genuine anger in his tone.

"You said yourself that she was an innocent. Vulnerable. He might have been right about how the jury would have felt about him attacking her."

"There are ways of showing that someone is lying without accusing them of it outright. There were questions he could have asked her that would have told the jury a lot, even if she didn't realize it. He didn't have to crush her; I wasn't asking for that. I could see the sense in not upsetting her too much. I mean, she had everyone on her side from the start without even trying. I was the one who had to prove my innocence, whatever they say about being innocent until proven guilty. She was giving evidence by video-link and the judge kept having to ask her to speak up, but it wasn't put on. She was genuine, you know? Not affected. Not looking for attention. Mortified by where she was and what was happening, but that made it all the more effective. Either she believed what she was saying or she couldn't bring herself to back down with her parents there in the public gallery and the police sitting in court, waiting for her evidence to put me away. Even though I knew she wasn't telling the truth, I was almost taken in a couple of times."

"But you're sure it wasn't malicious."

"As sure as I can be. There was no reason for her to be malicious. It wasn't a case of getting revenge on me for being hard on her because I hadn't been. I hadn't singled her out for attention in any way, in fact. When two police officers turned up at my house one weekend to tell me about the allegations, I couldn't remember who she was at first."

"Maybe that was the problem. No one likes being ignored."

"Do you honestly think she'd accuse me of having an affair with her just to get me to notice her?"

"It's possible. Haven't you ever considered that?"

"Not seriously. I wouldn't have thought even a teenage girl was capable of that."

"If this job teaches you only one thing, it's that people are capable of anything." For once, Derwent's mordant cynicism suited the mood.

"Well, by the time she got to court I'd definitely noticed her, but I don't think she was enjoying herself too much. I thought she was going to collapse a couple of times during her examination-in-chief, even though the prosecutor couldn't have been nicer or more gentle with her. She got over the nerves in time. She had this elaborate fantasy about the two of us, incredibly detailed, and she genuinely loved the opportunity to talk about it. I mean, it was insane, the things she said we'd done together. What I was supposed to have said to her. According to the prosecution I got a kick out of controlling her. I was supposed to have spun it out, this seduction process, so there were only two or three incidences of actual sex in her account. The rest of it was all hand-holding and swearing undying love. I don't know where she got it — pure Mills and Boon, most of it — but she was so sure of herself. Kennford just let her talk. His cross-examination was useless. And Isobel had two completely idiotic friends who worshipped her. They were willing to swear that she was telling the truth. I think they believed it too. I'd just come out of court every time and go into this horrible little room, this overheated hole, and listen to my solicitor and Kennford tell me what a bad impression the witness had made on the jury and how the whole thing was working out exactly as they'd planned, and I knew. I knew they were fucking it up and I was in real trouble."

"But you didn't get anywhere when you tried to say that."

"No. Like I said, they just told me I didn't know what I was talking about. I can still see it." He looked into the distance, a wry smile twisting his mouth. "It was January. Bleak as you like outside, rain or sleet every day. Inside it was worse. Someone had forgotten to take down the Christmas decorations in that room, and there was a bit of tinsel above one of the pictures that stuck up at an angle. It annoyed me. But it helped too."

"How so?"

"Every time Kennford ignored what I was saying or told me I didn't know what I was talking about and I just had to trust him, I'd stare at the tinsel instead of at him. I didn't want to have to look at his smug face. I just concentrated on the decorations, hating them, particularly this bit of tinsel." He laughed. "I'd promised myself that at the end of the trial I'd go back and get it. Save it as a souvenir. Not that I would really want or need any memories of the trial, but I wanted to have the satisfaction of ripping it down and stamping on it, or whatever, just to let off steam."

"I take it that's not how it panned out."

"No, in that I wasn't allowed to leave court after I was found guilty. The judge sentenced me there and then. He'd already heard all the character evidence during the trial, he said. All about my personal circumstances. He didn't need to know anything else about me to know that he was going to throw the book at me."

"But Kennford would have had a chance to reply. There's always mitigation."

"He was able to talk about the offense, but not about what a great bloke I was. That was a bit awkward because I was still saying I hadn't done it, so he was trying to talk about how the girl wasn't harmed by her experiences and how it was a far less serious crime than proper rape because she'd been a willing if naive participant, and I was sitting there shaking my head and saying 'no' as loudly as I dared until the judge got tired of it and sent me down."

"But if he'd already done the character evidence during the trial, there wasn't a lot else he could say. Especially if the judge was predisposed to be hostile."

"He did a crap job. It was halfhearted at best. His junior told me afterward he'd been preparing for another trial during the speeches at the end so he hadn't paid too much attention to which way the wind was blowing. He thought we couldn't lose."

"That was foolish of him."

"Wasn't it." Blacker matched Derwent's tone, flatly ironic. After a second the inspector grinned. He liked Blacker, I realized, and he believed his story, which was more important. So did I. Blacker had deserved better than to end up in a hovel teaching sums to well-off dunces and privileged high-fliers.

"So you did a year."

"I got four years, which meant I'd be looking at applying for parole in two. So I effectively served half of a sentence I didn't deserve."

"You must have started preparing for the appeal the minute you got sentenced."

"Wouldn't you?" He gave a bitter smile. "Prison isn't a great place for anyone convicted of abusing a child. The fact that she was fourteen didn't matter. I'm not what you'd call a fighter but I had to stand up for myself a couple of times."

"They wouldn't have let you into the general population."

"The prisons are packed. They don't have a choice about it, some of the time." He shivered. "Anyway, I preferred the decent

258

ordinary murderers and bank robbers to the sex offenders. They were worse, most of them. Evil. And not remorseful."

"Prison doesn't work for everyone."

"Prison is a place to put people so you can pretend they don't exist. Nothing more than that. But it's also a place where you get plenty of time to think, and that's what I did."

"What conclusion did you come to?"

"That I was going to get out. And I did."

"What was the basis of your appeal?" I asked.

"Two things. One was a remark the judge made during his summing-up. The appeal court agreed it was prejudicial and made the jury's verdict unsafe. The other was my representation. Philip Kennford was censured in the judgment for having failed to take notice of my instructions to him. They described him as arrogant and cavalier."

"Perceptive," Derwent commented. "So you got out."

"The Crown Prosecution Service decided not to go for a retrial. I think they were aware by then that Isobel might not be the strongest witness in the world. Her family made no objection to me being released, so they must have known." His face twisted. "But do you think any of them would have said anything if the conviction had been upheld? It took me all that time to realize that no one really cared about it. They just wanted it to go away

— the cops, the lawyers, the family, Isobel. Everyone. With me in prison, they could get on with their lives. With me out, everything was a lot more complicated."

"Did you try to contact Isobel?" I asked.

"No! Never. I don't care if I never come across her again. But they know they might bump into me now. I'm in their world again, even if I'm just looking on from the shadows."

Derwent was patting his pockets. "I think I've got a violin here somewhere."

"Yeah, I know. The pathos is getting to you." He shook back his hair. "I wanted to put it behind me. I thought I'd be happy once I got out, but I wasn't. Things were worse. I had nightmares — horrible, awful nightmares that I can still remember. I was living with my parents and they'd hear me screaming in the middle of the night. Mum said it was like having a baby in the house again."

"What were the nightmares about?"

"Going back. The appeal being overturned, somehow. Being chased and finding myself in a prison cell, or waking up there and realizing being free was all a dream." He was sweating, I noticed. The room was airless but it was agitation that was making him perspire, still, even just from talking about it. I did my job happy in the knowledge that the people I put behind bars deserved to be there, but Christopher Blacker was another matter and I wondered how Kennford had been able to be

260

so offhand about him, about the mistakes he had made that condemned an innocent man to months of hell.

"When did they stop? The nightmares, I mean?"

He looked at me with a funny smile. "I'm still waiting. But they got better after a couple of months. It wasn't every night anymore. Every other night, maybe." A slow headshake. "But that didn't mean I was free of it. It started to take over during the day. I'd be walking along the street and I'd find myself thinking about the trial, and Kennford, and suddenly I'd come to on a park bench, gazing into space. Lost time, I called it." Another twisted smile. "Made me pretty fed up, I can tell you, when I was the one who was owed time for the year in prison."

"I can understand you feeling bitter." Derwent reached into his tiny store-cupboard of empathy and produced a crumb of comfort that was all the more affecting for being a surprise. "Kennford let you down."

"I was more than bitter, mate. I couldn't stop thinking about him and his comfortable life, his career. I was just a misstep, a blip in his statistics. He'd forgotten about me the moment he left court. He was the one who'd fucked up but he'd lost nothing. I'd done my job, but through no fault of my own I'd been punished. I just couldn't seem to get over it. I was surrounded by people who wanted to help me — friends, my family. My ex-girlfriend even hung around for a bit until I told her to piss off. Everyone felt guilty about what had happened to me, but no one knew how to talk to me. I couldn't help them. I didn't know myself."

"Did you get counseling?" I asked.

"A few sessions. It was on the NHS — my GP set it up — so I had to wait a few months. I wasn't actually suicidal, you see, so I wasn't a priority."

"Did it help, when you did get to see someone?"

"I think I'd already gone through the worst of it." He looked sheepish. "And I found a way to relieve my feelings, which is why you're here I should imagine."

"You made threats against Philip Kennford. And his family."

"And his dog, and his car, and his house. You name it." He looked down at the floor, laughing a little. "I'm ashamed of it now. Turning up at his offices in a towering rage and demanding to see him, saying I had a right to get back at him for what he'd done to me. Thank God they didn't take it seriously enough to call you lot or I'd have ended up inside again."

"They told us it was never serious enough to be a police matter."

"I wandered into the reception area and frightened the life out of their receptionist."

"Blonde. Nice curves." Derwent, as he never got tired of reminding me, had an eye for the ladies.

"She was a brunette. Young. I doubt she's still working there, after what I did." He put his head in his hands. "I mean, I sent flowers, afterward, once I'd calmed down. But it can't have been fun for her to have me reeling around her nice little reception desk swearing blue murder and making threats."

"I'm sure it wasn't very pleasant. How did they calm you down?"

"A couple of the staff sat me down in a chair and held me there while an older one poured me a huge whiskey and told me to pull myself together. I drank the whiskey, got a grip on myself, started apologizing and left. I was waiting for a knock on the door, but he must have decided to turn a blind eye." A tiny glimmer of humor. "It was the least he could do."

Derwent leaned forward again, his hands clasped loosely between his knees. He looked as if he was halfway to getting up. That was one of his techniques: save the hard questions for the end when they think you're finished and they're home free. "What did you think, then, when you heard about Kennford's family on the news?"

"What do you mean, what did I think? Poor lady, poor kid. I didn't know at first it was his family. They didn't say." He sounded be-mused.

"You didn't think Kennford had got what he deserved, once you realized who they were?"

"That would be a bit harsh, wouldn't it? And a bit unfair on his wife and daughter. They hadn't done anything wrong." He shook his head. "I wouldn't have cried for long if something had happened to Kennford, espe-cially if he'd ended up in prison for some-thing. That would have been poetic justice, wouldn't it? But someone killed half his fam-ily. That's more than revenge. That's mon-strous."

Derwent levered himself up. He looked down at Blacker, seeming taller than I knew him to be. "I think we're done. Maeve?"

"One more question. Do you feel sorry for him?"

"No." The word hung in the air for a mo-ment before he elaborated. "But then I don't feel anything for him. Not anymore."

It was the first thing Christopher Blacker had said that I didn't believe.

CHAPTER ELEVEN

"I've got a treat for you."

I didn't usually spend a lot of time worrying about whether Derwent was happy or not, but I'd thought he deserved some fun when I was setting up our interviews for the day, and even though he obviously admired Miranda Wentworth, she was a bit long in the tooth for him. It was a shame I hadn't been able to get hold of Savannah Wentworth herself, but after five increasingly rude phone calls her agent had promised to get her to call me. I wasn't holding my breath. The next best thing was next on the list, Niele Adamkuté.

Derwent looked at the name without enthusiasm. "Who's he when he's at home?"

"Another of Kennford's clients."

"Someone else he let down?"

"In a way."

"How the fuck does this guy have a good reputation if he can't be bothered to do his job properly?"

"I think he represented Adamkuté successfully enough. It was what happened afterward that was more complicated."

"Oh." Derwent considered that for a few seconds. "No. I give up. What was he on trial for?"

"*She* was on trial for money laundering and got off. And then Mr. Kennford got off."

"Filthy hound." Derwent sounded, for the first time in relation to Philip Kennford, admiring. "What's she like?"

"If I knew that, I wouldn't be making you drive all the way to Poplar to find out."

"You're kidding." Derwent stared ahead of him at the traffic that was clogging every road in central London. "That's miles."

"She'll be worth it," I said with a confidence I didn't really feel, a confidence that would, in any case, have ebbed away under the onslaught of Derwent's grousing as we inched through London in the heat. Every car and shop window added to the glare and I had a headache from squinting before we'd gone very far. I found a pair of sunglasses in my bag and put them on, defying Derwent to mock them. Which, of course, didn't stop him.

"That's amazing. Where did you manage to find Stevie Wonder's cast-offs?"

"These are designer shades, I'll have you know."

"How much did they set you back?"

"A hundred and seventy quid."

He whistled. "They pay you too much."

"I like them, okay?" I was sounding defensive and I knew it, but I couldn't stop myself. "I don't spend a lot of money on clothes."

"You're not telling me anything I wouldn't know by looking at you."

I looked down at what I was wearing: gray trousers and a plain white shirt. Bland, forgettable, inexpensive but I'd hoped reasonably smart nonetheless. "I'd have to be insane to spend money on work clothes, doing the job I do. You don't want to be worried about your dry-cleaning bill when you're crawling around a crime scene."

"Doesn't have to be boring, though, does it?"

"I don't mind boring. I don't particularly want to stand out from the crowd." I wanted to watch people, not attract attention.

"You'd have a job to fade into the background," Derwent observed.

"Because I'm tall. Yeah, I know."

"You're quite eye-catching." He glanced across at me and looked away with a snort. "Sorry. I can't take you seriously in those. They're the size of bin-lids."

"Big is in," I said calmly. "Anyway, as I was saying, I don't spend much on fripperies. Plenty of people I know would have the deposit for a house if they'd saved the money they spend on bags and shoes."

"And have you saved enough for the deposit

on a house?"

"Not quite," I admitted, thinking with some guilt of my neglected savings account. "But it sounded good, didn't it?"

"It sounded like something an OAP would say."

"That makes sense. I think I nicked it from my mum, word for word." I shuddered. "Oh my God, I'm turning into her."

"All women turn into their mothers eventually. That's why I have a strict policy of only shagging girls under twenty-five. Before the rot sets in."

"That's creepy. And it's only going to get creepier as you get older."

"I'll probably go up to thirty once I hit forty-five. A twenty-year age gap is more or less sustainable, but anything more than that gets boring. You keep having to explain who people are and why they're famous." He grimaced. "The first couple of times it's cute. Then it just gets sad."

"Yeah, sad was the word that had occurred to me." I looked at him curiously. "Don't you want to find someone you can have a conversation with?"

"My priority isn't talking, Kerrigan."

"Even allowing for you being the world's greatest lover, you can't have sex all the time. You have to go out for a meal occasionally. Go on holidays. Drive long distances. Isn't all of that easier with someone who gets your

268

sense of humor and understands your cultural references?"

"To be honest, if I'm bored in the car, I just put the radio on."

I counted it down in my head. *Five . . . four . . . three . . . two . . .* Click. Freddie Mercury's voice filled the car, wanting to break free.

"Very funny."

"I'd let you pick the station but I don't want to listen to any old shite. Classic tunes, that's what I prefer."

"Who is this again?" I asked, feigning ignorance. "Is it the Beatles?"

There was the touch of a smile on his face. "Fucking Philistine."

Bickering with Derwent was a good way to distract from the tedium of traffic and in fact we were twenty minutes early for our appointment when we got there. Derwent stopped outside a newsagent and went in, reappearing with a bottle of water and a whippy ice cream for both of us. Mine came with a chocolate flake.

"What's this in aid of?"

"You've organized a treat for me. I had a sudden urge to be nice in return." He watched me attempting to eat the flake without dropping crumbs of chocolate down my front. "And I had a feeling it was likely to be a spectator sport."

"Give me strength."

"Go on. Work the tongue. Tickle the underside. Oh, yeah, baby, that's it." He humped the air.

"You aren't going to spoil this for me. And every word you say is going straight into my official complaint of sexual harassment."

"That file must be as thick as the phone book by now." He didn't sound particularly perturbed. He knew as well as I did that there was no complaint, and that there wouldn't be one. The last thing I needed was to get a reputation for being a humorless ball-breaker. He made remarks like that because it amused him, and because he could, and because he genuinely thought that way a lot of the time, and he wasn't going to stop. So I would keep batting back the rude remarks and he would keep making them, and in the meantime there was ice cream to eat. I made it my business to do so as unalluringly as possible.

Niele Adamkuté lived in a narrow street of terraced houses near Canning Town tube station. It was an area that had benefited from the development of Canary Wharf, the giant huddle of skyscrapers in the middle of the East End that exerted its own gravitational pull on the surrounding neighborhoods. People converged on it from all over London every weekday and abandoned it at weekends, and most of them never set foot in the heart of Poplar or Limehouse or any of the other places where property prices had spiked on a promise of new wealth in the area. The recession had delivered a sharp correction, but there were still plenty of people trying to make a fortune as property developers, turning a bargain buy into a des res for yuppies. Shetland Street, where Adamkuté lived, was halfway to being gentrified, which meant most of the houses didn't look their best. Skips sat on the road outside three of them. A couple of others were swathed in scaffolding and tarpaulins, and half-naked builders sat on the front steps of another two, smoking and soaking up the sun. Houses with neatly painted woodwork and immaculate front gardens butted up against ones that looked unoccupied, the windows dark and fogged with dirt, rubbish piled high inside the front gate. Adamkuté's house had all the hallmarks of a rental property: ugly double glazing, overflowing bins outside and a front garden full of gravel, the cheap no-maintenance solution to outside space. I rang the bell. Inside the house, just visible through the frosted glass of the front door, someone passed through the hall and ran up the stairs.

"Friendly."

"I rang to make the appointment. She knows we're coming." I leaned back to peer in through the front window, seeing bare walls and a minimum of furniture. "I don't think that was her. It looked like a man to me."

"And me. But I don't have high hopes of Miss Adamkuté. Kennford would fuck a hole in the ground if it was all that was available."

As he said it, the front door darkened, as if someone had been standing just beside it, hidden from our view. She couldn't have failed to hear what Derwent said, but when Niele opened the door, her face was composed. She looked at me.

"You are DC Kerrigan?"

"Yes. This is my colleague —"

"Josh Derwent." He lunged forward with his hand out. "DI Derwent."

The rank didn't seem to impress her any more than the hand he was offering her. She looked down at it as if she didn't understand what he wanted, then stepped back. "Come in."

"Thanks for agreeing to see us at such short notice," Derwent babbled, following me into the sitting room while Niele waited patiently to shut the front door. I could understand why he was flustered, because she was all I had been told and more. She was quite stunning — tall, reed-thin apart from a very well-developed bosom, elegant in tailored black trousers and a cream silk top. There was more to it than just good looks, although she certainly had those. She had a quality of stillness that was unusual, a reserve that was more intriguing than off-putting. Her eyes were incredible, slanting and green under arched eyebrows, and her hair was dark and glossy. A beauty spot high on one cheekbone was the only thing that marred the perfect symmetry of her features and it gave her face a touch of character it might otherwise have lacked. I knew that she was thirty-one but I wouldn't have guessed that she was a day over twenty-five, and I had a feeling Derwent would make an exception to his rule if he thought he had a shot. Her English was good, almost unaccented and idiomatic. She stood in the doorway while Derwent and I got ourselves organized, and I couldn't interpret the expression on her face. Not quite hostile, but definitely guarded, I decided. And the first words she said confirmed it.

"You're here to find out what happened between me and Philip Kennford, is that right?"

"More or less. We're trying to build a picture of his life and that means speaking to people who know him." I hesitated. "And who knew his wife."

"Her? I didn't know her. I met her once." The faintest trace of amusement was visible on her face for a moment. "We didn't get along too well."

"So I've heard."

"And I heard she's dead." She narrowed her eyes. "That's why you're really here, isn't it? You've heard that we had an argument and you want to know if I am responsible for killing her."

"Well, are you?" I was amused and a little surprised by how direct she was.

"Of course not. It was months ago that I argued with her. I haven't seen him since then and I don't want to." The pretty mouth snapped closed in what could only be described as a pout.

"You understand that we have to ask you about it, don't you? We need to find people who disliked Vita Kennford — who might have had a reason to kill her, and her daughter. And you do have a motive for murdering the first if not the second."

She laughed. "Why would I have waited until now?"

"Maybe you didn't have the opportunity before. Maybe you needed to plan."

"What is there to plan? You know people who can take care of that sort of thing, or you don't." An expressive shrug. "Of course, I don't."

"Of course," I agreed. All charges had been dropped halfway through her trial, I reminded myself. But that had been lack of evidence and some creative arguing from Kennford rather than being because of her shining innocence. I'd reserve my judgment for the time being.

"And of course I didn't want her to die.

But if you are looking for people who disliked her, you will have to make a list of everyone she met. She was not a pleasant person."

"Where did you meet her?" Derwent asked, not having been privy to Kit's description of their encounter. He had chosen a low armchair and now looked as if he regretted it since Niele hadn't sat down. She had taken up a position leaning against the wall, looking like a *Vogue* model.

"At his flat in Clerkenwell. She threw me out."

"Were you staying there?"

"He'd asked me to move in with him." She gave a tiny shrug. "I should never have said yes. I thought it would be better than sharing a house. *He* thought it would be better than sharing a house. He said this was like being a student again and he'd left those days behind him."

"Do you have many housemates?"

"A few." On cue, footsteps thudded across the floor upstairs, just over my head. "They come and go."

"Who are they?" Derwent asked.

"Why do you care?"

"I'm curious."

"Curiosity kills the cat. That's the expression, isn't it?"

"I'm more of a dog man."

The amusement was back in her eyes. "They're people from home. This is a good place to stay when you first come to the UK. Then they find work, move on."

"But you stay."

"It's convenient."

"It's a nice area," Derwent lied.

"Not really. But it suits me."

"Why's that?"

"I don't expect too much."

"A girl like you should expect nothing but the best."

Derwent was looking soulful. I suppressed my gag reflex for long enough to ask, "How long have you lived here?"

"Three years, off and on."

"So long?" I was surprised. The room was stacked with cardboard boxes in one corner, and the walls were bare. The furniture didn't match and there wasn't a lot of it anyway. It had the feeling of a temporary arrangement. "It doesn't look as if anyone's unpacked properly."

"It doesn't bother me. I'm not interested. I spend a lot of time out, at work or seeing friends."

"What do you do for a living, Niele?"

"I'm an administrator."

"What kind of administrator?"

"Office manager, I suppose."

"What's the office?"

"I'm not working at the moment. I'm looking for a new position."

Convenient, I thought, not believing her in

276

the least. She was about to learn that evasive answers generated more questions. "Where was the last place you worked?"

"It closed down. Very sad. Lots of people lost their jobs."

"What was the business?"

"A Lithuanian one."

"Selling . . ." I prompted.

"Transporting goods across Europe. Freight." She looked bored. "I don't really know much about that side of things. I just looked after the office."

"How are you managing for money if you're not working?"

"I have savings. And I do temping."

"With an agency?"

"It's casual work. Now and then."

"What do you do in the evenings? I can't imagine you like to hang out here."

I resisted the urge to glare at Derwent but I wasn't satisfied that I'd heard anything like the full story about where she had worked and what her job had been, and if it had been up to me she wouldn't have been allowed off the hook so easily. Then again, I wasn't as concerned with her social life as my boss apparently was.

"I do whatever I choose." She looked around the room. "But I don't stay here, you're right. I prefer to go out."

"Boyfriend?"

"Frequently, yes. But not at the moment."

I was waiting for Derwent to ask her out but belatedly he remembered what we were supposed to be doing there.

"How many people live here?"

"At the moment, five."

"How many men?"

"Why do you care?"

"Routine question. How many men?"

"Four."

"You're the only woman?"

"Yes. But that doesn't bother me." I waited to see if she'd say it. I could have mouthed it along with her, even if I couldn't have managed the sensuous movement of her body that accompanied it. "I've always got on better with men."

"Any romances?"

"I prefer English men."

To give him his due, Derwent only blushed a little bit. "Can you give me your housemates' names?"

"I could. Do I have to?"

"It'll make us a bit suspicious of them if you don't."

"I can't help your suspicions." She allowed herself a tiny smile. "But I don't want to get anyone else in trouble."

"They're not in trouble. I just want to know who lives here."

"Curious again?"

"It's an occupational hazard."

She shook her head. "I thought this was

about Philip Kennford."

"It is."

"So why are you asking me about the people I live with? Ask me about him."

There was a very good reason for us to ask her about the people she lived with; we were sitting ducks in her small front room if any of them wished us harm. I didn't like not knowing who else was in the house and I could tell Derwent felt the same way. We were on their territory, at their mercy, and Niele Adamkuté had certainly known criminals, once upon a time. The others who were on trial with her had been convicted. I was pretty sure that if the person stomping about upstairs didn't have a criminal record, that was nothing more than an oversight on our part.

Derwent wasn't about to give any of that away. Instead, he gave her the little-boy cheeky grin. "I suppose it's just force of habit, but we do like asking questions."

"Ask me about Philip."

"We'll get to that."

"That's all I'm going to talk about." There was something very stubborn about the set of her jaw that told me she meant it. Derwent spotted it too.

"Okay. Mr. Kennford. Tell us about him."

"He took advantage of me. He made a fool of me." It would have been more convincing if she had been more like a victim, but Niele Adamkuté didn't strike me as anyone's fool.

"When was this?"

"Last year. Nine — no, ten months ago."
She smiled to herself. "I hadn't thought it
was so long, but it was."

"How did you meet?"

"I was arrested and charged with money
laundering because of some work I did for a
friend. It was all a big mistake."

"Of course."

"My friend was very sorry that I was in
trouble because of the work I had done for
him, so he didn't want me to have legal aid.
He got me a very good solicitor who hired
Philip to represent me in court because he
was supposed to be the best person for the
job."

"But from what I've heard, it worked out
all right. You got off," I pointed out.

She shrugged. "There was no evidence.
That was all he had to say, that there was no
evidence. He sat there in court for days during the prosecution case and he didn't do
anything. Then he stood up and told the
judge I had to be allowed to leave, and the
judge agreed. He got thousands of pounds
and he did nothing."

"At least you weren't paying."

She made an extraordinary noise, pure
contempt. "There is always a payment, even
when someone does something for you as a
gift, or because they feel an obligation."

"Sounds sinister," Derwent observed.

"Not at all. It's how the world goes."

"So you weren't impressed with Kennford's work — but you ended up having an affair with him and moving into his flat. How did that happen?"

"I was stupid." She looked grave. "I was so pleased to be let go free, I went out for dinner with him. It was a very nice restaurant, very smart. Lots of celebrities go there. Hollywood stars, not TV." I appreciated the fine distinction. "And I drank a little bit too much. Besides, he is very charming when he wants to be, no?"

"And well-off. And handsome."

"Not really attractive. Old. But yes, he acted as if he was rich. He asked me to come to his flat, so he could show me where he lived. I thought it wouldn't matter if I did. I thought it would be fun." She looked at Derwent again. "I like fun, you know?"

"I can imagine." His ears had gone red.

"His flat was very nice. I spent the night there." A little shrug. "That was okay too. But I didn't think it would become anything important. He told me he would get in trouble if anyone found out. But then, I think he liked that."

"Thrill-seeker, isn't he. Mind you, I don't think anyone would need too many reasons to want to be with you, if you don't mind me saying so." Gallantry, from Derwent. I marveled, but kept it to myself.

"You are very kind." Her eyes rested on me for a second and I had the impression she wished I wasn't there. Which probably made two of them. I sat back in the sofa, very definitely not going anywhere.

"You didn't think it would turn into anything, but it did, is that right?" Derwent asked.

"We started to see one another, when we could. Mostly at his place. Once here, because I wanted him to see how I lived." She laughed, showing a completely unexpected dimple. "I knew he would hate it here. That's when he asked me to move in with him."

"Which you did."

"But I should have said no. He didn't like it that I was there all the time, once he had given me a key. He said it was like having two wives." She rolled her eyes.

"And how did you feel?" I asked.

"I didn't like it either. I like being independent. I had to ask him if I wanted to do anything. I had to be careful that no one saw me there, because he has friends who live in the same building. I wasn't allowed to answer the telephone or the door. It was like being kidnapped or something. Always hiding." She shuddered. "Not worth it."

"So when did it come to an end?"

"When I told him I was pregnant."

"Was it true?" Derwent asked.

"Oh, yes. I wouldn't tell a lie about that. I

was pregnant, with his child. I told him he needed to decide what to do. He could divorce his wife and marry me, or he could give me money."

"To look after the child." Derwent sounded deeply understanding.

A pitying expression came over her face. "To look after me."

"You mean you'd have got rid of it."

"I don't like children. I would have had it if he had wanted it, but he had to prove that by marrying me. Without a proper commitment, I wasn't going to go through with it. Too easy for him to say yes, I want you to have it, I'll love it and look after you both. Then there is nothing to stop him from walking away. And I am left with a baby and no figure, no money, no one to look after it." She shuddered. "No. I was stupid, but not that stupid."

"What did Kennford say?"

"He said he couldn't divorce his wife. He couldn't afford to because she had all the money and he wouldn't get any of it if he left her. He said he couldn't pay me, either. He told me I had to have the baby and have a DNA test to make sure it was his. Then he would give me an allowance for the child." She snorted. "I didn't agree."

"You didn't have the baby."

"No, of course not." She looked at Derwent as if the idea was completely insane. "I told him I wouldn't leave the flat until he gave me money to have an abortion and to make up for what he had done to me, or I would go to his wife and ask her for the payment I wanted."

"What did he say?"

"He laughed. He told me she wouldn't leave him, even if I told her about our affair. He said I had a week to get out." She folded her arms, which had the added advantage of maximizing her cleavage. Somehow, though, I thought she had lost quite a lot of her charm as far as Derwent was concerned. He tended toward sentimentality when it came to mothers and babies, I'd noticed, and all of this hardheaded negotiation would be a major turnoff for him. "I told him I wouldn't leave without my money and I couldn't get rid of the baby unless he paid me. Of course, I had already arranged for the termination but he didn't know that."

"But he wasn't worried about having another child," I said. "Or was it brinksmanship?" Niele looked blank and I realized her excellent English didn't include that word. "I mean that he was pretending not to care about whether the baby was born or not so you couldn't blackmail him, but actually he did care."

"I don't think he really minded another baby. He said he hoped it was a boy, if it was his, because he didn't have a son. And it was his," she added. "I was sure of that. But I was

284

also sure it wouldn't be born, so it didn't matter."

I thought of Kennford's daughters and how casual he seemed about them, and wondered if there were others scattered around the world. He was the type to like the idea of lots of descendants, a true alpha male intent on scattering his seed. In the case of Niele, it had fallen on very stony ground indeed.

"What happened at the end of the week?"

"He got some men to come." She looked affronted. "All of my things, they shoved them in bags and threw them in the street. I had to go too, or everything would have been stolen, and besides, they pushed me out. It was humiliating. I didn't think he would cause a scene like that, but he didn't seem to care anymore."

"And you retaliated," I said. She looked cagey. "Don't worry, we aren't interested in the details of that. It wasn't reported to the police so there's no crime to investigate."

"Some friends helped me. They were angry about what Philip had done to me. How he had behaved. They knew where I had been living so they went around there and . . . made it not so comfortable for him."

At her invitation, I was pretty sure. She acted like a fragile waif who needed protecting, but I didn't really believe in all of these "friends" who came to her aid when she needed it. She had whistled up some Baltic

285

muscle and they'd done the dirty work for her.

"They trashed the place, I gather."

"Maybe. I didn't see it afterward."

"But you went there, because that's where you met Mrs. Kennford."

"That was when I was most glad I had got rid of the baby. Imagine, the coward, he arranges for me to come and see him so he can pay me. Then he tells his wife to meet him there at the same time, and to bring her checkbook to pay for the repairs. She and I meet on the doorstep, but he never shows up. He knew she would see me. He knew we would talk. He knew she would pay me the money I wanted. He is a horrible, weak man, and if you want to know if he killed his wife, I say no, because he wouldn't have the courage." She wound up with a volley of what I assumed was Lithuanian. It was also a fairly safe assumption that it mostly consisted of swear-words, given her overall demeanor.

"Calm down."

I wondered if Derwent had ever found those two words to be effective in dealing with an angry woman. They certainly weren't now.

"I will not. I was so upset with him, and so was she. But she stood up for him. Her marriage is more important, her children need their father, on and on and on, and she offered me twice or three times what I had asked for."

"What did you settle on in the end?"

"I don't want to say. More than I had hoped."

"Worked out well for you, didn't it? Was it your first time to try a bit of blackmail, or is this a regular part of your income?"

"It wasn't blackmail. It was a gift from her to me."

"You said she wasn't a pleasant person," I reminded her. "That doesn't suggest someone who was being generous for the sake of it."

She pulled a face. "She was mean. She told me I was a whore and out to get what I could. She blamed me for her husband having an affair, instead of thinking about what she should have been doing to make him happy. She was aggressive from the start, when she didn't need to be. As far as I was concerned there were arrangements to be made, but I didn't want a fight with anyone. She wanted to keep me away from her husband and protect her family, so it was worth a few thousand pounds to her. She told me it meant nothing to her, she wouldn't miss it, so I might as well take it. But you could see she thought I was awful to get rid of the baby — she went on and on about her daughters. The twins, the twins, they mustn't know about their father." She laughed, sounding genuinely amused. "Just think, if I'd gone ahead with it, I'd have a baby now. Here.

Imagine! I had forgotten, truthfully, until you asked me how long ago it was."

"Charming," Derwent said heavily. I was right; the bloom had definitely gone off his Lithuanian rose.

"You cannot judge me. You don't know what you would do and you will never be in that situation." She looked at me. "You look like you care about your career. What would you do if you became pregnant?"

Panic. Swear. Sink into a nine-month depression. Call my mother and await delivery of multiple knitted items. The thought of it kept me awake at night, but I had no intention of sharing any of that with Niele. I settled for smiling at her blandly instead of answering. I had noted the little dig about being career-minded; I guessed she meant at the expense of my appearance. It was the second insult to my personal style in a couple of hours, and not calculated to win me over.

Recognizing that she wasn't going to get an answer, Niele stroked her stomach, which was as flat as an ironing board. "I am so glad I didn't go through with it. I wasn't sorry at the time and I'm not sorry now."

"Your body; your choice," Derwent said. "We get it. But what did you do with the money? If Vita was as generous as you say, you should have been able to move to somewhere nicer than this place."

"I told you, I like it. I like the facilities."

"What facilities?"

She swung open the door to the room and beckoned to someone who was standing on the other side. "You should meet Jurgis."

Jurgis, it transpired, was well over six feet tall and correspondingly broad, with hands like shovels. He was silent, but the expression in his small, dark eyes spoke volumes. We were no longer welcome in Shetland Street, I divined.

"One of your friends?" Derwent asked, getting to his feet. It only served to highlight the difference in size between the two men.

"A very good friend." She patted him on one giant bicep. "These are police, Jurgis. They need to leave now."

He advanced on Derwent, who stood his ground remarkably well.

"If we think of anything else to ask, we'll be in touch."

"I don't think I can help you." She caught my eye and sighed. "Look, I have told you the truth. I met Kennford's wife once. She was a bitch, but she paid me off and she had bigger balls than her man did, that's for sure. I didn't kill her. I don't think Philip would have killed her, or could have, even if he'd wanted to. That's all I know."

Jurgis put his hand on Derwent's shoulder and squeezed.

"Watch it, mate, or I'll arrest you for assault on a police officer." The pressure intensified, the giant hand clenching around Derwent's collarbone. He stood it for a second, then twisted out of Jurgis's grasp. "I mean what I say, Miss Adamkuté. If we need to talk to you again, we will, here or at the station. You've been arrested before — you know the drill. You're better off to cooperate." He put his card down on the coffee table and tapped it twice, meaningfully.

"This is what I have been doing." She looked amused, but I couldn't tell what was making her smirk. "I don't think I'll be seeing you again, DI Derwent." She picked up the card and read it. "DI *Josh* Derwent. But it really has been a pleasure."

"Mutual," Derwent said automatically, and blushed his way past her, back out to the car. He was already in the driver's seat by the time I got to the passenger door, gripping the steering wheel and staring straight ahead. "Don't say anything."

"Not a word."

He risked a look at me. "You can understand, can't you? You'd go lesbo for that."

"Not even in your dreams." I patted his arm. "Never mind. I think you were doing quite well before you embarked on your pro-life campaign."

"Pretty face, cold heart." He shook his head. "Kennford knows how to pick 'em."

"And apparently he's not firing blanks, with or without the aid of the little blue pills."

290

"Think she had Vita and Laura killed?"

"She'd have done it if it suited her, but I can't see why she'd have needed to."

"Me neither." He sighed. "Next time you want to make me happy, just book us a day trip to Disneyland Paris. That fucking Jurgis made me feel like one of the seven dwarves anyway. I might as well go and see if Snow White is up for a bit."

"I don't think the dwarves and Snow White had that kind of relationship."

"They did in the film I saw. Although come to think of it, that wasn't made by Disney. And it wasn't a cartoon."

It really never took Derwent long to recover from a setback, which was unfortunate from my point of view. I put my sunglasses back on and braced myself for a long trip back.

CHAPTER TWELVE

I got home to discover that Rob had made it back from work before me. He was lying on the sofa in the sitting room, wearing only his boxers, and raised a hand in salute as I stopped in the doorway. "We must stop meeting like this."

"I'd get up and greet you but I'm stuck to the couch."

"How attractive." I bent over him and kissed him briefly. "Been here long?"

"About half an hour. There's beer in the fridge if you want to join me."

"I'm not in the mood for alcohol just this second, but I'll get a drink once I've cleaned up." I glanced at the TV. "Must we watch golf?"

"Only for a bit," Rob wheedled.

"Fine. Enjoy." I left him to lounge, deciding I would take my time to get changed. Golf was up there with cricket as far as I was concerned — mystifying, time-consuming and ultimately boring. I made the most of my usual hot-weather routine: remove clothing, rehydrate, shower. Alone, on this occasion, though I told myself not to mind, and almost persuaded myself that I didn't.

It was nice to have some time to myself, anyway, to think about the case and the people I'd interviewed, and wonder what I'd missed. I didn't feel as if I'd made much progress. All I had learned so far was that Philip Kennford didn't waste much time on morality. That didn't mean that his wife and child had deserved to die. There was something missing, something I wasn't seeing about the family and how they were before the killings. The victims were still unknown quantities, and the more I found out about them, the less I felt I knew them. I wanted to talk to Lydia again, to see if I could get a better sense of Laura, in particular, but breaking through her reserve without shattering her fragile composure seemed like an impossible task. And I couldn't very well ask her the question everyone was wondering: why did you live when the others died?

Despite spinning things out as long as I could, the golf was still on when I went back to the sitting room. I was juggling an open bottle of beer and a glass of water as well as a stack of post, and had to do a sort of curtsey before he could rescue the beer. "Is it exciting?"

"In a word, yes. Do you want me to explain

what's going on?"

"Don't bother."

He grinned. "You should let yourself like it. You might get into it."

"I've had every opportunity to get into it. So far, nothing." I collapsed on a chair, stretching my legs out in front of me.

Rob sat up on one elbow. "Do you want to sit over here? I can make room."

"You look far too relaxed to disturb. And it's not as if I need to see the TV." I was leafing through the letters, working out which of them I could be bothered to open.

"Don't say I didn't offer."

"I won't," I mumbled, not really paying attention anymore, not that there was anything terribly diverting to read — a bank statement, a bill for my mobile phone, an offer of a new credit card with a crippling interest rate, a shrink-wrapped catalog from a company whose name I didn't recognize. I turned the package over, checking the label to see if it was meant for someone in one of the other flats, but it was addressed to me. I ripped open the polythene bag, pulled it out and began to flick through it.

"Did you sign me up for this?"

"What is it?"

"Lingerie." I raised my eyebrows at him. "There are subtler ways to hint I should make more of an effort."

294

"Not me." He held out his hand. "Let me see?"

"I'm not sure that's a good idea. You might want me to start buying this sort of crap." I paused on a particularly skimpy G-string, wondering how miserably uncomfortable the model had been. The expression on her face was far more wretched than sultry. She looked like a side of ham trussed up for the oven.

"That doesn't seem likely. You know me. I don't go in for that kind of thing. It just gets in the way." I threw the catalog to him and he thumbed through it, looking not particularly impressed. "Have you seen the prices? Who would have thought it would cost so much to look so cheap?"

"That's my boy." I leaned my head against the back of the chair, shattered. "I don't know how they came up with my name. If I don't buy anything from it, they'll probably stop sending it to me."

"They might. But once you're on a mailing list, they've got you for life. Are you absolutely sure you didn't sign up for it?"

"Absolutely positive. If you want me to dress up in nipple tassels and suspenders, by all means say, but I'm not going to volunteer to do it."

"What a tantalizing prospect." He looked back at the TV and I saw his eyes widen. "I don't believe it. It's over. I missed it."

"Oh dear." I peered at the screen, not recognizing anyone. "Did the right person win?"

"Nope." He took a deep breath and blew it out slowly, then smiled.

"Never mind. Want to watch something else?"

"Nothing specific." I watched him flicking through the channels. "This is weird. It's almost like we're people with ordinary jobs, relaxing after a hard day at the office."

He picked up his phone and waved it at me. "Except for these. We're never off duty really."

"Which is part of what you like about it. You love being that important."

"You got me."

"Do you want to go out?" I was still working my way through the post. The last thing was an envelope with a typed address label and I slit it open.

"Two nights in a row? Not unless you do. I'm not sure I can take the excitement. Anyway, I should take things easy. It's work drinks tomorrow night."

"Bonding with your new team?"

"Most certainly." He hesitated. "Do you want to come along? I'm sure they'd like to meet you."

There was something reluctant about the invitation, something that made me think no was the right answer. "I don't want to get in your way."

"Don't be stupid. How would you be in the way?" He was staring at the television, not meeting my eyes.

"I won't know anyone except you. If the point is for you to talk to your new colleagues, having me there won't be a help."

"You probably won't spend any time with me at all. Once they get a look at you —"

"They'll be queuing up to talk to me. Yeah, yeah."

"Seriously. Come with me. If you've got time." He was sounding more enthusiastic now, but I still wavered.

"I'll see what time I get finished, but I'll probably be working late. Where are you going?"

"Somewhere near Tower Bridge. I'll let you know where tomorrow."

I turned the envelope upside down and let the contents slide onto my knee.

"What the fuck is this?"

He sat up to see what I was talking about. "Are those photographs?"

"Yes. Of you." I held one up. "And some blonde."

"That's DI Ormond."

"Is it, indeed?" The picture showed a curvy woman in a low-cut top, smiling at Rob as they both sat in the front of a car. He was grinning back. It all looked very cozy.

"That was when we were doing surveillance. Who sent you that?"

I checked inside the envelope. "No note."

"What else is there?"

There was another photograph of the two of them in the car, this time taken from the side. It was recognizably the back of Rob's head. DI Ormond was looking at him, lips parted, eyes half closed. "She looks like she's auditioning for a porn film."

"Nothing so interesting." Rob held out his hand for the pictures. "Who sent these? Seriously?"

"I don't know. They were addressed to me. Someone wanted me to see them."

Rob shrugged. "Maybe a prank. A way of welcoming me to the team. Trying to cause some domestic trouble for me."

"It's a funny sort of prank. Or rather, not funny at all." I flattened out the envelope. "Besides, how would they know my name?"

"If I mentioned you?" He grinned. "It's not a state secret anymore. I do tell people about you."

"Hmm. Are you finished with the pictures?"

"Do you really want them back?" He raised his eyebrows.

"I wouldn't mind another look at them."

"Okay." He handed them to me. "But if it was up to me, I'd bin them."

"Don't you want to know who sent them?"

"Chances are I'll find out tomorrow at work. Or someone will confess in the pub once they've had a few beers." He shook his head. "Really, it's not worth worrying about."

"Okay." I stuck them in among the pile of envelopes I had set aside for the rubbish. It might have been my imagination but I thought Rob looked very slightly relieved. Or I was being paranoid again. I went quiet, letting him concentrate on a documentary about deep-sea diving that seemed to have caught his attention. The interview with Niele Adamkuté was playing in my mind, specifically the bit where she'd talked about Kennford going off her once they moved in together. It was like a stone in my shoe, irritating and impossible to ignore once I was aware of it. Rob was Kennford's polar opposite in almost every way, but he was a man, and men didn't like to feel trapped, as I understood it. Maybe moving in with him had been a mistake. It had been a spur-of-the-moment thing, a solution to the problem of a particularly persistent stalker I had acquired. I wouldn't have suggested it so soon if it hadn't been for that. In fact, there was a chance I wouldn't have suggested it at all.

In every relationship in my adult life, I'd been the one who called the shots. I'd been the one who was pursued, the one who was difficult to keep, the one who decided when we'd reached the end of the line. It was painfully obvious, even to me, that it was my way of protecting myself. I was pathologically afraid of starting to care more than my boyfriend did and, as a result, getting hurt. And with Rob, I was in new territory. For the first time, I didn't feel like I was in control, and I hated it. There was something Rob wasn't telling me, I was sure of it.

There was also the fact he had said he loved me the previous night. And had not repeated it, I reminded myself. People said stupid things in the heat of passion; I knew that much.

People also said stupid things when they were sitting in their living room watching television, as I proved a minute later.

"What would you want me to do if I got pregnant?"

"Huh?" He tore his eyes away from the screen and stared at me, utterly bewildered.

"It came up today. If I was pregnant. By accident, I mean. What would you want me to do?"

He looked down at the glass of water I was holding and raised his eyebrows. "Is this a hypothetical situation or do you have something to share with me?"

"Definitely hypothetical. Really." I was blushing, I realized, and wished I hadn't said anything. "Forget it."

"You asked. You must want an answer."

"Actually, I don't want to think about it. It's my worst nightmare."

"Funny, that. I had you down as the maternal type."

"Don't pretend you'd be pleased."

"It's not unthinkable," Rob countered. "It would be complicated, but people manage."

"Not in the job. Not if both of them want their careers to go somewhere."

Rob peeled himself off the sofa and crossed the room, hauling me to my feet so he could put his arms around me. I stood there stiffly, my own arms by my sides. "It's not worth worrying about it until it happens."

"That's just because you'd rather not think about it."

"I wasn't aware that you were worried about it."

"I wasn't. Not really. But someone I was interviewing asked me about it and I started to think about how it would be. The reality is, I'd get stuck with the responsibility of looking after the baby and it would make it impossible for me to do my job."

Rob was frowning a little, puzzled. "I don't think it would be the end of the world." He let go of me but stayed where he was, looking down at me. "What's this really about?"

I shook my head wordlessly.

"You're worried about getting tied down." His mouth thinned; I thought it might have been irritation, or even disappointment. "Always looking for the exits, aren't you?"

His talent for mind-reading was really

inconvenient now and then. "That's not it."

"Isn't it?" He sounded frankly skeptical, as well he might. He was getting far too close to what I really felt. "I thought you were happy here."

"I am."

"And that makes you feel panicky because . . ."

I let him wait for the answer while I sorted it out in my own mind. At last, I said, "I'm just not used to it. I'm not used to thinking about the future." *Whether I'm with you or not.* "To be honest, I don't know what I want."

I could see him debating the wisdom of pushing me to say more. He settled for keeping things simple. "Well, when you work it out, let me know." He kissed me once, gently. "I'll be here."

I was grateful to him for saying it, and I wanted to believe it, but I watched him walk out of the room with nothing but doubt in my mind.

By making a superhuman effort to act as if nothing had happened, we had a fairly pleasant evening. Rob cooked, we watched mindless television, then we went to bed in a companionable way, shelving passion in favor of sleep. A normal night for normal people — a privilege for us.

And somehow unsettling. I didn't get to sleep for a while. It was stiflingly hot too, and

I lay as far away from Rob as I could, not needing the extra body heat. When I finally drifted off it was a restless kind of sleep, frequently disturbed by noises from the street below. The window was wide open but there wasn't any air, even late at night. Sirens cut through the nearest intersection now and then, heading for bar fights and domestics and violence and all of the misery of a hot summer night in the city. It had been going on for too long, the heat wave. The novelty had gone and all that was left were frayed tempers and surfacing grudges.

It was almost a relief when a phone shrilled by our bed in the middle of the night, jerking me out of a dream about doing mountains of ironing in a hot, steamy room. I was sitting up before I realized I was awake, aware of Rob doing the same thing beside me.

"Yours."

"I know that," I snapped, checking the time and clearing my throat before I picked it up. The screen glared blue in the dark of the bedroom and I squinted at the name, wondering why DS Maitland was ringing me at three in the morning.

"Kerrigan."

His voice was loud and cheerful. "Sorry to wake you, but your presence is required. There's been another shooting."

"Whereabouts?" I scribbled the address on the pad Rob had handed me, and the detail

303

that it was close to Clapham North tube station. "Who's been shot?"

"Three lads. More of Goldsworthy's boys."

I felt my heart rate begin to drop. "Sorry, Harry. I'm not on that case."

"You are now. Godley wants everyone there. All hands on deck."

"I'm busy with the Kennford murders," I objected.

"Tell it to the boss, not me. Anyway, those bodies are cold. They're old news. Get over here while these ones are fresh. The blood's still wet."

I felt my stomach heave and shut my eyes, trying to think. "Has anyone called Derwent?"

"No idea. But you're on my list, and now I can cross you off. See you soon."

I stared at the phone for a second, reading "Call ended" without really taking it in.

"Trouble?" Rob switched on his light.

"Three shot in Clapham."

"More of your gang stuff?"

"So it seems." I got out of bed and discovered I was aching as if I had been lying on the floor all night. I stretched, joints creaking. "God, I'm too old for this."

"You're not even thirty."

"I feel about a hundred years old." I was opening and closing drawers, looking for a clean top. "Fuck. I really need to do some laundry."

"I'll put some on."

"You don't have to do my washing."

"I'm not going down to the river to scrub it on a rock. It's not a big deal."

I had found something that would just about do, a sleeveless top with tiny forget-me-nots embroidered around the neckline. It wasn't what you'd call hard-edged, but it was subtle enough that I thought I'd probably get away with it. And the blue would match the shadows under my eyes, so it was a winner all round. "Turn off the light and go back to sleep. It's the middle of the night."

"I don't mind."

"I do. You need your sleep." I gathered my things together and headed for the bathroom to get ready. "I want to hear snoring when I come back, okay?"

There was no reply, which I took to be agreement. About which I was quite wrong. By the time I got back from the bathroom, carrying my shoes in case I disturbed him, Rob was dressed and standing in the hall.

"Where do you think you're going?"

"I thought I'd give you a lift. Saves you trying to find someone else to pick you up on their way since you don't have any transport of your own."

My own car, my beloved Fiesta, had died an ignominious death on the hard shoulder of the M1 a couple of months earlier and I hadn't been able to replace it yet. For work, I could use the unmarked cars at the station, but I'd been planning to take a taxi up to Clapham as it was so close. "I can manage."

"Come on, Maeve. Let me drive you. It's not far, it won't take long."

I was torn between being pleased and suspicious. "Is this just because you're missing the murder squad? You want to get a reminder of what it was like to get three hours' sleep and then look at dead bodies?"

"Something like that," he admitted. "Is that all right?"

"I won't stop you." I grinned at him, suddenly glad of the company, happy to be leaving with him rather than leaving him behind.

Outside, the roads were quiet. The sky was still dark, the air warm enough that I didn't need to put on my jacket. It was the dead time, after the midweek drinkers had abandoned their carousing and before the first workers had left home. An occasional night bus blasted along, empty but for the driver, not needing to stop anywhere along the route but having to run it anyway. I sat beside Rob and chatted, thinking about other things. Specifically thinking that it could have been like that all the time if we hadn't been forced to admit our feelings for one another, if Rob hadn't had to leave the team. The two of us had been at enough crime scenes together for it to feel entirely normal that he was at the wheel, and it was a whole lot more pleasant than going anywhere with Derwent. I wondered again about whether he had been told what was going on. I'd have expected the inspector to call me, not Maitland. I knew he was fed up about being kept off the gang shootings. He had probably been so excited about this lot that he'd forgotten to call me, or hadn't wanted the delay of driving via Battersea to pick me up. Or he'd thought I'd make my own way there, which I should have as it was extremely close, but as Rob had predicted I might have struggled at that time of night.

It was a nice enough area, Clapham North — not as gentrified as some parts of the common's hinterland, but a popular middle-class enclave nonetheless. And everyone had a car, but nowhere to put it. The streets near the shooting were sealed off with blue and white tape, and inside the cordon ambulances and police cars spun their lights, jostling for access with unmarked cars. Outside the cordon, the residents had filled all of the spaces on both sides of the street. Rob pulled up half on the pavement, in a spot that was wholly illegal.

"At this time of night, I think I'll risk it. I won't be staying for long." He stuck the "Police on Duty" card in the windscreen anyway, and we headed for the barrier together.

It was a young and pretty PC who let us

through, her hair in a tight bun that sat under the rim of her cap like an illustration from the Met uniform regulations. She had a gap between her front teeth and it gave her a very slight lisp.

"You need to go down the street as far as the carpet shop, then take a right down the alley beside it. They're in the open space at the back of the premises."

"Thanks."

"You're most welcome," she said, and I glanced at her in time to see her eyeing Rob with interest. I didn't bother to look at him; he was used to that kind of reaction from women, and I was used to seeing him ignore it. I couldn't help listening, though, and heard him follow me without breaking his stride. I didn't know why I'd been worried about it; it wasn't as if he was stupid enough to flirt in front of me. To cover myself, I asked, "Are you coming all the way to the scene?"

"Do you want me to leave?"

"No. Of course not." I stopped, aware that as we got closer to the alley, our chances of being interrupted increased. "I just wanted to know."

"Well, I was planning to. I wouldn't mind a chat with Godley."

"What about?"

Rob hesitated for a second. "He put in a good word for me with DI Ormond. I just thought he might have heard whether she's happy with my work or not."

"Are you worried?"

"Always. I live on my nerves." He grinned at me, looking superbly unconcerned.

"All right, then."

"I've got your permission, have I?"

"To turn up at my crime scene? Yes. But it reminds me of how my dad used to pick me up from nightclubs when I was seventeen."

"All credibility with the door staff completely blown?"

"About two seconds after he got chatting with them," I confirmed. "The fake ID only ever worked once."

"Well, you don't need to worry about that this time. Since I'm the one that's not supposed to be here, I'll keep a low profile. Lead on, Kerrigan."

I did as I was told, passing houses with the blinds drawn, the occupants apparently unaware of the upheaval nearby or the emergency vehicles that snaked down the middle of the road. It wasn't difficult to find our way. There were only six shops on the street, an odd assortment gathered together about halfway down. Presumably the residents made good use of the newsagents and heavily shuttered off-license but I wondered how the specialist upholsterer survived, not to mention the tiny travel agent and the picture framer. The carpet shop looked as if it was on its last legs, the paint around the window flaking away in hand-sized curls. It was a big premises, though, double-fronted, and the alley at the side was wide enough for delivery vans.

If I had been unsure of my route, the presence of DCI Burt at the end of the alley would have been a decent enough signpost. She was on her mobile but waved hello with a surprising degree of enthusiasm.

"New DCI?" Rob murmured in my ear.

"What gave it away?"

"Your description of her didn't do her justice."

"Don't be mean." I felt protective of DCI Burt for reasons that escaped me. She was well able to look after herself — she had risen through the ranks with apparent ease and speed, after all. And I certainly didn't identify with her just because she happened to be a woman. It was probably as simple as the feeling I had that she was well disposed toward me, or at least not actually hostile. She had stood up for me in the briefing when Derwent was determined to tear me down, so I'd stick up for her when I got the chance.

The alley was surprisingly long and not well lit, and my torch batteries were starting to go. The space at the end was brightly illuminated with arc lights that ran on noisy generators, and the contrast made it even harder to see where I was going. I picked my way down it, glad that it was a carpet shop that stood next door and not a takeaway. Even so, I managed to avoid a broken milk bottle that glinted in the light but stepped in a burst plastic bag that reeked to high heaven. I could smell it over the diesel fumes from the generators and the cabbage smell of bins that pervaded the air.

"Oh, bollocks."

"I'm definitely not giving you a lift back now."

"If you were a real gent, you'd be going first."

"Doesn't fit with keeping a low profile. Sorry." He sniffed. "What even was that?"

"A cooked chicken, I think. Once upon a time." I scraped the worst of it off on a convenient doorstep, the back exit from the carpet shop. "Hideous. Give me good clean dog poo any day."

"Plenty of that around if you want it."

"Well, obviously I don't." I straightened my clothes and my shoulders, bracing myself for what lay around the corner. Three dead in a gang shooting. It wasn't going to be pretty. "Come on."

"Technically, you're the one that was holding us up, but okay."

We rounded the corner together and found a small square yard, the walls high and topped with broken glass set in concrete. "No parking" signs were on every flat surface but the driver of the shiny black Range Rover that sat in the middle of the yard hadn't cared. He also hadn't cared what happened to the car, I surmised, or he wouldn't have allowed someone to shoot out all the windows to the rear of the vehicle. The glass on the ground was pure black, so heavy was the tint on the windows, and the blood that splattered across it was, as Maitland had promised, still wet in places.

I had no idea when the car had been discovered, but someone had pulled strings to get every decent SOCO in South London to turn up, and most of the team to boot. That someone, I assumed, was Godley, who was watching them work with his arms folded. He was wearing a gray suit that looked as if it had just come back from the dry cleaners, every line of it sharp and unrumpled. His tie was perfectly knotted, his shirt a clean white. His hands were buried in his pockets and the look on his face was bleak. He glanced up and saw us, and for a moment his expression lightened. Rob detached himself from my side and went over to him, shaking hands and leaning in to say something to him that I couldn't catch. I didn't get much of a chance to stand around and watch, either, before Maitland bore down on me.

"House to house. We need to cover the buildings that the car might have driven past on the way to this yard, and that's hundreds of them. Someone must have seen something, or heard it."

"And you're expecting them to cooperate?"

"No one likes gang violence in their neighborhood. They'll do their duty."

"And no one likes being intimidated either, which is what they can expect if they're prepared to be witnesses."

"Well, don't tell them that now, will you? Make it look as if we've got this under control."

I nodded at the car. "What happened? What do we know?"

"Three victims. Happened around half past one but we don't have a specific time because the person who called it in — anonymously, of course — said they'd waited for a while in case the gunmen were still around. They'd seen the car come down the alley and hung around 'in case it was thieves planning to do a ram raid on the shop.' " Maitland's thick fingers raked the air to indicated the quote marks. "I think someone's been watching too much television."

"They were right about it being criminal activity," I pointed out.

"Well, they weren't much use, even so. No idea how many people were in the car when it went down the alley. No idea how many people came back out, but he did say they got into a silver saloon car before driving away. No model, no index plate, no descriptions, no further details."

"Marvelous."

"What we got when we turned up to check it out was two bodies in the backseat and one in the boot. The gunmen stood outside the car and shot through the windows — silenced weapons, we're assuming, because otherwise we'd have had half the neighborhood ringing 999."

"Who are the victims?"

"Three lads who were working for Ken Goldsworthy. We had their names already — I liked one of them for a killing over in Catford." He shrugged. "Probably right, wasn't I?"

That was no satisfaction when we'd never prove it and the case would remain open, unsolved. "Has the pathologist been yet?"

"On his way. But come and have a look. They've been doing the outside of the car while they're waiting, but I think they're done now."

I followed Maitland, unable to think of a reason not to look at the contents of the car. It was soaked in blood, blood I could smell as I got nearer, along with a ranker odor.

"This is Lee Wright, aged all of nineteen." The beam of Maitland's torch lingered over his face, the mouth hanging open, the eyes blank. He looked terribly young. He leaned forward at an angle, slumped over but held

314

in place by a seat belt. "You can't see it from here but their hands are tied."

"Why are his trousers around his ankles?"

"It's an old trick. Stops them from running if they get free. No shoes either. They're in the front footwell." The torch beam flicked over dirty toes, pale calloused skin. There was something pathetic about them, something infinitely human. He'd been nineteen years old and heavily involved in drug dealing, but he'd been a person too, for all that. He'd had a life ahead of him.

"On the other side of the car we have Curt Mason, all the way from Tottenham. Goldsworthy got in with a gang from one of the estates up there, recruited them for his own purposes. Convictions for violence, drug dealing, theft — you name it. Aged twenty-three." He was big, heavily built, his shoulders packed with muscle. His skin shone like polished ebony in the light of the torch. They had shot him in the head. Bits of his brain splattered across the back of the car, soaking Lee Wright's hair on that side.

"They wouldn't have been shot at the same time, would they? Too risky for the killers."

"Depends on the angle." Maitland stood back and extended his arm to show me. "If you stay back and keep your field of fire relatively narrow, you needn't come to any harm. Remember, they weren't going anywhere. You're not talking about moving

315

targets. I'd say two shooters, not three, because they left the lad in the boot until last, but you could certainly have had two of them firing at the same time. Less chance of attracting attention if it doesn't take too long."

"It's cold, isn't it? An execution."

"Professional. Nothing personal about it." Maitland moved around the car. "This is Safraz Mahmood, aged twenty, who got to ride in the boot. They left him until last, I'd guess, because he pissed and shat himself while he was waiting to die. He also battered the living daylights out of the boot trying to kick himself free. These things are like tanks — he didn't have a hope."

I looked in at him, curled up in the bottom of the car. His eyes were closed, the expression on his face sad. There were footprints all over one side of the boot.

"No gags on any of them. Whatever about the other two, he must have been screaming," I murmured, almost to myself.

"So you know what to ask about on the door-to-door inquiries. Shouts, loud noises or thuds, screams, car engines." He ticked them off. "Anything else strange they saw or heard."

"Right."

"Here's your list of streets. Both sides of the road, please, commercial premises as well as residential."

"This is going to take all day," I said.

"It'll take as long as it takes."

"I've got to do interviews this afternoon with Derwent, on the Kennford case."

"Then you'd better get a move on."

"Nice of you to drop in, Kerrigan." The voice came from behind me that I instantly recognized as Belcott's. "Whining about doing a bit of work already?"

I ignored him. To Maitland, I said, "What time are we starting to knock people up?"

"Six. Best chance of catching everyone before they leave for the day."

"What should I do in the meantime?"

"Same as everyone else. Hang around talking shit. Or drinking it, if you fancy a coffee."

"You're selling it to me. I should have brought my own."

"Like you brought your own company." Belcott hadn't taken the hint and now I registered that he was standing beside my elbow, glaring at Rob. "What's he doing here?"

"What does it look like he's doing? Come on, Belcott. Use your exceptional observational skills."

Rob was still deep in conversation with Godley, a conversation that had both of them looking serious.

"I wonder if he thinks you're worth it."

"I wonder why you'd care." I knew he was a bitter, venomous little man but he had an instinct for playing on your worst fears, no matter how deeply they were hidden.

"We lost out, didn't we? You got a boyfriend and we had to give up a good copper."

"I bet you wish I'd gone instead."

"I don't think there's any doubt about that. Not how the boss feels, unfortunately. But then Langton can't do the things you can do."

I turned around and glared at him. "For the last time, I'm not sleeping with Godley. Rob chose to leave. He got a promotion out of it, and he's doing really well. Now fuck the fuck off and don't come back."

It was poetic, really, that Maitland chose that very moment to break the news. "By the way, Kerrigan, you're teamed with Belcott on the inquiries. You'll be spending the day together."

"And don't think you're going to be able to duck out of it," Belcott hissed in my ear. "You're going to have to pull your weight for once."

I really couldn't see how my day could get any worse.

As it turned out, that was just lack of imagination.

CHAPTER THIRTEEN

It was during the fourth straight hour of knocking on people's doors that I began to despair. As usual, it was heartbreaking work — repetitive, time-consuming and frustrating. There was the occasional excitement of being called pigs, or being told to fuck off. There was the young mother who burst into tears because Belcott's aggressive ringing of her doorbell had woken her baby. There was the middle-aged woman who invited us in to tell us what she'd seen, who made us a cup of coffee with gravy granules and proved to be, in the words of her harassed husband, doolally. And there were the curtain-twitchers who had a good look at us and decided not to answer the door, for which I blamed Belcott and his clipboard.

"You look like a Jehovah's Witness. It's no wonder they don't want to talk to us."

"They still count as done." He forced a hastily printed leaflet through the letterbox ("MURDER — did you see or hear anything?") and scribbled something on the clipboard. He was more focused on ticking off addresses than on what we were trying to find out, and to begin with, that annoyed me. By the fourth hour, though, my feet were aching, my face hurt from smiling in an unthreatening way and my notebook was essentially empty. Most of the locals who had actually spoken to us were as helpful as they could be, which wasn't very helpful at all. It was the curse of murder investigations in London, the deeply ingrained desire not to get involved with one's neighbors or catch anyone's eye on the street. I understood the head-down mentality, having seen too many cases where attracting the wrong person's attention had resulted in death or serious injury. But I still wondered how the hell three men could be shot multiple times at half past one in the morning in an essentially residential area without anyone paying any attention whatsoever.

And speaking of not paying attention, I had missed the moment when Rob left, looking around to find him gone about half an hour after we'd arrived. I appreciated his delicacy in not coming over to say goodbye — I had told him to keep a low profile, after all, and there would have been comments from the team members who were gathering in the yard, bleary-eyed and rumpled to a man. But I still wanted to know if he'd got what he wanted from Godley, whatever that was. I had sent him a text and got no reply, which wasn't unusual because he hated texting. Also, it had been getting on for five in the morning and I half-hoped he was asleep. I would have given a lot to be back in my bed myself, and I was far from being the only one who was shivering with fatigue and too much caffeine. The yawning was constant and infectious. Only Godley looked truly awake, galvanized by the scene in front of him, talking to the SOCOs, the pathologist, the first responders and, later, a handful of the reporters who had been besieging us for hours. He needed to look dynamic, Maitland told me in a low voice, because the shit was about to hit the fan. There had been plenty of intelligence to warn us that this shooting was coming and we still hadn't been able to do a thing to prevent it.

"It's all right when it's just shitbags, obviously. But it's only a matter of time before there's collateral damage. A stray bullet goes through a window or across the street, hits someone innocent. A kid, even. Someone nice and middle-class and decent is what you'd get in an area like this, and the press would go crazy." Maitland shook his head slowly, his lips pursed in a soundless whistle. "Wouldn't want to be the one who's supposed to be in charge when that happens."

"He doesn't look worried." I was watching

him bending down to listen to what a boilersuit-wearing SOCO who looked exhausted was telling him.

"If he looked panicked we'd all be screwed, wouldn't we? No hiding that we're up shit creek then. He's got to look as if he knows what he's doing, but believe me, he's out of ideas. And we're out of luck."

After so many fruitless interviews, I was beginning to feel the same way. Another door, another blank face and shaking head. I came down the short flight of steps and resisted the urge to sit down on them so I could take off my shoes and rub my feet. We were on the shady side of the street at least, so it wasn't as hot as it might have been. Belcott was still dripping with sweat, his hair standing up in hedgehog spikes.

"How many more do we have to do?"

"The rest of this side. The other side. The next two streets that way. Then we're done."

The Victorians had known how to build high-density housing and that area favored long streets, so he was talking about hundreds of properties. We were working away from the crime scene, out of the likely area where anyone would have seen anything, and I couldn't manage to put any enthusiasm at all into it.

"Brilliant."

"Having fun?"

"More than you can imagine." I looked past

him, to a silver Mercedes that was cruising toward us. "Isn't that Godley's car?"

"Look busy." Belcott hurried up the steps of the house next door and rang the bell, scanning his clipboard with intense concentration.

The car was slowing down as it approached us. Instead of following Belcott's lead, I stepped out to the road and waved. It glided to a stop and the driver's window slid down. Godley was driving himself, and he was alone.

"Maeve. Just the person I was looking for. How are you finding it?"

"Not that useful, unfortunately. We haven't had much luck so far."

"Nor has anyone else." He shrugged. "It's the usual story, isn't it? Someone probably did notice something that would help us but they won't tell us about it, or they can't, or they haven't realized we need to know it."

A van was coming down the street behind the Mercedes, its engine noisy. With cars parked on both sides of the road, Godley's car was blocking the whole carriageway and there was nowhere to pull in. The van driver blasted a volley on his horn and I acknowledged it with a glare. As soon as I looked away, the horn blared again. Godley glanced in his rearview mirror and grimaced.

"Better make this quick. I want you to leave Belcott to finish off the house-to-house and come with me."

Rescue, at last. "Where to?"

"Wandsworth Prison. Tell Belcott and make it snappy, or that van is going to be parked in the backseat."

There were more glamorous destinations, but I didn't truly care. I nodded and hurried up the steps to interrupt Belcott, who was embroiled in a lengthy conversation with an elderly man. He couldn't hear a word Belcott was saying and Belcott couldn't understand his answers when he did manage to get a question through to him. Another typically rewarding encounter.

"I'm going. Godley's got a job for me."

"What?" He turned round and glared at the car, then at me. "Why am I not surprised?"

"Don't get any ideas, Belcott. It's not what you think."

"Where are you going?"

"Prison, not that it's any of your business."

"Why?"

If I'd answered, I'd have had to reveal that I didn't know why we were going to prison, who we were going to see or why I was included. Ignorance was not anything to boast about; it was much better to let Belcott think I was withholding information deliberately. I skipped back down the steps. "Good luck with the inquiries."

It would take him hours to complete the

list of addresses, and he would fill in the time by imagining what I was doing with Godley, in the vilest terms possible. I couldn't stop him from thinking the worst of me. I couldn't bring myself to feel bad about leaving him in the lurch either. Godley's car was air-conditioned, and comfortable, and I sat into the passenger seat with a beatific smile.

"So who are we going to see?"

"An old friend." Godley revved the engine. "A very old friend indeed."

It shouldn't have been that hard to guess who the boss meant. There was, after all, one person who knew exactly what was going on across South London, given that he had set it in motion. One person who I knew, and Godley knew better still. The notorious gangster, murderer and thief John Skinner, detained at Her Majesty's pleasure for the remainder of his natural life, but not content to go quietly. Especially since it was his archrival Ken Goldsworthy who stood to benefit from Skinner's current whereabouts. If I was slow on the uptake it was because as far as I knew Skinner had been moved out of London a couple of months earlier, once he'd started his sentence. The London prisons struggled to accommodate their share of inmates, between the large numbers of remand prisoners and those who were just starting their sentences. They had to be held close to the courts where they were being tried, but it placed a strain on overcrowded and outdated facilities, and the usual practice was to send as many as possible off to far-flung corners of the country once they had got used to the idea that they weren't going home. It was something that upset their families and the inmates themselves, but part of their punishment was that they had no control over where they ended up. I felt more sorry for their children and partners, condemned to long, frustrating journeys or no visits at all, through no fault of their own. But as John Skinner had no living children and his estranged wife was unlikely to visit, that really didn't apply to him. Still, it was useful that he was back, and so close to the current crime scene. Not quite close enough to hear the sirens, probably, and certainly not the shots, but close enough to feel like he was a part of it, maybe. And we could be certain about one thing: he was up to his neck in it.

Wandsworth Prison was one of London's Victorian jails and far too useful to be put out of service, even though it was showing its age. It was the largest in the city and one of the biggest in Europe, sprawling over the top of a hill in the otherwise plush area that bordered the green and shady beauty of the nearby common. From the road there was little enough to see, the bulk of the prison extending a long way back. Large containers of flowers were a jaunty addition to an otherwise bleak open courtyard, which was dominated by a double-height paneled gate that led into the prison itself. The walls were gray and almost windowless, somber even on a glorious summer's day. I had never visited a prisoner there before, though the procedure was much the same everywhere. I handed over my phone and anything that could be used as a weapon, passed through a security arch, submitted to a further pat down, and eventually followed Godley down a tiled corridor that smelled of school dinners and bleach. The meeting room that awaited us was wholly unremarkable. There was nothing as grand as a glass wall between us and the far side of the table, but there was a guard on duty outside the door, a reminder that Skinner didn't have much to lose.

I had stayed quiet for the short car journey once I'd found out who we were to see, thinking about the handful of encounters I'd had with him. Silence seemed to be what Godley preferred anyway. He drove with precision and great concentration while I sat beside him wondering why he had wanted me, why I had been selected to go with him. I doubted the gangster would remember me at all.

The ticking of the clock on the wall was making me edgy. To break the silence, I said, "I thought Skinner was up in Lincolnshire."

"He was until a week ago. I had him moved

down here."

"Why?"

"Easier to get to talk to him, for one thing. And I thought it might disrupt communications with his lieutenants. However he's managing it, he's got an open channel with his thugs. He's still telling them what to do, even now."

"Hard to see how you could stop it, unless you got him put in solitary. He couldn't stay there forever, anyway. And once he got out —"

"He'd be up to his old tricks," Godley finished. "Yes, I know."

"So what are we doing here? Appealing to his better nature?" I said it jokingly, but the expression on the superintendent's face told me I was right. It also told me that I would be wise to backtrack, and quickly.

"Do you have any better ideas?"

"No. I mean, I think it's a good idea. It's definitely worth a try." I sounded like the worst kind of sycophant. "I'm not sure he has a better nature, that's all. I think we saw the best of him when his daughter went missing."

"Around the time he started a campaign of torture and murder. It's not what most people would characterize as good behavior." Godley shoved his hands into his pockets and paced up and down the room, burning off some nervous energy. "I just want him to call a halt, that's all. It's so pointless. All of these young men dying, and for what? Dead bodies don't make money, and John Skinner was always all about money."

"But he's out of all that now. He can't spend money in here. And he's not supporting his wife, is he?"

"They split up."

"So he can't enjoy it, and she's not going to spend it for him. What does that leave? Pride, I suppose."

"That's a good insight." Godley stopped pacing. "I might be able to use that."

I blushed to the roots of my hair, but I wouldn't have been able to live with myself if I'd taken the credit for it. "Oh, well, actually DS Maitland said it first."

"Not to me, and not at the right time." He smiled, ridiculously handsome even under the horrible prison lighting that seemed designed to emphasize bags under eyes and jowly chins. "I knew there was a reason I brought you."

"I'm glad," I managed, fighting back outrage. I felt like some sort of talisman, a good-luck charm Godley had decided to take with him on a whim. Was that it? The off chance I might say something useful? I sat down on one of the starkly uncomfortable chairs to wait for Skinner and went back to saying absolutely nothing in the meantime.

Skinner had changed in the couple of

months since he'd been inside — that was the first thing that occurred to me when he finally appeared. It was hard to tell how much of that was down to the surroundings, to the prison uniform he was wearing instead of a thousand-pound suit, to the loss of his exile's tan. His hair had been collar-length, thick and iron-gray, but now it was clipped almost to the skull and what was left of it was dirty white. The short hair did nothing for his features, which seemed to have blurred a little, softened from enforced inactivity. His cheeks were puffy, his jawline soft. His eyes were the same, though — hooded and reptilian — and I couldn't suppress a jolt of nerves as they swept over me, lingered for a second, moved on.

"To what do I owe the pleasure?"

"I think you know, John. Have a seat." Godley was still standing, but when Skinner sat down he did the same.

"I don't know, actually. I'm beginning to think I might know why I was moved, though. Your idea, I take it."

"Sorry about that."

"Back to London. Back to good old Wandsworth nick." He grinned, a crocodile smile. "Did me a favor, Charlie. Put me back in touch with a few old pals. Better than being stuck out in the middle of nowhere."

"Don't pretend you're pleased to be here."

One shoulder lifted in a shrug. "It's all the

same to me, mate. I go where I'm told."

"Good as gold, that's you."

"I wouldn't say that. But one place is much like another."

"How are you doing it, John? How do you communicate with them?" There was a note in Godley's voice that I'd never heard before, a kind of desperation that he was cloaking in fake bonhomie. It wasn't fooling me and it certainly wasn't working on Skinner, who laughed.

"You'd like to know, wouldn't you? Moving me around won't stop it, that's all I'll say."

"What will?"

"I don't know. Made any arrests? That might help."

"We're pursuing a number of lines of inquiry." Godley stopped himself. "What do I sound like? You know we're a long way behind. Everyone I want to arrest is already dead. Or in prison."

"Might as well be dead." He didn't sound troubled by it, but the words were bitter.

"I'll be honest with you. I've come to ask you to put a stop to it."

"To what?"

"The war. You and Goldsworthy. Dead bodies all over South London. Any of this ringing any bells?"

"I know what you're talking about, but I don't know why you you think I'd be able to stop it." There was a surpassingly sly expression on Skinner's face. He was enjoying this, I realized.

"Because you set it in motion. There's too many of them, John. Too many young kids."

"You know I can't do anything about it. I'm in here."

"Don't pretend you're not in touch with it. You knew about the deaths this morning before I did, I'm sure of it."

"I'd heard something was coming." He looked at me again. "Where do I know you from, sweetheart?"

I had to clear my throat to answer. "The investigation into your daughter's disappearance."

"You were in the interview room. And the flat, before that." He clicked his fingers. "Now I've placed you."

The hairs were standing up on the back of my neck. I tried to look unconcerned. I wasn't usually intimidated by criminals, especially ones who were locked up on a whole-life tariff, but Skinner had a well-earned reputation for taking revenge on people who crossed him. And that included Superintendent Godley.

"What's your name, darling?" Skinner's expression was pleasant but his eyes were cold.

"Leave her alone. She's not important." Godley's voice cracked through the room like a whip before I could even draw breath. I wouldn't have dared to answer Skinner even if I'd wanted to.

"But I'd like to know more about her. She must be good or you wouldn't have made her come along. Or is she just here for decoration?"

"She's a junior member of my team and not likely to be of interest to you now or in the future. She happened to be free to join me. That's all."

I kept my face neutral, watching Skinner's reaction. He didn't look convinced, exactly, but I could see his interest was waning. It was another way of yanking Godley's chain, that was all, a cheap trick to divert attention away from Skinner's murky dealings. But the boss wasn't so easily distracted.

"Three of them dead this morning, John. Three young lads. Different backgrounds, different families." He snapped his fingers. "Gone."

"Very tragic. They must have picked the wrong side."

"There's no such thing as the right side in this mess. No one's winning. Not you. Not Ken."

"Ken's doing all right for himself."

"I doubt that. He's desperate for this to end. Has he reached out to you?"

"He tried." Skinner looked pained. "I told him what I'm telling you. I can't stop this now, and I don't want to."

Godley shook his head. "Do you really hate him that much?"

"He's been knocking off my missus."

"That's personal. You've never confused personal issues with business before." Godley leaned on the table. "You're making mistakes, John. These Eastern Europeans you've brought in — they need stopping. It's time to give them their marching orders."

"You've got it wrong, Charlie. I don't employ them. It's a bit of freelance work they're doing. Speculative stuff."

"They can't kill everyone who's associated with Goldsworthy."

"Kill enough of them and no one will want to be associated with him."

"Is that what you told them to do?"

"Not exactly. They worked it out for themselves." He stretched. "I'm not in touch with them, whatever you think. I don't make the decisions. I may have pointed them in a certain direction, but what they do is their own business."

"Who are they?"

"No one you'd know."

"Where are they from? We know they're European, from one of the former Soviet bloc countries, according to my sources."

"Your sources don't know shit, if you'll pardon my French."

"We'll find out who they are. We're getting close."

"That's the nice thing about subcontractors — I don't have to care. If you catch up with them, fair enough, they're fucked. But as long as you don't, they're doing a good job at pissing Kenny off, and pissing you off, and that's fine by me."

"They're out of control. They're not playing your game. They've got one of their own running."

"That's what I'm trying to tell you. You're right, they are out of control. And they're not going to stop until they've got what they want, which is everything Ken has and then some."

Godley shook his head. "Not good enough, John. You can't let it go on. You've got to step up. You started this, you have to finish it."

"I can't help you."

"Yes, you can."

The two men stared at one another for a long moment. Eventually, Skinner looked away.

"You haven't made it clear to me why I should bother. What's in it for me?"

"My undying gratitude."

"And?"

"There's no deal to be done, John. I can't make your sentence go away. You pleaded to some very serious crimes and you've got to take the consequences. I can get you moved out of here to a more up-to-date prison, probably, but I can't guarantee that you'll like it."

335

Godley's forehead wrinkled. "To be honest, the whole situation confuses me. I can't see why you would want to hand over everything you've worked for. I can't see why you're happy to let it all go. Someone else is going to take advantage, if you're not doing your business and Ken can't, whether it's these Eastern Europeans or someone else. I can understand you hating Goldsworthy, and I can understand you not being particularly interested in making money anymore, given that you won't get to spend it. But I can't understand the logic in standing back to watch your territory burn, just because you're banged up, and you've always been logical, John. We've always had that in common."

"I'm welling up." Skinner brushed away an imaginary tear. "It's still logical, Charlie, even if you can't see it. I want chaos. I want fighting. I want deaths. I don't care about the money or the power — I never did. I just want to know that my enemies and their mates are fucked, and my new associates have been doing an excellent job."

"If you say so. But it's time to stop." Godley got up and knocked on the door. "I'll be in touch, John. Make contact with them in the meantime. Tell them you've changed your mind."

"They're not good listeners."

Godley's face was grim. "Then they need to learn. Find a way to make them hear you."

I couldn't stop myself from turning to look at him, wondering if I'd heard correctly. *Find a way to make them hear you . . .* It was the sort of thing I'd expect to hear on a surveillance tape, one criminal speaking to another.

"You're the boss." Skinner was smiling again, definitely amused by his own private joke.

The superintendent drew in a breath as if he was going to say something in reply, but he settled for banging on the door again, harder this time. We left Skinner sitting in his chair, still with that strange smile on his face, and I didn't care if I never saw him again.

Godley had parked under a tree across the road from the prison, but the time we had spent with Skinner had cost us the shade. The sun had raised the temperature inside to the point where I recoiled on opening the door.

"We'll wait. Leave the door open and let some fresh air in."

I did as I was told, then leaned my elbows on the roof for no longer than a second. "Ow."

"Careful. Don't burn yourself." He was back to his usual self, civilized and pleasant. I refused to be charmed.

"What were you asking him to do?"

"You were in the room. You heard." His eyes were steady on mine.

"I didn't like what I heard."

"Why's that?"

"It sounded like you want the people who are responsible for these killings dead, if there's no other way they can be stopped."

"I want them brought to justice."

"With respect, sir, that's not what you said to Skinner. You more or less asked him to have them killed."

"With someone like Skinner, you have to speak the language they understand. He is a killer, not a lawyer."

"So you weren't saying they should be murdered." I sounded uncertain, even to myself.

"Of course not. Why would I?"

I didn't know. I didn't want to think about it. "What do you think he'll do?"

"Intimidate them. Warn them off. Maybe persuade them to leave the country." He smiled. "Don't worry, Maeve. I'm sure no harm will come to them."

"Why did you want me there?" The question burst out of my mouth before I had time to think about the wisdom of asking it. Godley's eyebrows drew together.

"Would you have preferred to be doing the house-to-house?"

"No, obviously not. But I don't understand why you needed me to be there. I didn't say anything. I didn't contribute anything."

"That's not true."

"I'm not a child. I don't need to be praised when I haven't earned it."

"You earned your place there."

"How?" I demanded.

"I needed someone to be there to vouch for me. Someone to say I didn't do anything illegal or suggest that something illegal be done by Skinner's men."

"You should have brought a tape recorder."

"I prefer the personal touch." He was watching me, his eyes bright and guileless in the sunshine. "You can vouch for me, can't you?"

"I can say what I saw and what I heard." I sounded priggish, but I couldn't help myself. "I'm still not sure what that amounted to."

"Anyone would think you weren't pleased to be included." I didn't say anything and Godley smiled. "I have a lot of time for you, Maeve. I think you have the makings of a great police officer, no matter what anyone says."

The last part stung. "What do they say?"

He looked away. "In case you hadn't noticed, I'm a bit busy at the moment. I don't have time to give out career advice, or gossip with you, just because you're quite good at what you do."

Quite good . . . ouch. I was wounded by Godley's remark, and angry with him for dragging me into his vendetta against Skinner — if that was their relationship. There was something about it I couldn't quite understand, some nuance that I was missing. "Speaking of being good, why isn't DI Derwent on this case?"

"He's busy."

"We're all busy," I pointed out. "But Derwent is one of the only people on the team who has experience of gang killings. He should have been at the scene this morning."

"He doesn't need that kind of stress." Godley sounded as if what he said was final, but I pushed some more.

"He thinks he does. He thinks he's being sidelined deliberately."

"Well, he might be right."

"Why? Why would you do that?

Godley got into the driver's seat instead of answering me straightaway. I got in on my side and looked at him expectantly.

"I didn't want him involved, Maeve."

"Why not?"

"For his own good."

From the way his mouth tightened, that was all Godley was prepared to say on the subject. I stared blindly through the windshield, too confused to ask anything else as we drove away.

I was pretty sure I'd just been done over, but I couldn't for the life of me work out why.

CHAPTER FOURTEEN

"I don't know why you even bothered to show up, to be honest with you. It's not as if I can't manage on my own. Besides, you look like shit."

Derwent was in a foul mood, and taking it out on the nearest person came naturally to him, especially when that person was me.

"The reason I look like shit is because I had three hours' sleep," I said patiently. "The reason I bothered to show up is because I wanted to meet Gerard Harman."

"Think he's a credible suspect? A man in his sixties? A widower whose dead daughter never got justice, thanks to Philip Kennford? Think he's capable of slaughtering two people?"

"I don't know yet. I'll wait until I meet him." We were sitting in the car outside Harman's address, a small bungalow near Reigate that wasn't quite far enough from the M25. With the windows down, the traffic noise was constant and constantly jarring, too loud for it to turn to background sound no matter how long we sat there. "He had every reason to feel bitter about Kennford. And there's a certain poetic justice to killing his daughter, isn't there?"

"He's an old man." Derwent shook his head. "Doesn't matter how angry he is. I don't think he'd be able to chase down Vita and stab her multiple times once she'd seen him kill Laura."

"Plenty of men in their sixties are strong and fit. If he was active —"

"No fucking way. This is another wild goose chase." Derwent was tapping the steering wheel, obviously edgy.

"You'd rather be somewhere else."

"I'd rather be doing something useful, yeah." He glanced at me. "At least you got to do something this morning. And got an invite to the boss's latest big idea, which sounds like bullshit to me. Asking Skinner to stop killing people is like asking a fish to stop swimming."

"I was a bit surprised by it."

" 'I was a bit surprised by it,' " he repeated in an idiotic voice. "Well, I was a bit surprised to hear you were there in the first place."

He had been snappy since I'd found him having lunch alone in the team's room, take-away hot dogs slick with grease and onions. The food smelled like warm coins. By dint of patient questioning and perseverance I gathered he had spent the morning at Southwark Crown Court giving evidence, so I hadn't missed anything in the Kennford case. Not that that made up for my being asked to attend the North Clapham crime scene, it was quite clear. It was almost a relief that he was prepared to talk about it — he had absolutely refused to ask me anything up to now, contenting himself with glowering at me and being as rude as only Derwent could be.

"I don't know why Godley wanted me there. I don't know why you didn't get a call to the crime scene this morning. It seems to me you're the one person who should be involved in the gang murders, and it doesn't make any sense that you aren't. But the person you need to ask about it is the boss."

He snorted. "Brilliant suggestion. I have."

"What did he say?"

"Fuck all."

"Really? He told me it was for your own good." I could have bitten my tongue out as soon as I said it.

Derwent looked at me, his expression unreadable. "You asked him about it?"

"Briefly. After we'd met Skinner." I was staying very still, taking the line that Derwent was basically an animal, so sensing my fear might make him attack. *Please don't notice how scared I am.*

"It's none of your fucking business, is it?"

"It is my business when the boss isn't using

the resources at his disposal effectively. It is when you're being sidelined for no reason that I can see."

"Thanks for caring."

"Look, you might not like it but I do care. It's frustrating to see you being left out. This Kennford case is a weird one but anyone on the team could investigate it and do just about as well as we've been doing. The drugs murders are different. You have the experience of dealing with them before. It doesn't make sense that you're not involved."

"Well, you know why that is, don't you? I'm not enough of a lady." Derwent's voice dripped sarcasm. "Una Burt, on the other hand, is technically female, so she gets the go-ahead to run the investigation as Godley's number two."

"He's being pretty hands-on, if it's any consolation."

"It isn't, really." Derwent was calming down, his anger fading out to puzzled disappointment, the dog chained up in the yard barking himself to silence. "I shouldn't have to find that kind of thing out secondhand because I should be where Burt is."

It would have been wise just to be glad he was cheering up. I certainly shouldn't have said anything to provoke him. Somehow, though, I couldn't stop myself from pointing out the obvious, even though I knew there'd be trouble. It was more of the stupid loyalty I felt to Una Burt, just because she'd managed to succeed as I hoped to.

"DCI Burt is senior to you, though. It's not like you're equals. She might still have been Godley's second-in-command even if you'd been on the case. You'd have been reporting to her."

"Do you think I don't know she outranks me? I know all about taking orders from people I don't like and don't respect — I was in the army for long enough, and there were plenty of ignorant assholes queuing up to put me down."

"Must have been tough."

"It was the making of me."

"Evidently."

"What's that supposed to mean?"

"Absolutely nothing," I said promptly, not wanting to give away what I'd been thinking, which was *No wonder you're such a tosser.* "But things are different in the police. You're a senior officer too, not a private. I bet you were pretty young when you joined up."

"Just turned eighteen."

"Yeah, well, you're not a teenager anymore. I don't think DCI Burt has the power to intimidate you into doing what she wants if you disagree with her."

"So?"

"So maybe Godley doesn't want you clashing with her. Maybe he wants to keep you away from her so the situation doesn't arise, and that's what he meant by it being for your own good to stay out of it."

He shook his head, stubble scratching against his shirt collar. "It's a big investigation. There's enough for both of us to do. More than enough. I wouldn't have to see her, except at briefings, and I can hold my tongue if I have to."

"Really? I'd never have guessed," I said sweetly. It was a gamble, but I was feeling reckless. Derwent whipped around again, death-glare at the ready, but subsided into a snort of laughter that seemed to take him by surprise.

"All right. I'll admit I don't generally have that reputation."

"And you earned your reputation the hard way."

"Hard for everyone else. I don't mind being a twat."

"You might even say it comes naturally."

"Do you really think that's what he meant? That he doesn't want me upsetting Burt?" He sounded hurt, his emotions unguarded for once.

"It sort of makes sense."

"Nothing else does."

"No," I agreed.

"Why did he go to see Skinner? What was he trying to achieve?"

"I don't know."

"Why did he take you?"

"I don't know that either."

We sat in the car for another minute or so, listening to the heavy goods vehicles rumbling along in one lane, and a police car with its siren screaming racing past, unseen. Derwent stretched and checked his watch.

"We'd better get on with this."

I looked at him questioningly. "Not looking forward to it?"

"Not much." He pulled a face. "Grieving parents are always a tough interview."

"She died eight years ago."

"That's the thing, it doesn't matter if it was eight hours or eighteen years. They never stop grieving."

At first glance, Gerard Harman was not in the grip of grief. More importantly for us, perhaps, he was neither a doddering old man nor exceptionally fit. He was tall and thin with short gray hair, his face grave behind thick glasses. He was wearing a long-sleeved check shirt with the cuffs done up, some kind of brushed cotton that looked soft, but far too warm for the hot day. Green cords and brown walking boots completed the country gentleman look.

"You're late. I thought you weren't coming. I was just about to take the dog for a walk." As if it proved something, he waved the lead he had been holding, and I became aware of a scrabbling sound coming from the door at the back of the hall.

"We won't take long." Derwent had put his foot over the threshold, casually, as if it was how he preferred to stand. I knew he was ready to stop Harman from closing the door in our faces.

"You'd better come in." Harman had a particularly colorless voice, a monotone that gave little away, but I thought he was nervous. He turned and led the way into a small sitting room to the right, followed by Derwent, who left me to close the door. The bungalow smelled clean but stale, as if the windows were never opened. Probably they weren't — even with the double-glazing there was no way to ignore the noise from the road. The house hadn't been redecorated for a while but it was shabby rather than dated, the original choices of wallpaper and carpet bland enough to have lasted well.

"Do you live here alone?" Derwent asked, staring around the room.

"Since my wife died."

"When was that?"

"Ten years ago next month."

"That's a long time to be on your own. I'd have thought you'd have spinsters and widows chasing after you."

"I'm not interested in that kind of thing." It was impossible to tell if he was offended; even his rate of blinking didn't change. He turned to me. "Do sit down. I won't be able to offer you anything to drink, I'm afraid. I can't let Pongo out of the kitchen now. He'll never settle. He saw the lead."

"What kind of dog is he?"

"Mostly a springer spaniel, but not entirely. I got him from a local animal shelter."

"Springer spaniels are lovely dogs."

His face lit up. "Yes, aren't they?"

"Can we bring this meeting of the Kennel Club to a close? Then we can get out of your hair." Derwent sounded bored.

"Of course." Harman sat down in an armchair and lifted one leg over the other, using both hands. He saw me watching him. "I had a mild stroke a couple of years ago. This is the only souvenir."

"It must make it hard for you to manage Pongo."

"He's usually quite understanding of my shortcomings. I got him so I had a reason to go for walks. The physios insisted I needed the exercise, but I found it terribly dull when there was no purpose to it."

"Does it stop you from doing much?" Derwent asked, and I knew he was thinking of the crime scene, of the overturned tables and the way Vita had been hunted down. "I didn't notice you limping."

"I drag my foot a little when I'm tired, and there isn't a lot of strength in the leg at any time. That's why it needs a bit of help with crossing over the other one." He looked down at it and tapped it gently. "Not so bad, really. Much improved from how it was."

Inconclusive. Derwent evidently felt the same way. "We're here to talk about Philip Kennford, as I mentioned on the phone."

"Yes. I was surprised." He pushed his glasses up to the bridge of his nose. "It was a name from the past."

"Not a name you like to hear?"

"It doesn't have positive connotations." Harman's eyes went to a picture on the mantelpiece, a photograph of a teenage girl holding a rabbit and smiling.

Like Derwent, I had seen it as soon as we walked into the room and recognized the dead girl. Knowing the answer, I asked, "Is that your daughter?"

"Yes. That's Clara."

"How old was she when that was taken?"

"Sixteen or seventeen." He smiled a little. "It was hard to find a good picture of her. One just of her, I mean. I have some with her mother, and some with me, but that was the only one of her on her own that was good enough to frame. Of course, she didn't really look like that at the time she died."

"She was twenty-four."

"Yes. Still young. She had her whole life ahead of her, really." Behind his glasses, his eyes glistened, and I thought for one awful moment that he was going to cry. "But there we are. She had the misfortune to meet the wrong person and there was nothing I could do to warn her."

"Did you try?"

"I had my concerns, so I tried to talk to her, yes. Maybe if her mother had been around, she might have confided in her. But she wouldn't admit to me that there was anything wrong." He made a gesture with his hands that somehow conveyed absolute helplessness. "She was in love. She didn't want to hear what her old dad thought. And to be honest, I didn't have any idea what he was really like. If I had, I'd have kidnapped her and locked her away until she came to reason."

Derwent cleared his throat in a hold-on-a-second-must-I-remind-you way. "Harry Stokes was acquitted."

"He put her in hospital three times before he killed her." The stark statement was enough to silence Derwent, no mean feat.

"Wasn't that mentioned at the trial?" I asked.

"She lied about how she'd injured herself whenever she had to see a doctor. Never made a complaint to the police." Harman shook his head, still bewildered. "He broke her nose and she said she'd tripped. He broke her wrist and she said she'd fallen downstairs. He gave her concussion and she told the doctors she was just clumsy."

"It's not that unusual for victims of domestic violence to pretend it didn't happen."

He nodded. "The prosecutor got someone from a women's refuge to testify about that. She said it took an average of thirty-six violent incidents before the victim would make a complaint. Maybe Clara had more fortitude than that, or maybe she was scared, but she was with him for two years and she never told anyone the truth."

"Not any of her friends?"

"He made sure she didn't have any. He wouldn't let her speak to them or have a phone of her own. She used to call me now and then from a pay phone and tell me she didn't have any credit on her phone, but it was because he'd taken it away from her. He isolated her first. Then he made her dependent on him. Then he killed her."

I had skim-read the file, but I asked, "How did she die?"

"She bled to death."

Derwent came back to life. "Sounds like murder to me. How did he get away with it?"

"Well might you ask. He claimed he'd been out with friends and came back to find her lying in a pool of blood." A convulsive swallow. "He did go out, but she was already dead."

"What was the story? She tripped and landed on a knife?" Not having done his homework even to the limited extent that I had, Derwent was genuinely curious.

"It wasn't that far-fetched, unfortunately. They had a glass door to their kitchen and she went through it."

"Not safety glass, then."

"It should never have been installed, but that was the landlord's fault. He was a DIY enthusiast. He made it himself. A sheet of glass that was too thin to be used for that purpose superglued into a frame, so when she hit against it and it broke, there were long shards sticking up. She severed an artery in her leg. The pathologist said it wouldn't have taken her long to die. A minute or two."

"You should've sued the landlord."

Harman blinked at Derwent. "What would be the point? Stokes was going to kill her one day. If it hadn't been the door, it would have been something else."

"But he wasn't convicted. I suppose they couldn't prove it wasn't an accident."

"That was Kennford's doing. He made a big fuss about forensics — there was no DNA on the door from anyone except Clara. Why should there have been? Stokes didn't need to touch the door to push her through it. But the jury thought that was important. I could see them nodding when he talked about it in his final speech. Too much faith in him, not enough thinking." He tapped his forehead with a finger that shook very slightly, the strain of the conversation showing in the sweat pearling on his forehead and the tension that vibrated through him.

"Kennford was just doing his job." Derwent sounded as if he was solidly on the QC's side. No one would have guessed how he really felt about him.

"He was doing what he calls his job. But it was so cynical." Harman drew a long quivery breath and let it out again. "He didn't believe Stokes was innocent, you know. He said as much to me one day in a café near court when I happened to bump into him. He said, 'Everyone deserves a proper defense, Mr. Harman, no matter what they've done or what sort of shit they are.' And then he laughed and asked me not to tell anyone that he'd said that about his own client. I asked him if he thought he would win and he said no, the prosecution case was too strong. But he pulled it apart. Worse than that, he made Clara out to be a drunk, unstable, and said that was why she had left her job. She was a hotel receptionist before, but it was Stokes who made her leave. He didn't like her talking to other men when he wasn't there. Didn't like her having her own income either. It was another way to control her."

"I believe that's very common in domestic cases too," I said sympathetically.

"She spoke three languages, you know. She was going places. She wanted to manage a hotel someday, but she was happy enough to start at the bottom and learn the trade. That was the sort of person she was — no sense of entitlement, a gentle girl. She was quiet but she always had lots of friends because she was loyal, and caring, and never had a bad word to say about anyone. Kennford said she was a loner and unsociable, and that was why Stokes had to go out to drink with his friends alone."

"Explaining why he left her in the house. But that doesn't explain how she happened to fall through the door or why she was always getting injured," I pointed out.

"She was covered in bruises when she died — all at different stages of healing, so there was a history of it; it wasn't a one-off. The prosecutor said it proved that she was living in a dangerous environment. Kennford said she was clumsy — accident-prone, because of the drinking. And Clara was *never* a drinker."

"Had she consumed alcohol before she died?"

"She was over the legal limit to drive, but only just. She'd had two glasses of wine, the pathologist estimated. It was a Friday night and they used to open a bottle of wine then." Harman stopped for a second and squeezed his hands together, agonized. "I bought her a case of red wine for Christmas that year. One of those special offers from the paper, you know. I thought she'd enjoy it, because she had picked up a taste for it when she spent a year in France. Kennford suggested to the jury that she was a raging alcoholic who would have been barely able to stand with the amount she'd had to drink. And he *knew* it wasn't true." Harman pointed at the picture. "You can't tell from that, but she was very slight. She'd been a gymnast as a teenager and she still had that physique, small and slender. The very thing that made her most vulnerable to Stokes was what Kennford suggested had killed her, that she was too small to cope with the amount of alcohol she had drunk. I thought it was loathsome."

"It must have been very difficult for you to sit in court and listen to that," I said.

"It wasn't easy, but I went every day. I owed her that much. Her mother would have wanted me there too. I went for both of them." Harman took his glasses off and rubbed his eyes. "I didn't get a lot out of it, I must admit."

"I still don't see that Kennford did anything other than his job." Derwent, bullishly controversial.

"You're right. He was doing his job. It was cynical, the way he went about it, but that's not against the rules. What bothered me was that he didn't care about the consequences. He put a guilty man on the street."

"The jury acquitted Stokes. And you can't be sure it wasn't a genuine accident."

"Can't I?" Harman's mouth twisted with

something like amusement. "Do you know where Stokes is now?"

Derwent looked at me but I didn't know either. "You'd better tell us."

"Prison."

"Why?"

"He was convicted of attempting to murder the girlfriend he had after Clara. He fractured her skull. She'll have some degree of physical and mental impairment for the rest of her life." Harman's voice was harsh. "She was an estate agent, before. She owned her own home. Now she's in sheltered housing so there's twenty-four-hour support available for her, and she'll probably never work again."

"Okay. That is horrible." I could see Derwent struggling not to tell Harman how he really felt. With an effort, he said, "But you can't hold Kennford accountable for what his client did after the trial was over. That's up to him."

"I agree. I don't blame him for Stokes being a killer. But I do hate him for the fact that he helped to free him without a thought for the consequences. And for the way he did it."

"Hate is a strong word," I said, disturbed.

"Not strong enough. Kennford lying about who Clara was and how she lived killed her all over again."

An awkward stillness settled over the room. I hadn't the heart to ask any more questions, and Derwent seemed to be lacking in the killer instinct too. The dog barked in the kitchen and collided with the door again with a solid thump, followed by silence. I wondered if he'd knocked himself out.

Harman cleared his throat. "Are you finished? I should really take Pongo out. He's been waiting for a while."

Derwent looked at me but I shook my head. As close to shamefaced as he ever got, he said, "I might as well ask, what did you do to Kennford's car?"

"I scratched a word into the bonnet with a chisel. It was easy to do. He left it parked in the Temple, near his chambers. It's an area where the public can come and go relatively freely during the day. I didn't have anything better to do once the trial was over, so I watched him for a few weeks to make sure it really was his car — a green Jaguar, a lovely one — and once I'd confirmed it, I bought a ticket for a concert in Middle Temple Hall. Baroque music. I had no intention of going, of course. The ticket got me past the guard and gave me access to the whole of the Temple when it was dark and more or less deserted. It didn't take me long to find the car and do it."

"What was the word?"

"Liar." Harman shrugged. "Short and sweet."

"How did they know it was you?"

"I went to the police the next day and handed myself in." Another wry smile. "They handed me straight back out again. Criminal damage isn't as serious as I thought it was."

"Why did you do that? They'd never have traced you if you weren't on CCTV." Derwent sounded almost disappointed that he hadn't put up more of a fight.

"You probably think it was guilt, but it wasn't." Harman looked down at his hands. "I went to a pub after I'd done it and had a tot of whiskey — knocked it back — but it was more because I felt I should be in a state of shock than because I actually needed it. I felt fine. It didn't make me feel better, of course. Nothing was going to do that. But I just didn't care about what I'd done. I'd never even got a parking ticket before, but I was behaving like a master criminal or something. Clara would have laughed at me." Harman laughed a little too.

"So why did you go to the police?" I asked.

"Well, then I got to thinking about it, and I realized there was no way Kennford would know why I'd done it or what I'd meant by it if he didn't know who had done it. That just wasn't good enough. He needed to understand why it had happened. So I went to my local police station and told them what I'd done. Pleaded guilty at the trial. And the bastard had the cheek to tell the judge to go easy on me. He asked for my emotional state to be taken into account. I said I didn't want any special treatment, especially at his bidding, but maybe it did make a difference. I don't know." He took his glasses off and rubbed his eyes. "I was glad I didn't have to go to prison, when it came to it. I'd made my point, I thought. It got in the papers — a human-interest story, they told me. So at least he was publicly shamed."

"Were you satisfied with that? No other thoughts of revenge?" Derwent asked.

"Of course I wasn't satisfied. It felt like an empty gesture, and it was, but I couldn't think of anything that would make up for the way he robbed me of justice for my daughter. Not to mention that poor girl who Stokes injured next."

"Did Kennford represent him at that trial, do you know?"

"No, he didn't. He only likes cases he can win."

"So you don't think it was because he felt bad about representing him the first time round," I said.

"I wish that were the case, but no, I don't think so. Even at my trial, you could see he had almost forgotten about Stokes. My daughter was part of history as far as he was concerned. He said to me afterward, 'I hope you can put this behind you and move on.' The man couldn't understand I could never put Clara behind me, or move on. But I don't know what would have taught him that lesson short of killing his daughter and letting him see what it's like."

I shot a look at Derwent, who was sitting very still. I took that as an indication that I could do the honors. "Do you know why we've come to see you today, Mr. Harman?"

He looked bewildered. "Following up?"

"No. Not that." As gently as I could, I explained to him what had happened to Philip Kennford's family, and the fact that he was one of the barrister's known enemies. "It did get quite a bit of coverage."

"I don't watch the news or read a paper, you see. I listen to the radio sometimes, but not always. I find it upsetting."

"That's understandable."

Derwent had had enough of being sensitive. "Where were you on Sunday evening, Mr. Harman? Between six and midnight, let's say."

"I was here."

"Alone?"

"Except for Pongo."

"Speak to anyone? See any neighbors?"

"No. I'm sorry."

"Don't apologize. I just have to ask. Doesn't matter to me if you don't have an alibi."

"I had no idea I'd need one."

"Course not."

"The poor woman, though. That poor girl." The dog made a strangulated noise, halfway to a howl, and Harman turned his head to listen. "I really should get on, I'm afraid."

"Is that it? Your greatest enemy gets what's coming to him, and you're worried about walking the dog?"

Harman turned his pale, watery eyes to Derwent. "How else should I be? Did you want me to celebrate? Or weep for him?"

"I was expecting a reaction of some kind."

"It's too late for that." Harman shook his head as he put his hands on the arms of his chair, ready to lift himself up. "It's much too late for that."

"What happened to your arm?" I asked sharply. The movement he'd made had pulled the sleeve of his shirt up, the cuff sliding over a bony wrist to reveal a long angry gouge in Harman's skin. He looked at it as if he'd never seen it before.

"Brambles. In the garden. I was cutting them back. Why?"

"Can I see?"

He unbuttoned his sleeve and pulled it up a couple of inches. The scratch was long, livid, and flanked by two others further up his arm.

"That looks nasty," Derwent observed. "When did you do that?"

"Sunday." He pulled his sleeve back, leaving it to flap loosely around his hand. "Now, if that's really all I can do for you, I need to go."

"You've been very helpful," I murmured automatically, my mind elsewhere. "Thank you for your time."

Derwent added a slightly confused thank-you as we headed for the door. The two of us stepped outside and, as one, headed around the corner of the house to look at the garden, which was neat and orderly without being particularly enticing. Shrubs had grown tall around a strip of lawn that was as perfect as a bowling green. We walked back to the car in silence. I waited until Derwent had shut his door.

"No brambles that I could see?"

"Not even anywhere they might have grown."

"What did those scratches look like to you?"

"They could have been from anything."

"I've seen fingernail scratches that looked like that. The parallel lines."

"Think he was lying, then?"

"I have no idea," I said truthfully.

We watched as Harman let himself out of the house, the dog leaping and groveling in excitement. He set off down the road without acknowledging us, though he must have seen us sitting there. One leg dragged very slightly; if I hadn't been looking for it, I might not have noticed.

"We should follow up on his medical history. Find out if he really did have a stroke or if it was just a story to make us think he wouldn't be capable of killing them."

"This fucking case." Derwent shook his head. "I'd just like to be able to cross one person off the list, you know?"

"But why would he say that about killing Kennford's daughter if he did it?"

"To throw us off the scent? Who knows? Who gives a shit?"

"Did you like him?" I didn't really know why I was asking, but I wanted to know.

"As a person? Yes. I did." Derwent sounded surprised at himself. "I thought he was a decent old bloke. Lonely, probably. Loves his dog."

"The dog's all he's got."

"At least Kennford's still got one daughter."

"Two, if you include Savannah."

"That's right." Derwent perked up at the thought. "Any luck getting hold of her?"

"None so far. Her agent keeps promising me she'll get in touch."

"Bugger." Derwent stared out through the windshield, back to morose.

"The thing is, none of our current suspects is really a serious contender. None of them seems to be angry enough to kill anyone, let alone a teenage girl and a defenseless woman." I stretched, easing tense muscles in my shoulders. "We've got this list of Kennford's supposed enemies, but when it comes down to it, they're all just grudges and issues about his professionalism."

"What about our lovely Lithuanian? She had access to pretty seedy gang types who wouldn't think twice about teaching someone a lesson by snuffing their nearest and dearest for the most trivial reasons. Some of the stories I've heard about the Lithuanians would make your hair curl." He eyed me. "Scratch that. Maybe they would make yours go straight."

"Very funny. You're right, Adamkuté could have set up a contract killing, probably without leaving her house. I just don't see why she would have wanted to. She gave me the impression she was glad to be out of her relationship with Kennford. A lucky escape, basically."

Derwent looked at me pityingly. "You don't think we're getting the full story from any of these people, do you? They're hardly likely to tell us how they really feel when we're running a murder investigation and they count as possible suspects."

"Harman didn't even know about the killings."

"So he said." He shook his head, marveling. "You really did come down in the last shower, didn't you?"

"No, but I believed him."

"Because he was so open and honest? Fu-u-ucking hell."

"Look, I'm pretty good at spotting when someone's lying to me, okay? And I didn't

365

get that feeling from most of what Gerard Harman said. The thing that bothers me is that we've been focusing on Philip Kennford because he's a high-profile target and we could see someone being pissed off enough with him to want to harm him, probably because we're biased against him ourselves. We haven't found out anything about Vita except that she was hard-nosed, wealthy and apparently liked dirty sex. Or didn't, if you believe what Miranda Wentworth says. And we haven't scratched the surface with Laura. Either one of them could have been the real target, as I've been saying all along."

"Do you really think this isn't to do with Kennford?"

"No. I mean, I think he must be a part of it. I just can't see how."

"I think it's more likely that Kennford ran across the wrong person in his professional life than that a rich, dull housewife got herself into a relationship with a homicidal maniac."

"A relationship that was so secret no one knew about it."

"Did she have any friends? Anyone she confided in?"

"None I've been able to trace. Acquaintances at the tennis club don't really count. I have tried," I said lamely, seeing Derwent's frown. "I spent a couple of hours on it yesterday. I talked to a few of her phone contacts, but they weren't what you'd call friends. She didn't have any hobbies, she wasn't in any book groups or clubs apart from tennis and the gym, she didn't go out. She was completely wrapped up in her family." I hesitated for a second. "I know you don't like him, but I still can't see a motive for Kennford to kill his wife, you know. It does seem to me he was telling the truth — she was far more use to him alive."

"Unless she was planning to divorce him."

"There is that. But why would she bother? She'd dealt with his pregnant Lithuanian mistress — that doesn't leave a lot that she would regard as a deal breaker."

"Something to do with the kids," Derwent said wisely. "That would do it."

"Which makes me think we should be focusing on the twins." I frowned. "There's something there, you know. Something we haven't worked out. Laura was the favorite and Lydia was born to be a victim, but Laura died and Lydia was unharmed. I wish I had a better relationship with Lydia or her aunt. It would really help if I could talk to her again and gain her trust."

"What do we know about Laura? What do we suspect?"

"We suspect we don't have a clue about her. Her friends haven't been a huge help. You were there for the Millie Carberry interview and none of the rest of them have been any better."

"Who's been doing the rest of the interviews?"

"Liv's been running through the list Lydia gave us. A lot of them are away on holidays so it's taken a while to track them down. No one knew anything, or no one would admit to knowing anything."

"So Laura lied?"

"It doesn't help us. We knew she was lying about having a boyfriend already. All we know is that she was supposed to be out, she'd set herself up with a reason to be out, and she ended up staying in and getting killed. We still don't have her phone, or any idea who the boyfriend was."

"Okay. Well, that gives us something to look at. We'd better talk to Lydia again. I'll come along this time. See if that makes a difference."

My heart sank. "Please don't try to terrify her into talking. She's vulnerable, you know."

"I can be sensitive."

I raised my eyebrows. "This is a talent you keep well hidden."

"I have a fatherly manner. Teenagers find it reassuring."

"Firstly, you're what — thirty-five?"

"Thirty-six."

"Less of the pipe-and-slippers thing, then. You're barely old enough to be her father."

"I got started early."

I let that one go. "Secondly, you've never

reassured anyone in your life. You depend on making people so uncomfortable they'll tell you anything just to get rid of you. Thirdly —"

Before I could go on, my phone rang in my pocket and I dug it out, noting automatically that the call was coming from a withheld number.

"Hello?"

"DC Kerrigan? This is Savannah Wentworth." Her voice was soft but clear. "I believe you want to talk to me."

I concentrated on making the arrangements for her to come in and speak to us later on that afternoon, but I couldn't help smiling at the expression on Derwent's face when he realized who I was speaking to. Christmas morning had nothing on it.

CHAPTER FIFTEEN

Due to that weird osmosis of information that seems to be common to all police stations everywhere, by the time Savannah Wentworth set foot in the place everyone in the building knew who she was visiting, and why. There had been time on the way back for Derwent to get his hair cut. I thought he'd looked better before — the short version made it hard to miss how much his ears stuck out — but I wasn't going to interfere. Meeting Savannah was the only thing that had cheered him up for absolutely ages, and a happy Derwent was an altogether nicer one. Personally, I wasn't gripped by the hysteria that seemed to be fairly universal. I didn't really see any reason to be awed by the prospect of meeting someone whose main claim to fame was looking good in designer clothes — or out of them. Still, I couldn't help enjoying the buzz. Derwent and I practically got a standing ovation when we walked into the team's room.

"Oh my God, oh my God, oh my God."

Liv ran over to my desk and started to jump up and down on the spot. "Do you realize she is just my ideal woman? I mean, I have wanted to see her in person *forever*. She can't possibly be that good-looking in real life, can she? Or maybe she can. Oh my God. What do you think she'll be wearing?"

"Clothes." I was going through my in-tray. "Do you think you could get a grip, Liv? It's just that you're being insane."

"Oh, come on. You have to admit we don't usually get anyone remotely glamorous here. This is *exciting*."

"It's *routine*. She's helping with a murder inquiry. And not willingly, if it comes to that."

"I'm sure she has better things to do than come down to this hole in the ground. Do you need anyone to take notes?"

"I think we can manage."

"Maeve." Godley was standing in the doorway of his office. "A word."

I made my way across to him, feeling that frisson of tension that comes from not knowing if you're in trouble or not.

"To what do we owe the pleasure of this three-ring circus?"

"Savannah Wentworth is Philip Kennford's daughter by his first wife. He managed not to mention that to us but I found out from one of his colleagues. She was in town for a meeting so I arranged for her to come in and speak to us."

"Do you seriously think she might be involved in her half sister's death?" Godley sounded scathing.

"I don't know, sir."

"It doesn't seem likely, does it?"

"Again, I won't know until I've spoken to her." I had the feeling I was standing on a very small piece of rock in high seas, and every wave washed away another piece of it.

"I don't like drawing attention to the team like this." He went to the window and looked out. "Do you know there are photographers across the road?"

"Someone must have tipped them off. Maybe she did it herself."

"I doubt that." He sighed. "There must have been a more discreet way to have this conversation."

"Meeting here was Savannah's suggestion, sir. She lives in rural Sussex when she's in the UK, so it seemed to make more sense to see her here, given that she was happy for us to speak to her in central London."

"Get her out of here quickly, Maeve. We're getting enough attention from the media as it stands because of these shootings. I would rather not make the front page of every tabloid in the country because Savannah Wentworth happens to be related to some murder victims."

"I have no interest in spinning it out, sir."

A knock on Godley's door from Derwent,

who looked to be fizzing with excitement. "Kerrigan, she's here."

There was no need to ask who he meant. I left him to get his own pep talk from Godley, hoping that he might have calmed down a bit by the time he made it into the interview room I'd booked. It was on the ground floor and windowless — not quite what Savannah Wentworth was used to, probably, but she would have to cope with it. I stomped down the stairs, feeling prickly with irritation. Godley was picking on me. There was no reason to tell me off for arranging a routine interview in a routine way. I was pretty sure it had to do with putting me in my place for asking about Derwent's exclusion from the other investigation. It was even more of an insult that Derwent himself hadn't been remotely grateful. I came into the reception area in a bad mood and found it to be unusually crowded. It took me a second but I spotted a very tall, very slim dark-haired woman with her back to me, standing up by the seats.

"Savannah Wentworth?"

She turned and smiled. "No. I'm Zoe Prowse." She was mixed race and exceedingly pretty, with pale-brown skin and striking light-blue eyes. She had a scattering of freckles across her nose, which was pierced, and white, even teeth. She also had a row of hoops the length of one ear, and her hair was shaved in horizontal bands on that side.

"I'm Savannah." I hadn't noticed her at first because Zoe had been doing a good job of blocking her from view, I realized. I wasn't the only person in the lobby who was looking for her, even if I was the only one who had a good reason to want to identify her. She stood up, and up, and up, so that I felt like a midget. I was used to being taller than most women — and men, for that matter — but Savannah and her companion had inches on me. Both of them were dressed casually in jeans and flat sandals, but on Savannah the outfit looked as if it had come straight from the pages of a magazine. She was far more conventional in her style than Zoe — one piercing in each ear, impeccably groomed hair — but I couldn't stop staring at her because in person she was flawless, with that angular beauty that's somehow otherworldly. She was exceedingly slender, her skin stretched over cheekbones that were razor-sharp, but it suited her. She wasn't wearing any makeup at all and her skin was perfect, her coloring delicate. She did resemble her father but there was some genetic quirk that had refined his features to make them out-standingly beautiful in her. I thought it would probably be impossible to take a bad picture of her, which was presumably why she was such a star.

Reminding myself why I was there, I stopped gawping and introduced myself, aware that everyone in the lobby was trying their hardest to eavesdrop. I had been expecting a diva but what I got was a serious young woman who seemed a little anxious, fiddling with the cuffs of her long-sleeved top.

"I'm sorry this took a little while to set up. I know it's really important. I've been really busy for the past few days."

"It's just a chat," I found myself saying, wanting to reassure her. "No need to worry."

"Is it okay for Zoe to come in with me? I think she would be really helpful."

"I'm sure that would be fine." If she needed her assistant to remind her of dates and times, that didn't surprise me. The celebrity lifestyle had to be a confusing one. I led the way to the interview room, noting as soon as I opened the door that it stank of aftershave. It didn't take a supersleuth to trace it to its source, which was a nervous DI Derwent, rubbing his right hand on his trousers to dry it before extending it to Savannah.

"Miss Wentworth. It's a pleasure to meet you." He pumped her hand enthusiastically as she murmured something that might have been "Thank you" and sank into one of the stained plastic chairs. Zoe sat down in the corner behind her, unnoticed. She was probably used to being ignored when in Savannah's company.

"Thank you for coming in to see us today." Derwent was still laying on the charm for all he was worth.

"I thought it was best to get it over with when I was free this afternoon. I'm hard to get hold of. I travel a lot."

"Part of your job, isn't it?"

"Yes. Not my favorite bit, actually." She crossed one long leg over the other, swinging her foot. "It has its moments, though. I've just come back from South Africa. Beautiful place."

"When did you get back?"

"Last Saturday." She looked over her shoulder to Zoe, who nodded agreement. "I did an editorial shoot for a new magazine on Monday, all day. Since then, lots of meetings and a bit of downtime. It was good that I wasn't supposed to be traveling, given what happened to Vita and Laura. You'd never have tracked me down."

"When did you find out about it?" Derwent asked.

"My mother rang me on Monday as soon as she heard about it." Savannah bit her lip, looking frail and anguished. I recalled that a lot of modeling was basically playing a part, and wondered how deeply she really felt about them. "It was such a shock. I mean, I didn't know Laura very well, but I'd seen her and her sister grow up, off and on. And Vita — she wasn't my favorite person in the world, but I wouldn't have wished her harm."

"When did you last see them?"

"A couple of years ago, maybe? I'm not totally sure."

"From what I understand, she was the reason you fell out with your father," I said. Derwent being reverent was amusing up to a point, but we couldn't let Savannah walk out without finding out more about her relationship with Kennford's second family, even if it made her angry.

Anger, however, did not seem to be the dominant emotion. Savannah's expression changed from one second to the next, the sorrow replaced by mocking amusement. "Who told you that?"

"Gossip," I admitted.

"Well, your source was a bit off on that one. I mean, I'm sure she wasn't weeping into her pillow about it, but I don't think she was particularly bothered about the real reason Dad didn't want to talk to me anymore. I thought it was all coming from him, from the way he reacted."

"What was the reason, then?" Derwent demanded.

"I don't want it to go outside this room."

"You have my word." It certainly sounded as if he meant it, and at the time he probably did. He would have promised a lot to get the inside story on Philip Kennford.

Savannah looked again at Zoe, turning around in her seat to do so. Zoe nodded, her expression neutral.

"Dad found it impossible to accept that I prefer women to men."

"As in . . ."

"As in I sleep with women. I am a lesbian. A dyke." Savannah's voice had risen and Zoe leaned forward in her chair to put a hand on her shoulder. The model covered it with her own hand for a second, then released it. "Sorry. I shouldn't shout."

"I didn't know that." I could almost have felt sorry for Derwent, whose face seemed to have frozen in an awkward half-smile. Since he didn't seem to be capable of speech, I went on. "That's a well-kept secret, isn't it?"

"It's no one else's business." Savannah spoke tartly and I saw her father's personality in her for the first time.

"Who knows about it?"

"You. My parents. Zoe. My agent. No one else." She hesitated. "Having said that, I presume Dad told Vita but I asked him not to tell anyone else.

"Why's that? Do you think it would be bad for your reputation?"

"No. At least, I don't think it would be. My agent found out by accident — it wasn't as if I went and told her to see what she'd say. She wasn't bothered but she agreed not to talk about it to anyone."

Derwent leaned back in his chair, recovering his composure a bit. "Can't see why you need to make it into a big secret in this day and age. People are used to that sort of thing. It wouldn't be much of a scandal."

"I just didn't feel I needed to tell the world, that's all. There are some things that are better kept private. And my job is all about how I look. People can make me into anything they want. The less they know about the real me, the more intrigued they are. I don't do press interviews. I don't give quotes to magazines. I keep my personal life to myself. It makes people focus on the image, not the reality, and that works for me."

"Don't you owe your fans the truth?"

The blue eyes were ice cold. "Just because I make a living out of being famous doesn't mean everyone is entitled to know every detail of my private life." She turned to me. "I bet you don't tell everyone at work what you get up to behind closed doors."

Derwent got in before I had a chance to reply. "She doesn't need to. It's common knowledge."

I glared at him. "There are no secrets on the team, but it would be nice if there were some." To Savannah, I said, "I can see your point."

"Well then." She looked from me to Derwent and back again, not really understanding what either of us meant. "What happened with me and Dad was that I came out to him last year and suddenly he wasn't so keen to boast about how I was his favorite daughter.

It was ironic, really, because you'd think fancying women would be something we'd have in common."

There was a world of hurt in her voice but she would have died rather than admit it.

"He's pretty open about it," I said.

"Has he tried it on with you? No? Give him time." She rolled her eyes. "No one's safe. He made a pass at my teacher once, at a parent-teacher meeting, in front of Mum. That didn't go down too well. Other people's mothers at parties and school concerts. When I was older, friends of mine too. Teenagers, I mean. It's gross, when you come to think about it."

"Did he ever do anything? Try it on with someone underage?" Derwent asked.

"Nothing illegal. But he'd make comments. You know — you've turned into a very lovely young lady, someone's going to be lucky to get you. He thought it was charming." She shuddered. "You get a lot of that in modeling, when you're young. Clients and photographers, mainly. You get used to it, but it's never nice. I wouldn't have liked it, and I'm sure it pissed off my friends. He's just an old creep, when you come down to it."

"Do you miss him?" I asked.

There was a long silence. "I miss the person I thought he was. Nothing has disappointed me so much as his refusal to respect me and my identity. I always made allowances for him. I believed in unconditional love, no matter how angry I was about things he'd done. I always tried to see the good in him. I accepted the fact that he was a womanizer and no one was off-limits. I forgave him for leaving my mother, even though she was really hard work when I was growing up." Savannah's eyes filled with tears, which she blinked away. "Sorry."

"There's no need to apologize. This must be difficult for you," I said gently.

"It's all old news." She sniffed a couple of times before Zoe leaned forward again, this time with a tissue. "I met Zoe last year and fell in love, and Dad couldn't deal with it. He wouldn't even meet her when I asked him to. And Zoe was really looking forward to getting to know him too."

I looked at Zoe, who had a strictly noncommittal expression on her face. It wasn't usually the girlfriend or boyfriend who was too bothered about what the parents thought, whether they were gay or straight. I had a suspicion it had been Savannah's idea all along.

"Still, I don't regret any of it." She blew her nose loudly, somehow managing to look elegant rather than a pink snotty mess, as I would have been. "He didn't seem to understand that it doesn't matter to me that Zoe's a woman. She could have been anything. I fell in love with the person, not her gender.

You can't help who you fall in love with. It's about a mental and spiritual connection, not a physical one. And Zoe and I were meant to be together. We're soul mates. When we met, it was like I was looking in a mirror and seeing Zoe look back. We had so much in common it was crazy. I couldn't have stopped myself from falling for her even if I'd wanted to."

Derwent was looking frankly skeptical. I hurried to get in before he could say anything awful. "Was your dad shocked, do you think?"

"Repulsed. I'd had boyfriends before, you see. I didn't think I'd ever be attracted to a woman." She shook her head. "I'm still not. I always feel like a fraud when I say I'm a lesbian, and that's why I don't want anyone making a big deal out of it or labeling me. I just love Zoe."

Zoe herself was looking remote, as if she'd tuned out. I wondered how she felt about Savannah's comments. Her sexuality was none of my business, but I found it strange that she didn't seem to be at ease with it, for all her anger with her father. Savannah seemed to be trying to say that she didn't even see Zoe as female, which struck me as borderline insulting. The woman was ultra-feminine, despite the piercings and the hard-edge haircut. I couldn't imagine what it would be like to find yourself attracted to a member of the same sex, but I thought of

Rob, and the physical effect of being close to him — that knee-quivering, heart-stopping excitement that hadn't diminished over the months we'd been together — and I couldn't separate that from the emotional side of our relationship. It certainly wasn't unimportant to me. I wondered if it was the strength of her father's reaction that had made Savannah Wentworth so defensive and secretive about her romantic life, or if she was inclined to be protective of her privacy anyway.

"How did your mum react when you told her?" I asked.

"Predictably. No grandchildren, poor me." Savannah grinned. "Firstly, I wasn't exactly broody before. Secondly, you'd think she hadn't ever heard of sperm donors. It's not an insurmountable issue."

"But she wasn't as upset as your father."

"It's different, I think. She was pretty unmoved. I imagine she thinks it's a phase and I'll grow out of it. Anyway, she's too wrapped up in herself and her own world to have the energy to think about me. *He* didn't like the fact that I was turning my back on men. He was always proud of people fancying me — which I'm not even going to try to pick apart because I personally think he needs years of therapy for various reasons and it would take a professional to understand that particular little quirk. Also, I don't know this for sure, but he might have been worried I'd be a bad influence on the twins. Tempt them away from the straight and narrow path." She rolled her eyes. "He's stupidly strict with them. I never had any of the rules they have to obey. No boyfriends, no social life to speak of. I'd have kicked off massively if he'd tried any of that shit on me."

"Why do you think he didn't?" Derwent asked.

"He wasn't around for my rebellious phase. He had already got together with Vita and the twins were really young. He just didn't get the chance. Or he didn't mind either way and the discipline was all from Vita."

"Tell me about Vita. What was she like?"

"The ice queen. She didn't care about anything except really uncomfortable interior design and the twins. She didn't like me. Too much competition for her girls. Like I say, I don't think she had anything to do with Dad not wanting to talk to me, but I don't think she was sad about it."

"She stopped him from going to your catwalk shows, I heard."

Savannah raised one eyebrow. "Same source of gossip as before?"

"Well, yes," I admitted.

"It's more accurate this time. She didn't like him being away from home for no good reason, and I quote. I started doing the European fashion week shows — that's London, Paris and Milan — when I was sixteen. I was a baby, really. My agency looked after me okay, but it meant a lot to have someone in the crowd who was there to see me. He'd take me out for dinner and tell me how great I'd been." She looked vulnerable now, her bottom lip quivering. "It was the one thing that gave me security, knowing he'd be there, in the audience and afterward. And he hadn't been around for so long, it was like meeting him for the first time when he started to show up. I remember thinking, I really like him. He's my dad and he's really cool." She grimaced, embarrassed. "I was young, like I said. Too young to find it shameful that my dad was trailing me around Europe trying to cop off with pretty young women."

"Was that why he was there?" Derwent asked.

"Oh, I don't know. I could be being cynical. I think he genuinely got a kick out of seeing me in the spotlight. It just so happened that he got to take advantage of where I was and who I was with. He loved the attention he got in restaurants and clubs when he turned up with two or three girls, never mind that one of them was his daughter."

Derwent shook his head. Almost to himself, he said, "The more I hear about him, the more I wish I had the chance to give him a good slap."

She laughed. "You don't want to listen to

385

me. He's not that bad, really. I'm just a bitter castoff. Not one but two cuckoos in the nest meant there was no room for me."

"Did you resent the twins?" I asked.

"Sure. Massively, at first. I sulked for months after they were born. But they were cute little things and they won me over. They were like little monkeys when they were small. Sweet little scrunched-up faces. Hard to believe when you think how grown-up they are now. Or were." She looked stricken. "I can't actually believe that Laura is dead. And what I've read about it makes it sound as if she died in a really horrible way."

"There's no good way to die when you're fifteen." Derwent was right but that didn't make it any less brutal. "Where were you on Sunday night, Miss Wentworth?"

"At home, which is in the middle of the middle of nowhere in Sussex. I was catching up on my rest after being away. I slept for fourteen hours that night. I must have been shattered."

"Were you alone?"

"Zoe was around." She turned to address her. "You were working, though, most of the time." To me, she said, "Zoe designs jewelry. She has a studio beside the house, on the other side of what used to be the stable yard."

"So she wasn't with you," Derwent said heavily.

"I was thirty yards away." Zoe's voice

wasn't loud, but it was definite. "Savannah didn't go anywhere on Sunday night. I'd have heard the car."

"She couldn't have missed it. And I'd have needed the car to go anywhere. It really is the back of beyond. It's down a mile-long track that isn't paved. No one would know the house was there unless they knew, if you see what I mean."

"Sounds perfect," I commented.

"It is. Too big for the two of us, really, but we like it."

"I'd have thought you'd need to be a bit closer to the center of London."

"Not really. It's forty minutes to the M25 from where we are. Manageable. And I always stay in a hotel in town if I've got an early start."

"Nice for some," Derwent said.

"One of the perks of the job. It's like being a footballer, though; it doesn't last forever. I have to make the most of it while I'm at the top."

"I suppose we should let you get back to it." Derwent looked at me. "Anything else? No? Thank you for your time, then, Miss Wentworth. Miss, er?"

"Prowse," Zoe said. "Zoe Prowse."

Savannah put her hands on the table, her fingertips beating a soundless tattoo on the wood. "Look, there was something I wanted to ask you before we go."

"Fire ahead."

"It's Lydia." The fingers tapped. "How is she?"

"She's doing okay," I said, which was sort of true.

"I doubt that. I doubt she's coping well at all." Savannah's eyes were fixed on me and I felt she could read the truth from my face.

"She's struggling a bit. But I think she had difficulties before the murders took place. They just won't have helped."

"That and you lot interrogating her, I imagine."

"We've been doing our best to be sensitive," I said quickly.

"The best thing you could do is leave her alone."

"I'm afraid we can't. Not yet. We need to talk to her again about what happened."

"Why?" Savannah demanded.

"Because we can't find out what we need to know about Laura and her mother from anyone else."

"What about Dad?"

"He's helped as much as he can."

"In his own world, I suppose. No real idea of what his kids are like. That's typical."

"He wouldn't be the first father of teenagers to be a bit clueless about what's going on in their lives."

"I suppose not." Savannah dug her nail into

a crack in the table, worrying at it. "Where is she?"

"In Twickenham with her aunt. Vita's sister."

"Renee? She's a fucking bitch." The vehemence surprised me; my mouth popped open and stayed that way for a fraction of a second too long.

"She's been very helpful."

"Don't even start." Savannah picked at the table, furious. "She's awful. Poor little Lydia."

"You've met this Renee, then," Derwent said. "I haven't had the pleasure."

"She's cold-blooded, like a lizard. What's Dad thinking?"

"He doesn't have custody of Lydia at the moment," I said.

"Because he's a suspect? Jesus. What a mess." She tapped her fingers again, this time at high speed. "Look, I want to take Lydia. I want to get her away from London and anything that reminds her of her mum and her sister. She needs space to grieve, and she needs time, and she needs distance from this horrible state of affairs."

"I'm sure you're right. But —"

"But what? It's not difficult." Savannah glared at me. "She's my half sister. Call her. Ask her what she wants to do. Ask Renee if she minds handing her over — I guarantee you, she won't give a flying fuck."

"What about your father? What will he say?"

"I don't know and I don't care. This isn't about him." She looked at Derwent. "Please. Just ask them. Ask Lydia first, then ask Renee. I guarantee both of them will agree to it." This was more like the demanding diva I had been expecting, but she was still charming, still pleasant in her manner. Usually, that wouldn't have made a blind bit of difference to Derwent.

"We could," he said slowly.

"Then do it. Come on. I have an alibi." She gave a glorious, wicked giggle that brought a smile to Derwent's face. "She'll be safe with me, I promise. And happy, as far as she can be in the circumstances."

"We just feel we might be able to help," Zoe said softly. "If she feels she's in a safe place she might open up a bit."

"That's true," I said, looking at Derwent. It wasn't the worst idea I'd ever heard.

"We'll ask her and her aunt. But I'm not making you any promises. I'm not going to try to convince either of them if they say no."

"I wouldn't ask you to." Savannah crossed her legs again, settling back in her chair. "We'll wait here while you go and call them."

"What, now?"

"No time like the present."

As if in a daze, Derwent stood up and went to the door. I followed, knowing that as soon as his brain kicked in, he'd realize he didn't know Renee's telephone number or address.

He was silent all the way back to the office which was fine by me since I was trying to walk and copy her details from my notebook at the same time. Just outside the door, he stopped. "What am I doing?"

"What the pretty lady told you to do." I handed him the page I'd been writing on and patted his arm consolingly. "Better make it snappy. You don't want to keep her waiting."

"Fucking hell." He said it without his usual conviction, though. "I feel like I've been run over by a Ferrari."

"But it was worth it just to get that close to one, wasn't it? Now remember, not a word to anyone about what we've just heard." I held the door open for him.

"Don't worry, I couldn't even if I wanted to." As he walked away, I heard him mutter in all seriousness, "Some things are just too tragic to say out loud."

CHAPTER SIXTEEN

"Now this," Derwent observed, "is all we
need."

"This" was Philip Kennford, striding
through the room with his jaw squared, heading for Godley's office. I slumped down in
my chair a couple of inches, not quite hiding
behind the computer screen in front of me
but definitely trying not to attract his attention. Derwent was even less subtle, plunging
under the desk opposite mine as if he'd
dropped something. I rolled back my chair so
I could see him.

"Are you going to stay there until he's
gone?"

"If I have to."

"I know he hit you, but I wouldn't have
thought you'd be scared of him."

"I'm not." Derwent showed me his watch.
"It's almost eight o'clock. I'm tired, I'm fed
up with doing paperwork and I'm hungry.
What I don't want is to get stuck in a slang-
ing match with twatface in there."

"Or another punch-up."

"I wouldn't dignify what happened last time with the word punch-up. He took a shot at me when I wasn't looking."

"It wasn't fair."

"No." Derwent narrowed his eyes suspiciously. "Are you laughing at me?"

"Never. I wouldn't dare. Even though you're crouching by the bin."

"The minute I come out, I'll get collared."

"You're paranoid." I looked across at Godley's office. "The door's shut. You could make a run for it while he's in there."

"Why didn't you tell me earlier?" Derwent backed out from under the desk and straightened up, dusting his knees off. "God, it's filthy under there."

"You can't get the cleaning staff these days."

"Don't blame them, love. Those are your crumbs."

"I don't eat at my desk," I said with dignity. "The last person who ate in here was you. I don't need to be a forensic expert to know that's the remains of your hot dog."

He squinted at the floor. "You might be right."

"I know I am. I saw you drop the crumbs."

Derwent picked up his jacket and slung it over his shoulder, hooked on one finger. His shirt sleeves were rolled up, his tie stuffed in one trouser pocket. He looked like an extra from a budget edition of *Miami Vice*. "Right.

Work's for losers. I'm out of here for the day."

Godley's timing was impeccable. "Josh? In here, please. You too, Maeve."

Derwent's shoulders slumped. "Ah, fuck. I knew this would happen."

"Come on. Time for the rematch." I led the way to Godley's office, wanting to get it over with. The boss had sounded tired but not angry, which I counted as a good sign. There was always the chance that he'd exhausted his irritation with me earlier when I'd got my not wholly warranted bollocking over Savannah. I slightly despised myself for caring, but I couldn't pretend that I was unmoved to be on Godley's shit list. I wanted him to respect me as a member of the team, not just a box ticked on some equal opportunities form, but some days that seemed like a very futile aspiration. Today had all the hallmarks of being one of them.

I picked up on the atmosphere in the room as soon as I walked through the door. Kennford was standing beside Godley's noticeboard, a scowl on his face. He glanced at me, then returned to studying the close-up shots of dead gangsters. He was more formally dressed than usual, as if he had come from court, though it wouldn't have been sitting for hours. His black pinstripe suit was tailored to give him a perfect V-shaped back and made the most of his height. Dressed to impress, I gathered, and wondered what he was there to say.

"Sit down, Maeve. Josh, get a move on." Godley had already sat down behind his desk. Derwent was taking his own sweet time about coming into the office, making a big deal out of closing the door quietly. It wasn't as if there were many people left to disturb; the place had emptied out for the day.

Godley leaned on his desk, tenting his fingers in front of his face so I had to guess at his expression. "Mr. Kennford is here because he wants to make an official complaint about you."

"With regard to what, exactly?" Derwent demanded, flinging himself into the chair beside mine like a stroppy teenager.

"With regard to placing my daughter in an unsuitable environment." Kennford turned around and glowered at Derwent. His hands had bunched into fists, I noticed. I also noticed I was directly between them. I really wished I'd picked somewhere else to sit. "Who are you to make decisions like that for her?"

"I didn't make any decisions for her. Nor did DC Kerrigan. Your other daughter asked if she could provide Lydia with a place to stay. I simply got in touch with your sister-in-law and passed on the offer."

"I'm sure she didn't even stop to think about it."

"She said it was up to Lydia, actually. She said she didn't mind either way."

She had said a lot more than that, I happened to know. She had had quite a lot to say about the strain it was placing on her family to have Lydia there, and the constant harassment from the media, and the inconvenience of taking Lydia to have her cut dressed as an outpatient, and the frustration she felt at the amount of time it was taking to find somewhere else for Lydia to go. She was a busy woman and Lydia needed more than she had to give. It was hard to see how Lydia was better off with her aunt than with her half sister, but I was interested to hear how Kennford would justify it.

"Yes, why not leave it to the self-harming, grief-stricken fifteen-year-old to decide where she goes and what happens to her?" Kennford ran his hands through his hair. "Why am I the only person who sees this as a problem?"

"Maybe because you're the only person who doesn't like her half sister." I hadn't meant to sound caustic, but Kennford glared.

"You don't know what you're talking about."

"I know Savannah was able to offer her a complete break from her normal routine, which is probably what she needs. I know Lydia didn't take very long to accept. I know Lydia definitely needs a lot of love and attention after what happened to her. Incidentally, did you get around to visiting her in hospital? Or were you too busy?" I was too angry with Kennford to think about whether what I was saying was appropriate.

"She was released before I had a chance to get there. I was in court."

"She was there overnight. Court finishes at four in the afternoon."

"Ever heard of visiting hours?"

"They wouldn't apply to you. You're her father."

"Well, I didn't know that."

"Because you didn't bother to find out."

"Maeve. That's enough." Godley's voice was thin with exhaustion.

"Is it?" I jerked my thumb in Kennford's direction. "He's come here to complain about us finding somewhere for Lydia to stay, and he didn't even bother to go and see her when I had told him about her injuries. I don't think that's fair. Do you?"

"Fair or not, Mr. Kennford is here because he has genuine concerns about his daughter's safety."

"What concerns?" I turned back to Kennford. "Do you think Savannah was involved in the murders?"

"I didn't say that," he snapped.

"If you're concerned about her being involved, you need to tell us why." I folded my arms. "You've left us in the dark, Mr. Kennford. You didn't even tell us about your other daughter. You know more than you've been letting on. If you genuinely think Lydia's in danger, you must tell us now."

"She had an alibi." Derwent yawned vastly after he'd spoken, not bothering to cover his mouth.

"Who did?" Godley asked.

"Savannah. She was home alone with her partner."

I was watching Kennford's face and saw his eyelids flicker at the last word. "Is that it? You're worried she'll turn Lydia into a —"

"Now, now." Derwent interrupted me, tutting. "You know we're not allowed to talk about that."

"I'm sure Superintendent Godley won't tell anyone else."

"That's how these things get out. You promise not to say anything, but then you tell one other person who you trust, and they tell one other person, and before you know it, it's common knowledge."

"Could someone please tell me what's going on?" Godley said in a tone that suggested he was running out of patience.

"Mr. Kennford has a problem with his eldest daughter's sexual orientation. Savannah has a girlfriend. But it's a secret." Derwent put his finger across his lips.

"I don't have a problem with it." Kennford sounded pained.

"You're a great big homophobe, Mr. Kenn-

398

ford. That's fine, though. I wouldn't be pleased either if my beautiful daughter turned out to be a bean-licker."

"For God's sake, do you have to be so crude?"

"It's not for His sake," Derwent said gravely. "I enjoy it."

Kennford turned back to Godley. "Look, I'm appealing to you as a father. I don't want Lydia with her half sister. I don't want to go into the reasons, but I'm not convinced it's a good environment for her. I want you to stop this before it goes any further."

Godley shook his head. "It's a family matter, Mr. Kennford. We need to know where Lydia is, and that she's safe there, but beyond that we aren't involved in her life. We're the police, not the social services. If you have any reason to believe Miss Wentworth is likely to threaten your daughter, please do tell us. If you have any evidence to prove Miss Wentworth was involved in the murders of your other daughter and wife, again, I hope you'd tell us. But you can't expect us to intervene in a family feud."

"You will when it suits you, I've noticed." Kennford turned around and stared at the noticeboard again. I had the impression he wasn't seeing it. "What do you suggest I do?"

"Speak to Lydia. Share your concerns with her, if you like." Godley leaned his head on his hand as if he couldn't hold it up any longer. "Where are you staying now, Mr. Kennford? Still in the Temple?"

"No. With a friend."

"Is it suitable for your daughter to stay with you?"

He wavered, but came down on the side of the truth. "Not really. I don't think either of them would like it. It's a female friend, as it happens."

"A close friend?" Derwent couldn't have been expecting an answer and he didn't get one, unless you counted Kennford's nostrils flaring.

"Well, as you're not able to provide her with a safe home yourself," Godley said gently, "perhaps it's for the best that she's with a family member. Someone close to her in age, rather than her aunt."

"You think so."

"In the absence of any evidence to the contrary, yes."

"Who is this friend you're staying with?" Derwent demanded.

"No one you would know."

"One of your old clients, maybe?"

Kennford stiffened. "What's that supposed to mean?"

"We had an interesting chat with one of your ex-girlfriends, DC Kerrigan and I. A Miss . . ."

"Adamkuté," I supplied. Derwent couldn't or wouldn't get his head around her name, even for the pleasure of revealing to Kennford that we knew about her.

"Niele?" Kennford rocked back on his heels, looking shaken, then tried to smile. "Where did you dig her up?"

"Never you mind." Derwent frowned and scratched his head, pretending to be puzzled. "Here, it wasn't strictly ethical what you did with her, was it?"

"It was a private matter. Nothing happened until she was no longer my client. The only point of interest is how we met, and lots of people form relationships with those they meet through work."

"You were bloody lucky she never got around to making an official complaint." Derwent turned to me. "Did you get the feeling she was still a bit annoyed, Maeve? Because I had the impression all she needed was a little bit of encouragement to take it further."

"You could be right."

"Do you think we should go round and speak to her again? Maybe see how she's feeling since we raked it all up again?"

"You can play games with me all you like but you can't pretend that Niele isn't a criminal. No one will believe anything she says." The color had risen in Kennford's face.

"Ah-ah, Mr. Kennford. Not a criminal. All charges were dropped at halftime, weren't they? Because of your brilliant advocacy, it appears."

"What about the fact that she's an extortionist? How would that go down?"

Derwent shrugged. "You tell me. Did you report her for it at the time?"

"No."

"Did you give her any money yourself?"

A muscle in Kennford's jaw twitched as he clenched his teeth. "Vita paid her off."

Derwent shook his head, all in sorrow. "But Vita's not such a great witness anymore, is she? Niele can say the money was a gift. It's probably a defense you'd be happy to run with, if you were her barrister."

"She's a drug addict. Did you know that? And she runs with a bad crowd. Serious criminals, I mean. The sort of people who do violence like that." He pointed at the noticeboard that hung behind him, the pictures a symphony in gray and red. They blurred into one image from a distance. Blood on the pavement tended to look the same no matter who had shed it.

"Her being a druggie and into gang stuff — none of that stopped you from shagging her blind," Derwent pointed out.

"Which was my mistake, I'll admit. But aside from an error of judgment, I did nothing wrong. It was consensual and it ended. She is exactly as reasonable about it as you would expect her to be, given that I dumped her. Don't tell me you fell for her 'he took advantage of me' line, because it's bullshit."

"She got pregnant, didn't she?" Derwent sucked air through his teeth. "Would have thought you'd have been more careful, given all you knew about her background and so forth."

"Accidents happen."

"Accidents leave medical records that will corroborate her case."

"She didn't do a DNA test."

"How do you know?" Derwent dropped the false bonhomie. "Listen to me, Mr. Kennford. You come in here and threaten us with a formal complaint when we're just doing our job, so you have to be prepared to get the same treatment. If you want to take this further, feel free. But I will personally go round and sit with your Lithuanian lovely while she writes her letter to the Bar Council, and help her spell all the long words. And even though I might not believe you took advantage of her, I think she'll convince them very nicely."

"You're a *shit.*" Kennford was trembling with anger.

"No, Mr. Kennford, I'm a copper who's trying to work out who killed your wife and your daughter, and I'm doing my best not to let your frankly annoying attitude put me off. They deserve answers and so does Lydia."

"And what do I deserve?"

"Oh, Mr. Kennford. You ask questions for a living. You should know better than that."

403

Derwent shook his head, grinning widely. "I'd start telling you but we'd still be here at midnight."

"Is that all we can do for you, Mr. Kennford?" Godley was as urbane as ever, ultra-civilized in contrast with his DI. "Or was there anything else you wanted to talk to us about?"

"There was one thing." He slid his hand inside his jacket and took out an envelope that he flicked across the table to Godley. "I'd like you to have a word with this prick."

"What is it?" Derwent was straining to see.

"A sympathy card." Kennford's jaw was clenched. "It came in the post this morning."

"To which address? Your house?" Godley asked.

"Chambers."

Godley opened the card to read it, so I could see the image on the front, a white lily leaning on a cross. "With Sympathy" was looped across the top in silver cursive script. It was just the wrong side of tasteful. " 'I'm sorry to hear of your bereavement. Jesus will look after them, and he'll look after you if you let him into your heart. Maybe this is an opportunity for you to come to Him. I hope you find happiness. C. Blacker.' Do you know who that is?"

"Yes, and so should you," Kennford snapped.

"Christopher Blacker," I explained, not

404

actually surprised that the boss had forgotten his name. "He was unhappy with the job Mr. Kennford did when he represented him on a rape charge. We spoke to him yesterday."

"And told him what had happened, presumably. So I have to put up with patronizing shit like that." Kennford pointed at it, his finger shaking. "Tell him to stay the hell away from me."

"You could take it at face value, mate. Forgiveness, as sold by Clinton's Cards." Derwent tweaked it out of the superintendent's hands so he could read it himself. "Think he was serious or ripping the piss? He told us he's a Christian. He might have meant it."

"I don't care if he meant it or if he didn't. I view it as harassment. I don't want to have anything to do with him and I'd appreciate you telling him as much."

"I'll have a word," Derwent said, not looking as if he thought it was particularly urgent. I thought that was probably for effect, though — he would be more concerned than he was letting on to Kennford. I was bothered by it myself. There had been something about Chris Blacker, still waters that ran too deep for comfort. Sending a card to Kennford was a passive-aggressive move in my book, but one that was calculated to draw attention to himself, which surely wouldn't be his intention if he was the killer.

Then again, Blacker was certainly clever enough for a double bluff or two.

"Can I keep this?" Derwent asked, waving the card.

"I don't care what you do with it. *I* don't want it." Kennford was looking irritable. "Look, are you going to help my daughter or not?"

"You haven't given us any reason to interfere with her wishes. As far as we know, she's going to a safe place and happy to be there."

Kennford swore under his breath but didn't say anything.

"Look, Mr. Kennford, I don't want Lydia's well-being to be compromised. I'd like to ask you again if there's any specific reason for her not to stay with your other daughter." There was a pause before Kennford shook his head. "Then there's nothing else I can do."

The barrister looked at each of us in turn, but again with that sightless gaze that made me think he wasn't quite with it. Moving with great dignity, he went straight to the door and walked out.

"Thank you for your time," Derwent called after him. "Do drop in whenever you like."

"Josh, do I really need to tell you not to taunt him?" Godley sighed. "Look, both of you, I hope you know what you're doing. Is Lydia safe where she's going?"

"As far as I know," I said. "If Savannah's

an actor, she's bloody good. I thought she was genuine and honest."

"Me too. And you know I don't think anyone is honest," Derwent added.

"We've offered to drive Lydia to the house tomorrow anyway, so we'll get a chance to see how the two of them get on."

"Why did you decide to do that?" Godley asked.

"Basically so we could have a nose around Savannah Wentworth's house," I admitted. "But also so we could talk to Lydia in the car. I thought not being face-to-face would take some of the pressure off and we might get a bit more out of her."

"Do you think she has more to tell you?"

"I'm sure of it."

Derwent yawned again. "What do you think his problem is?"

"Kennford? No idea. But we can't take his concerns seriously until he's prepared to talk to us." Godley shook his head. "If he'd seemed more bothered about Lydia's safety from the start, I might be a bit more understanding now. But he didn't even bother to go to see her in the hospital. I can't understand that."

"If it had been your daughter nothing would have kept you out of there."

Godley didn't answer, his face grim, and I remembered that his daughter was one of the subjects he considered to be off-limits. Derwent must have recognized that he'd made a mistake, because he moved on.

"I'll give Blacker a call. Tell him to mind his own business."

"Do you think it's strange that he sent the card?" Godley asked.

"Hell, yes. Don't you?" Derwent slid it into an evidence bag, holding it gingerly. "It hasn't been treated with the care you'd want for an exhibit but I'll give it to Kev Cox. See if he can use it for comparative purposes against any of the material he recovered from the Wimbledon house."

"Good idea."

"There is one other reason why Kennford might have turned up here to shout at us," I said.

"What's that?" Godley asked.

"To get an update on what we've found out so far. To throw us off the scent, if we were even close to being on it. To distract us and make us suspicious about Savannah instead of him."

"Are you still suspicious about him?"

"No reason not to be, as far as I'm concerned." Derwent tapped the edge of the evidence bag on the desk, considering it. "And it's not just that I don't like the job he does. I haven't liked him from the start."

"You don't like anyone," I pointed out.

"True. But I know when someone is trying to bullshit me. And that's all I got from him, from start to finish." He jerked his thumb in the general direction Kennford had taken. "We've only got half the story, believe me. And when we get the rest of it, I promise you, we'll have our case."

I have no idea how it happened, but I ended up asking Derwent if he wanted to come out for a drink. It was something to do with the way he loitered by his desk, flicking through the folders on it in an aimless way. I got the feeling he had nowhere to go once he left the office, despite his rush to leave earlier. Whether I was right about that or not, he had agreed to come before I got halfway through a slightly awkward invitation.

"I don't even know if it'll be a good pub," I was still saying when we were halfway to London Bridge on a packed Tube train. "Or what the company will be like. I haven't met any of them before."

"These are your boyfriend's new colleagues, aren't they? I know a few guys on the Flying Squad. Don't worry about me. You won't have to hold my hand."

"Definitely not." I didn't have to fake being appalled at the idea.

Derwent dropped a heavy arm across my shoulders. "And I won't leave you to be a wallflower either. You stick with your Uncle Josh and I'll make sure you have a good time."

"I don't need you to make sure I have a good time." I used the swaying of the carriage as it rattled over some bumpy track to duck out from under his arm. "I just thought you deserved a drink, that's all. It's been a tough few days."

"You don't know the half of it."

"I don't want to know any details of your personal life. Just to avoid any doubt about that."

"Of course you're curious. Why wouldn't you be? Working closely alongside me, you must wonder occasionally what's going on inside my mind. Who I'm thinking about. What I get up to in the evenings, when we're not together."

"No, really." We pulled into a station and I peered to see where we were. "Waterloo. Oh, shit. The platform is packed."

"Get ready for a crush." As Derwent said it, a great swell of people began to push past us heading for the doors. I turned my head sideways, acutely embarrassed as the DI's body pressed against mine. "It's nothing personal, Kerrigan."

"Of course not."

"Still, I've had worse experiences on the Underground."

"I'm not sure I have." I absolutely refused to make eye contact with him from a distance of six inches, even though I could feel him staring at the side of my face. The carriage was filling up behind him, the passengers who'd been waiting forcing their way on despite the fact that the doors were already beeping to indicate they were about to close. He gave a snort of laughter and moved back slightly as the doors finally slid home, leaving a platform full of reproachful faces behind.

"You should see your expression. Pure misery."

"It's about fifty degrees down here and I'm enduring full body contact with my boss. Why are you even surprised I'm miserable?"

"Oh, I'm not, really. It must be torture for you, being so close to me."

"It is," I said, my tone absolutely sincere. "But I'm fairly sure it's not in the way you're thinking."

"Always fighting it, aren't you?"

"And I always will."

"Yeah, you don't want to get a reputation for shagging your colleagues."

"Which is the only reason I'm not tempted, let me tell you."

Derwent grinned, knowing full well I wouldn't dream of having anything to do with him. "Right. Well, let's enjoy being out of the office and away from this shitty case for once. The first round is on me."

He was as good as his word, fighting to the bar through a packed pub when we eventually emerged from the Underground and located it. The street outside was full of drunk

411

people talking too loudly and smoking as if they were getting paid to do it. Inside, it was hotter still but the fug of smoke was pleasantly absent. I could only imagine what it would have been like in there before the ban. I jostled through the crowd to stand in what seemed to be the only free space in the entire bar and checked my phone. While I was reading my messages a tall, frosty glass of gin landed on the shelf beside me with a clink of ice cubes. A bottle followed.

"Tonic. Add your own. I'd go for as little as you can stand and take the evening from there."

"Top advice, boss." Desperately thirsty after the journey, I emptied the bottle in anyway and drained it in one go. I surfaced gasping. "Was that a double?"

"It was indeed." Derwent handed me another glass that he'd had tucked under his arm. "Here's another. Get it down."

"I'd quite like to be not blind drunk when I meet Rob's colleagues, thanks."

"Whatever." Derwent had lined up a pint for himself to follow the one in his hand. "Any sign of them?"

"Rob's just texted me. They're in the back room, apparently. I can't face the struggle to get there. I said we'd wait here until the crowd thinned out a bit." I looked around. "These are post-work boozers. They'll be hungry by now and this place doesn't serve food. I reckon half an hour will see us right."

It was a small enough pub, a weird combination of traditional boozer and swanky bar. I guessed it had been redecorated recently and the tiny chandeliers, blue velvet banquettes and wooden floor were new. The big mahogany bar was emphatically not, dented and scratched by generations of drinkers. Mirrors ran down both sides of the room, doubling the reflections of hundreds of people all crammed in, shouting at the tops of their voices. I craned to see the room at the back, getting a vague impression that it was even more crowded than the part we were in. I couldn't see Rob anywhere.

"When did they get here?"

"An hour ago."

"Great. They'll be softening up nicely. No one will be able to remember to be discreet." Derwent scooped up his second drink. "Come on. I could waste time talking to you, but there's gossip to be had. Faint heart never won fair Flying Squad."

"You go first," I urged.

"Shy?"

"No, but you're bigger than me and people are more likely to get out of your way."

"True. Stick close."

I did as he said, staying within touching distance of his back as he shouldered through the crowd, leaving a variety of shaken and annoyed drinkers behind him. He made it to the doorway of the inner room and stopped dead, so that I crashed into him. I leaned forward and said into his ear, "What's up? Can't you see them?"

Instead of answering, he turned around, and it was as if a switch had flipped in his head. The jovial fellow drinker was gone; he was back to being the faintly sinister superior officer I found so unsettling. "Look, I've turned a blind eye to this so far but I can't ignore it anymore. This is unprofessional behavior and I'm surprised at you."

"What?"

"It's completely irresponsible to go out drinking when we're in the middle of a big case. Two, if you count the gang stuff. I might get to work on that yet, and I don't want the Kennford case to get forgotten, even if you're not too concerned about the fact we have a double murder to solve."

"What are you talking about?" I looked at him, bewildered.

"I'm just surprised how unprofessional you are."

"Unprofessional," I repeated stupidly.

"You can't do your best work if you're tired and hungover."

"No, but I wasn't planning on a big one." *And you were the one buying doubles . . .*

"You should get out of here." He started to move forward so I had to step back. "We both should. Best thing you can do is go back to

414

the office and read the notes on the interviews again. I want a report on them on my desk first thing tomorrow morning — anything that bothers you, any major points you think we need to revisit."

"I don't understand. What's going on, Josh?"

"It's up to you. If you want to prove you take your job seriously, you'll leave now. If not . . ." he shrugged. "Then I'll know where you stand."

It was probably the gin that made me slow to catch on. He had been moving me away from the back room as he spoke, but I was taller than Derwent and still had a good view over his shoulder.

A view that, at that moment, consisted of my boyfriend sitting in the corner of the room, turned away from me. A fair-haired woman stood behind him, her hourglass figure flattered by a tight-fitting skirt and top. Unseen by anyone at the table, she was running her hand down the back of his neck and along his shoulder in a gesture that spoke of familiarity, and affection, and intimacy. I was fairly sure I recognized her from the photographs I'd seen the previous night. Rob's ears were red and as I watched he leaned forward so his elbows rested on his knees, moving away from her.

But then, he did know I was in the pub. And however much he enjoyed sneaking around, he'd hardly want to get caught. Derwent had obviously seen my face change. He risked a glance over his shoulder, then turned back to me. "Ah. You've seen them."

"I have."

"It was worth a try."

"To save Rob from getting in trouble? Big of you. But I suppose that's how it works. You boys stick together and try to fool us. After all, we're just stupid birds. We deserve what we get."

"That wasn't what I was trying to do." Derwent shook his head. "Ah, fuck. I think I'd better go. What's your plan?"

"I don't know, exactly. Mark my bloody territory, that's for sure."

"Just don't make a scene."

"Why shouldn't I?"

There was an unfamiliar look on Derwent's face, a look that I slowly recognized as sympathy. "Because if I'm not mistaken, Blondie is Rob's boss. So you might be the official girlfriend, but you don't have the advantage, do you? And whatever she's up to, you might have to bite your tongue for his sake. If you really care about him, I mean."

I thought that was his parting shot, but I was wrong. He had one left, and he delivered it as he moved away, heading for the door.

"Not much of a choice, is it? Fuck up his career or kiss your relationship goodbye. It sucks to be you, Kerrigan, and no mistake."

I really, truly wished I didn't agree with him.

If I hadn't seen what Derwent had been trying to hide from me, I might not have noticed anything strange was going on, which was actually the opposite of reassuring. Rob turned his head and saw me about two seconds after Derwent faded into the crowd, so I had no alternative but to smile, and make my way through the back room toward him, and allow myself to be folded into his arms for a kiss that tasted of cold beer and went on much longer than I would have expected.

"That's a big welcome," I said, when I could speak.

"I missed you."

Oh, yeah, I thought, looking into his eyes and seeing nothing but sincerity. *Or this is your way of warning your boss to back off because your current girlfriend has just arrived.*

"I only saw you this morning."

"That was a long time ago."

He wasn't wrong. I felt as if I'd been up for days. I was jittery from lack of sleep and spoiling for a fight as a result, but I made myself talk to him civilly about my day, and his, and what I had missed by getting to the pub a bit late. I was fairly sure he hadn't noticed anything wrong when he offered to introduce me to his colleagues. Of course, it was sod's law that the first person we encountered when he led me to the corner table was Deborah Ormond, who turned to look at me with a wry, red-lipsticked smile that I longed to smack off her face.

"And who's this?"

"This is Maeve, my girlfriend. She works on Charles Godley's murder squad."

"So you're the reason Rob left and came to join us."

"One of them," I agreed.

"Then I suppose I should say thank you."

"There's no need for that." I smiled thinly. "Rob made up his own mind to go."

"He knows his own mind," she said with a quick look at him that I couldn't quite interpret. His face was unhelpfully neutral when I glanced at it. I swallowed down the hard knot of anger that was threatening to close my throat and agreed with her with a little laugh that made me sound like I was a total airhead.

"Well, I'd better not monopolize you." She made it sound like the excuse it was. I knew what she meant. *This conversation is boring me and you are too gauche for words.*

"That's right," Rob said easily. "You've got to meet a lot of people, Maeve. They've been asking about you."

"You'd better tell me what you've been saying." I smiled at him again, ignoring DI Ormond as she stepped sideways, out of our path, but I was acutely aware of her scanning me from head to toe, and doubtless being unimpressed with what she saw. I had already noted her very good highlights and expensive haircut, not to mention the fact that enough buttons were undone on her shirt to show off more than a hint of lace underneath. I had also noticed that she had been pretty and was still very attractive, but that there were crow's feet around her eyes and lines around her mouth. Somehow, that didn't help me as much as it might have. She was older than me, true, but she had experience to show for it, and assurance. Maybe Rob wanted something different. Maybe he was hoping to get found out so I would take the hint and leave him his freedom. And maybe the photographs had been someone's way of tipping me off.

I met five or six of his new colleagues and talked to them without taking in a single name or anything they said. I drank another gin and tonic and laughed at jokes I hadn't heard or understood, and everyone seemed to think I was delightful. Every time I looked at DI Ormond she was deep in conversation with someone, or checking her phone. We never made eye contact but I had the impression she was watching me all the same. And Rob never let go of me, keeping one hand in the small of my back or wrapped around my waist, which wasn't his usual style at all.

"Another one?" A brick-faced DS pointed at my glass and I realized it was empty.

"No. I'm going to hit the road."

"Really?" Rob sounded surprised. "So soon?"

"I know. But I got so little sleep last night." I yawned, not actually pretending to be tired. "If I keep drinking I'll fall over sideways."

"More booze for you, then," the DS said with a loud laugh.

"Seriously, I'm going to head off. I have a long day tomorrow."

"I'll come with you." Rob put down his pint.

"Don't be silly. You're having a good time. You don't need to escort me home." I squeezed his arm affectionately. "Stay."

"It's no big deal." He was frowning a little. I made a bigger effort to look as if I didn't have a care in the world apart from being a bit short on sleep, and lowered my voice.

"You don't want to get a reputation for being on a short lead, do you? What would the boys say if you left now?"

"Who cares?" He shrugged. "I've never worried about that kind of thing before."

"Well, it's a new team. New rules. And I don't want to be the reason you get a bad reputation. I feel guilty enough as it is."

"I keep telling you, it was my choice to go." He sounded irritated, which was good. There was a far better chance he'd let me leave alone that way, and all I wanted was to be alone so I could think. Not to brood, I assured myself. Just to review the evidence and decide if I was being paranoid.

"I know. But I still worry about it. Even though your new colleagues seem lovely."

"I'm not so sure about that." He grinned. "Are you sure you don't want me to come with you?"

"Absolutely. I have stuff to do, and you're having fun." I leaned over and kissed him, resisting the urge to look around halfway through so I could check if DI Ormond was watching. "Try and find out who sent the pictures, if you haven't already."

"I will."

"I'll see you later on."

He was still holding my hand as I walked away, but I broke free and didn't look back.

Once I was out of the pub, in the fresh air, I began to regret leaving him to Deborah Ormond. I had no doubt that she would talk to him about me. Say something patronizing, probably. That seemed to come naturally to her. I plunged down into the hot, airless Underground and got a seat this time, changed trains without thinking about it and emerged for the walk to Rob's flat hopping mad. She was a very attractive woman, if you liked them on the weathered side of experienced. Maybe it was a power thing for him, sleeping with an older woman. Reducing her to shivers of pleasure. Taking her breath away. I wrapped my arms around myself, fighting back tears I really didn't want to shed, and when I found myself on our street I couldn't remember how I'd got there.

I let myself into the building and stopped by the post boxes to collect our letters. Another catalog slithered out of the box, fat and glossy in its shrink-wrap. Bloody mailing lists, I thought, taking the stairs three at a time.

The really annoying thing was that I hadn't wanted to believe Rob was like the others. I'd wanted to believe he'd meant what he said, and I'd thought it was my problem that I couldn't accept he loved me. The triumph of self-doubt over years of experience of disappointing or lying or cheating men. Or men who did all three at the same time.

"Never ignore the bad feeling. Never pretend everything's okay." I said it out loud as I let myself in and let the door slam behind me. It was all very well to focus on the good things, but that didn't mean ignoring the bad ones. That didn't make me a pessimist, I told myself, putting my bag down. It didn't make me impossible to love. It made me sadder and wiser than most.

I started to sort through the post, listening to the messages on the phone at the same time. Two from Mum featuring thinly disguised nagging, as usual; one from an old friend, Aisling, to let me know she was both engaged and pregnant. I paused in the act of ripping open a fat envelope addressed to me. It looked like business post, the label typed and coded, but there was no company name on the stationery.

". . . which I know is completely the wrong way round but I can't honestly say I'm sorry about it. We're just so happy."

She sounded it. I tried not to think cynical thoughts — and I was genuinely pleased for her — but I decided not to phone her back for a few days. Just until things had settled down. And they were bound to settle down soon, one way or another.

I turned the envelope sideways to tip the contents out onto the kitchen table. "Shit."

With the end of a pencil, I spread it all out, sifting through the pile of slippery photographic paper so I could see everything laid out in black and white. It didn't get any better on closer inspection. In fact, it was a whole lot worse than I'd thought.

And I had no idea what to do.

CHAPTER SEVENTEEN

"You can't keep me in suspense."

"I don't want to talk about it." It was the same conversation Derwent and I had been having since he got to work. After forty minutes in the car in morning traffic, it was really starting to grate on me.

"You just need to let it out. Talk it over with an objective listener."

"If I wanted to do that, I'd find a better listener than you."

Derwent looked wounded. "Who's a better listener than me?"

"Almost anybody?"

He considered it for a second. "Fair point."

The one thing I'd decided the previous night was I wasn't going to let Derwent know anything more than I had to.

We had been heading toward Twickenham, but suddenly Derwent pulled across the road into a McDonald's.

"What are we doing here?" I said over the blare of a truck's horn. Derwent hadn't left as much space to make the turn as the Highway Code — or sanity — recommended.

"I'm hungry. I want a coffee."

"Look on the bright side," I said sourly. "At least your discretion means you got an early night and no hangover."

"And you didn't?" The keys jangled as Derwent pulled them out of the ignition, as if I'd just leave him there and drive off if he didn't pocket them before he got out. The idea was tempting now that I came to think about it. "Come on. I want the details. You look tired. What time did you leave?"

"None of your business." I looked tired because I hadn't come close to sleep the night before, but that wasn't from worrying about what Rob was getting up to. I had far bigger problems than that, not that I intended to discuss them with Derwent. Or anyone else, until I'd worked out the best course of action. Even thinking about it sent a chill over my skin, a faint sense of unease that shivered over me like a breeze on water.

"You're not hungover." He sniffed. "Weather like this, there's no hiding the booze sweats the morning after."

"I didn't stay that long," I admitted.

"Not having fun?"

"Not a lot."

"Did you manage to winkle your boyfriend out of the pub or did you leave him there?"

"I went home alone. By choice."

"Oh yeah."

"It's true. I didn't want to spoil his evening."

"You seemed to be set on doing just that when I left you."

I shook my head. "Not like that. I didn't want him to leave early because I didn't want his new team thinking I was clingy and controlling."

"Yeah, that's not you."

I couldn't tell if he meant it or if he was being sarcastic, but sarcasm was always a good bet with Derwent. "Look, I really don't want to talk about it, okay?"

"Okay. I get it." He opened his door. "You didn't tell me he was working with Debbie Ormond."

"I didn't think it would mean anything to you."

"Oh, it would have meant a lot, believe me."

I knew he was being cryptic on purpose to annoy me, but I couldn't stop myself. "Do you know her?"

"Know her? Better than most, as it happens. I know her very well indeed." He gave me a big, raised eyebrows grin, lots of teeth on display, and got out of the car before I could ask any follow-up questions. He sauntered into the McDonald's and spent an eternity scrutinizing the menu, then chatted to the teenage cashier while he was paying and stopped to read the headlines on a

426

discarded newspaper on his way out. I wasn't even slightly mollified by the fact that he returned to the car with two coffees stacked in one hand and a paper bag in the other.

"Croissants?"

"I'm not hungry."

"Coffee?"

I took it from him without saying thank you.

"No need to be sulky, Kerrigan. It's not like you to shoot the messenger."

"I wouldn't mind if the messenger actually passed on some information instead of pratting about."

The grin again. "Got on your nerves, did it?"

"As you intended." I sipped my coffee, which was far too hot to drink and burned the tip of my tongue. "Ow."

"Come on. You want to know about Debbie Ormond, and I want to know if it all kicked off after I left. Fair exchange." He peered at me. "No visible scarring or bruising so I'm guessing it didn't turn violent."

I ignored him. "It's not far to Renee Fairfax's house. I'm not going to talk about it in front of Lydia."

"Wouldn't expect you to. She is a minor, after all, and I don't want Philip Kennford to accuse me of trying to lead her astray by discussing dirty adult things."

I wavered. I did really want to know what he knew about DI Ormond. "You can have the short form if you want."

"I need details, Kerrigan. I can take a detour." He raised his cup. "Got to drink this before I can face Renee, anyway, so we might as well take our time. They're not expecting us for half an hour."

"And I bet Renee would be just as cross if we were half an hour early rather than late." I sighed. "Look, let's stay here so we can have breakfast and I'll tell you all about it. But you have to go first."

"You mean you want the sordid details of my fling with Debs?"

"For once, yes. Not in too much detail, if you don't mind."

"Nothing that would make your mother blush. Okay. Can do. Food, please."

I passed him the bag. "You can have both of them."

"I shouldn't. But I'm doing a ten-mile run later, so I can burn it off."

"I don't know how you can run in this heat."

"You don't notice if you're going fast enough and you stay out of the sun. It's when you stop you have to watch out. You can overheat like that." He snapped his fingers.

If it had been anyone else in the car with me I might have made some mordant comment about how life was like that — you thought everything was okay while you were too busy to consider it but as soon as you

428

stopped to think about it, it was actually a disaster. All in all it was a good thing I was stuck with Derwent, who wouldn't be inclined to give a stuff about my newfound life philosophy.

"Tell me about Deborah Ormond."

"Well, she was Debbie when I knew her." He examined the chocolate croissant he was eating. "I think this is stale, you know."

"That's tragic. When did you meet Debbie?"

"My first posting after training, in Kentish Town. We're the same age, same length of service more or less. She was in the intake before mine at Hendon."

"And?" Derwent seemed to be more interested in his breakfast than in talking.

"And I shagged her a few times. Or rather, she shagged me. I didn't stand a chance once she decided she was going to have me."

I managed to keep from wincing even though the words stung. "You don't sound too distressed about it."

"I was a young lad and horny as hell at the time so it suited me fine to be used and abused by Debbie. She had a thing for public places, I remember — backseat of the car if it was dark enough, or in offices in the station with a chair jammed under the door handle." He grinned. "She liked a risk, did Debbie, and I never minded. But she also liked getting her end away and when I wasn't free

429

she'd call the next person on the list, or the one after that. She didn't really care who she slept with. I know she broke up one marriage while I was there, a DS whose wife had just had twins. Never thought twice about sleeping with him despite his personal situation."

"I can't stand people like that."

He shrugged. "I asked her about it. According to her, she was a free agent so she could do what she liked. It was up to the guys if they wanted to say no. She didn't force anyone to sleep with her. Not that you had much choice if she decided she wanted you."

"None of this is making me feel better," I pointed out.

"Hold on, I'm remembering more stuff, if it was her." He thought for a second. "Yeah, that was Debbie. She was double-jointed so she could get herself into insane positions. It was like a party trick. Bet she hasn't lost that, even though she's put on a bit of timber over the years."

"She's getting on a bit," I said bitchily. "And she definitely hasn't kept up with applying eye cream, whatever about her fitness."

"She always liked the sun. Used to go to nudist resorts on holidays so she didn't have any tan lines." He sighed. "Tell you what, I haven't thought about her in years, but she used to bang like a shit-house door in a hurricane."

"Again, more detail than I need. What happened in the end?"

Derwent sipped his coffee, hiding a smile against the edge of the cup. "I'm not sure I want to admit this."

"I won't tell anyone."

"She got a bit much for me. A bit too demanding."

I raised my eyebrows. "She doesn't sound like the type to want a commitment."

"Not that. It was all about the sex. She always wanted to try something new, or she'd raise the stakes by making it more risky. When she started pestering me to do a threesome with her and another colleague, I backed out."

"That's not like you. I'd have thought it would be a dream come true. Unless the other colleague was a man."

Derwent was blushing. "I mean, I'm as open-minded as the next person. But I didn't even like talking to the bloke."

"You are not remotely open-minded." I grinned at him. "I'm still a bit surprised you didn't try it."

"Fuck off." He was still red.

"I just mean that it's not that unusual, is it? Two men and one woman? It wouldn't have meant you were gay or anything."

Derwent completely missed the irony in my voice. "Yeah, but it wasn't just us doing her. She wanted to watch us. Being together."

"Oh."

"Yeah."

"She sounds lovely."

"She was well pissed off with me for dropping her." Derwent shook his head. "I had to request a transfer in the end."

"You ran away?"

"Fast as my little legs would carry me. Why do you think I got into running marathons?" He grinned. "I haven't seen her since, to be honest. The Met's big enough to avoid someone like that. Hadn't heard she'd joined the Flying Squad. I wonder when that happened."

"I think she's new, from what Rob said. Still settling in."

"How's she doing?"

"Honestly? Not that well." I told him about the surveillance operation that had gone wrong. "I think they're a bit hacked off with her."

"Yeah, and by the looks of things she hasn't learned any lessons about not sleeping with people she works with." He saw the look on my face. "Sorry, Kerrigan. I didn't mean —"

"Rob? Yes, you did. But I don't think they have slept together."

Instead of answering, Derwent sipped coffee.

"Okay, you don't have to believe me."

"What did he say about it?"

It was my turn to concentrate on drinking rather than talking.

"Don't tell me you didn't ask him."

"I have to wait for the right time."

"And last night wasn't it?"

"Definitely not." He'd got in at four, by which time I had been pretty sure I wasn't going to get any sleep at all. I let him think I was out cold, and when I'd left earlier, he'd been facedown in the pillow himself. "There just wasn't a good opportunity."

"So what makes you think he's not scratching her itch?"

I shuddered. "That is a vile expression, but if you must know, it's because I don't think he would do that."

Derwent snorted. "Too honorable?"

"Too honest." I flinched from the look on Derwent's face. "He is, okay? He's always been completely direct with me. Not one for games, usually. Besides, he made a big deal out of me being there. No one could have missed the fact that we were together."

"Trying to persuade Debbie to back off while you were there."

"Or he might have been trying to show her that he is in a serious relationship and just not interested in her."

"You'll have to talk to him and find out, won't you?"

"Mm." I wasn't looking forward to it. "It does make sense though. There's been something bothering him since he started working there. What if Debbie has been chasing him since the start?"

"Seems likely. He's a good-looking lad, objectively speaking."

"I've always thought so." I couldn't resist it. "You and Debbie still have the same taste in men, I see."

"That's bang out of order, Kerrigan." He glared, not even slightly amused. As so often with Derwent, his revenge wasn't slow to come. "It's tricky for him, though. Because Debs was never big on taking no for an answer. Once she'd decided she was going to have someone, she wouldn't back down. And Rob's just joined the Flying Squad so he's not going to be keen to transfer, is he? Looks as if he's going to have to keep playing hard to get until she gets bored and moves on, or give in."

"For what it's worth, I don't like option two."

"For what it's worth, I don't think Debbie is going to like option one. Interesting times, Kerrigan. Keep me in the loop, won't you?"

When hell froze over and not before, I promised myself silently, but all Derwent got was a smile.

I'd never seen anyone more eager to leave anywhere that wasn't a prison. Lydia was sitting in the hall of her aunt's house waiting for us, and gave every sign of having been there for hours.

"I'm ready." She stood up and shouldered a bag that looked far too heavy for her. "Can we go?"

"I'd like to have a word with Mrs. Fairfax first, if she's about." Derwent looked inquiringly at the housekeeper, but it was Lydia who answered.

"She's probably busy."

"Not too busy to say goodbye to you, surely." Derwent was pouring on the charm again; I really wished he wouldn't bother.

"I don't think she's available," the housekeeper murmured.

"What does that mean? Is she here?"

"Mrs. Fairfax is working."

"Well, tell her it's time for a tea break."

"She's with a client."

"What is she, a dominatrix?" He saw the look on my face. "Sorry."

"She probably could be if she wanted to." Lydia gave us a tight, self-contained smile as we turned to stare at her.

"You shouldn't even know what that word means," Derwent said.

"I'm fifteen, not five."

And she'd got her self-possession back in a big way, it seemed. I was starting to think I should have brought Derwent with me for the original interview, as he'd wanted. Lydia was tapping her foot.

"Look, can we go? I don't want to be late."

"Not yet, sweetheart. But we can put your

bag in the car." He turned to the house-keeper. "Listen, love, I want to talk to Mrs. Fairfax. You go and get her, and I'll be back in five minutes."

The housekeeper opened her mouth to argue, then closed it again, recognizing that Derwent was not prepared to be reasonable. I didn't envy her. I wouldn't have wanted to piss off either of them.

At the car, Lydia made to get into the back-seat.

"You can sit in the front."

She looked at me, then at Derwent. "What about you?"

"I'm driving. DI Derwent is going to be in the backseat." We had agreed it on the way to the house, on the grounds that Lydia was more likely to talk to me, and it would be easier to stop her from tuning out if she was sitting beside me.

"I like the back of the car," Derwent explained. "I can catch up on my paperwork."

"He means sleep," I said, and got a wan smile from Lydia. I looked past her. "There's Mrs. Fairfax."

"Lovely." Derwent sounded more confident than he should have, given the expression on her face. She was in gray trousers and a black shirt today, in silky material that billowed around her slender body, and her arms were folded tightly. She stood in the doorway, watching.

"I don't think she's coming over," I said diffidently.

"Then we'll go to her."

I turned back to Lydia, to find that she had disappeared into the car like a tortoise retreating into its shell. I bent down. "Are you okay? Do you mind waiting while we talk to your aunt?"

A nod.

"Want to say goodbye?"

She shook her head.

"Is everything okay, Lydia?"

"I just want to go." Her voice had dropped to just above a whisper.

"We'll be on our way soon."

It took far longer than I had anticipated, even though Renee wasn't prepared to give us long, and Derwent didn't want to take more than the bare minimum of her time once he'd been exposed to her brand of charm for a minute or two.

"Good riddance. She's been nothing but trouble."

"That's not very charitable, Mrs. Fairfax. She's a victim, isn't she?"

"I don't know about that. All I know is that we have suffered unwanted attention of various sorts since she's been here. I've had meetings disrupted. I've had to take her to hospital to have her stitches done again — did you know that? She got blood all over an antique pillowcase before she told me she needed help. And no one has been the slightest bit interested in finding out about the strange man who was trespassing in the garden on Tuesday night."

"What strange man?" Derwent was looking bewildered.

She snorted. "Typical. They haven't even told you about it. I saw a strange man down there." She pointed a long, bony finger in the direction of the river. "Late at night. He was *lurking*."

"What do you mean by that?"

"He was wearing black. Hiding behind bushes. Spying on the house."

"Did you call the police?"

"Of course."

"What happened?"

"A police car turned up forty minutes later, after I had done their job for them."

"What did you do?" I asked, alarmed.

"I went out with a torch to show the man we knew he was there. He ran away."

"That was brave," Derwent said. "Considering what happened to your sister and niece not that long ago."

"I'm not going to hide in my own home. If someone wants to loiter on my property, they're going to need to explain themselves."

"He didn't try to talk to you?"

"No. Ran like a rabbit."

I looked at Derwent. "Journalist, maybe?"

"Could be. Did he have a camera?"

"I didn't search him. I rather thought that was your job."

"But the response car didn't find him, I take it."

"He was long gone by then."

"I'm going to need a description," Derwent said, leaving it to me to go to the trouble of writing it down. Renee didn't manage much detail. Dark clothes. Aged twenty to thirty, she thought. Average height. Dark hair. Caucasian.

"And I do mean white," she said. "Very pale."

"What time was this?" I asked.

"Ten. Half past. Something like that."

"It would have been pretty dark."

"So?"

"Skin tone can be hard to judge at dawn and dusk." It was my diplomatic way of saying that the main point she had been able to recall about her mystery man wouldn't necessarily help us to track him down. "Can you remember anything about his hairstyle? Or his features? Or what he was wearing?"

"I've told you all I know. I didn't really get a good look."

"And no sign of him since," Derwent checked.

"Thankfully, no."

I looked at Derwent meaningfully. It could be our killer. It could be nothing. Either way, we had no chance of tracing him based on what we'd been told so far.

Renee looked past us to the car. "I don't want to sound unsympathetic but I wish we hadn't been involved in this whole mess. I don't understand why Philip thought I'd be the right person to look after her."

"I think he was desperate," Derwent said with more truth than politeness.

"And still is, if he's got his other daughter to take her on." Renee shook her head. "Now she is a bad influence."

"What do you mean by that?" I asked.

"Vita told me about her and her *preferences*. Disgusting. But then, what do you expect with a father like that?"

"That's what you were going to say the other morning." It had been bothering me. "You stopped yourself, but you were going to refer to her being a lesbian, weren't you? You didn't want to in front of Lydia."

"I didn't want to talk about her in front of the girl. Vita asked me what I thought of Savannah and I made it quite clear I thought she shouldn't be allowed anywhere near the twins. Even before she declared herself a lesbian." She shook her immaculate hair back from the smooth white forehead. "Not the sort of person you would encourage teenagers to emulate."

"She's very beautiful and very successful," Derwent pointed out.

"She's an unpleasant little scrubber. I met

her at Vita's house once. I wasn't impressed."
She sniffed. "Philip traded up when he met
Vita. Miranda had no class and nor did her
daughter. I told Vita she would drag her girls
down into the gutter, and thankfully she
listened to me."

"You brought about the estrangement
between Philip Kennford and his daughter,"
I said.

"That was one positive influence I was able
to bring to bear on them, yes."

"Is it fair to say you're a bit of a snob?"
Derwent asked, completely deadpan.

"Fuck off, Detective. Just fuck off."

"You know there are people who'd pay to
be sworn at by posh birds, don't you? You
could make a fair bit. Phone sex is what I
mean. Don't knock it until you've tried it —
at least it's clean work."

The color was standing in her cheeks, but
her lips were pressed together as if she was
keeping a torrent of words back, with difficulty.

"I'm only joking." He wiped away the sweat
on his forehead with the back of his hand to
provoke a grimace of disgust from Renee.
"Did you ever give your sister any good advice?"

"I told her not to have anything to do with
Philip's bastard offspring."

"The Lithuanian girl's baby," Derwent said.
"She paid her off anyway."

"Was she Lithuanian? I thought she was black, but I probably had that wrong." Renee looked vague for a second. "I don't recall, I'm afraid. The girl turned up last year. Vita asked me what to do. I said ignore, deny, reject until she goes away."

"Did Philip know about her?"

"I told Vita if she was wise she wouldn't say anything. You never know when a man is going to lose his head over a child, whatever they look like. She had a hard enough time to get him to acknowledge her and the girls."

"Which explains the running and face creams and sex toys," Derwent said. "To get him to pay attention to her."

If Renee had been capable of a full frown, she'd have produced one at that point. "I don't choose to think about that aspect of my sister's life."

"Sex?"

"Quite." She looked chilled. "It's none of your business either."

"Everything is our business." Derwent said it flippantly but there was a truth to it.

"Well, my business is luxury, and luxury includes not having to wait around. So if you're finished, I have clients waiting for me."

"Time we went." He doffed an imaginary cap. "Thank you for your input, Mrs. Fairfax. Very helpful."

I think she would have liked to tell him to screw himself, but didn't quite want to run the risk that he'd find it kinky. She settled for slamming the door as hard as she could. Derwent stared at it.

"That went well, I think."

"Better than last time I met her, believe it or not."

"That's because you don't do charm, Kerrigan."

"And charm is telling someone they'd make a killing at phone sex?"

"She loved it." He shook his head. "I knew I should have been here all along. Watch Lydia fall for me."

"Like a ton of bricks, I'm sure." I read over the description again. "What do you think of the man?"

"The dark stranger? Media or a figment of her imagination, five'll get you ten."

"I'd never gamble with you."

"I've got the luck."

"You'd cheat." I hesitated. "So nothing to worry about."

"Probably not." He shrugged. "How are you going to trace him, Kerrigan? Even if he was picking his nails with a machete while he was standing in the garden, we'd still have to find him to talk to him, and scary Renee scared him off."

"Worth double-checking what the response team were told. They might have more on him."

"Yeah, you might as well waste your time

that way as any other."

"The description didn't ring any bells for you?"

Derwent's forehead crinkled as he considered it. "Not much to go on. It's the classic dark stranger."

"It's a description that matches Christopher Blacker quite well, I thought."

"Fuck. You're right."

"Yeah. It might be worth showing her a picture of Mr. Blacker."

"Even though she didn't get a good look at him."

"Well, you never know if a photo might remind her."

"You think we should be more interested in Christopher Blacker, don't you?"

"I don't want to think that," I said, being honest. "I liked him, or I thought I did. He was pretty charming."

"But maybe that was the plan. Charm you, pretend not to be bothered about his life turning to shit, plot to destroy Philip Kennford's."

"I couldn't have put it better myself."

"I think we should go and see Mr. Blacker. Just to say hello."

"We don't have any evidence," I pointed out. "Not a hair to prove he was here. Nothing that connects him to the crime scene. And if you do confront him without any evidence, you're just warning him to be more careful."

Derwent rubbed his eyes. "Okay. I'll put in a request for surveillance on him. Get them to monitor him for a few days. I doubt I'll get permission to do it for longer without having anything against him."

"We could try for a search warrant. Have a look through his flat, see if there's anything suspicious there."

"Like a great big knife? I'd love to, but then we'd have to let him know we were interested in him." Derwent sighed. "Leave him in ignorance a bit longer, Kerrigan. Let him think we've forgotten all about him. If he steps out of line, we'll be ready."

We crossed the gravel to the car, where Lydia was waiting.

"That Renee. What a cow." He said it to me but Lydia heard, and a smile flashed across her face. He bent down. "Good to go?"

"Yep."

"Then let's get out of here."

It was easier said than done. The traffic was appalling all the way to the M25 where roadworks had closed two lanes, causing mayhem. Derwent was asleep before we'd got through the chaos, head back, snoring uninhibitedly. I glanced across at Lydia.

"See? I told you he'd pass out."

"Does he always do that?"

"What, sleep in the car? No. But that's just because he's usually driving."

"So why isn't he driving now?"

Because I was hoping you'd confide in me.
"Because he's tired, I suppose."

"Oh." She looked out of the window at an estate car that was loaded with holiday clutter: suitcases, buckets and spades, and bikes bolted to the back. There were three children in the backseat. I had already peered in to check they were all strapped into their car seats. It was sheer habit. "Do you think they're going or coming back?" Lydia asked.

"Going, by the looks of things."

"How can you tell?"

"The car's pretty tidy so they took their time over packing. And they all look happy." The child nearest us turned and saw us watching them. He stuck out his tongue as far as it would go. "Charming."

Lydia laughed and waved at him. "We deserved it. We shouldn't have been spying on them."

"It's the only good thing about being stuck in traffic. You can be properly nosy about other people's lives."

"That's your job, isn't it?"

I looked at her, surprised. "I suppose so. That and trying to make sure people who have done bad things get punished."

She looked out of the window, away from me. "What would happen to the person who killed Laura and Mum if you caught them?"

"Prison."

"For long?"

"Forever, potentially." I hesitated. "It would depend on the circumstances."

"What do you mean?"

"How old they were. Why they did it."

"If they had a good reason?" She sounded uncertain.

"No. More if they were ill, and that was what made them do it, they might end up in hospital instead of prison."

She nodded and went back to looking out. She had washed her hair that morning and it blew in the breeze as we got clear of the traffic and picked up some speed. It was whipping around her face so I couldn't see her.

"Lydia, do you know who killed Laura and your mum?"

"No." The answer was immediate.

"What about Laura's boyfriend?"

"What about him?"

"Do you know his name?"

"I told you I didn't."

"Yes, but that was a few days ago. I thought maybe you might have remembered."

"How could I remember if I didn't know about him?"

"I suppose you couldn't."

"You don't believe me, do you?"

I shrugged. "It wouldn't surprise me if you knew more than you let on to us. It wouldn't surprise me at all if you were trying to protect Laura. It's just frustrating for us because we really need to talk to him, to rule him out."

"You think he might have killed them?"

"I don't know, but I know better than to discount the possibility before we've talked to him. People do strange things for love. We know Laura was supposed to be meeting someone the night she died, but whoever it was, she kept it a secret from her friends. Maybe it was him."

"Maybe."

"If we had Laura's phone we might be able to trace him."

She didn't say anything.

"We still haven't found it, Lydia. We're still trying to get access to Laura's e-mails too. At the moment we don't know anything about her, really."

"I don't know what you want me to do." I had to strain to hear her over the engine.

"Just talk to us, Lydia. Trust us. You can't do anything to hurt Laura or her memory. The best thing you can do is help us to find her killer."

"I would if I could." Her hands were knotted in her lap and I felt terrible; I was basically bullying her.

"Just give it some thought."

She didn't answer and I settled down to concentrate on making time, pushing the car as fast as I reasonably could. When she spoke, it was so soft that I almost missed it. "Laura was angry with Mum about something."

"What?"

"She was upset about something Mum had done last week."

"What sort of thing?"

"I'm not sure."

"How do you know?"

"I heard her talking to someone on her phone last Thursday. I was in the bathroom between our bedrooms, brushing my teeth. I don't think she knew I was there."

"What did she say?"

"I don't remember exactly. Something like, 'It's typical of Mum. I can't believe she won't even let you talk to him.' "

"Anything else?"

"She said it was none of Mum's business anyway and she'd try to sort it out. And then she said 'Sunday night.' "

"Are you sure?"

"Positive. Because then when she said she was going out, I assumed it was connected."

"Do you think she might have been talking to her boyfriend?"

"I don't know." Lydia picked at a bit of dry skin beside her thumbnail. "Maybe. She said, 'I really want to see you.' It could have been him."

"What if Laura wanted to introduce him to your parents and mentioned him to your mother first to see what kind of reaction she might get? Is that likely?"

"Maybe. Laura found it easier to talk to Mum, even though it often ended up with them shouting at one another."

"So it wasn't unusual for her to be angry with her."

Lydia shook her head. "Not like this. She basically didn't speak to Mum after that call. Until the night she died, I mean. Laura was more the kind of person who would scream and throw things, so it was weird."

"What did your mum think?"

"She tried to talk to her. She asked me what was wrong, but I didn't know."

"Did you ask Laura?"

"No. I knew she wouldn't tell me. She liked having secrets. She was always the leader and I just followed her. Or not."

"People always say twins are so close."

"We weren't, really. We didn't have a lot in common. But I loved her and she loved me." Lydia swallowed. "I think she was trying to protect me, you know. I don't think she wanted me to know what was upsetting her so I wouldn't get involved. She was always trying to look after me. Like she was two years older than me, not two minutes."

"Was she more grown-up than you generally?"

"I suppose." Lydia was looking out of her window again, her head turned away. "She was in a hurry to grow up, Mum used to say. She couldn't wait to leave home. She thought Dad was deluded about keeping us under control."

"Which explains her rebellion. Having a boyfriend, I mean."

"That and everything else she could think of." Lydia sounded far older than her years sometimes, austere and disapproving like a maiden aunt. "She was always pushing them. She liked to find some way of getting at them — some way of challenging them. It didn't matter what it was. She loved getting them to be angry with her."

"Sounds like fun."

Lydia shivered. "I hated it. Every meal out, every car journey, it was always the same. She'd start a fight to see what would happen. Mum said she'd inherited it from Dad, but he said he wasn't going to take the blame for it."

"And you just wanted to be left alone."

"Exactly." Lydia looked at me in surprise. "How did you guess?"

"Just the impression I had."

"Well, that's how it was."

So Laura had found something — or someone — to use to torment her parents. And Lydia hadn't wanted to know what it was. I gritted my teeth, trying not to show my frustration. There was no point for one thing; that opportunity had been lost. Besides, there was a good chance that if she'd been a bit more curious about it, we might have found ourselves investigating her death too.

The two of us relapsed into silence, a

silence that was only broken by gentle snores from the backseat until we turned off the motorway and on to some winding country lanes. Derwent woke up with a snort.

"Where are we?"

"Good question." I slowed to negotiate a humpbacked bridge. "If you hadn't broken your satnav, we might have a clue."

"You don't need satnav if you've got a map." Derwent scrabbled for the road atlas he kept on the back window.

"I seriously doubt this road is marked on your map. I haven't seen a name. Besides, you need to know where you are in the first place. And we're lost."

"Didn't Savannah give you directions?" Lydia asked.

"They don't seem to make a lot of sense." I handed her the sheet of paper with scribbled instructions on it.

"Turn right at the white gate," she read. "Take the second left after that, beside the brown cow."

Derwent brightened. "Is that a pub? They're always good landmarks. We can ask some local yokels to direct us."

"I think she means an actual cow," I said.

"What? That's ridiculous."

"Well, it's what we've got."

"Have you got a phone number for her?"

I had my phone tucked between my head and my shoulder as I drove. "I've got her voice mail."

"Well, tell her she's a mad bitch."

"Shut up," I snapped just before the recording kicked in. I left a terse message asking to be called back.

"Why didn't you tell her we're lost?"

"Because we shouldn't be. If you hadn't broken your satnav —"

"You shouldn't have to rely on satnav. There was a time before it, you know."

"Well, I wouldn't have needed satnav if my navigator hadn't been asleep in the backseat." I pulled into a gateway and stopped. "Look, show me the map. I'll see if I can recognize any landmarks."

It whirled between the two front seats and slammed into the dashboard like an injured bird. I had opened my mouth to snarl at Derwent when I heard a tiny whimper from the seat beside me.

"Lydia? Are you all right?"

"I don't know why you have to be so horrible to one another." It came out as a wail.

"We're not really being horrible."

"Yeah." Derwent plunged forward between us like an overly enthusiastic Labrador. "It's a sign of affection, really."

"I wouldn't go that far." I tilted my head so I could see past him. "But really, it's not because we're properly angry with one another. Just a bit fed up about being lost."

Lydia nodded, wiping away tears. "I'm sorry."

"No need to apologize, darling." Derwent ruffled her hair and then slid back to his seat. "Any ideas, Kerrigan?"

I flicked pages, finding where we'd left the motorway but almost immediately losing the trail. "Not a clue. We could just keep driving."

"Your phone's got reception, though, hasn't it?" Lydia said. "Because if it does, you could use it to check where we are."

"Genius," I exclaimed, poking at it. "But actually no signal."

"I'll see if I've got anything." She burrowed in her bag and produced a phone, switching it on. It took a minute to connect to the network while I sat and stared at it, and her, and debated whether to say anything. A look at a serious Derwent in the rear-view mirror decided me.

"Lydia . . . I thought you didn't have a phone."

She looked up at me guiltily. "I don't use it."

"That phone belongs to you, though?"

A mute nod.

"You said you didn't like them."

"I don't call anyone. Ever. I just have it for emergencies." She was bright red. "I don't even know the number. It's just for dialing 999 and finding where I am if I get lost. Mum made me have it. There isn't anything in the contacts, even. Look." She turned it round so I could see it was empty.

"That's a nice phone to use for emergencies," I observed. It was a Samsung, top of the line.

"What do you call this if not an emergency, Kerrigan? Give the girl a break." Derwent had stretched his arms across the backseat, his posture exceedingly relaxed.

"How right you are. I'll shut up and wait for directions." I sounded too cheerful. I looked into the mirror again and saw the same expression in Derwent's eyes that I knew was in my own.

Suspicion.

CHAPTER EIGHTEEN

It was Zoe who came to meet us when we finally arrived, Zoe with a wide smile on her face and a warm welcome for her girlfriend's half sister. A forbidding five-bar gate stopped the car from going any further than where we were idling on the pitted track that led to the house, but through it I had a vague impression of old, huddled buildings made of worn red brick, the paintwork peeling, the roof uneven and spilling tiles with gay abandon. Above all, my main feeling was that I was somewhere homely. There were pink flowers in the window boxes and red geraniums spilling out of an old milk churn by the door, and Zoe stepped over a fat cat snoozing on the doorstep on her way to unlock the gate. She came round to look through the car window.

"Sav's asleep, believe it or not. Come in and I'll wake her up."

"It's nearly midday." Derwent had the disapproval cranked up to eleven.

"So?" She shrugged. "No reason for her to get up. She's got the day off and she had early starts the rest of the week."

"Nice work if you can get it."

"Yeah, well, the reason she can get it is because she's unique." Zoe was still looking at Lydia. "Do you want the tour first or do you want to get settled in?"

"Tour, please."

She glowered at the backseat. "I wasn't actually talking to you."

"I know." Derwent wasn't wasting any charm on her, not that he had much to spare, but I could read his thinking quite easily, and I doubted Zoe was having any trouble. *No point being nice to a dyke, is there?* "But since you're offering."

"Yes, but I wasn't." Without getting flustered she was holding her ground.

"Look, we have to check the place out. Make sure it's a safe environment for Lydia."

"You don't look like any social workers I've ever seen."

"Oh yeah? Seen many?"

"A few." Her eyelids flickered and I had the strong sense that she regretted going down that conversational path. "Okay. It can't do any harm to show you around. Maybe you can tell Lydia's dad that this isn't a den of iniquity, or whatever he seems to think it is."

"Oh, you heard about that, did you?" I

grinned. "We got in a bit of unexpected bother."

"I know. We're grateful." She went back and held the gate open and I drove carefully into the yard, pulling up by the front door, close to where a very nice silver Audi was parked. The yard was a cobbled square that was sprouting weeds in places. It was lined with stables but all the doors were closed and there was no smell of horses.

"This used to be a stud farm," Zoe explained. "It hasn't been used for that in a decade."

Derwent had unfolded himself from the backseat of the car and was stretching. "Typical. No use for males of any kind."

"Did you say something?" There was a real edge to Zoe's voice and I smothered a smile, amused to see Lydia doing the same.

"Carry on." Derwent waved a lordly hand. "Where's this studio of yours?"

She pointed to the opposite side of the yard from the house. "It used to be a pigeon loft. Savannah had it fitted out for me as a surprise."

"Where's the door?"

"In the corner. That green one. But you can't go up there," she added quickly.

Derwent was already halfway across the yard. "Why not?"

"Because it's private. Besides, there's nothing to see. It's just a room with a drawing table and some boxes in it."

"I'm not interested in what's in the room. I'm interested in the view."

"Savannah's alibi?" She pressed her lips together tightly. "Fine. Help yourself."

Derwent didn't need any further encouragement. He shot through the door and rattled up the stairs.

I turned to Zoe. "Don't you make your own stuff?"

"Sometimes. I can do the simple things. But I generally design things and get other people to make them. I'm good at drawing and concepts. Not so great as a silversmith." She shrugged. "Knowing your limitations is always a help."

"It must help that you and Savannah are in a relationship. I bet it's easy to get free advertising."

"Savannah wears some of my things, but she wears lots of other stuff too." She smiled brilliantly at Lydia. "Do you wear jewelry?"

"Not much."

"You should wear pink tourmaline. It would be stunning on you."

Lydia looked down, embarrassed, as Derwent came back toward us. He shrugged at me. Inconclusive.

"Are there any other outbuildings or is this it?" I asked.

"There's a garage on the other side of the house. And a barn. We don't use them much."

"Do you always leave your car here?"

"Usually." She looked at it as if she'd forgotten it was there. "I suppose. It's easiest."

"Show me the garage," Derwent demanded.

"Why?"

"Because I asked you to. And I asked nicely, for me." He rubbed the sweat off his hairline. "Look, don't make this into a big deal. It's too fucking hot for that."

"Fine." Zoe walked toward the side of the house with long angry strides. For the first time I noticed a black sheepdog lurking in the shadows near us.

"Doesn't he mind the cat?"

"Who? Beckett? No. They ignore each other. The cat regularly produces kittens and she's cranky when she's in heat, and when she's pregnant, and when she's got a litter on the go. So that's all the time, really. She's taught him to leave her alone."

The dog drifted along behind us with all the mass and weight of a flake of soot, licking his nose occasionally with a long pink tongue. I held out my hand to him and clicked my fingers but he ignored me.

"Does he like people?"

"Not a lot. I got him from a shelter. He didn't have the best start in life."

"Is he your dog?"

"Yeah. Savannah doesn't really like dogs, but she likes me to have the company when

460

she's off traveling."

"He looks like Mollie." It was practically the first time Lydia had spoken. "Dad's dog."

"She's black and white, isn't she?" I said.

"Yes. But her head's the same shape."

"You must be an artist," Zoe said. "To notice that, I mean."

"She does fantastic drawings." I sounded like a proud mother, I realized, and dialed it back a bit. "I think they're good, anyway."

"It's just a hobby," Lydia muttered.

"That's how I started out. And now I make a living from my hobby."

"That and shagging a multimillionaire supermodel." Derwent was straight to the point. I glanced at Lydia to see if she was embarrassed, but her expression was studiedly neutral. "Don't tell me you could afford a place like this on your own."

"Probably not," Zoe said evenly.

"Did you design jewelry before you met Savannah?" I asked.

"Not for a living."

"What did you do?"

"This and that. I worked as a waitress. Did a couple of seasons as a ski instructor in Switzerland. I trained as a chef for a while." She shrugged. "Whatever took my fancy, really. I hadn't settled to anything in particular."

"Did you go to university?"

"Couldn't afford it."

"You could go now," Derwent pointed out. "Your girlfriend would pay for it."

"She might, but I wouldn't take the money." Zoe glared at him. "Stop trying to make out I'm with Savannah for what I can get."

"Fair assumption."

"Not really. Not fair at all."

She had led us away from the house a little, to where a track snaked up to a collection of buildings. We walked through long grass, crickets whirring on either side of us, the sun fierce on my head. Invisible, multilegged things crawled on the back of my neck and under my trousers. Imagination, I told myself sternly.

"The garage. As requested." Zoe gestured at it with a flourish.

It was an old-fashioned wooden structure, a barn with a glass window above the door and rooflights all the way round it. Built in the early days of motoring, it really needed a Model T Ford to be parked in the middle of it to look right. The door was open, revealing that there was nothing inside but a spreading oil patch. The walls were shelved, loaded with cans of petrol and engine coolant and oil. It made sense that they needed to have the wherewithal to fix minor problems with the car; it would be a long walk to the nearest garage. It also looked as if it was past time to deal with whatever was causing the puddle on the floor. Derwent went in and crouched beside it, smudging it with one finger.

"That's fresh. Got a problem with a leak?"

"Intermittently."

"It's a big enough puddle. You must park the car in here a fair bit."

"Yes. I said that, didn't I?"

"You said you *usually* parked it in the yard. But this garage looks well-used."

"Well, it's probably about half and half." She sounded irritated. "I don't see the problem."

"Where was it last Sunday night?"

"I can't remember."

"Because if it was parked here, you wouldn't have heard it leave, would you? Not from the other side of the house."

"Well, if I said it was in the yard, that's where it was."

"But you're not sure."

"I am sure." She was standing in the sun and now she lifted a hand to shield her eyes. It had the added advantage of guarding her expression.

"You just said you couldn't remember," Derwent said.

"I made a mistake."

"When? Yesterday when you told us it was in the yard, or today?"

"Today."

"You do see this is important, don't you? You do know why I'm asking."

"Of course."

"You are Savannah's alibi."

"I understand that." Zoe looked down at Derwent, which was a long way given her height. "If you're asking me if I think Savannah went to London and killed Vita and Laura, the answer is definitely no."

"I'm asking you where the car was."

"In the yard."

"You're sure?"

"Yes."

"No doubt at all?"

"None."

"Right. Just wanted to clear it up."

"I'm glad I was able to help." She raised her eyebrows. "Seen enough?"

"You said there was another barn," I pointed out.

"An old one behind the garage. We don't use it for anything. The roof is falling in. Other than that, it's just the house."

The four of us turned to look at it, seeing a long, low building that was evidently older in some parts than others, though none of it was what you could call new. The bricks were hundreds of shades of red, the windows small and low, haphazard in their distribution. The side we were on was more sheltered than the yard and eight or nine small trees stood behind the house, unripe apples a sharper green among the leaves.

"Lovely." I hadn't meant to say it out loud, but Zoe smiled at me.

"We think so."

"It doesn't look like somewhere anyone rich would choose to live." Derwent was not sounding impressed.

"That just shows your lack of imagination. It's perfect for Sav. She spends all her time in cities or on planes. This is the complete opposite. No one to see what she's wearing. None of the neighbors care that she's famous. She can really relax."

"Good way of keeping her all to yourself too, isn't it?"

"I don't need to keep Savannah away from the rest of the world to know how she feels about me." Zoe spoke quietly, but with total conviction.

"Can we go inside?" Lydia asked.

"Of course. I don't know what we're still doing out here. Come on." Zoe strode back down the path, her long legs scything through the grass. Lydia scampered after her like a Jack Russell, looking her age for once. I followed more slowly, aware of Derwent behind me swearing under his breath. It might have been the heat that was annoying him, or the uneven terrain, but I had a feeling it was Zoe herself.

A shriek of metal on metal made me look up to see one of the windows under the eaves swinging open. Savannah leaned out of it, waving. Her hair was all over the place and she was wearing a white vest without a bra.

She was laughing, and she looked utterly ravishing. "Lydia! You've come! You're here!"

"Doesn't miss much, does she?"

I looked round at Derwent. "Bitter?"

"About what?"

"Her lack of interest in men?"

"Fuck that. I'm more bothered by the alibi that isn't." He pointed in the general direction of the yard. "I'm going to look under that car when we're leaving. I'll bet you a lap dance there isn't an oil stain under it, or anywhere else in the yard. That car's never parked anywhere other than the garage, except today when they knew we were coming. All of that was just window dressing."

"I'm stuck on who's supposed to be doing a lap dance for whom."

"Don't flatter yourself, Kerrigan. If I'm right, you're paying a professional to do one for me."

"And if you're wrong?"

"Then we both get the pleasure of sleeping easy, don't we?" He shook his head, his jaws working as he savaged a piece of gum. "I wish I knew what Philip Kennford isn't telling us. I wish I could be sure leaving Lydia here was the right thing to do. Something about this bothers me a lot."

The two in front of us had reached the house already and Lydia was standing just beside the back door while Zoe opened it. Her arms were wrapped around her tiny frame as if she was cold. The sun's glare made it impossible to see anything inside when the door swung open. Zoe disappeared into the darkness without a glance in our direction, and after a second's hesitation Lydia followed, dropping out of view as completely as if she had been swallowed up forever. I wished it didn't feel like an omen.

I hated it when Derwent was right.

What we found inside the farmhouse was a strangely appealing mixture of vintage shabby chic and out-and-out junk, faded chintz and vases full of wild flowers. The floors throughout were wooden, the walls oak-paneled or cream-painted, and where the ceilings weren't strung with low, dark beams they had the cottage-cheese lumpiness of properly old plaster. Antique linen and lace hung at the windows — old sheets and tablecloths remade into curtains — and the rugs on the floors were handmade, doubtless expensively. The kitchen was the heart of the house, a big room with a huge scrubbed table at its center and an extraordinary range of copper pots nailed onto the walls. It had cost a fortune, I thought, looking at the fine carpentry that was pretending to be old shelves and cupboards, and the double-width Belfast sink. Predictably, there was an Aga, red and showroom-glossy. One wall was taken up with an inglenook fireplace, a wooden-framed sofa on either side of it, and that was where Zoe indicated we should sit. She headed to a scullery off the kitchen where a vast American fridge hummed.

"Homemade lemonade?"

"That sounds good," I said, ignoring a glower from Derwent.

"Coming up."

The fridge clanked as ice cascaded into a jug; living in the country in bucolic bliss was obviously fine as far as it went but there was no reason to forgo the little luxuries of modern convenience. It occurred to me to check my phone and I wasn't surprised to find I had full signal and instant Wi-Fi. We weren't as far from civilization as all that.

"Did you do all this yourselves?" I asked when Zoe came back with a tray.

"No. The previous owner did it." She looked around. "I wouldn't have the patience to haunt antique shops and auctions for all of this copper tat, but she loved it. She was doing an interior design course and this was her show house."

"And Savannah bought the lot."

"She liked it. She wouldn't have had time to put it together herself either, but it appealed to her." Zoe grinned. "It's very different from her other homes."

"Where else does she live?"

"New York and Paris. There's a villa in St. Lucia. She used to have a house in Chelsea but she sold it when we found this place."

"Every little luxury money can buy." Derwent sounded bitter.

"She invests in high-end property. This is the only place she bought because she fell in love with it."

"I thought it was because she fell for you and you needed your privacy so no one else would find out."

The color washed into Zoe's cheeks. "I suppose that's true. In a way."

"Does it ever bother you that she wants to pretend you don't exist?"

"It's part of the deal." She occupied herself with pouring cloudy lemonade into tall glasses, concentrating on what she was doing with perhaps more care than was strictly necessary.

"Bit different from your house, isn't it, Lydia?" Derwent said.

The girl nodded, taking it all in through owl-like eyes that widened still further at the patter of bare feet on a creaky wooden staircase. The door swung open and Savannah breezed into the room, now dressed in a cotton flowered dress but still with unbrushed hair.

"I'm so sorry I was still in bed. I told Zoe to wake me when you got here." She put her arms around her half sister and gave her a quick hug. "So glad you came, darling. We'll try to make it nice for you."

"I don't need anything." There was a note of something approaching panic in Lydia's voice. She had turned her face away, but I could tell that she was blushing. I recalled the pile of magazines in her room and wondered if she had collected them because they featured Savannah. It couldn't be easy to meet your hero, even if she was related to you.

"Well, we'll try to make sure you have somewhere nice to stay. Have you seen your room yet?"

Zoe answered. "We've only just come inside. I was waiting to take Lydia upstairs."

"Waiting for what?" Savannah's eyes fell on me and Derwent. "Oh. You're still here."

"Don't mind me." Derwent looked more or less as if he had taken root in his corner. He knocked back his drink and gave an appreciative burp that instantly tainted the air around him with acrid lemon. "Refreshing."

"I'm glad you liked it." Zoe set her glass back down on the tray as if she couldn't face sipping it after Derwent's performance. "Sav, you could show Lydia her room now, I suppose."

The model clapped her hands. "Yay! Come with me."

I took the invitation that hadn't quite been extended to me and followed them out of the room, gambling that Savannah was too nice to tell me I wasn't wanted. She led us up the narrow, creaking stairs to a long landing that ran the length of the house, with windows overlooking the little orchard on one side and bedrooms on the other. The window where I had seen her was still open, the curtains quivering in a breath of wind that wasn't strong enough to cool the air. It was close to being unbearably stuffy up there, the pitched ceiling giving a clue that we were right in the roof space.

"Sorry it's so hot. No air con, but you can leave your window open all night."

"I don't mind hot weather." Lydia's voice was a whisper.

"That explains how you can stand to wear black. Long sleeves too. You really mean it, don't you?" Lydia hung her head miserably. The older girl dropped an arm around her sister's shoulders and squeezed. "If you feel like getting out of the whole Goth look, just let me know. I've got plenty of stuff if you want to borrow anything. It'll be long on you, but we can make it work."

"I'm okay."

I thought Savannah was going to pursue it but she gave her a slightly dubious look and then carried on. "You're in the end room because it's the nicest. Wait until you see the view."

She carried on down the corridor, pointing out her bedroom on the way past. The door hung open, showing off a huge four-poster bed, which was unmade. There were clothes piled high on a chair in the window and a rickety table was covered in cosmetics of various kinds. "Zoe thinks I'm awful because I never pick up after myself."

"Does she do it for you?" I asked.

"She's my girlfriend, not my slave." Again there was that flick of scorn in her voice that reminded me of her father.

"I thought she was your assistant."

"She does the admin." Savannah shrugged. "It just makes sense for tax purposes if I employ her and pay her a wage. It doesn't mean I take advantage of her."

"But she runs the house here."

"I suppose so." She opened the door at the end of the corridor and stood back. "Have a look, Lydia."

I let the two of them go in first, Lydia walking slowly. A wide bed piled high with pillows and cushions took up a lot of the space. It faced the window, which was large and framed a stunning view across the fields to some low wooded hills in the distance. To make the most of it, there was a roll-top bath in front of it, and I would have loved to lie in it gazing out at the sunset, preferably while sipping a cold glass of wine.

Savannah was watching to see Lydia's reaction. "There's a bathroom too. Loo and shower in here." She opened a door in the corner and flicked on the light. "You don't have to use the bath if you don't like it."

"It's fine." Lydia's voice was low, but I thought she was pleased. She cleared her throat. "Laura would have loved it. She always wanted a bath like that."

"Me too. It's what made me want the house."

"Why don't you use this as your room, then?" I asked, genuinely curious.

"Because the other one has a walk-in wardrobe and a huge bathroom on the other side, and I'm too spoiled to settle for a teensy chest of drawers if I don't have to." She shrugged. "What can I say? I live down to the stereotype now and then."

"I'm going to go and get my stuff." Lydia was halfway out the door already. "I want to get everything moved in."

"There's no hurry." Savannah sat on the edge of the bed. "But if it makes you happy."

"I'd prefer it."

I thought Lydia was like a newly rehomed animal, desperate for reassurance that she was really staying, wanting to show how grateful she was but unable to say it. I listened to her move away down the corridor, a soft hiss the sound of her hand running along the wall as she went. When I heard her reach the bottom of the stairs, I walked around to face Savannah.

"How much do you know about Lydia's . . . problems?"

"What do you mean? The murders?"

"No. Although that won't be helping." Briefly, I explained about the eating disorder and the self-harm, one ear open all the time for the sounds of Lydia coming back.

Savannah's eyes filled as she listened. "The poor little duck. It makes even less sense that Dad left her with Renee."

"Your father isn't very sympathetic. He feels she's brought her troubles on herself."

"Typical."

"Lydia needs a lot of support and she hasn't really had it up to this point."

"That much is obvious." Savannah looked away from me toward the view, looking lovely but remote.

"You do realize that it's a massive responsibility, looking after her." I could feel myself losing my grip on my temper. "If this is just your way of getting back at your father, you'd better tell me now so I can find somewhere else for Lydia to go. You need to be serious about giving her the care she needs."

"Don't patronize me," Savannah spat.

"I'm not. It's just —"

"Do you think I haven't seen plenty of eating disorders in my line of work? And cutting? Burning, even?" Savannah got up to pace around the room. "It's hardly unheard of. Models aren't the most stable people."

"I wouldn't have thought you could get away with self-harm if your body is your job."

"You can always find somewhere to hurt yourself that doesn't show. Between the toes is an old favorite. Inside the mouth. The genitals, even."

"You do sound familiar with it. More than me, I have to admit. What about you? Have you ever tried it?"

"Me?" She laughed. "No. I'm too much like Dad for that. I don't do self-destructive. I just destroy other people."

"What does that mean?"

She shrugged. "It sounded good in my head."

"Come off it, Savannah," I snapped. "What did you mean?"

"Just that Zoe doesn't have it easy. And the boyfriend I broke up with to be with her — he wasn't too pleased." She sighed. "I try not to do any harm, but I take after Dad. I take advantage of people and I can see myself doing it but I can't stop."

"It must be hard. Looking the way you do, I mean."

"Why?"

"Because people want to please you. Or they want you to live up to their fantasies."

"That's it. They have expectations." Savannah frowned. "How do you know?"

I hesitated. "Let's just say I know all about unwanted attention and leave it at that."

"Unwanted attention? I really doubt you do know about it. I've had ten or twelve stalkers in the last year alone. Proper, serious, police-involved harassment."

"I'm sorry about that." I wasn't going to compete, even though I could have tried.

"Comes with the territory, like I said." She laughed humorlessly. "That's why I'd like to be normal, really. Do an ordinary job; look ordinary, even. So I didn't have to put up with that kind of thing."

"I hate to break it to you but plenty of ordinary people have to cope with being harassed. And most of them don't have your resources. They can't afford to hide away in rural splendor with their secret girlfriend."

"This wasn't my idea, actually. Zoe suggested it."

"Really?" That wasn't the impression I'd had.

"Look, I grew up not knowing one end of a cow from the other. I've never lived in the country. I can't get used to how quiet it is out here, or how far you've to drive to get a pint of milk. This is completely not my kind of place but I like it. It makes her happy. And that makes me happy." She shook her head. "How did we get on to talking about this?"

"Because I wanted you to be aware you may need to keep an eye on Lydia." I opened the door, checking that she was still downstairs.

"Keep her away from sharp knives, you mean?" Savannah bit her lip. "God. That sounds as if I think she did the murders. I don't, obviously."

"Obviously," I agreed.

"But there's no way she could have, is there? I mean, the injuries she had — they weren't from a fight."

"I don't believe so," I said carefully. It intrigued me that Savannah was bothered about it. "Why do you ask? Do you have concerns about her being involved?"

Savannah shifted restlessly. "I don't know. Not really. I mean, she's just a kid. But it was something that Zoe said to me that made me wonder about it. And now you say she had a serious cut on her arm and it makes me edgy. I just thought I'd ask."

"I'm a bit surprised you didn't think about it before you asked her to stay with you."

"Well, I didn't."

"Are you still happy to have her here? Because if you want us to take her away —"

"No! I want her here. I really do." Savannah wriggled again. "Besides, what's the alternative? Back to Renee?"

"Probably."

"There's no way."

"What do you have against her?" I asked, curious.

"There's no warmth in her. No caring. The only thing that worries her is her reputation. And her precious family. She was the one who made Vita tell Dad to cut me off."

"How do you know that?"

"He told me. I only met her once. I thought she was a witch, and I was right. You know, I asked Dad once why Vita stayed with him. He told me she asked him for a divorce a couple of years ago, then backed down on Renee's instructions. Renee told her she'd made her choice and she had to live with it. Not what I would want to hear from my big sister, if I had one."

"Me neither. I did wonder why Vita stayed in the marriage."

"I think it was her obsession. That and the girls. But it was Renee who guilt-tripped her into staying with him through thick and thin. She basically gave him a license to behave as he wanted and he took full advantage. You'd think she liked him or something."

"Not the impression I got."

"Maybe he shagged her and then never called." Savannah's eyes widened. "Hey, you don't think —"

"Lydia's coming back." It was with genuine regret that I called a halt, but there were things Lydia didn't need to hear about her parents, and it was all pure speculation anyway. From the thumps and bumps and low-pitched swearing, she had recruited Derwent as a porter.

"You need a lift." He shouldered the door open and threw the bag at the bed, just missing Savannah. "This is all right, though."

"Thanks. I'd have thought it was a bit girly

for you."

"And I'd have thought it was a bit girly for you." He swiveled on the spot. "Where's the TV?"

"No TV."

"You need a little plasma-screen job just there." He pointed to a space on the wall near the bath. "Sit in the bath with a cold beer, watching Man U getting thumped — I'd die happy."

"As long as you died, I wouldn't care how." Savannah wasn't bothering to hide her feelings for Derwent anymore. "Is there anything else I can do for the two of you or are you prepared to leave us in peace?"

"Couldn't make me stay." He looked at me. "Ready, Kerrigan?"

"I think so."

Derwent and I took our leave of them with varying degrees of politeness, Derwent making no attempt to be subtle as he double-checked Zoe's story about the car. I sat in the passenger seat waiting while he lay full-length on the ground, searching every inch with his torch. Zoe and Savannah watched without comment. Lydia had wandered over to stand by the gate, accompanied by the dog who seemed to have adopted her. When Derwent eventually got into the car, the look on his face was pure triumph.

"Nothing."

"And that's good news."

"Well, objectively no." He had the grace to look mildly ashamed. "It does mean Lydia may be in danger, I suppose."

"But more importantly, you were right."

"That's where I was coming from, yeah."

"You're a prince among men."

"Finally, you're prepared to admit it." He started the engine and nosed forward, giving Lydia time to unlock the gate. "I knew I'd wear you down."

"But if you think they're lying —"

"To be honest, if I thought she was in danger I'd have her out of here in a heartbeat, but I can't see it. I think these ladies thought we needed there to be an alibi and cooked one up, just to reassure us. The physical evidence says they're lying about it, but that doesn't mean the clotheshorse is a murderer."

"Give it a rest." I put my hand on Derwent's arm. "Just stop for a second."

He braked beside Lydia, enveloping her in a cloud of dust. "Whoops."

I put down my window and handed the coughing teenager a card. "Sorry about the dust. I just wanted to tell you to put my number in your phone, since you do have one after all."

"Okay."

"You know how to add someone to the contacts, I presume."

"I'll work it out."

"And use it if you need it."

She nodded. "Thank you."

"You know where to find me."

She ran back to the gate, closing it behind her so we were shut out again. Beside me, Derwent stirred, putting the car into gear.

"It was interesting about the phone. Would you have picked her for a liar?"

I didn't need to stop to think about it. "Actually, I would."

"Why's that?"

"Because it seems to run in the family."

Derwent grunted his agreement. The car bumped slowly down the track while I watched the house getting smaller in the mirror and thought about deceit, and suspicion, and family secrets, and whether anyone really wanted us to solve this case at all.

CHAPTER NINETEEN

"Okay, what's wrong?" Liv plumped down on the edge of my desk.

"Do you mind? Those are important." I extracted a sheaf of forms from under her rear end.

"Come off it. It's not like you to be pissy about paperwork. What's up?"

"Nothing."

"You've been staring into space for the past twenty minutes."

"Thinking."

"There's a little puddle of drool there." She pointed. "Brain activity close to nil, I'd have said. What's up?"

I put my face in my hands and groaned. "Take your pick."

"Is it work or personal?"

"Both."

"Bad?"

"The worst."

"I was going to offer to buy you a can from the vending machine to cheer you up. This sounds a bit more serious."

"You're not wrong." I checked the time. "Too early to hit the pub, unfortunately. The vending machine it is."

The one major advantage of the machine was that it was located in a small alcove two floors down from the team's room. That and the fact that the refrigeration unit was as noisy as an oil rig made it possible to have a private conversation there without attracting too much attention, provided you kept it brief. We rattled downstairs in silence, by mutual consent, and Liv did the honors. Two cans clattered down into the slot and she fished them out.

"Spill the beans."

I took a deep breath. "Rob may be having an affair with his boss, Derwent and I possibly just put a key witness in danger, and something really, really bad happened last night."

Liv blinked rapidly. "So the first two don't count as really, really bad?"

"Not in the context of the third." I popped the ring-pull and sipped orange fizz, wincing at how sweet it tasted. "God, this is rank."

"It's all that was left. I can't believe they haven't restocked the machine. It's not like we're in the middle of a heat wave or anything." Liv hadn't opened hers yet and was holding it to the back of her neck, trying to cool down. "You'd better start with the third thing, then, although I'm pretty sure you're wrong about Rob."

"I wish I was." I squeezed the sides of the can, flexing the thin metal. "Do you remember Chris Swain?"

"As in your creepy stalker, Chris Swain? As in the guy who lived in your building and filmed you and Rob —"

"Shagging. Yes. And keep your voice down."

A man I didn't know was walking toward us with a preoccupied air and a handful of coins, but just because I didn't know him I wasn't prepared to assume he didn't know me. We fell silent while he in his turn discovered the lack of choice, struggled with his disappointment and also settled for orange. As he disappeared around the corner, I turned back to Liv. "Swain's been out of sight since Belcott and Vale found the wiring in my old flat. He disappeared before they got a chance to interview him."

"I remember that. They did a pretty thorough job looking for him."

"Yeah, Colin Vale doesn't do any other kind of job, and Belcott was just insanely curious. They put in the hours all right, but they didn't find a trace of him anywhere — his passport hasn't been used since, nor have any of his credit cards, and there was no activity on any of the accounts he had in his name. I don't think it's safe to assume he killed himself from shame and we just haven't found the body."

"He was ready to go underground, wasn't he?"

"Had it all planned." I drank a little bit of orange, regretting it as it fizzed up in my sinuses. "Anyway. I was starting to think he was gone for good."

Liv's eyes were round. "He didn't turn up."

"Not in person."

"How, then?"

"I've been getting weird things in the post at home. Underwear catalogues, that kind of thing. I thought I'd got on a dodgy mailing list."

"That happens. It's a bit weird, but it does happen."

"Yeah. It does. But there were pictures too, of Rob and his boss. Not doing anything in particular," I added quickly, seeing the look on her face. "Just looking a little bit more friendly than you might expect. Rob passed it off as a prank, but I don't suppose he thought it was Chris Swain's work either. I wouldn't have put two and two together if I hadn't found an envelope with our post when I got home late last night."

"From him?"

"I think that's a safe assumption."

"What was in it?"

I set the can down beside the drinks machine, suddenly nauseous. "Photographs."

"Of you, presumably."

485

"Mostly. And other people. Pictures of me at work the other night, in Clapham, at the crime scene. Pictures of me and Rob that were taken in the street and with a long lens looking into our flat. He'd cut Rob out of them, Liv. I mean physically cut out his face."

She was looking disturbed. "That's so creepy."

"It's worse than that, isn't it? It's a threat."

"Or he just wanted to swap Rob out and put himself in. I presume these were intimate moments he'd captured. You know, your face here, that kind of thing."

"There was a note."

"What did it say?"

" 'You're worth more. If you can't see that, let me show you the truth about him. If you still don't have the wisdom to get rid of him, he's a dead man.' "

"Is that word for word?"

"For some reason it stuck in my head," I said wryly.

She shook her head. "Maeve, it's not worth worrying about. He's a run-and-hide kind of weirdo. A peeping Tom. He's not going to attack anyone. Just get some decent blinds and try to persuade Rob not to wander around naked anymore."

"It's not just him I need to worry about, and he's plenty of trouble on his own. Remember the Web site he was running? There were tons of freaks on it who wouldn't think twice about doing his dirty work."

"Rob can take care of himself."

"Can he?" I winced. "I don't know. And I don't know if I want him to take the risk anyway if he's cheating on me."

"You can't believe he's cheating." Liv's voice was flat. "You're not going to take a stranger's word over his, are you? A stranger with a hell of an agenda to boot? You can't let him dictate what happens to you. That's the whole point, isn't it? You're just playing into his hands if you do break up with Rob."

"What if he *is* having a fling with his boss?"

"Well, this is how I know you've lost the plot completely. What are you talking about? How could he be having an affair?"

I filled her in on what I'd seen and what Derwent had said about DI Deborah Ormond. Liv's response was immediate.

"Talk to him."

"But —"

"You know better than to jump to conclusions without actually knowing what's going on."

I rubbed my eyes with the heels of my hands. "I just think it might be for the best to walk away. Just draw a line under it and move on."

"Wouldn't be the first time, would it?" Liv raised her eyebrows. "That's your usual way out, as I understand it."

I shook my head. "We did things too fast.

We moved in together because I needed a roof over my head, and then I lost him his job."

"You didn't. Godley found out about your relationship because of Swain spying on you, not because of anything you did wrong. And Rob chose to leave. You were halfway out the door too, as I recall."

"But Rob was the one who ended up going. He's not the sort to kick me out even if he's fallen for someone else. He's waiting for me to notice there's something wrong and act accordingly."

"That doesn't sound like Rob."

"Why else would he invite me to the pub when he knew Deborah Ormond would be there? Why else would she maul him in front of me? Someone was sending a message."

"And it didn't occur to you that it might be Rob showing DI Ormond that he's taken? Proving to her that he's got a stunning girlfriend already and is off the market?"

"It's possible that he wanted to warn her off somehow." I admitted it grudgingly.

"Is it also possible that the pictures and the note were sent by someone other than Chris Swain?"

"Who else would bother?"

"A certain nymphomaniac DI trying to freak you out? Someone playing a practical joke?" Liv tilted her head back to drain the last of her can. "I think you're way off, for what it's worth. You're getting in a state about nothing."

"About Chris Swain or Rob?"

"Both," she said crisply.

I checked the time. "We'd better head back. Thanks for the support, by the way."

"I am being supportive. I just don't think you should be in a panic." Liv's eyes were troubled, though, and in any event she ruined the effect of her careful nonchalance with her next question. "Am I right in thinking you don't want to mention the letter and photographs to Godley?"

"Absolutely not."

"You should tell as many people as possible. Make a fuss. Get it investigated. Scare off whoever thinks it's funny to freak you out, and get some reassurance at the same time. At the very least you should tell Derwent because he's the one who's with you most of the time. He's most likely to see someone hanging around if Swain is following you at work."

I shook my head. "I don't want to say anything to anyone until I know more. If you're right, and I'm wrong, it's not worth worrying about. And if I'm right —"

"Then by the time you find out, it might be too late."

"That's not what you said just now."

"I was trying to reassure you so you didn't freak out."

I pushed open the door into the stairwell. "Tell you what, Liv, next time you think I need cheering up, don't bother."

She crossed her arms, nettled. "Charming."

"I wasn't looking for a lecture," I pointed out.

"I wasn't trying to give you one."

"That's how it sounded to me."

"I'm surprised you could hear anything over the voice in your head that tells you you're right all the time."

"Ladies, ladies. Please." Ben Dornton jogged past us, heading up the stairs. "There's no need to fight here where no one can see you. Take it to the team's room so we can run a book on who'll win."

"Piss off," I said.

"It's none of your business," Liv called after his retreating back.

"Lovers' tiff?" echoed down the stairwell.

"Definitely not," I said, earning myself a glare from Liv.

"Don't flatter yourself."

"That's what Derwent said too. For the record, I don't think either of you are attracted to me. Does that help?"

"Profoundly."

I leaned against the wall, suddenly exhausted. "Oh, shit, Liv. It's not your fault."

"No, it isn't." She was still looking annoyed, but less so. "I still think you need to talk to Godley, but start with Rob. Is he around?"

"He should be back by late afternoon."

"Perfect. Tell the boss you've got a headache and you need to go home early."

"No word of a lie. But I don't think he'll be too sympathetic."

"What are you talking about? He loves you."

"Not anymore. I've blotted my copybook."

"How's that?"

"Standing up for Derwent. I know, it doesn't sound likely."

She laughed. "Don't tell me he's starting to grow on you."

"Like mold." I sighed. "When am I going to learn that doing the right thing isn't always the right thing to do?"

"When it's chiseled on your gravestone." She patted my shoulder. "Come on. Let's disappoint the lads by being friends again, instead of needing to mud wrestle to settle our differences, or whatever it was Dornton had in mind."

"I don't want to think about what Dornton had in mind, thank you." I followed her up the stairs, though, feeling better and worse at the same time. She hadn't laughed it off, and that bothered me. But it bothered me even more that I couldn't tell if I could trust Rob or not.

I knew there was someone in the flat as soon as I pushed open the door. There was some disturbance in the air, something too subtle

491

to be a noise. I stood on the threshold, listening, every sense straining. It had been a jumpy enough trip back from work; I hadn't been able to stop myself from looking around every time the train stopped and people got on or off. Walking back to the flat, I found myself taking a circuitous route, one that had lots of sharp corners where I could stop and wait to see if anyone was following me. I hated the paranoia; I hated the fact that it was justified.

At the flat, I had just got as far as thinking about where my CS spray was (my locker at work, unfortunately) when the bathroom door opened. I knew it would be Rob but my heart still jumped and the look on my face must have been the opposite of pleased because he stopped a couple of feet away.

"What's up?"

"Nothing." I forced a smile. "I'm fine."

"Why are you standing there?" He reached out and very gently pulled me into the flat. "I thought I heard your key in the lock, but then you didn't come in."

"I was trying to work out if you were here or not."

"Here, but going out. I thought I'd head to the park for a run, as you might have guessed."

"I noticed the gear." I put my own belongings down and blew my hair off my forehead where it was sticking to me. "Rather you than me. It's too bloody hot."

"I'm sick of being stuck indoors. Besides, I didn't think it was as bad today. And I won't notice when I'm actually running."

"Just when you stop, Derwent says."

"Does he indeed? Well, he'd know."

"You need to drink lots of water. And don't run in the sun."

"I'll be under the trees. Plenty of shade. Plus, it's late enough that I don't think the sun is too strong at this time of day." He shook his head, bewildered. "What's wrong, Maeve? You're talking like you're on autopilot or something. Did anything happen at work?"

"No. Not at work." I didn't know how to start talking about any of it but I was suddenly, unhelpfully angry with him.

"Cagey." He went into the sitting room and I followed, watching him lace his trainers as he sat on the edge of the sofa. "Are you going to tell me what's going on?"

"I was sort of hoping you might start."

He frowned, twisting round to look at me. "What do you mean?"

"Does this ring any bells?" I leaned forward and began to run my hand up and down his back using the approved Deborah Ormond technique.

"Knock it off." He leaned away. "What are you doing?"

"You seemed to like it when your DI was doing it. I thought I'd have a crack. If there's anything else she does for you that you want me to try, you only have to ask."

He stood up. "Are you talking about DI Ormond?"

"The very same. I saw her mauling you in the pub."

"You didn't say anything about it last night."

"I didn't get the chance. I wasn't going to raise it in front of her."

"Maybe you should have. Then she could have told you the same thing I'm going to. You've got the wrong end of the stick." His eyes were wary.

"Have I? Derwent got the same impression. He saw her too." I laughed. "You must think I'm blind, or stupid, or both. Did you really think I wouldn't notice there was something going on?"

"There's nothing going on."

"Bullshit."

"I promise you."

"I know what I saw, and it wasn't just me, it was Derwent too, so you can't claim we were both mistaken. I just don't know why you'd bother to deny it."

He ran his hands through his hair. "Look, it's not what it looked like."

"Finally, we're getting somewhere. You're prepared to admit there was something to see."

"I'm prepared to admit nothing," he

snapped. "But what I will say is that DI Ormond had been drinking for a while that night. She's on the tactile side even when she's sober, and when she's boozed up she gets grabby."

"I spoke to her, remember. She wasn't boozed up. She was absolutely sober."

He laughed. "Really, she wasn't."

"Well, obviously I don't know her as well as you do. But I didn't hear her slurring her words and she didn't seem to have any trouble focusing." I took off my shoes and stalked into our bedroom. Over my shoulder, I said, "I also didn't see her touch anyone else while I was there."

"Maybe you weren't looking."

"Again, not blind, not stupid." I was getting changed, pulling off clothes and yanking on whatever was closest to hand without much regard for the overall effect.

"Pigheaded, though."

I turned around. "Look, why are you bothering to deny it? You got caught, Rob. Either you hadn't briefed her to leave you alone in front of me, or you didn't care about me realizing what you've been up to. I would have expected a bit more in the way of honesty and courtesy, but I can promise you I won't break down if you just tell me the truth. I can take it."

"You've made up your mind about this, haven't you?" He sat down on the end of the bed. "You don't know what's going on."

"Well, try telling me." I leaned against the wall. "Come on, Rob. I know there's been a problem since you started your new job. You haven't been yourself. I thought you were just finding it hard to settle in, but there's more to it than that, isn't there?"

"That was part of it." He dragged his eyes up to meet mine. "What did you notice?"

"You haven't been sleeping well, for starters."

"No one sleeps well in this weather."

"Come off it, Rob. You haven't been around much, but when you've been here you haven't been what I'd call chatty about work. Not as much as you should have been if you were enjoying it, anyway. I thought it was because you didn't want me to feel guilty about you having to transfer out of Godley's team, but I was way off, wasn't I?"

"It wasn't the work. Or not exactly."

"It was her."

"It was DI Ormond."

"You can call her Debbie if you like. I gather that's how she prefers her boyfriends to address her."

"I don't call her Debbie." He said it flatly. "Where did you hear that?"

"Derwent. He's her ex."

"One of many, from what I've heard. Bit of a coincidence, though."

"Not really. It seems she goes for anyone

she works with — always has. And she's been around for long enough to get through a fair proportion of the Met."

He sighed. "Look, I didn't want to tell you about it because I didn't want to worry you and I didn't want you to be upset on my behalf and I didn't want to even mention it in case you thought it mattered, but she's been doing her best to make my life difficult since we both joined the squad. She's got a nasty reputation for playing favorites and picking on anyone who doesn't go along with what she wants. And I wasn't prepared to go along with what she wanted."

"Because what she wanted was you."

"Basically. From the first day she laid eyes on me, and not because of anything I did or said, before you jump to any conclusions. And I wasn't going to cooperate."

"Well, how laudable."

He stood up. "I didn't ask you for a medal. I wasn't even going to tell you about it, remember?"

"Until you got caught out."

"If I'd really been worried about keeping the two of you apart I would have come up with some reason for you to stay away from the pub the other night."

"I've been wondering why you didn't."

"Because I didn't have anything to hide."

"So hiding it was just for practice."

"Don't be such a bitch."

I raised my eyebrows. "It's not like you to throw names like that around."

"It's not like you to be so unreasonable." His eyes were as hard as flint. "Seriously, Maeve, get over yourself. You know I didn't lie about anything important. You know I was keeping it from you for good reasons, and not because I was trying to play the field."

"Good reasons being that you didn't trust me not to overreact."

"Well? You're not proving me wrong."

"Fucking marvelous." I started to walk out of the room and he stepped in front of me.

"Don't leave. Don't just walk away. This is too important."

"It *is* important. You need to start treating me like an adult. Like your equal, even."

"That's how I see you."

"It's not how you treat me. You've always been the one who acted like you were in charge. Even saying that you loved me — that was your way of distracting me from what was really going on."

"You cynic." He frowned down at me. "What else is going on? What aren't you telling me?"

"Don't turn this around on me."

"What's going on?"

"Nothing." It was my turn to be on the back foot.

"It's never nothing with you." He was still staring at me. "There's more to this than you

498

overreacting about DI Ormond. You've got something else on your mind."

"Oh, stop with the telepathy, for once. There's no more to this than the bare fact that you didn't trust me enough to tell me you were having problems at work. And that's no basis for a relationship in my book."

"You're not breaking up with me over this," Rob said softly. "Don't even pretend it's enough of a reason."

"It sounds like reason enough to me."

"Don't get me wrong, this conversation isn't over, but I don't see the point in prolonging it now. I'm going to go out and run until I don't feel like murdering you anymore. You can do what you like, but I suggest you meet me in the park — say at the café by the lake in about an hour — so we can talk about this like human beings. Being in here doesn't seem to be doing either of us much good."

It was a good suggestion, better than he knew. I had just been about to ask if we could go somewhere else to talk. If my stalker was staying true to form, the flat could be bugged if not wired for video, and I didn't want to let Chris Swain know too much if I could avoid it. What I wanted was for him to believe Rob and I were finished, and it was starting to look as if it would even be true. I just wished I could be more pleased about it. It was for Rob's sake, I reminded myself, and made myself go on.

"All right. I'll see you there. I'll even buy you a bottle of water. But I don't think a change of scenery is going to bring about a change of heart."

"We'll see." He picked up his keys and his phone, and checked the time. "Right. One hour, or thereabouts. I'll see you there."

I listened to him go, wincing as he slammed the door. He kept his emotions on such a tight rein that it was the only sign of how upset he was.

Doing the right thing had never felt so hard.

CHAPTER TWENTY

If I didn't quite enjoy the walk through the park, I was still able to acknowledge that it was a lovely place to be. Battersea Park suited the long warm summer evening, with children playing under the tall plane trees and locals strolling hand in hand down avenues of beeches. There were dogs everywhere, all kinds from pedigree to pure mongrel, mostly up to no good. Most of them seemed to have been in the lake at one point or other, and some of the owners looked more than a little damp around the edges.

The park had been planned with rambling in mind and I took advantage of that on my way to the café. The lake was surrounded by lush planting and featured islands covered in what was apparently wild woodland. I took my time wandering around, watching teenagers squabble in hired rowing boats while the ducks looked on sagely from the banks, staying well out of it. Romantic champagne picnics seemed to be in fashion; almost every bench had its cooing couple. I wondered how many of them would end up staying together for the long haul. I wondered how many of them were lying to each other. I wasn't really in the right mood for lovebirds, understandably enough.

I crossed a humpbacked footbridge onto one of the islands in the lake and found a free bench at last, just opposite the café. The great table-legs of Battersea Power Station's chimneys stuck up behind it against the fading sky, a reminder that London in all its grime wasn't too far away despite the acres of trees and grass that surrounded me. There was no sign of Rob, who was presumably pounding his regular route around the outskirts of the park. The path bordered the Thames on one side and it would be a nice place to run at that time of evening, I thought, with the best chance of a breeze. Certainly there was no breath of air on the lake. The leaves hung limply above me and the grass was piebald brown where the sun had scorched it during the long summer days. Dragonflies and midges shimmered above the surface of the water and I sat and watched them, thinking about the Kennford case, and Rob, and whether a glass of wine would help with our forthcoming conversation. The café was busy; most of the tables outside were full. The hum of conversation was audible from where I sat, and the setting sun cast a golden light over the scene, making everyone look ten times more glamorous and beautiful than they deserved to. A London summer at its best, you could say, if you didn't mind the heat or could avoid it during the days. It was one of the curses of being a police officer that we were out in all weathers. Bodies never seemed to turn up on temperate days, early on in a shift, when there was light and time to deal with them. Murder was not a convenient speciality but I was increasingly aware that it was all I wanted to do. I had been warned by one of the older detectives on the team when I joined it that it was the professional equivalent of a smack habit. "It'll break your heart and take everything you value in your personal life but you won't be able to quit." Typical old CID hyperbole, I had thought at the time. Now I wasn't so sure.

A jogger ran past — not Rob. Then another two, women running together, talking about weddings. One was lean and slim-hipped; the other profoundly pear-shaped and out of breath but pounding along with good grace. A personal trainer, I thought, with a highly motivated bride who still had a bit of work to do. A cyclist sped past, a vision in emerald-and-white Lycra and fly-eye sunglasses, his wheels whirring like the insects in the undergrowth. Another jogger, this one stocky and perspiring heavily. On the far shore I saw a figure in blue shorts and a dark top. It could have been Rob and I squinted, watching his arms and legs move in a steady but fast rhythm, as measured as engine pistons. He was running off his temper, I recalled. He would be moving quickly.

A prickle at the base of my skull made me look around; it was that feeling of being watched that I had learned not to discount. How it worked, I didn't know, but I had been right too many times to think it was a fluke. At first, I couldn't see anyone. There was a homeless man in the shrubbery behind me, a bundle in dark woolen clothing that I hadn't noticed before I sat down. He was probably the reason the bench had been unoccupied, but he was far enough away for me to ignore him, and anyway, he was asleep. I scanned the trees and bushes around me, feeling ridiculous but also feeling my heart thud in my throat. I edged my mobile phone out of the pocket of my jeans, just in case. Nothing on the right, I was sure. I turned my head and looked to the left, very casually, as if I was just taking in the scenery.

He was on the bridge, fifty yards away, and he had a camera. The cyclist who had passed me earlier, anonymous in shades and his helmet. Now that I saw him again I knew who it was, even without seeing his face. He had grown a heavy beard but I recognized the sandy hair and the narrow build. The give-away was the lens that was pointed straight at me. From that distance I couldn't hear the click as he took pictures, but I had no doubt he was doing more than look through the lens. I turned my head away again and peered at my phone, flicking through the contacts, choosing a name.

Please pick up.

It rang.

Please.

Another long ring. Another two and I'd get his voice mail.

Maybe he wouldn't answer. Maybe he would be too angry, still, or he'd wonder why I was bothering him ten minutes before we'd arranged to meet.

And it rang.

Maybe he wouldn't hear the phone. Maybe I should have rung someone else.

"Hello?"

"Rob?" I couldn't keep the distress out of my voice.

"Maeve? What's wrong?" His breathing was labored.

"It's Chris Swain, Rob. He's watching me. He's here."

"Where?"

"On the bridge to the island in the lake," I started to say, but looked back halfway through the sentence to see the bridge was empty. "Shit. He's gone."

"What's he wearing?"

I described him as best I could, and the bike.

"I'll see if I can cut him off. Do you know which way he went?"

"No." I had got to my feet and moved forward to the water's edge. "Where are you?"

"Near the café. I can see you."

"Wave," I said, scanning the shore. "Oh, okay. I've got you." He was pacing back and forth, obviously desperate to get moving for all the calm in his voice.

"Have a good look around. Look at the paths. If he's on a bike, he'll be moving fast but he can't go everywhere in the park. Watch the gaps in the trees."

I was doing as he suggested, straining to see. A brief flash of white and green drew my attention and I peered across the water until my eyes stung with the strain.

"Okay. I've got him. He's heading toward you, on your right at the moment. Coming fast."

"On this path?"

"The one behind, I think." I watched as Rob took a shortcut through a flowerbed, vaulting over some railings. He had hung up on me, unsurprisingly — he would need all of his energy for the chase. And he was tired already, I remembered with a pang.

And if he caught Chris Swain, what was he going to do? Fight him? Rob wasn't armed but there was every chance Swain was carrying a weapon. I was already regretting that I'd involved him. I should have called 999, but it didn't come naturally to me to ask for help like an ordinary member of the public. In the middle of a park, miles from my radio and equipment, that's exactly what I was, though. And so was Rob. I dialed the number and explained who I was, where I was and why I needed urgent assistance. Without shame I mentioned Godley's name to add weight to the report. The operator assured me it would be treated as a priority.

Having called in the cavalry, I didn't have much to do beyond standing by my bench chewing my bottom lip, waiting for my phone to ring. I didn't want to move until I'd heard from Rob or someone else. All around me people carried on talking and running and laughing, as if nothing strange was going on at all, and my nerves were being stretched to snapping point. When my phone did vibrate I answered it on the first ring.

"Lost him." I could barely hear him.

"Are you okay?"

"Fine. Angry."

"Did you see him?"

"Yes."

"Did he see you?"

"Probably." A couple of deep breaths. "I almost got him."

"Oh, Rob. Where did he go?"

"Out one of the gates. He's gone."

"I'll tell the control room."

"No need. Just been talking to a response car. They're on it."

"Oh, well done," I said inadequately.

"Where are you?"

"Still on the island. I was waiting to hear what happened. I can come and meet you."

"By the Rosary Gate."

Again, I was left holding a dead phone. I started to jog along the path heading for the bridge where I'd seen Chris, dodging between slow-moving pedestrians. There was no urgency but I wanted to see Rob, to make sure he was really all right. If any harm had come to him . . . but it hadn't. Down the other side of the bridge and across the grass, between picnickers, through an impromptu football match with a muttered apology to the nearest players. My sandals had thin leather soles that weren't ideal for running and I had to be careful not to slip.

The phone rang again.

"Kerrigan."

"There's no need to hurry. You're not missing anything."

The voice was mocking, more self-assured than I remembered, but instantly recognizable. I stopped. "Chris?"

"You knew it was me." He sounded genuinely pleased.

"Funnily enough, I find you easy to remember." I turned around slowly, trying to pick

508

him out of the crowds, knowing he was there somewhere. "I take it you can see me."

"You're right."

"Why can't I see you?"

"Not looking in the right place, I expect. It's a common problem for you and your colleagues."

"We've been doing our best."

"It's a very clumsy effort, Maeve. The bank accounts and computer traces, I mean. Nothing I can't avoid. Anyone with half a brain could manage it."

"I'm sorry to hear that." I could feel sweat trickling down my back. They wouldn't be covering the exits of the park. They thought he had gone. There were too many gates, too many places where he could have ducked back in. It was the best chance we'd had to corner him and I was stuck on the phone, talking to him. I started walking, heading for the Rosary Gate.

"Did you get the pictures I sent you?"

"I thought they looked like your work." I swallowed. "You've got to stop this, Chris. It's not fair."

"No, what's not fair is losing my job and my website. What's not fair is having to leave my home because you decided to get your mates to search the house. Just because you're a police officer, you think that makes you special."

"You'd been spying on me. And everyone's

entitled to their privacy."

"There's no such thing."

"You like to pry into other people's affairs but you don't like it when you're the one who's investigated. You've just been complaining about it. Try to be a bit more consistent, Chris."

"You're not challenging me, are you, Maeve?" He tutted. "You don't want to do that. You don't know what I'm capable of."

"No, I don't." I was shaking, from adrenaline more than from fear. "All I know is you're determined to make my life a misery."

"Not at all. I just don't want to see you waste your time on someone who isn't worthy of you."

"This has nothing to do with Rob," I said quickly. "This is between you and me."

"I wish it was. But he's here, isn't he? He's pounding around looking for me, your knuckle-dragging hero. I don't like him, Maeve, and I don't like that you're still with him. I thought I'd shown you what he was like."

"I saw the pictures. They were doing surveillance."

"Is that what he told you?"

"Look, you don't have to worry about him. I told you. We're breaking up."

"Moving on? Got someone else lined up?"

"No." I said it with as much force as I could muster.

"I don't believe you. Girls like you always have the next one ready. You don't like being alone, do you? You like being looked after." A plaintive note crept into his voice. "I could look after you, you know."

"That's never going to happen."

"Never say never, Maeve."

"You're not my type."

"You just don't know what your type should be. You need someone who'll be there for you. Someone faithful. I've been loyal to you since the minute I set eyes on you. I've barely looked at another woman. Not like that miserable bastard you've been with."

"I told you, forget about him. He's old news."

"He will be."

I felt the pit of my stomach drop away. "What does that mean?"

"You'll find out." He gave a little laugh. "I've got to go, Maeve. I'd better not hang around too long. Eventually someone will work out I'm here, or you'll manage to get a message to one of the officers standing around looking for me, and then the hunt might actually be on."

"They're looking for you already," I said.

"They're looking for the wrong person, in the wrong place. I've got rid of the bike, and the outfit. I'm sorry you saw me like that. It wasn't the most attractive getup but it suited my purposes. You wouldn't recognize me now, I'll tell you that."

"Are you close by?"

A giggle. "You can't imagine."

I couldn't stop myself from looking around again. I had gone beyond strategy and cool surveillance to genuine terror, worse as always because it wasn't on my account. "Please, leave me alone, Chris. I don't deserve this."

"You can beg if you like. I love it when women plead. You'll promise anything to get out of a tight spot. No morals, when it comes down to it. No courage." He sighed happily. "I'll be in touch, Maeve. Warn your little fuck-pal he needs to start looking over his shoulder."

"Listen to me, Chris," I said urgently. "We've split up. I'm moving out."

"That's good. But I owe him a lesson." He sounded amused. "It's too late, Maeve. I like you for trying to save him, but there's nothing you can do. Nothing at all."

"Chris, please." My throat was tight with unshed tears, mainly of rage and frustration. "Just let it go."

"Not now, not ever. I'm with you until the end, Maeve. Until the end."

I opened my mouth to argue, but it was too late. The conversation was over. He was gone.

I shouldn't have been worried about Rob — I had spoken to him, after all, and knew he was both all right and in the company of rather a lot of police officers — but I was irrational enough to keep running until he was in sight. I slowed down then, partly because the stitch in my side was making me gasp for air and partly because I couldn't think what to say to him. He was talking to a uniformed officer and had his back to me, so I had plenty of time to try to come up with an opening line. What I managed, however, when he swung around, was a gasp at the blood that was streaking down the side of his head from a gash above his ear.

"What did he do to you?"

"It looks worse than it is."

"Let me see."

"Leave it." He jerked his head away irritably. "It's not a big deal."

"It looks like a big deal to me."

"I'd better go and clean up, then. PC Michaels wants to speak to you." He walked off without another comment to me and I watched him go until the officer cleared his throat apologetically.

"I just need to take a statement from you, really, so I can write up a report."

"Of course." I answered his questions automatically, explaining something of the history between Chris Swain and me and giving some clue as to why I had reacted that way to him appearing in a public place.

"Did he make any threats against you or

anyone else?"

"Specific threats? No." Nothing I could use against him, anyway.

The officer was unfailingly polite, but I could tell he was baffled by the entire situation. It was a relief to get to the end of our conversation, even though the alternative was Rob, who was sitting on a bench with his arms folded, a forbidding expression on his face. He had accepted a bandage from one of the officers but refused their offer of proper medical attention. I went over to stand near him.

"Don't you think you should let them get some paramedics to check you over?"

"I didn't lose consciousness and it's not particularly deep. It just bled a lot. It looks better now I've cleaned it up."

"If you say so."

"Really, it's fine."

"What happened?"

"I should be asking you that." He glared at me. "When were you going to mention that Swain was back?"

"I've only just found out."

"What, today?"

"Yesterday," I admitted. "When I came back to the flat last night. But I wasn't sure it was him."

"Start talking."

I told him about the defaced photographs of the two of us, and how I thought he had signed me up for the catalogues I'd received. "He probably sent the pictures of you and Deborah Ormond too."

"And was disappointed with your reaction, presumably."

"I imagine I was supposed to storm out."

"I should have made it easier for him by letting her have her wicked way with me."

"It would have helped."

He stared into the middle distance. "In the flat, earlier — I knew there was something more to it. I knew you wouldn't throw away everything we've got because you were annoyed about DI Ormond."

"Don't kid yourself. This isn't about Chris Swain."

"That's a shame. If you want us to break up, I'd have hoped you'd have a good reason."

"I don't want us to break up at all." I realized it was true as I said it. "The reason I'm so angry with you is because you didn't trust me enough to tell me about your problems. You didn't want me to know."

"No, I didn't. I didn't want to worry you."

"And if it was the other way round and I didn't tell you, how would that make you feel?"

"I don't know."

"Well, you do, because you're livid I didn't talk to you about Chris. And I didn't even know he was back until last night. You've been dealing with the Deborah Ormond situation for months, on your own, and the fact that you couldn't tell me about it makes me feel pretty shit, actually."

"I was trying to protect you."

"You weren't letting me be there for you. You didn't think I'd understand." I shook my head, trying to blink back tears before he noticed them. "You don't think much of me, do you?"

"Maeve."

"No, Rob. Don't try to persuade me I'm wrong about this. The best thing we can do is walk away from all of this and be glad we found out now that we're not meant to be together."

"I'd dispute that."

"Which bit, exactly? Because Chris Swain is violent, unhinged and seriously angry with you, so you should be running for the hills, even if it wasn't for everything else."

"I don't believe in running away." He was staring across the park, into the distance. "Not from you."

"I suppose that's reassuring."

He put his hand out without looking at me, and after a moment I put my hand into his. He didn't say anything, just held on to me, and the feel of his palm against mine was more comfort than any words could have been.

We were still sitting like that when a Mercedes pulled in through the gate and stopped short a few yards from us.

"This doesn't look good," Rob observed, as the driver and passenger got out and slammed the doors.

"I'm not surprised the superintendent is here. I am surprised about the other one," I had time to mutter before they were close enough to overhear.

"What the hell's going on?" Godley was in a towering rage, and Derwent didn't look much calmer.

"I'm sorry," I started to say.

"Sorry's not good enough. You're being harassed by Chris Swain again — am I right? And when he actually turns up — not before — you decide to involve the police, even though you know there's an outstanding warrant for his arrest, that officers on my team were tasked with finding him and any developments in the case, any at all, should have been brought to my attention."

"It all happened so fast," I said.

"If it's any consolation, she didn't even tell me." Rob stood up and shook hands with Godley, then Derwent. "Good to see you again."

"I could wish for better circumstances," Godley said heavily.

"What happened to you?" Derwent was staring at the bandage on Rob's head.

"I was a bit too slow and a bit too ambitious. I tried to pull him off his bike and he straight-armed me into a tree."

"Ouch."

"It was the tree that did the damage," Rob said quickly. "Not him. He just got lucky."

"He's been lucky twice now and it pisses me off." Godley turned back to me. "You need to do some talking, DC Kerrigan. Fill in the blanks for me. The next time I get a call from the shift commander to tell me one of my team is in trouble, it would be nice to know what's going on."

"I'm sorry I didn't say anything. I didn't want to make a fuss about nothing."

"What happened?"

I described the events of the previous few days and the photographs and wound up with Swain's phone call.

"How did he have your number?" Rob asked.

"I don't know. I didn't give it to him."

Godley shook his head. "That's the sort of thing he could find out in his sleep. I'm not surprised about that. What I do find surprising is that he would show his hand like this."

"Maybe he's got bored with hiding," I said.

"Maybe he thought you were looking too happy," Derwent suggested. "When he found you, I mean."

"Or he thought it was worth it to tell you what was going on between me and my new boss." Rob caught Godley's eye. "Which is nothing, by the way."

"I'm beginning to understand why you were asking me for a reference the other night."

I turned to look at Rob, eyebrows raised. "A reference? Moving on?"

"Considering my options," he said evenly.

"I know Debbie Ormond of old, mate, and I can understand you needing an escape route. You'd chew your own leg off to get away from her." Derwent shoved his hands in his pockets, his feet wide apart to demonstrate just how much space his balls needed to air themselves. "You might need to, as well. Once she's got you in her sights, you're fucked."

"I've managed to avoid getting too close so far. Swain seems to have picked up on it somehow — he took photos of me with DI Ormond that looked borderline compromising. I assumed it was my new colleagues' idea of a prank."

"And I accepted that story," I explained. "I didn't have any reason to think they'd been sent by anyone else. It was only last night when I got the other pictures — the ones that were defaced — that I started to think differently."

Godley frowned at me. "You still should have said something."

"To one of us, at least," Rob said. "Instead of trying to sort it out on your own."

"You didn't even say anything to me." Derwent sounded genuinely wounded.

"I do try to leave my personal life out of our day-to-day work." Not to mention that Derwent was still the last person I would ever confide in. I wrapped my arms tightly around myself, feeling chilled in spite of the warm evening. "I know I should have done things differently, but I had a lot of other things to think about, and it's not as if the team isn't busy at the moment with the gang killings, and the Kennford case."

"So?" Godley's eyes were cold. It had not been tactically wise to mention the gang investigation. I hurried on.

"So I accept I got it wrong but the main thing I'd like to know is what I should do now. He made a threat against Rob, even if it wasn't anything specific we can act on. He knows where we live. He knows where Rob works. It seems pretty obvious to me he has grown in confidence since the last time I encountered him. I wasn't scared of him before — pissed off at having my privacy invaded, and angry that Rob had to leave the team, sure — but I didn't feel scared."

"Scared is a step forward in my book." Rob put an arm around my shoulders. "You're too willing to risk your own safety."

"Oh, and are you prepared to start watching your back? Change your routine? Do you want to move to another part of London and start again?"

"I will if I have to."

"What would make you do that? Because I heard the way he talked about you. He's not your biggest fan. And if he's prepared to come out of the woodwork for the sake of making sure I get the message about you and DI Ormond, he's prepared to take risks to get rid of you permanently."

"You told him you were breaking up with Rob, didn't you?" Derwent looked at him meaningfully. "You might like to start working on dropping the public displays of affection for a while, if there's a chance he might believe her."

Reluctantly, Rob took his arm away again. "He said it didn't make any difference to him if we were together or not."

"He said a lot. It might help." I looked at him beseechingly. "I couldn't forgive myself if anything happened to you because of me."

"Nothing's going to happen."

"Still, there's no point in putting yourself in harm's way. I definitely don't want either of you staying in that flat at the moment." Godley looked at Rob. "I'm not your boss anymore, but I want you to take my advice and stay in a hotel for the next couple of nights. Don't make it easy for him to attack you."

"I don't like doing what he wants us to do."

"Well, I don't like picking up the pieces when a tragedy's happened and I want you to review your security arrangements. New locks. Consider getting an alarm system if you don't have one. I'd recommend fitting one with a personal attack button. That's if you're determined to stay."

"I like my flat," Rob said mildly. "And you do too, Maeve, don't you?"

"It's a nice flat." And I wasn't making any promises about staying there. "I do think it's a good idea to stay out of it for a while, though. Work out what we need to do. Maybe they'll catch Swain while we're away."

"We'll do our best." Godley looked from Rob to me. "You need to take this seriously. Don't think that you're immune just because you're serving police officers. You bleed just as easily as anyone else."

Rob nodded. "I take your point. The thing is, sir, I'd really rather like the chance to talk to Chris Swain."

"Talk?" Derwent looked skeptical. "I don't think you'll be doing a lot of talking."

"Not as such, if I have anything to do with it." The expression on his face belied the calm words; I had never seen Rob look so completely dangerous before.

"Let's not talk about that now."

"Fine. As you say, we do have other things to worry about." Godley gave me a thin-lipped smile. I wasn't completely forgiven yet, I could see.

"Any developments in the drugs shootings,

sir?" Rob asked.

"All quiet so far."

"It can't last," Derwent said helpfully. "It won't have burned itself out yet."

"Thank you for your valuable insight." Godley turned to me. "Can you sort yourselves out for tonight?"

I nodded.

"Right. Well, I'd better get back. Do you want a lift, Josh?"

"Might as well." He caught my eye and obviously realized I was wondering what he was doing there in the first place. "I was in the team's room when the boss came steaming out of his office and said you were in trouble. Thought I'd come along for the ride, if it was going to be exciting."

"Sorry to disappoint you."

"That's okay." He started to head for the car, then turned back. "I'm glad you're all right, you know."

"How touching." But I was grateful to him for riding to the rescue even if he wasn't my idea of a knight in shining armor.

I turned back to Godley. "Thank you for coming out. I'm sorry I made a mess of things."

"I can understand why it happened. But don't let it happen again, will you?"

"Definitely not."

The phone in my hand came to life again and I smothered an exclamation, staring down at the screen. Not a number I recognized. I was peripherally aware of Rob leaning in to see it, of Godley stopped a few steps away and Derwent with one foot in the car, one on the road, all frozen as if they were playing Grandmother's Footsteps.

"Answer it, for fuck's sake." It was Derwent who said it, inevitably, but it was what I needed. I did as I was told.

"Kerrigan."

The voice at the other end was faint — so weak I could barely hear it. "Please . . . *please . . .*"

"Who is this? Hello?"

"Please." It was barely a whisper. "Help us."

"Lydia?" I looked up to check that Derwent was paying attention, which he was, concern in every line of his face. "Lydia, is that you?"

"Yes."

All of the hairs were standing up on my arms. "What's happened? What's wrong?"

Silence, a silence that seemed to last forever. Then, two words, but they were more than enough.

"He's here . . ."

CHAPTER TWENTY-ONE

The initial instinct to rush to the rescue was one thing; reality was another. It was Sussex Police who responded to Lydia's cry for help, not us. Godley drove us back to the station so we could pick up a car, politely but firmly declining to drive us to Sussex once he knew the situation was under control. He did drive at top speed to make up for it and made a valiant attempt to run every red light between Battersea Park and the nick.

"I want to get there alive, boss."

"Stop whining, Josh." Godley looked at me in the rearview mirror. "All right, Maeve?"

"I'm okay." It lacked conviction, as he noticed immediately.

"There's no need to worry about Lydia's safety."

"I'm not worried about her. Well, I am, but only because I think she hasn't been honest with us so far."

"Worrying about Chris Swain?"

"A bit," I admitted. And about Rob, but I

wasn't going to say that. He had gone back to the flat to pack bags for us; he would let me know, he said, where he found to spend the night. I could join him if and when I got back from Sussex. Or not, presumably.

"What do we know about the individual in custody?"

I repeated what Sussex CID had told me over the phone when I'd got hold of them. "He's nineteen. It's Seth Carberry."

Derwent turned in his seat to give me a look. "Who's that?"

"He's the brother of Laura's best friend. He let us into the house when we went to interview her — remember?"

"Not in any detail," Derwent said grumpily. "What was he doing down in Sussex?"

"From what Lydia said, I think we're about to confirm the identity of the boy from Laura's camera."

"The mysterious boyfriend." Godley's knuckles shone white as he gripped the steering wheel and I could have guessed what was on his mind before he said it. "If I found out my daughter was up to that sort of thing, I wouldn't be answerable for what I did."

"This is a good reason to keep Philip Kennford in the dark about it." Derwent sighed. "It would all make so much more sense if it was the boyfriend and the girl who'd died, and Kennford who'd done it. Why would Carberry want to kill his girl and her mother?"

"And why is he hanging around her sister?" I added.

"How did he know where to find her?" Godley asked.

"Good point. We only drove her down to Sussex today. No one should have known she was there except her dad, her aunt and the two ladies and I don't think any of them would have told him where she was."

"No one could have followed you, I take it."

I could answer that one. "Definitely not. It's down a dirt track a mile long. Anything moving leaves a cloud of dust behind it. It's flat countryside, and we got lost so we doubled back on ourselves. No way were we followed."

"Well, that's your first question for him."

"The second is whether he's been in Twickenham recently," I said.

"Renee's stranger?" Derwent nodded. "That would make sense."

"If he found her in Twickenham, that leaves Savannah and Zoe out. They didn't know she was there until we told them."

"Yeah, well, the obvious person to tell him where she is is Lydia herself."

"She was terrified," I pointed out. "She rang me in hysterics."

"Doesn't mean she didn't bring him to her door." Derwent looked back at me again.

"She's an attention-seeker, isn't she? Not eating, cutting herself — that's all her way of getting people to focus on her instead of her sister. Calling you in a panic fits in with that. She must have known we wouldn't be able to help her directly. She should have been calling 999, not you. And getting him to follow her around fits too. She gets to take over from her sister, step into her shoes. Be the popular one for a change."

"I'm not saying you're wrong, but you didn't talk to her. She sounded genuinely scared."

"We'll see."

"All right." I looked out of the window at streets that were familiar, not really seeing them except to register that we hadn't far to go. Almost to myself, I said, "There is another reason she might have been faking."

"Go on," Godley said.

"If her accomplice had just got nicked, I imagine Lydia would have wanted to be very clear that he was nothing to do with her. There's no better way to distance herself from him."

"You think they were in on it together?" Derwent asked.

"I don't know. I can't imagine Lydia killing her mother and her sister, but we don't know that she didn't. Or that she didn't set it up." I tore at a nail that had a ragged edge, suddenly irritated by it. "I mean, she survived.

She wasn't harmed at all. Even Philip Kennford got a mild concussion out of what happened last Sunday night. We've been pussyfooting around her because of all her issues but, as you say, they're all part of the same thing — wanting attention. This is pretty much the best way to make sure she's number one on her father's list, isn't it?"

"Because she's the only one?" Derwent shook his head. "You're a cynic."

"It's been said before."

"Do you really believe Lydia was involved in the killings?" Godley asked.

"I'm not ruling it out, that's all."

"Then I won't either," Derwent said. "Not if the famous Kerrigan intuition says I should be suspicious."

"She's been right before." Godley pulled into the yard and stopped near Derwent's car. "Do you need to get anything from the office before you go?"

"Probably, but I can't think what."

"Don't worry, Kerrigan. We'll manage with what we've got." Derwent was sounding almost kind, I thought, off my guard completely. It was, as usual, a mistake to relax. "All you really need is a notebook and a pencil so you can take notes for me. I bet even Sussex CID can rise to those."

They had taken Seth Carberry to the nearest police station to Savannah Wentworth's house, in a small market town. Derwent spent the drive down there speculating on whether it would be a thatched building, or if there would be more than one cell, and was pleasingly bemused to discover it was an extremely modern building bristling with phone masts with the latest in BMW response cars outside.

"I'd say they can afford a pencil all right," I observed, and got a glare.

"This is just window dressing. Reassuring the community by looking slick. Don't be fooled. They're all bumpkins."

"Have a heart. We're still in the Home Counties."

"These are all coppers who wanted to join the Met. Wait and see. We're going to get shit off them like you wouldn't believe, just because they wish they were us."

"We certainly will if you go in with that attitude." I looked at him curiously. "Do you really think every police officer in the world wishes they worked for the Met?"

"Why wouldn't they? Best force around. Best resources. Best crimes."

"That's debatable."

"Fittest female officers too." He grinned. "I'm only joking. Fittest police dogs, I meant to say."

"You'll never change."

"Better hope not." He got out of the car and stretched, then strode into the building with a swagger, the big copper down from

London to show the locals a thing or two. I followed more slowly, wishing I was there with someone else. Anyone. On my own, even. He was a liability at the best of times and a pain in the arse at all times, and I was starting to wonder if I'd be better off working with someone else. DCI Burt, for instance. She seemed sensible, pleasant and professional. Derwent fell into the "none of the above" category.

By the time I made it inside, Derwent was leaning on the counter doing his level best to charm the receptionist. She was very young, wore her fair hair long and straight, and showed off a mouthful of metal when she smiled or spoke. I anticipated the smile would decrease in wattage the longer Derwent spent with her.

"Don't imagine you're usually this busy on a Thursday evening. Lots of people coming and going tonight."

"It's about the same as normal."

"Really? Even with ugly mugs like ours turning up from the Met?" He leaned on the last two words for extra emphasis. Remarkably, she didn't seem to be impressed.

"We get officers from all over."

"From London?"

"From abroad, even." She widened her eyes at him, feigning awe. Not the pushover she looked, I thought, and wanted to give her a round of applause. I settled for joining Derwent at the counter and showing her my ID.

"Do you know if Lydia Kennford is here?"

The response came from behind me. "She's in one of our interview rooms."

He was a thickset man with a weather-beaten square face, middle-aged but with a mop of dark curly hair that seemed to belong to a younger man. It gave him a curiously mismatched appearance.

"DS Saunders. Barry Saunders." He shook my hand, a brief but agonizing squeeze. I watched, fascinated, as Derwent struggled not to react when it was his turn. "I spoke to you on the phone, I think, if you're DC Kerrigan."

I had already recognized his voice and the soft burr of the local accent. "You did indeed. Thank you for reassuring us about Lydia's safety."

"We made good time. He didn't have much of a chance to do more than look through the windows. And then one of the girls on the farm overpowered him. Had him all trussed up waiting for the response team to take him away."

"Was that Zoe?" I asked. I couldn't imagine Savannah tackling anyone.

"That's right. Zoe Prowse. Nice girl."

"I bet that's not what Mr. Carberry thinks." I could see Derwent was itching to tell the other detective that Zoe was a lesbian and therefore not such a nice girl after all. I pitied

532

the person who had done his diversity training. There was nothing you could teach him about respecting other people's lifestyles, race or sexuality. I liked to think Barry Saunders might be a little bit more enlightened.

"He says she overreacted." He pulled a face. "Not sure I would blame her. Three young women living miles from anywhere, and a lad comes wandering around the house uninvited. He parked his car well away from it too. Didn't want anyone to know he was there, I'd say. Until he was good and ready at least."

"Did you search him?" Derwent demanded. "And the car?"

"Of course." Saunders let that response stand for a moment, before relenting. "No weapons on him but there was a knife in the car."

"What sort of knife?" Derwent's voice had gone up an octave, all the way to hysteria in the space of a single sentence. So much for being the cold-as-ice detectives from the awe-inspiring Metropolitan Police.

Saunders looked amused. "A small one. Two-inch blade — something like that. It was in a toolkit in the boot. It was on a multiuse tool — screwdriver, pliers, scissors, that sort of thing. He said he'd never noticed it was on there."

"Nothing to get excited about, then." Crestfallen was not the word for Derwent's demeanor.

"I wouldn't bother getting in a state about it, no. Like I said, the car wasn't near the house — twenty minutes away on foot, so if he was planning to use the knife, you'd think he'd have brought it with him."

"We'll still take it. Get it checked by our forensics guys. You probably don't have access to a police lab, do you?"

"We use a private one. Only for the most serious crimes because of the cost. This probably wouldn't count, given that he didn't actually intrude on the premises." There was a quirk to Saunders' mouth that made me think he wasn't taking Derwent entirely seriously, which was good, because if he had been inclined to be offended we could have been in serious danger of getting thrown out. "But you're more than welcome to run whatever tests you like. Have a look at the rest of his belongings before you speak to him. You might pick up on things someone like me would miss, not being familiar with the case."

I cut in before Derwent could say anything else undiplomatic. "What we'd really like to do is talk to Lydia first, then Seth Carberry."

"I've got her waiting for you."

"You didn't arrest her, did you?" Derwent asked.

Saunders looked genuinely surprised. "Why would I? DC Kerrigan mentioned that you'd like to talk to her so I invited her to come and wait for you. She seems like a nice enough kid."

"Is she on her own?" I asked.

"She's got her half sister waiting with her, I believe."

I looked at Derwent. "Will Savannah do for an appropriate adult? Because I don't fancy your chances of getting Renee to turn out tonight, and you didn't want to involve her father if you could help it."

"We'll make it work. She's just giving us a bit of insight, isn't she? We're not treating her as a suspect. At the moment."

"What could you suspect her of? If you don't mind me asking." Saunders' broad face looked baffled. "Doesn't seem the sort to say boo to the proverbial."

"We're not sure. Maybe nothing." Derwent narrowed his eyes and lowered his voice, trying to impress the detective. "Maybe murder."

"Is that right?" Saunders shrugged. "Takes all sorts, doesn't it?"

It wasn't the response Derwent had been hoping for, but he went with it, striding down the corridor. "Let's have a look at her, anyway."

"It's this way, actually," Saunders called after him, pointing in the other direction. "But if you want to take the long way round, don't let me stop you. That might be how you do it in the Met. I wouldn't know."

It was the second time I'd seen Savannah in a police station and for the second time I was struck by how she managed to transcend the dingy surroundings. Slender in khaki shorts and a white top, with her hair scraped back in a ponytail, she was leaning against the wall when we went in. Lydia was sitting at the table, her head buried in her arms, and Savannah raised one finger to her lips.

"She's asleep."

"Too bad. We'll have to wake her."

"Give her a minute. She's exhausted." Savannah stood up straight and stuck her hands in her pockets, tilting one foot so she was balanced on the edge of it. She looked coltish and very young, and I was quite prepared for Derwent to go along with whatever she asked. To my surprise, he dragged a chair out from the table, the legs shrieking on the tiled floor. I glared at him but it was too late; Lydia had lifted her head and was staring at us blearily.

"How are you?" I asked.

"Okay." She whispered it. Her face was pale, her eyes red, and I wondered if she had been crying or if it was just how she looked when she'd woken abruptly.

"Let her wake up." Savannah spoke sharply. "Don't interrogate her until she's ready to talk."

"No one is interrogating anyone. We just want to find out a bit more about what happened tonight." I said it as much for Derwent's benefit as for Lydia's. He needed to keep in mind that we had no evidence against Lydia — nothing that would be a reason to arrest her. Without evidence we were relying on her cooperation, and while I couldn't imagine Lydia flouncing out of the police station in a huff, I could certainly visualize Savannah doing just that.

"Then you should speak to him. That *freak.* Creeping around, terrifying us."

"I gather Zoe dealt with him pretty effectively."

Savannah's face lit up. "She frightened the life out of him. I don't think he even tried to fight her. By the time he knew he'd been spotted he was facedown with his hands tied behind his back."

"So she wasn't injured?"

"Not at all. But we agreed it was better for me to come to the station with Lydia so she had someone from the family with her. Moral support." She looked past us. "Is Dad coming?"

"We haven't informed him of the events of this evening yet. We wanted to know what happened ourselves before involving him." I looked at Lydia. "Did you want him here?"

"I don't mind."

"She'd have liked him to show he cared, I

think." Savannah's mouth was incapable of looking thin-lipped but it came close at that moment.

"I'll get in touch with him when we're finished here. Probably tomorrow, at this rate. It's getting pretty late, after all." I smiled at Lydia, who was looking a little less wan. "Do you need anything, Lydia? A drink, or something to eat?"

"No. I'd just like to get back and get some rest."

"We'll try not to keep you for long." Derwent leaned across the table, crowding her a little bit. "But you need to do some talking, don't you?"

"What do you mean?"

"How did he know where you were? Not just this time. When you were in London too." Derwent tapped the table with one finger, more or less under the girl's nose. She leaned back to get away from him. "You had to have been in touch with him, Lydia. You told him where to find you."

Her face crumpled and for a couple of minutes there was no sound in the room except for sobbing. After a while Savannah moved over and stood beside her, patting her shoulder in a slightly awkward way. It might have helped; certainly Lydia got herself under control and wiped at her eyes with her sleeve.

"All right. You're right." She was barely audible.

"You were in touch with this Seth Carberry all along."

"He got in touch with me."

"How?"

"Laura's phone."

"You had it," I said softly. She nodded. "Where is it now?"

I hadn't noticed it but Lydia had a bag on her lap, a small satchel. She opened it and took out an iPhone, then slid it across the table to me.

"The password is one two three five."

"Thanks." I turned it off without looking at it.

"Don't you want to see what's on there?" Savannah asked.

"I do, but it has to go for technical examination." I shrugged. "They don't like us fiddling with the evidence. I'm not an expert. I might lose something important."

"Or add something. You couldn't trust her." Derwent grinned at me. "Only joking."

"What did Seth want with you? And what did you want with him?" I asked Lydia, ignoring Derwent.

She looked revolted. "I didn't *want* him."

"You told him where to find you."

"Because you wanted to know who he was. You asked me if I could help you, and I did. I thought I was doing the right thing."

"You should have given us the phone and let us track him down. You could have put yourself in danger."

"I thought I could get him to talk to me. That's what he wanted. To talk about Laura."

"And pick up with you where he left off with her?" Derwent asked.

Lydia blushed to the roots of her hair. "No. Not at all."

"Were they still in a relationship when she died?" I asked.

"She'd broken up with him, he said. She told him she was too busy to see him. She had other things to do with her time. She couldn't be bothered to sneak around anymore."

I frowned. "That doesn't sound as if she was campaigning to introduce him to your parents, does it?"

"I suppose not."

"Were you in touch with him before Laura died? Did you know him then?" I asked.

"No. I'd never met him. I spoke to him twice this week, on the phone. That was it." She sounded definite, her eyes guileless. So much for my theory about them being in cahoots.

"Did he tell you anything else about Laura, or their relationship?"

"No. He just wanted to see me to talk about her." Her face puckered again. "He said he missed her. And I miss her too."

"Of course you do." Savannah put her arms

around her sister's neck. "Can we stop this now?"

"Fine." Derwent glowered at Lydia. "But you need to start being honest with us, young lady. Is there anything else you've been holding back?"

Instead of answering, Lydia looked up at Savannah. She seemed to be about to say something, but settled for shaking her head.

"Right, then." He leaned across and chucked her under the chin. "You'll do, missy. But don't try to do our jobs for us, will you. That's what we're paid to do. Now head off home and don't get in any more trouble."

She nodded, gazing up at him as if the sun shone out of him. It was nice that someone shared Derwent's high opinion of himself, even if I couldn't imagine why. He made a most unlikely father figure. Then again, Philip Kennford was not what I would describe as ideal either. In comparison with him, even Derwent might look good.

They had taken Seth Carberry down to a cell in the basement of the police station to wait — not the most pleasant place to be, so he was as cooperative as he was going to get when he appeared in the interview room. On the other hand, that didn't mean that he was prepared to be cooperative at all. I hadn't been clear on what to expect from Laura's secret boyfriend but it wasn't what I got. Carberry was small and wiry, and his skin was pure white as if he never saw daylight. He had unruly black hair, heavy eyebrows and an awkward nose that he was still growing into, but there was something hypnotic about his eyes, which were very dark indeed — so much so that I strained to see his pupils. I had seen him before at his family home and failed to notice much about him, but looking at him now without the beanie hat I was sure I had seen him on another occasion and I couldn't quite recollect when. It bothered me, twisting at the back of my mind like a forgotten name. I tried not to think about it and naturally I couldn't then think about anything else. It wasn't from the pictures in Laura's camera, because he hadn't been the star by any means. He had been a triangle of torso, a flat stomach with a meager trail of hair down the center, a strip of thigh in the corner of an image. I had imagined him to be older, not least because Laura had been a pretty girl, and outgoing, and I had expected her to find someone worthy of her. Seth Carberry didn't even come close to it. That didn't seem to have occurred to him. He had as much natural arrogance as a gamecock, and gave me and Derwent the same unimpressed look down his bony nose. He was wearing a gray T-shirt that had obvious sweat marks under the arms and jeans that were at least one size too big for him, with very dirty sports socks. I was inclined to forgive the grubbiness; police stations weren't the most antiseptic places. On the other hand it was the second time I'd seen him looking scruffy. Teenage chic, I presumed, and was glad the men I met generally knew their way around a washing machine and shower.

"What's this about? Why do you want to talk to me? I thought I was in trouble with the locals, not the Met."

"Sit down." Derwent pointed at the chair opposite us and then fiddled with the recording equipment. "You know what it's about, don't you? It's about you turning up at Miss Savannah Wentworth's house and snooping about, and whether that's connected with the case we're investigating. The murder of Vita and Laura Kennford." He ran through the official preamble for the benefit of the tape, including the fact that the boy had waived his right to have a solicitor present. It didn't make either of us think he was innocent or anything other than naive, but it made life easier. "Mr. Carberry, you were arrested for attempted burglary of Miss Savannah Wentworth's premises at Godetts Farm, Sussex, on Thursday the nineteenth of August at eight p.m. What were you up to?"

"Nothing. I didn't even know it was her house."

"What were you doing there?"

"I wanted to see Lydia. To find out what happened to Laura, not just what was in the papers and on TV. She'd said she'd see me, but when I got there she wasn't around."

"And Zoe jumped on you."

"Is that her name? We weren't introduced. I didn't get the chance to explain I was there by invitation." He frowned. "I wasn't really snooping, either. It was still daylight. If I'd wanted to hide, I'd have come at night."

"Is that what you usually do?" I asked.

He shifted in his seat. "I don't do that kind of thing usually."

"But you did go to Laura's aunt's house in Twickenham, to try to see Lydia. And you ran away when you were challenged."

"Yes." He admitted it reluctantly, but he did admit it. I flicked a glance at Derwent who narrowed his eyes very slightly in return. Not Christopher Blacker in the garden, then. And yet I still didn't feel easy in my mind about him.

"You didn't intend to harm her on that occasion either," Derwent said.

"I just wanted to talk to her, as I said. And I thought she wanted to see me. She gave me that impression."

"Did you get in touch with her or did she contact you?"

"She contacted me. Freaked me right out when I got a message from Laura's phone, but I realized what was going on pretty quickly."

"Had you met Lydia before?"

"Fuck, no. She's a massive weirdo, isn't she? Doesn't go out much. Doesn't have friends. My sister had told me about her so I wasn't all that keen. Then Laura didn't even want me to meet her, so it didn't matter."

"Laura wanted to keep you a secret. Why was that?" I asked.

"She had her reasons, I assume. And I didn't mind. I wasn't exactly keen for everyone to know about us when she was so much younger than me. It wasn't going to do a lot for my reputation, put it that way."

"But now that Laura's dead, you do want to talk to Lydia."

"Like I said, I'm curious about what happened. I want to know how she died." He shrugged. "It's not that weird, is it?"

"You went to the Kennfords' house in Wimbledon the night Laura died." It had taken me a little while but I'd placed him at last. The boy in the baseball cap.

"How did you know that?" He looked at me as if I was clairvoyant. Beside me, Derwent was doing the same.

"You were in the crowd by the gate when we arrived. You were watching the police coming and going."

"There's nothing suspicious about it."

"We'll decide that, son," Derwent said. "What were you doing there?"

"I'd gone to the house to see her — to speak to her, not because I thought something had happened to her. We were supposed to meet last Sunday night. It had been arranged for ages, and then she canceled."

"Did that annoy you?"

"Yeah, it did." The dark eyes met mine. "It was my birthday, actually. I'd gone to a fair bit of trouble to make it a nice evening for us — I'd borrowed a mate's house so we wouldn't be disturbed, and I'd bought champagne for a kind of picnic dinner. I was pissed off when she canceled."

"Pissed off enough to take it out on her?" Derwent asked.

"What do you mean by that?" He fidgeted, rubbing his hands over his knees as if he was trying to wipe something away on the denim. "Enough to kill her? Obviously not."

"Did you argue with her?" I asked.

"We had a fight."

"What sort of a fight?"

"The kind where you break up at the end of it." He gave me a pitying look, the arrogance undented.

"Did it get physical?" Derwent asked.

"I don't think I understand the question."

Derwent stood up, surprising even me, and leaned across the table. "Understand this. I am asking you if you hit Laura when you argued with her, or at another time. I am asking if you laid hands on her in a violent way."

Seth looked wary. "Why do you ask?"

"There was bruising to her face. It was identified at the postmortem. It happened a day or so before her death, so the timing fits. Was it you?"

"I don't want to get in trouble."

"You're already in trouble," I pointed out. "Start talking."

He shrugged. "I gave her a little tap."

"A little tap," Derwent repeated, sitting down very slowly. I could tell he wanted to lunge across the table at the boy. "Tell me about it."

"Nothing to tell. I slapped her." He mimed an openhanded blow. "Pow."

"Why?"

"Because she rubbed me up the wrong way. She told me she wanted to finish with me. She wanted more, apparently, than I could offer." He laughed. "She thought a lot of herself, did Laura."

"You hit her because she broke up with you." I didn't even try to keep the disgust off my face. "Looks like she made the right decision."

"She'd have come back."

"Why do you say that?" I asked.

"Because she would have. It wasn't over."

"Sounds like it was pretty much over to me. How long had you been in a relationship?"

"Seven weeks."

"Is that all?" Derwent ran his hands over

547

the sides of his face as if he was testing out how his shave had lasted. "Bloody hell, I thought it was some kind of great love affair."

"Seven weeks is a long time when you're a teenager," I said to Derwent. Seth bridled.

"I'm nearly twenty."

"And there's a point," Derwent said softly. "What were you doing with a fifteen-year-old?"

"She's a friend of my sister's. You know that. She came to our house once to work on a project and we got talking."

"Then you made your move. On a girl your sister's age." Derwent's tone was pure disgust, but I was pretty sure he was faking that. He'd have done the same in a heartbeat and called it shooting fish in a barrel.

"She was the one making all the running, believe me. I wouldn't have tried it on with her if she hadn't been flirting with me. I thought she was pretty but she was young and inexperienced. She didn't really know what she was doing at first, which was sweet." He gave me a smile that made my stomach clench in disgust. "That kind of innocence — you just want to teach them what to do. And you can. They'll do anything you say."

"She was only fifteen."

"She didn't act like a fifteen-year-old."

"I know. We've seen the pictures." Derwent was straight in with that.

"Oh." He flushed a little, obviously aware of what we'd seen.

"That is you in the photos with her, then. On her camera."

"Probably. Unless she was sleeping with someone else. I'd have to see them to be sure."

I looked at Derwent, knowing he was going to be cross. "We don't have a set with us."

"We can arrange for you to see them. Confirm it is you in the pictures."

"It looks like you," I said, and wished I hadn't as Seth's mouth curled into a smile.

"What did you think of them?"

I glowered. "I thought they were images of an underage girl having sex with someone who was old enough to know better."

"Pretty sexy, though. You'd have to say."

"Pretty illegal is what occurred to me." He flinched a little, visibly on edge for the first time. I pushed harder. "What did you do with them? Did you put them on the Internet?"

"No. Nothing like that. They were for personal use only."

"Yours?"

"Laura's. It was her idea."

Derwent snorted. "The fifteen-year-old virgin wanted to commemorate her first experiences in the nasty world of sex, is that right?"

"Basically."

"Sorry. I don't believe you."

"It's true. Laura had a list of things she wanted to do. She watched a lot of porn."

"Where would she get hold of that kind of thing? She wasn't old enough to buy it."

"Um, for free, all over the Internet?" Seth's tone was scathing, as if he couldn't believe what a dinosaur Derwent was.

"Did you watch it together?" I asked.

"Sometimes. If we had time. I'm more of a doer, myself." He smiled again, obviously thinking that it came across as charming, but the dead eyes would have put me off even if his personality hadn't been so repellent. "Laura was the big fan."

"Why was that?"

"She'd found a collection in her parents' house when she was thirteen and that got her started on it. It made her curious. By the time I met her, she just wanted to do everything she'd ever seen. She only knew the theory. It was time for the real thing. And I was happy to oblige if I could."

"You must have thought all your dreams had come true," Derwent said dryly.

"It was all right. Got a bit boring sometimes." He propped one foot up on the other knee. "She got a kick out of talking about her parents afterward, like, 'What would they say if they could see what I just did?' Earning their disapproval seemed to be the point, you know?"

"Being a rebel was important to her, then."

I was thinking about what Lydia had told me, about Laura picking fights with her mother and father.

"It was how she got through the day. She told me her mother was on her case all the time, her dad was never there and had tons of affairs, and her sister was halfway to crazy. I think she was lonely. It wasn't much of a family, she said. She was looking for something more."

"And she ended up with you." Derwent shook his head. "Poor Laura."

"Me or someone else."

"Are we back to you not being the star of the photos?" I asked. "Because I would be surprised if it wasn't you."

"Thanks for that." He ran a hand through his hair. "She was seeing someone else."

"How do you know?" Derwent asked.

"Found messages from him on her phone."

"Did you indeed?"

"She was getting texts from someone and she was excited about it — kept going for her phone to check if he'd sent her something and she'd missed it."

"Did you find out who he was? A name?"

"No. They weren't signed. It could have been anyone."

"Someone you knew, though."

"She said it wasn't. She said I was being ridiculous. But I read the messages. It was all 'I think about you all the time' and 'I need to see you' and 'We'll make them understand they have to let us be together' — stuff like that."

"Sounds like competition," Derwent observed.

"That's what I thought. To be honest, that was part of what we argued about on Friday. I couldn't deal with how she reacted when I confronted her. She thought it was funny."

· "I bet she wasn't laughing after you hit her," I said with a thin smile.

"No. No, she wasn't. Um, that was it, really. That was the last time I spoke to her. I saw her on that Sunday but not to talk to her — she was just walking through the village talking on her phone. She didn't see me."

"And you went to the house on Sunday because you thought you could talk to her," I said.

"I went because I thought he was going to be there."

"Her father?" I was lost.

"No. The guy she was in touch with. Something in one of the messages made it seem as if they'd arranged for him to come to the house that night. I thought it was so she could introduce him to her parents and that made it worse, because she'd told me straight out she was never going to let them know about me, that her dad wouldn't like me and her mum would be too suspicious of me to be polite." He shook his head, still hurt. "I wanted to know what made him better than me. I'm going to Cambridge in October, for God's sake. I'm not the sort of boy that parents don't like."

"Oh, you're a real catch," Derwent said. "What are you going to study?"

"Law."

"You might want to think again, son. A conviction for trespass isn't going to help your career ambitions."

"That had occurred to me." His jaw was clenched.

"I'm beginning to see why you wanted to meet Philip Kennford," I said.

"Yeah, obviously. When I met her first, I thought Laura would be a useful contact. I thought she might be able to arrange some work experience for me with her father. That was why I showed an interest in the first place. But it's been nothing but trouble from start to finish." He was an arrogant little shit, but I could tell he meant what he said next.

"I wish to God I'd never met her."

CHAPTER TWENTY-TWO

The hotel room door was the sort that was impossible to open quietly, the key card humming and clicking to itself as I slid it into the lock. The handle required brute force to turn it. I slipped in as silently as possible, trying to get the door to close without banging, which proved to be beyond it too. A rustle from the bed behind me made me wince. Busted.

"What time do you call this?"

"Time I was in bed." I was almost glad he had woken up; it was reassuring to hear his voice sounding normal when nothing else was. I began to take off my clothes without putting the light on. "Did you pack pajamas for me?"

"Do you need them?" Rob yawned. "There are some, somewhere. I haven't bothered, myself."

"Toothbrush?"

"In the bathroom."

It was a small bathroom and the lighting made me look old before my time. I brushed my teeth with my eyes closed and quickly, aching all over. We had finished with Seth at one in the morning. Derwent had then moaned all the way back to the large, soulless chain hotel off the busiest roundabout in Wandsworth where "the missing member of Take That," as he put it, was waiting for me. It had annoyed Derwent that Rob had been wearing running kit, it seemed. Running was his territory. Rob standing around posing in shorts and a vest top had just been attention-seeking. I had let him rant, glad of a lift and preoccupied with the interviews we had just conducted. I was worried about Lydia. I was disgusted with Seth Carberry. I was hopelessly confused about the Kennford case. And I was completely out of ideas.

The air-conditioning was blasting when I came out of the bathroom in a T-shirt and pants. "I think this is the first time I've been cold since the hot weather started."

"Bliss, isn't it?" He mumbled it into the pillow, half asleep again. "I could almost be grateful to your stalker for the opportunity to sleep in comfort."

"Don't even mention him to me." I got into bed, already bothered by the street lights shining into the room and the red gleam of the standby bulb on the television. Beyond tired, I spent a restless couple of minutes trying to get comfortable.

"What's wrong?"

"The pillow is too soft." I thumped it crossly and lay down on my back, staring up at the ceiling. "The air-conditioning is too loud."

"This is a temporary measure. We'll find somewhere else to stay tomorrow." He yawned. "Go to sleep."

"I can't."

"Of course you can."

"I hate this." A tear slid out of the corner of my eye and down into my hair. I sniffed, then sniffed again. "I'm so sorry about it."

He rolled toward me. "Don't be stupid. It's not your fault."

"You should be doing the job you love and enjoying life in your own flat, not camping out in a crappy budget hotel. And all of it is my fault, if you think about it. If you weren't involved with me —"

"Spare me the guilt." He said it gently, though. "I've always made my own decisions, Maeve. And one of those was that you were worth a bit of hassle." There was a pause. "I could get tired of you trying to break up with me for stupid reasons, though."

"It seemed like the right course of action." Another tear joined the previous one.

"It always does."

"It's not because I don't care about you."

"I know."

I couldn't help laughing. "Oh, do you indeed?"

"It's because you don't like depending on anyone else. For anything."

"Not so."

"You like to think you're too tough to need me." He raised himself up on one elbow and grinned down at me. "But you're wrong. It's too late. You're committed."

"I could walk away at any time."

"No chance."

"How bigheaded are you, exactly?"

"Oh, very." He leaned down so he could kiss me. "Completely."

"Cocky git." I hesitated. "We should talk."

"About what in particular?"

"Trust?"

"Oh, that."

"Yes, that." I imitated his bored tone of voice and it made him laugh. I waited him out, though, wanting a serious answer.

"I made a mistake," he admitted. "I thought I could deal with the DI Ormond situation without involving you. I thought I could wait her out and she'd lose interest, but she's not really like that."

"You should have told me."

"I know. I'm sorry."

"I wouldn't have freaked out."

"Yeah. Except that you did."

"Only because I was cross with you for not being honest with me."

"I was afraid to be honest. I was afraid you'd leave me." He slid his hand along my

557

leg. "I would miss you too much."

"I bet." I picked his hand up and gave it back to him.

"Like that, is it?"

"I should go to sleep."

"Me too." After a moment his hand returned to my knee. This time I let it stay where it was. And move. And linger. And move again.

"What are you doing?"

"Nothing."

"Oh yeah? It doesn't make everything better, you know."

"I know. But it's a good way to pass the time."

"So is Scrabble."

"Shame we don't have a board." He leaned over and kissed me again. "We'll have to think of something else."

I made it easy for him sometimes, really I did, but it worked out rather nicely for me too. And I did get to sleep without too much trouble in the end, so there was that. All in all, things could have been a lot worse.

Rather inevitably, they became worse almost immediately. Not very many hours later — before six, it turned out — the two of us sat up at the same time in response to a phone ringing. It was how I woke up more often than I cared to calculate.

"Where is it?"

"The floor."

"Mine, then." I slid off the bed and went hunting through the clothes I'd shed earlier, shaking them out. Rob turned over with a groan and buried himself in the pillow, which was exactly what I would have liked to do. The phone was still ringing, vibrating against the floor, and I saw it in the end under the bed because the screen was lit up.

"What do you want?" I said it before I answered, not quite brave enough to say good morning to Derwent in those terms, settling for a neutral, "Kerrigan."

"Woke you, did I?" His voice was loud and I winced.

"Of course you did." My voice sounded rough; the air-conditioning had dried out my vocal cords.

"Tough shit. No more sleeping. You need to get your arse in gear and meet me. We've got a job."

"What job?" I rubbed my eyes, trying not to yawn into the phone.

"We've been invited to a crime scene."

"What's that supposed to mean?" The tiredness was receding as the old familiar tension flooded my body.

"It means one of our witnesses just turned up dead."

The street didn't look much better for being full of police vehicles instead of builders' vans. Derwent parked near the end, swearing under his breath, and I decided not to bother teasing him about the distance we had to walk. He had been in a bad mood since he picked me up, a mood that was showing no signs of lifting, and I didn't feel much like laughing anyway.

We were out of our territory and neither of us knew any of the local CID, so it took us a while to get through the various cordons and get into the house itself. Standing in the hall, I found myself struck by how unchanged the place was, how familiar from our previous visit, the same coat hanging on a hook, the same stack of unopened junk mail in the corner by the door. Then the differences began to filter through. There was a smell in the air that hadn't been there before, something I recognized from other murders I had attended: blood, chiefly. There were sounds from upstairs — many feet moving around — and boiler-suited SOCOs were working in the living room. This would be a big case for someone and they weren't stinting on manpower. I stood beside Derwent, waiting to be told where to go. We had paper shoe-covers but that didn't mean we could or should roam through the house. Everyone who passed us seemed to have something better to do than talk to us.

"Can I help you?" It was an officer in a dark-blue suit, a youngish man with thinning hair and heavy-framed glasses who was coming down the stairs at speed. Instinctively I felt I wouldn't like him — there was something in the timbre of his voice, the tight-arsed posture he affected that made him seem like the teacher's pet, all grown up.

"DI Josh Derwent." He moved in front of me, which was his usual technique — far be it from him to do anything as useful as introducing me. I stepped to the side so I was still visible.

"Ah. We found your card."

"Yeah, I thought that was why I got a call."

"We thought you might be able to help us out. Fill in some details for us. I'm DS Bradbury. Andy Bradbury." He held up gloved hands. "I've been searching bodies. You won't want to shake."

"You're dead right." Derwent didn't look as if he was particularly sorry about it either.

Bradbury looked at me. "And you are?"

"DC Maeve Kerrigan."

"Do we need you to be here?" He raised his eyebrows at Derwent. "You didn't need to bring an entourage."

Derwent folded his arms. "Tell you what, mate, if she goes, I go."

"There's no need for that. I just wanted to make sure there was a reason for her to be here, that's all. We can't have too many people milling around."

"Well, she was here with me the last time so she knows what I know, if not a bit more."

"Right. Right. Well, that's fine, then," Bradbury blustered.

I was feeling a completely unfamiliar warm glow at being defended and the knowledge that Derwent would soon do or say something unspeakable to make me dislike him again made it all the sweeter. I winked at him as Bradbury turned away, and was gratified to see him look surprised, then pleased.

"It's a clean sweep, you said on the phone. How many bodies are we talking about?"

"Five." Bradbury pointed into the sitting room. "One in there. Three upstairs, in their beds. Your one in the kitchen." He went for his notebook, thumbing through the pages. "What was her name?"

"Adamkuté. Niele Adamkuté." I had been about to say it but Derwent got there first; he had actually learned her name, then, at some stage.

"How were they killed?" I asked.

"They were shot. Using a silencer, I would presume, given that none of the neighbors heard anything. The victims didn't have any warning by the looks of things. All very professional. They didn't know what was happening until they were already dead."

"Did they all live in the house?"

"As far as we can tell. We're trying to ID them, but some of them have two or three passports so it's not easy."

"Find any weapons?" Derwent asked.

"Yep. Knives, several handguns, a ton of ammo, a couple of shotguns. And cash. And amphetamines in large numbers, bagged up, ready for retail. And what looks very like stolen gold jewelry in a couple of hold-alls under a bed." He grinned. "No one is going to be crying for this bunch."

"If you say so." Derwent's jaw was tight. Like me, he seemed to be having trouble with the fact of Niele's death. She had seemed so tough, so indomitable, and it shouldn't have made a difference that she was beautiful, but it did. "We only met two of the occupants so I can't help you with identifying the others, but we'll tell you what we can."

"Come and have a look anyway." He pushed past us and went into the sitting room. "Can I let these officers see the victim in here?"

"Help yourself. He hasn't moved." The nearest SOCO was bearded and paunchy with drooping eyes that looked like they'd seen too much. Specifically, too much of Andy Bradbury.

"He was asleep, looks like. The TV was on in here when the first responders arrived." It was still on, showing baseball from Japan. Niche programming, I assumed. Opposite it on the sofa lay a large-framed man that I recognized as Jurgis, but only with some difficulty. His face was pulled out of shape by the damage done to his head. The back of his skull was more or less gone. Blood and brain matter had sprayed across the cardboard boxes that I had noticed on our previous visit, and one SOCO was meticulously recording each gobbet of tissue, each fragment of bone.

"That's our mate Jurgis, isn't it?" Derwent said to me.

"I'd have said so." I looked at Bradbury. "We only got his first name, I'm afraid. Did you find any ID for him?"

"There was a passport for a . . . Jurgis Jankauskas." He read it out of his notebook again, mangling it more than a little bit.

"Sounds about right," Derwent said. "She wouldn't have had any reason to use a false name for him when she was talking to us, would she?"

"Probably not. You never know, though."

"Looks as if they were up to all sorts of bad behavior. She might have made a habit of lying," Bradbury offered. "Especially knowing you were coppers."

"Possibly." Derwent was looking irritable. He had liked Niele, liked her more than he wanted to admit, and calling her a lying criminal was a bad way for Bradbury to ingratiate himself with the inspector. Even if it was true.

I hurried in with, "That name looks like a good place to start, anyway. There's a lot of damage, isn't there? What ammunition were they using?"

"Hollow point."

"Not messing about, then."

"Not at all." Bradbury leaned forward, angling his pen toward what had been the roof of Jurgis's mouth. "He was lying with his mouth open. The barrel of the gun would have been where my pen is — bit closer, probably. Pull the trigger" — he mimed it — "guaranteed kill shot."

"Is that what the pathologist said?" Derwent asked.

"Er, yes. It is." He seemed a little bit disappointed to have to admit he hadn't worked it out for himself.

"Do you think he was the first victim?"

"Probably not. I'd be inclined to think your lady was the first. They came in through the back."

"And she was in the kitchen?"

"Sitting at the table, it seems." He went back out into the hall, without waiting to see if we would follow. Derwent hung back to let me go next, which was unusually chivalrous for him. I didn't make the mistake of looking sympathetic, but I wasn't exactly keen to see Niele's body either — not having seen what had happened to her large friend — and I dragged my feet as I went down the hall. The kitchen was as bleak and unloved as the rest of the house, with cheap white units and dated appliances. A couple of the doors were damaged, showing the chipboard under the veneer. Not the best quality, and not well treated either. There were crumbs on all the work surfaces, stains on the floor and an overflowing bin in the corner. The sink was piled high with pots and pans soaking in cold, greasy water, and the top of the cooker was a disaster area, plastered with layers of burned food.

"Is this really how criminal masterminds live?" I said to Derwent over my shoulder. Bradbury answered, though.

"These were foot soldiers. They do the work and send the money home. I bet all of them had nice houses in Lithuania. They put in the time here for a few years, then retire and live in the lap of luxury."

"You sound like you know all about it," Derwent said.

"I worked on an organized crime unit for a bit. We had a lot of trouble with them." Bradbury shook his head, then pointed down at the floor. "This is your witness, isn't it?"

She was behind the table where she had fallen, sprawling on her side, her legs bent. Her face wasn't damaged at all, but in death she had the creepy perfection and pallor of a mannequin. Her eyes were open, staring at nothing.

"Has she been examined by the pathologist?" Derwent asked.

"Yes, but he put her back the way he found her. He's got a thing about leaving the scene intact as much as possible."

"Useful." Derwent crouched down, staring at Niele's body, which was dressed in jersey trousers and a strappy vest. She had Ugg boots on her feet and I thought she would have chosen to die in more elegant shoes, if she'd had the chance to dress for the occasion. "*She* wasn't asleep."

"That's why we think she died first."

"She was painting her nails." I had already seen the uncapped varnish bottle on the table, the cotton wool and remover set to one side with an orange stick and emery board. Thorough, meticulous, perfectionist: it all fitted with the impression I'd formed of her. Looking at her hands, I saw she had been halfway through the first coat, a stinging fuchsia pink. The unpainted nails were a dull blue by now. "Was the TV on in here?"

"The radio. Someone's turned it off since we got here. God-awful stuff — some pirate channel with Eastern European pop."

"Maybe she was homesick," I suggested. No one responded. "What time do you think it happened?"

"Late. Between midnight and two, we think."

"She was a night owl, then." Derwent was still staring at her.

"So it seems. The other victims were all asleep." Bradbury shrugged. "We know they were alive at midnight because a neighbor came round to complain about where one of the men had parked — the guy was blocked in and he needed to move his car."

"What gives you the two-hour window?"

"The pathologist suggested it."

"Is that it?" Derwent looked distinctly unimpressed. "They can't usually be so specific. Sounds like crap to me."

"Hardly." Bradbury squared up to him. "He's basing it on the facts. Body temperature, mainly."

"I've always been told that's unreliable, especially in this sort of weather." I knew Derwent was thinking of Glen Hanshaw, who would hem and haw about providing a time of death until we were tired of asking.

"Well, there's also the fact that we got tipped off by an anonymous caller who rang in at four and said they'd been dead a couple of hours, so we've got that to corroborate it."

"Is that how you found out? A call? So someone wanted you to know about the deaths." I looked at Derwent. "That's not usual, is it?"

"Not with a professional hit. But maybe they needed the message to get out there. Killing them all like this — it's a bit extreme."

"What sort of message, though?"

"A warning to anyone else, perhaps. Don't try and play with the big boys." Derwent sighed. "Guns and drugs and stolen gold. The fucking glamour of it all would make you throw up. What a waste."

568

I knelt beside him to look more closely at Niele's body. "Shot in the chest?"

Bradbury nodded. "One shot."

"No misses." Derwent's face was grim. "Professional standard of shooting. She's still holding the brush. She didn't have time to do more than look up. They must have blasted her as soon as the door was open."

"At least she wouldn't have known what was happening. She probably wasn't afraid."

"That girl wouldn't have been afraid of anything." Derwent tilted his head sideways, staring at her for a long moment. Then he stood up. "It's a shame, that's all. Where did you find my card?"

"In her room. Do you want to have a look?"

"Might as well."

"The other three bodies are upstairs too." Bradbury headed out of the kitchen, striding jauntily. "You can have a look at them before you see her room."

"Do we have to?" Derwent muttered. Out loud, he said, "Not sure there's much point, mate. We didn't meet anyone else when we were here."

Bradbury was not the sort to be put off. "Worth a squint, probably. You never know."

I shared a woebegone look with Derwent. We trudged into the hall, up the stairs and through three more crime scenes featuring bodies in various states of undress and disarray, along with a large number of policemen and forensics investigators, none of whom seemed particularly pleased to see Bradbury. The first had been asleep in a single bed that took up most of the tiny room he occupied. The bullet had entered his head just behind his left ear and buried itself in the mattress. The room was stifling and a plywood wardrobe blocked half of the window. The wallpaper was almost hidden behind pictures of naked women, some torn from magazines, some advertising the dubious delights of the local prostitutes, the kind you found in phone boxes.

"Cheap décor," Derwent commented.

"This is how I imagine your flat looks."

"Oh, thank you very much." He scanned the display. "Why is it you just can't get tired of looking at tits?"

"I think I could."

"Do you mind looking at the body?" Bradbury sounded fed up. Derwent looked at him instead, a long look that would have made me squirm. Yet again, I stepped in to keep the peace.

"I don't recall seeing this man before."

"Me neither," Derwent agreed.

"Next one, then."

It was a bigger room and a bigger man, a giant who made Jurgis look positively fragile. Two shots this time, one to the stomach, one to the chest.

"Overkill. One would have done it." Bradbury shook his head, as if deploring the waste of a bullet.

"I wouldn't want to risk him getting up, would you?" Derwent leaned over to look at the man's face. He had died with a frown, his brow furrowed, his face puffy and sullen. "Not one I know."

"Me neither."

"He had guns under his bed."

"I'd let him mind my gun, if I had one. Better than a safe any day." Derwent turned to examine the room. "No sign of a burglary."

"No. We were the ones who searched the place. It was a kill job, pure and simple. Or they found what they wanted without having to hunt for it."

"My money's on the former, for what it's worth," I said.

"Yeah, well I won't bet the house on your opinion if you don't mind. I might wait to see what more experienced officers have to say."

Bradbury was fast becoming one of my least favorite colleagues, and there was competition for that slot. I stepped away from the bed. "They did what they came here to do, did it well, and made sure you found out about it sooner rather than later. After you, I bet they tipped off the media."

"They were here not long after we arrived," he admitted.

"I'd feel a bit manipulated if I were you.

You're just tidying up someone else's mess." Bradbury opened his mouth to argue but I raised my eyebrows. "Next one?"

It turned out the pathologist was still with the last victim, so we were allowed to glance in and duck out again having denied all knowledge of the man in question. He was young and fair-haired, with a crucifix around his neck on a gold chain, and he had been naked and asleep when his life ended. There was something vulnerable about him, something that reminded me of the boys who had died in the Range Rover in Clapham. I shook my head as I turned away.

"What's wrong?" Derwent asked.

"He's too young to be dead for a row that probably wasn't anything to do with him."

"Don't be fooled by the pretty face. He was probably a violent thug."

"You'd like to believe that."

"I would. I wish all murder victims were criminals. It would make it that bit easier to do this job."

"Finding it tough?"

"Today, yeah." Derwent looked exhausted, I thought, his eyes puffy from lack of sleep. "And I could do without the fucking tour guide."

Bradbury had lingered in the room behind us to ask the pathologist a few questions about the fifth victim, receiving monosyllabic answers. He joined us in the hall.

"Ready to see Niele's room?"

"About half an hour ago." Derwent rolled his head around his shoulders, stretching his neck. "I told you that would be a waste of time."

"You never know."

"Bullshit. I knew it before I started. Do you get paid by the hour or something?"

"There's no harm in being thorough." Bradbury pointed past Derwent. "That's your witness's room in there."

"Finally." Derwent barrelled through the door, then stopped. "All right, guv?"

"Josh." I recognized Godley's voice before I saw him, leaning over an open drawer with a couple of T-shirts in his gloved hands. The room was spotless but not luxurious in any respect. The bed was iron-framed and narrow, and the walls were bare, painted white. It was austere in the extreme. I remembered that Kennford had described it as being studenty, and felt inclined to agree with his opinion.

Derwent didn't seem to have noticed anything except the superintendent. "What are you doing here? How did you even know about it?"

"It seems to be gang-related. I was informed about it as a matter of course, given the other investigation."

"Who informed you?"

Godley frowned. "I fail to see why it matters, Josh."

"Sorry, we haven't been introduced." The DS oozed past me. "Andy Bradbury. I know who you are, of course."

"Good." Godley looked at him without enthusiasm. "Are you running this case?"

"I'm in charge of the crime scenes. I'm here to make sure everything is done properly."

"That sounds like a fine and important job. Please, don't let us distract you from it." Godley smiled pleasantly, but he wasn't going to let the other officer stay and Bradbury knew it. Muttering something about checking up on the pathologist, he left, not bothering to say goodbye to Derwent or me.

"Thank Christ for that. I bet they did leave him here to mind the crime scene. I'd put him in charge of counting the paper clips if I had to work with him." Derwent stretched up like a meerkat to peer at what Godley was doing. "What have you got there?"

"Nothing much. I'm just searching the room."

"What are you looking for?"

"This and that." Godley must have been aware that his reply fell a bit short of the politeness for which he was famed. "A phone, mainly."

"Isn't it downstairs?" I frowned, trying to remember what had been on the kitchen table. It was like a parody of the party game where you have to remember what was displayed and what's gone missing. I was sure the phone had been lying beside the bottle of varnish on the table.

"There was one. Not the right one, though."

"Do you want any help?" I asked.

"By all means."

I started to check the bed, lifting pillows and the duvet to make sure it wasn't hiding anywhere obvious. Derwent stood for a moment, watching us, then left the room without further comment. I heard him going downstairs and wondered what he was doing. Behind me, Godley had moved on to the wardrobe and was opening bags.

"Is this a business phone or something?"

"Could be."

"Do you know what model it is?"

"Not a clue."

I ran my hands under the mattress, sliding them along. It would be near the edge, I thought, recalling Niele's immaculate manicure. She wouldn't want to go digging for it every time it rang. At the foot of the bed, I touched something metal and drew it out carefully.

"Bingo."

"You found it?" Godley put out his hand. "Good girl. Give it to me."

"Shouldn't I bag it up?" I stared up at him. "It's evidence now, isn't it?"

"I need to check something. Make sure it's the right one." His hand was still outstretched and I couldn't see a way to say no without fatally harming my career prospects. I put the phone into his palm and watched as he pressed buttons. "No password. Good stuff."

He turned away from me then, hiding the phone from me with his body. I looked past him to the mirror that hung on the wall and watched him running through menus. It was the address book he wanted, it transpired, and I could feel my eyes getting wide as he checked through the list of contacts, deleting two. My boss or not, there was no way I wasn't going to challenge him.

"That's not right, is it? You shouldn't be doing anything to the phone."

"Don't worry, Maeve. It's fine." He tucked it back where I'd found it.

"Are you leaving it there? Why aren't we recovering it? It's evidence."

"Let's leave it for Bradbury's team. They get depressed if they don't find something." He put his hand under my arm and guided me out of the room, toward the stairs. "Good work, Maeve."

"Was it?" I pulled away. "We didn't exactly finish, did we? I hadn't looked in the bedside table."

"Leave it for Bradbury," Godley said again. "It'll do as it is. Besides, I've got to go."

I dearly wanted to demand to know what he had been doing, and why, but I knew I wasn't going to get a satisfactory reply. We collected Derwent on our way out and the two of us stood to watch Godley's departure. The Mercedes had been double-parked, as if Godley had been in too much of a hurry to find a proper space. He nodded to us before driving off, and I thought he seemed pleased with his morning's work.

"We should go too." Derwent's face was expressionless.

I frowned. "Is that it?"

"What more do you want?"

I waved a hand in the direction Godley's car had taken. "That was odd, wasn't it? I mean, not usual."

"I wouldn't know."

"What do you think —"

He interrupted. "Don't ask me. Don't mention it to me again. It didn't happen."

"What didn't happen?"

"I don't know. And neither do you." He walked away, chewing gum aggressively, and none of the journalists outside the final cordon were stupid or desperate enough to attempt to draw him into conversation.

CHAPTER TWENTY-THREE

It was a frankly toxic journey back to the office, made worse by the morning traffic. The delay didn't bother me as much as it might have, and nor did the silent rage emanating from the seat beside me. With nothing to do but mind the map I could sit quietly and rest, half-asleep as the sun streamed into the car. I was chronically short on sleep, not functioning at anything like my best, and I assumed Derwent was in the same condition. We stopped for petrol after traveling a mile in just under an hour, and Derwent came back to the car with a bottle of aspirin.

"Fucking childproof cap." He wrestled with it, spinning the top ineptly.

"Give me that." I twisted the cap off on my first attempt, having actually looked at the bottle and worked out how to do it. "How many do you want?"

"What's the maximum dose?"

"No idea."

"Read the label, then. Whatever it is, double

it." He started the car and pulled out of the petrol station, using the entrance instead of the exit. The traditional volley of horns and shouted abuse followed.

"If you ever get tired of being a policeman, why don't you set up as an unlicensed minicab driver? You have all the skills."

"Because I don't like the smell of those little air fresheners that look like Christmas trees, and I can't stand drunk people when I'm sober."

"No need to drive sober, is there? I'm sure most of them have a drink or two before they start work." I was skimming through the instructions. "I don't think it would be safe to double the dosage. Headache?"

"No thanks, I've got one already."

"Along with a cracking sense of humor."

"That's me. Funny and clever and handsome. It's not right that one man should have so many advantages in life."

"They sit lightly on you." I gave him two pills and a bottle of water. "Drink the whole thing. You're probably dehydrated."

"I'm not hungover," he snapped.

"I didn't say you were. It's a hot day." I looked at him curiously. "Did you have a drink last night when you got back?"

"One."

"It was late for that."

"It helps me to sleep. I bet you found your own way to relax, didn't you? Nothing like sleeping in a strange bed to make you feel frisky."

I could feel myself blushing despite wishing quite fiercely to remain unmoved. "Sorry. You're way off."

"Am I? I don't think so."

"I should call Philip Kennford." I said it more or less at random, to change the subject. "I promised Lydia and Savannah I'd let him know what happened last night."

Derwent groaned. "Don't involve him. He'll just want to give me a bollocking about something or other. I can't be arsed, honestly."

"We should talk to him about Niele too."

"I'd rather stick my bum in a beehive."

"He might know something."

"About what, exactly?"

"Why she died." I shrugged. "How do we know he's not a viable suspect?"

"It doesn't connect." Derwent was scowling. "For one thing, no one is mad enough to wipe out five people for the sake of shutting up one who had already spilled her guts to the police. If Niele was the sole target, she would have been the only one to die. There was no reason to kill anyone else when they were all tucked up nice and quietly in bed. Anyway, I had a chat with one of the other detectives while you were upstairs with Godley. The word is that Niele's house was the headquarters for the Eastern Europeans

Skinner recruited to do his dirty work."

"You're kidding."

"Not at all. That's why Godley was involved."

"You mean those men killed the Clapham boys?"

"I wouldn't know. I'm not involved in the investigation, remember?" He relented a little. "Probably. They're going to try to match the ballistics. The weapons are the right caliber, so that's a start."

"So who killed them? Ken Goldsworthy's lads?"

"If he has anyone that slick on his team, which I doubt." Derwent's forehead was furrowed. "It looked familiar to me, that crime scene. I've seen killing like that before. Cold, clinical, detached. Not getting excited, even though there are five of them to slot. I went to a crime scene in Shepherd's Bush once that was just like this — straight shooting, no messing. Three dead that time."

"Did you catch the killer?"

"Couldn't put a case together, but I was pretty sure who'd done it."

"And it was?"

"Someone who worked with John Skinner. A guy named Larch. Tony was his first name. One of those people who looks like a killer — mad eyes, the bloke had, ice-blue and staring. He was bald by choice, I always thought to avoid shedding hairs at crime scenes, but also because it made him look like a hard bastard. He wasn't a big lad but he scared the crap out of me. When Skinner moved to Spain, Larch left the UK too. He spent a bit of time in South America, then the Caribbean, and then we lost track of him. Kept his nose clean so we didn't really have a reason to follow him around, more's the pity, because he had good taste in holiday destinations."

"Do you think it's worth finding out if he's back in the country?"

"Probably. But it's not my case, remember? Anyway, why would one of John Skinner's associates take out his new partners in crime? I can't see him doing Goldsworthy's work for him."

"Maybe because Skinner's lost control of them and even he's worried about it."

"John Skinner doesn't care about what happens to his empire. He doesn't care if there's a shooting a day for the next year. He's in prison for the duration. His best chance to get out is to come down with something terminal and get compassionate release so he can die in relative comfort." Derwent shrugged. "Can't happen to a more deserving person. I won't be weeping for him."

"It must be difficult to give up on it. He's worked hard all his life — on the wrong side of the law, but he's still a businessman, when all's said and done. I can't understand why he handed over the fight to the Eastern Europeans in the first place."

"Because they were the only thugs more brutal than his own, I reckon."

"And then he changed his mind?"

"Or someone changed it for him."

"Like who?" I started to say, but I knew who. My boss. Superintendent Charles Godley, a man who was above suspicion, a man who couldn't be bought, you'd have said. And unless I was very much mistaken I had heard him make the suggestion that had resulted in Niele Adamkuté's death. Not half an hour before, I had unwittingly assisted him to destroy evidence, because whatever had been on the phone had to have been important for him to turn up at the crime scene like that to delete it. I couldn't deal with it at that moment. I pushed it out of my mind with an almost physical effort.

"Anyway, Kennford. Do I call him?"

"You do not."

"Then Lydia is going to wonder why he doesn't care enough to get in touch with her."

Derwent snorted. "No guarantee he'd follow it up anyway."

"Still."

"No. That's an order."

I could see there was no point in arguing when Derwent had made up his mind, but I wasn't happy about it, and when we got to the office and found Philip Kennford there, I was relieved.

"DI Derwent." He had been waiting in reception, watching the door, and when we walked in he got to his feet with a jerk, as if he was spring-loaded. Derwent stopped for a second out of sheer surprise, then continued toward the lift.

"Sorry, Mr. Kennford. I don't have time to talk at the moment."

"Don't walk away from me."

Derwent turned around but kept moving, walking backward. "I really do need to go."

"You don't even know why I'm here." There was a note of desperation in Kennford's voice, a strain I hadn't heard before. I looked at him curiously, noting that he was red-eyed and pale with fatigue. "I need to talk to you."

Derwent might not have been the most sensitive of people, but even he was able to spot that Kennford was in difficulties. He hesitated for a moment, then nodded. "I've got a few minutes. Start talking."

"Here?" Kennford looked around. "Like this?"

"I could try to find us an interview room so we can talk to Mr. Kennford in private," I suggested.

Derwent glowered at me. "What a good idea." To Kennford, he said, "Come up to the team's room. But I meant what I said. I don't have much time this morning."

The barrister followed us into the lift. "I

gather you were at a major crime scene in Poplar. That's what your colleague said when I rang."

"That's right." Derwent popped a piece of chewing gum into his mouth.

"Who were the victims?"

"Why do you ask?"

"You know very well."

The lift was moving especially slowly, it seemed. Derwent chewed his gum. Kennford waited. He was good enough at asking questions to let the silence grow until Derwent couldn't stand it any longer.

"I'm sorry, but it was Niele. And the men she was living with. Five bodies."

"How?"

"They were shot."

"Did she suffer?"

"Looked like it was instant. She didn't get much time to react anyway."

"That's something."

"Yeah, it's a consolation." Derwent gave it maximum sarcasm. Kennford shook his head. "You play with fire, you have to expect to get burned."

"What do you mean?"

The lift doors opened and Kennford followed us out. "I mean that she was up to her neck in organized crime when I knew her. I'm presuming nothing had changed."

"Seems not."

"Poor old Niele." There was something

585

perfunctory about his impromptu epitaph, something unfeeling, and it nettled me.

"She could have been the mother of your child."

"Not her. She got rid of it at the first opportunity." He looked down at me. "Besides, I wouldn't have had anything to do with the child."

"Wouldn't you care about it?"

He shook his head.

"What about the fact that someone you helped to create was making their own way in the world?"

"She was on the pill, she told me. I took her word for it. I didn't want another child and it was nothing to do with me that she made a mistake and got pregnant. I can only take responsibility for things that are actually my fault."

"It must be lovely to be so free of guilt."

"I have plenty of guilt about other things." The shadow was back on his face. "Look, I can make this quick, but I do need to tell you a few things I should have mentioned before."

"You surprise me." Derwent held open the door for him. "Have a seat, Mr. Kennford, and I'll let DC Kerrigan work her magic to get an interview room."

I turned to do as I was told and saw Godley in the conference room with Kev who was talking at a hundred miles an hour, and a very pretty forensics investigator I recognized from the Kennford house. Godley glanced up at more or less the same moment and beckoned me to join them, leaning sideways to see if Derwent was at his desk. He saw Philip Kennford beside him and frowned, then held up two fingers and beckoned again. *Both of you, in here, now.*

Taking the view that Kennford didn't need to know where we were going I leaned down and muttered in Derwent's ear that we were wanted, and for once he didn't bother to argue.

"What's going on?" I asked, shutting the door of the conference room behind us so Kennford couldn't overhear anything.

"Kev has some preliminary results he thought we needed to know about from Philip Kennford's house."

"Thanks to my brilliant investigator here."

"Caitriona Bennett." She shook hands with me and Derwent. She was a bit younger than me and tiny, with bobbed fair hair and clear freckled skin that blushed easily. With a name like Caitriona she probably had one Irish parent, if not two, but it didn't seem like the right time to ask about it. "I didn't do anything particularly brilliant."

"I disagree." Kev was bursting with pride. "Have a look at this." He handed me an evidence envelope, brown paper with a plastic window so I could see a small silver shape inside it.

"What is it?"

"It's called a bail."

I folded the bag so I could see it more clearly, a triangle of metal with a loop on top. The whole thing was no more than five millimeters long. It had a delicate pattern chased into it. "What does it do?"

"It's a jeweler's fixing. You attach it to something you want to make into a pendant and that's how it's suspended from the chain. This one is actually platinum, which is pretty unusual. It's the sort of thing you would use for high-end design. Specialist stuff."

"That's what it is! I thought it looked familiar." It was strange how seeing it out of context made it hard to recognize. I looked up. "Something you use to make jewelry?"

"Yep. But it gets more interesting," Kev said. "Tell them about where you found it."

"It was on the stairs to the first floor of Endsleigh Drive, in a footprint." I remembered her working on the stairs when we were touring the crime scenes, meticulously examining every inch of the tread where she was sitting. "Looking at it, I think it had been caught in the tread of a boot in some mud — we recovered some dried dirt in the same place. Chalky soil. We're analyzing it to try to narrow down the area it might come from."

"Would Sussex fit?" Derwent asked.

"I'm not an expert on soil." And she wasn't going to speculate. I knew Derwent was thinking of the great chalk escarpments of the South Downs, and I knew why.

"To be honest, that's not the most exciting thing about it. Tell them about the DNA." Kev was rocking back and forth on the balls of his feet.

"We recovered some skin cells from inside the loop. We only have enough for a partial profile at the moment but we're working on that too. It's taken us a few days to get this far but the initial results show that the DNA belongs to someone related to Laura Kennford, but not to her mother. A half-sibling."

"If we got DNA from a half-sibling could you match it to the sample?"

"That would be ideal."

Derwent looked at me. "We know about a half-sibling, don't we?"

"One who lives with a jewelry designer."

"One who was her father's favorite before his pesky new wife intervened."

"One whom he might have wanted to protect."

"Time to talk to Mr. Kennford, I think, since he's here," Godley said. "And this time, no more crap. I don't mind arresting him for attempting to pervert the course of justice, if that helps to jog his memory."

Kennford actually needed very little in the way of persuasion to tell us what he knew, especially when Caitriona had run through her account of finding the bail and what it signified. His face crumpled, and I thought it was the first time I'd seen him experience an honest emotion since I'd met him.

"What could I do? I love Savannah. I didn't want to believe she was involved."

"What made you think she was?" I asked.

"I saw her. In the mirror. Before she hit me." There was a short, meaningful silence. "Not properly. Not enough to be sure it was her."

"You must have been fairly sure or you wouldn't have bothered to lie to us."

"I only saw her for a moment. Just her arm, really, and she was wearing gloves. I wasn't sure, but the more I thought about it, the more I was convinced that it was her. It was the way she moved, and the height, and the fact that she was so slim. I'm going on my instinct here, but I don't think I was wrong. I know her well, you know."

"Not as well as you used to before you dumped her."

"I made a mistake about that. I should have stood up to Vita." He began to sob. "My poor little Savannah."

"What about poor little Laura? And Vita?"

He nodded. "I got it wrong. They paid the price. Vita brought it on herself, but Laura was an innocent bystander."

"Maybe not such a bystander." I turned to Derwent. "The messages Seth Carberry saw on Laura's phone — 'I want to see you,' that kind of thing — they could have been from Savannah. Not a boyfriend."

"Looks like it."

Turning back to Kennford I said, "What if Laura was trying to set up a meeting between Savannah and you and Vita to confront you because she was fed up about being kept away from her sister? Savannah could have taken advantage of that to get into the house and attack your family."

"Only half of it."

"Because Lydia was out of sight in the pool. And Laura was supposed to be out, wasn't she? Maybe Savannah thought Laura was Lydia and Laura was the one who was supposed to survive."

"Or maybe she was looking for Lydia when she encountered you." Derwent's forehead was crinkled with worry. "And she didn't keep searching after she hit you since she couldn't take the risk of hanging around until you woke up. You wouldn't be so easy to attack if you were on your guard."

"She didn't hurt me. Not really. She loves me."

"It's a strange version of love, if you don't mind me saying so." Derwent was chewing rapidly. "What are we going to do about Lydia? She's got to be in danger."

"That's why I was trying to stop you from letting her move in with Savannah."

"It might have helped if you'd been honest

with us," Godley said heavily. "As it stands, we have a teenage girl living in the same house with someone who wanted to kill her not quite a week ago."

"That was one of the things that convinced me I was right. Savannah was so determined to get her to move in with her. I know she doesn't like Renee — no one does — but she'd shown no interest in Lydia before." Kennford sighed. "I can't protect her anymore."

"Don't feel bad," Derwent said, the sarcasm heavy in his tone. "We'd have got there without you in the end."

Godley turned to Derwent. "What do you want to do, Josh? Get Sussex CID to pick her up?"

"I'd rather we did it. Surprise her and maybe get a confession." Derwent tapped a finger against his lips. "Kerrigan could call Lydia. Find out if everything's okay after last night. Maybe try to get her out of the house for the morning so we don't have to worry about where she is. If you can find out where Savannah is likely to be, so much the better."

"Okay."

"We'll head down to Sussex ourselves and arrest Savannah."

"I'm coming too." Kennford had got to his feet.

Godley shook his head. "I'm not sure that's a good idea."

"It's a fucking awful idea." Derwent glanced at Caitriona. "Sorry about the language, darling."

"I've heard worse."

"It's not a bad idea," Kennford insisted. "I might be able to help get you your confession. She won't be expecting me to turn up." He looked imploringly at Godley. "Please. I've let her down so many times. The least I can do is be there for her. Show her I haven't forgotten about her, that I do care."

"And make sure Lydia's all right." Derwent's tone was Sahara-dry.

"Of course. That's a priority."

Derwent leaned in, getting in Kennford's face. "You put Savannah first, Mr. Kennford. You chose the murderer over the innocent girl, even though you knew Lydia was in danger. You played a game with your daughter's life, and you're bloody lucky you didn't lose. Now, I don't know how you're planning to get to Sussex, but you're not coming in my car. If I have to spend another minute in your company, I'll puke."

"My car's parked outside."

Godley looked pained. "I can't stop you from coming, in that case, but you will need to travel with us. I don't want you to get there first. You could cause us some serious problems."

"I think I know better than to get in the way of a police operation," Kennford said stiffly. "I'll do as I'm told."

"First time for everything, I suppose." Derwent walked out before Kennford could reply, leaving an awkward silence and the lingering smell of ill-judged aftershave. He had a diva's instinct for making a big exit.

Without wasting any more time, I rang the farmhouse and got Zoe, who told me Savannah was still in bed. Lydia was having a late breakfast but she was delighted to come to the phone, and still more delighted at the prospect of going shopping with Zoe.

"She's taking me out to get some new clothes. I didn't really pack enough when I was leaving the house."

"That's understandable. You were under pressure. But going shopping sounds like a good idea. It's good to get out of the house now and then."

"I'll tell Zoe you said that. It's exactly what she said to me."

"Sensible woman."

"I'll tell her you said that too."

"Your dad wants to come and see you, by the way. He's been asking about how you are."

"Really?"

"He was pretty concerned about you."

"Tell him I'm fine. But I'd love to see him. Show him the farm. He'd love the dog too."

She sounded like a normal teenager I thought with a pang as I hung up. For the first time, she seemed at ease with herself. And we were going to blow her world apart again, because we had to, because we didn't have any other choice.

It didn't make it any easier.

We took the lead on the drive to the farm-house, me and Derwent and Liv in one car with Godley and Ben Dornton in the Mercedes, and Kennford behind them. It was better to go in mob-handed, to have some extra muscle in the shape of Dornton and another female officer in case Savannah needed to be searched or monitored and I couldn't do it for some reason. The gate was open when we got close to the house.

"What do you want to do?" I asked Derwent. "Drive in?"

"Yeah. We can park in the yard." It was the longest sentence he had spoken since we left London.

"It's good that the gate's open. It looks as if Zoe and Lydia left it that way when they went out."

"Possibly."

"Do you think Savannah's still in bed?"

"The house looks shut up," Liv offered when Derwent still hadn't responded after parking the car.

"The curtains are closed up there." I shaded my eyes, peering up at the house. "That's Savannah's bedroom, I think."

The second car pulled in behind ours, and then the third. The three men got out.

"What's the strategy?" Godley asked Derwent, who shrugged.

"Knock on the door. Take it from there."

"Are you okay, Josh?"

He didn't answer straightaway, and when he did it was without looking around. "Just keeping quiet until I have something to say."

"I should go first." Kennford strode toward the front door.

"I'm sorry. That's not appropriate." Godley turned to me. "Is there a back door?" I nodded. "Take Dornton. Go round that way. If you can gain access, do. We'll meet you inside."

"Okay." I jogged around the house, taking the path we had used when Zoe showed us the grounds. Dornton was puffing behind me.

"You're mental. It's too hot to run."

I ignored him. I was on edge, too jittery to walk. It was oppressively hot, though — he was right about that — and when we came round the corner of the house, he whistled.

"Look at that sky."

It was dark gray and as heavy as lead. The sun was still shining and the hills were a blistering shade of green and mustard yellow. The grass in the orchard had withered away almost completely and my shoes were covered in dust.

"Do you think it'll rain?" Dornton was staring at the clouds, fascinated.

"Why are you talking about the weather when we're here to arrest a murderer?" I hissed.

"Dunno."

"Can you try to concentrate for a few minutes?"

"Yeah, all right. Keep your hair on." He looked affronted. "I was just saying, it looks like rain."

"Brilliant. If the whole policing thing doesn't work out for you, why don't you retrain as a meteorologist?" We had made it as far as the back door, which was painted black and looked intimidatingly solid.

"Because I failed my science GCSE." He gave a gusty sigh. "I'd have loved it."

"Is babbling nonsense your usual response to stress?" I was straining to hear whether the others had made it into the house yet; I didn't think they had. I put one hand on the door to test it, and was somehow unsurprised that it swung open.

"Not even latched. Not very security conscious, are they?"

"I'd have said they were. But we're in the country now."

"Are we going in?"

I hesitated, trying to decide. On the one hand, we had been told to meet Godley in the house. On the other hand, there wasn't a sound coming from inside, which suggested they weren't having any luck with gaining access. Even as I stood there, a thunderous knocking made me jump.

"They're still trying to get her to come to the door."

"Let's go in and see if we can move things along." I went first. "The front door is that way, through the kitchen. You could let the others in."

"Where are you going?"

"Upstairs." I pointed. "If she's still asleep with that racket going on I'll be very surprised. I think the house is empty, but I'm going up to make sure."

"Be careful."

"Send Derwent up when you let him in. He knows where to go."

I was glad to be rid of Dornton, and also pretty confident that I wasn't in any danger. There was no point in trying to be quiet on my way up the stairs because every step had its own individual creak or snap. It sounded like an old organ played by an arthritic incompetent and I rattled up as quickly as I could, my head up to make sure there was no one waiting for me at the top in the best tradition of horror films. The corridor was empty, the windows tightly closed this time. It was airless and incredibly hot; I could feel sweat trickling down my back. Nothing ever went according to plan. Of course, Savannah had got up and gone shopping with Lydia and Zoe. That was the obvious explanation. There was no reason to think anything was wrong just because the house was quiet, with the exception of the others tramping through the rooms downstairs, talking in low voices.

I did a standard search, routine, checking inside every room along the corridor. I hadn't noticed that Savannah's door was ajar, and as I stepped toward it, there was a creak from inside the room. My heart stopped.

And started again as a piteous face peered at me through the gap.

"Come here, boy." I tried to remember the dog's name. It was something bookish, I thought. I clicked my fingers. "Come here, Beckett."

The dog panted, then licked his nose and I remembered that he was nervous around strangers. He gave a tiny whine.

"If you won't come out, can I come in?"

He backed away from the door as I approached, but his hackles were down, his tail wedged firmly between his legs. He didn't look much like a threat, so I decided to risk it. The room was dim, the curtains still drawn. Beckett sank down in the corner with his head on his paws as I came through the door, looking guilty, but he had no reason to. He was certainly not responsible for what had happened in that room, I could tell from a single glance.

I didn't know who had cut Savannah Wentworth's throat, but I was fairly sure they were human, even if only in the most technical sense.

CHAPTER TWENTY-FOUR

"I want to see her."

"I don't think that's a good idea."

"I should remember her as she was, not as she is now, is that it? Spare me the touchy-feely crap. She's my daughter; I want to see her."

I blew my hair off my forehead, or tried to. It was so hot that it had stuck in several places. How completely typical that I had been left to try to cope with Philip Kennford, to soothe him and prevent him from crashing into the crime scene that the others were investigating even now. Women's work, they called it when they thought no one was listening. Making tea and holding hands. There was more to being a family liaison officer than that — and there were plenty of male officers who counted it among their skills too — but I'd never done the necessary course to qualify. There was no point in limiting myself to a nurturing role if I didn't absolutely have to.

"This is a murder investigation, Mr. Kennford. The only people who should be upstairs are the investigating officers and the pathologist, when he gets here. Anyone else who is in the room runs the risk of contaminating the scene." Despite myself, I could feel irritation start to build. "And you know this better than I do."

"Because I've used it to get murderers off." He laughed harshly. "By God, someone's teaching me a lesson about that now. I'll be a campaigner for the death penalty in future. I'll never do another murder trial, unless I'm prosecuting."

"Is that your take on why this has happened? To influence your career?"

"I don't know. Maybe. It makes as much sense as anything else." He walked back and forth, pacing like an animal in too small a cage. I was standing at the foot of the stairs, my arms folded, with what I hoped was a stern expression on my face.

"Look, there must be something you can do. Let me see her. I should identify her officially, shouldn't I? I'm her closest relative."

"There will be a formal identification process, yes, but not here and not now." I looked at him, curious. "Why is this so important to you? It's really not a pleasant sight."

"I don't know. To say goodbye. To believe she's gone, maybe." He shrugged his shoulders a couple of times, turning it into a twitch that I didn't think he could completely control. "Oh, fuck. I'm sorry, but I just think it would be better if I saw her."

"You don't want to do that, mate." Derwent came down the stairs behind me. "We're not talking a little nick here."

"I want to know what happened. Was it the same way Laura died? The same type of wound?"

I didn't have to think about it; I had already compared the two. Laura's neck had been cut down to the bone, which was not the case with this one. Nevertheless, I hedged a little. "We'll have to wait to hear from the pathologist, but it's not as deep."

"Or as long." Derwent was standing behind me, and now he lifted my chin, drawing his finger across my throat. "Laura's injury was from ear to ear, essentially. Savannah's is more of a stab to the jugular." Two fingers rested on the vein, pressing a little bit more firmly than necessary, I thought. "The knife was moved from side to side to widen the hole but it's less of a slash, more of a stab, if you see what I mean."

"God." Kennford had gone very white.

"You asked for the details." He let go of me. "Want to go up and have a look, Kerrigan? You didn't get much of a chance to see."

I went, not because I wanted to gaze at Savannah's dead body but because I wanted to get away from Philip Kennford, and from Derwent. My neck tingled where he had touched it, and not in a good way — more as if I had just had a close encounter with some poison ivy. Derwent was being typically provoking in sending me upstairs when the man in front of him was literally twitching with his desire to do the same, but Derwent would enjoy that. He would also enjoy keeping Kennford downstairs, I thought. And would do it far more effectively than me.

Savannah's room seemed very crowded when I went back in, with Godley leaning over the bed staring down at her. Liv and Dornton were standing well back, gloved hands crossed in front of them.

"Maeve. What are you doing here?"

"Derwent sent me back up." I crossed to the foot of the bed, watching Godley's torch play over the dead woman's throat. Her eyes were closed and her teeth were caught on her lower lip; her last pictures would not be as beautiful as usual. In the light of the torch, I could see that Derwent had been telling the truth about her injury. The blood had flowed down both sides of her neck, pooling under her head and soaking the mattress. She had been sleeping naked and the sheet was tangled around her waist. There was something vulnerable about her unclothed torso, something uncomfortably skeletal about how thin she was when she was no longer animated and gracefully alive. "What do you think?"

"I think it was recent. She's still warm."

I checked my watch; we had been there for almost twenty minutes, no more than that. "The back door was unlocked. Could have been an intruder."

"Could have been." Godley sighed. "Glen is going to get here as fast as he can, and I've asked Kev Cox to come too. We might as well keep the same team on it on the assumption that we're looking for the same killer."

"But are we? It's a different kind of injury. Probably a different knife too."

"I'd like to hope there aren't two murderers running around picking off members of the Kennford family, if that's all right with you." He sounded deeply irritable and I stepped away from the bed, confused, to look into the en-suite bathroom for the sake of having something to do that would take me away from him. The glass walls of the shower cubicle were streaked with water and I opened the door a crack, using my pen to pull on the handle. Warm air greeted me, scented with flowers. I peered at the tiles, then crouched down to examine the shower tray.

"Find something?" Derwent was leaning over me.

"Maybe." I pointed. "That's blood, isn't it?"

There was a watery streak down one tile in the corner, dripping over the edge and onto the shower tray where it dissolved and disappeared. It was very faint and pale pink rather than red.

"You could be right. Well done, hawk-eye."

"Safe to assume the killer showered, then."

"Seems likely."

"And changed his or her clothes."

"Or did the job while they were naked, got dressed afterward. Easier to clean up, and some of them love the feeling of the blood on their skin. Especially when it's fresh."

"That's disgusting."

"That's murderers for you." He straightened up. "We need to know what time Lydia and Zoe left."

"And where they were going." I rubbed the back of one gloved hand over my forehead, sweating again in the oppressive damp heat of the bathroom. "She just said shopping, but it could have been an out-of-town shopping center or the nearest market town or somewhere big. I didn't ask."

"Give her a call." Dornton leaned into the bathroom to join in.

"I did. No answer."

"I don't like not knowing where she is." Derwent was looking concerned.

"Me neither."

"Did you check the rest of the house?"

"I did." Dornton again. "No sign of anyone

up here. Which room did she have?"

"The one at the end of the corridor."

"Unmade bed but otherwise tidy."

"That sounds right." Derwent nodded. "She was neat as anything in her own house."

I sat back on my heels. "Remember her bed though? Hospital corners and you could bounce a tennis ball on the coverlet, it was so taut. Leaving her bed unmade doesn't sound right."

"Maybe she was in a hurry to go."

I stood up and edged past Derwent, careful not to touch any surfaces. "It didn't sound as if they were rushing when I spoke to them. She was just having breakfast."

"We found dishes in the sink downstairs," Derwent said, following me down the corridor.

"So they had breakfast and didn't wash up, which is possible, I suppose." I went into Lydia's room and frowned at the rumpled bed. The pillows and cushions were mostly on the floor and the duvet was slipping sideways. I checked the bathroom. "Her toothbrush is wet." There was a faintly bitter smell in the room that I traced to the lavatory. The water had a gauzy quality, as if there were tiny particles floating in it. "I think that's where breakfast ended up, but Kev could confirm it."

"Are you actually sniffing the toilet?" Derwent looked disgusted.

"I'm trying to work out what happened this morning. She came upstairs, she threw up, she brushed her teeth. Ready to go shopping." I walked back into the bedroom. "Something happened. Something made her stop what she was doing. Look at the pillows. She was in the middle of making the bed when something interrupted her."

"This is her bag, isn't it?" Derwent held it up. "She'd have needed that for shopping.

"You'd have thought." I looked at him, troubled. "What happened here?"

"I don't know. But Zoe's car wasn't in the yard." He shrugged. "Not worth getting too excited over it, is it? It probably took Lydia longer to upchuck her porridge than she'd bargained for."

"And her bag?"

"It's heavy. Maybe she had a smaller one, or she just took her wallet or something."

"She's a teenage girl. She would want all her clutter."

Derwent was rooting in the bag. "Fuck. Here's her wallet." He opened it. "Cash card. Money. Her phone. All right, that is a bit strange."

"More than a bit, surely." I went back into the corridor and peered through one of the dormer windows. There were too many trees between me and the garage for me to be sure of what I was seeing. "I can't see inside the garage, but I think the doors are open."

"You'd leave them open if you drove out."

"Yeah." I stared at it, troubled. "We need to search the property."

"Dornton and Liv are doing the yard at the moment."

"Let's try out the back, then."

"Make sure the car isn't there."

"Exactly."

Derwent was silent as we cut through the house and stepped out of the back door. The heat was incredible, the air crackling with tension as the clouds massed overhead, heavy with rain. I had a headache already, a tight band around my forehead that no painkiller would touch. It was fear, fear and not knowing what we had missed. Savannah was our suspect, and Savannah was dead. Which meant that there were two killers, or we had been wrong about her. "But she fitted the DNA profile."

"What did you say?" Derwent demanded.

"Thinking aloud." I went ahead of him along the path toward the garage, which was more trampled than it had been the previous time we'd been there. Something moved in the grass beside the path, something big, and I stopped.

"What now?"

"Nothing. Just the dog." My heart was beating erratically; for the second time that day Beckett had terrified me. He was hardly stealthy, crashing through the undergrowth at the same fast pace that we were keeping, looking up over the feathery tops of the wild grass now and then to check that we were still there. Up ahead of us, the garage door banged.

Derwent gave me a tight smile when I looked around. "Just the wind."

"I'm sure you're right." There was a breeze but it was hot air that didn't refresh me in the least. "Dornton thinks there's going to be a storm."

"Does he?" Derwent managed to get precisely the same lack of interest into his voice that I had shown earlier, and I blushed, concentrating on keeping my footing on the last part of the path. The door banged again as we came around the side of the garage, which was empty.

"They're gone."

"Thank Christ for that." Derwent said it like he meant it.

"She still hasn't had the oil fixed." I pointed at the floor, where the puddle had grown and spread.

"Something stinks." Derwent frowned. "Petrol."

"They had a can of it on the shelf. Must have been running low."

"I wouldn't keep petrol around the place. Not if I had a garage made of wood."

"I wouldn't have taken you for a health-

and-safety type."

"Just common sense." He backed away. "Didn't she say there was another building?"

"A barn. Behind here."

"I'll go and have a look there."

The door banged again. I went to look at how the catch worked and found that it was straightforward, a metal bolt that slotted into the ground. It would inconvenience Zoe a little bit to have to open it again when she got back, but she would have other things on her mind, I thought. She would see the cars in the yard and know that something had happened, even before someone got to her to tell her the news. I hoped it wouldn't be me.

The door fixed, I wandered into the garage, waiting for Derwent to get back. The stuff on the shelves had to have been left by the previous owner, or the one before it; there was some extraordinary stuff. I paused over some tongs that looked like medieval torture equipment but were probably veterinary tools. Next to them was a coil of barbed wire, and beside that a tin of paint that was surely never going to be usable again. The lid was crusted on with dried paint and the sides of the tin were streaked with rust. From the style of the logo, it dated from the 1960s. There was being thrifty, I thought, and there was being a hoarder. I passed on to the back wall of the garage, which was tools and spare car parts, mainly. And stopped, my head cocked to one side, listening.

Derwent was saying something. The window above my head was broken, explaining why I could hear him even though he still seemed to be in the barn. He sounded calm, conversational even, but I couldn't hear a reply.

He spoke again.

Someone else was in the barn with him. The dog, possibly. Beckett had disappeared when we came close to the garage, nose to the ground. I was not going to get overexcited for a third time that day about a sheepdog, no matter how nice his nature.

On the other hand, it wasn't like Derwent to bother talking to an animal.

And there was no harm in looking to see what he was doing.

Once I was outside the garage, I saw the others gathered at the back of the house, heads together. I waved and Godley broke away from the group, shading his eyes to see what I was doing. I pointed to the side of the garage and he nodded. They would have finished the first search down at the house. They would be waiting for Glen Hanshaw, or for Zoe to return. The house would be off-limits until the crime scene specialists had checked it over. We had trampled around enough already, I thought, hacking through nettles and tall cow parsley to get to the barn door. I wasn't used to being the first responder at a murder. The response teams were better at it, the uniformed officers who spent their time racing to answer 999 calls or being despatched to concern-for-safety calls, where someone hadn't seen their elderly neighbor for a few weeks, actually, and the TV was on all hours of the day and night, and they were just worried there might be a problem . . .

Derwent sounded especially calm. I was walking softly. I didn't want to startle the dog. Or Derwent. Or even reveal to him that I had heard him saying, "It's okay. Really, it's all right. You're not in trouble. Everything is going to be fine." He was a soppy git under all the bluster, as I had always suspected. I was half-smiling as I stepped into the barn, which was dark and effectively derelict. The roof was nothing more than bare rafters in several places, and pigeons had colonized the space completely. The smell of old straw and damp was pungent.

And overlaid with another smell.

Petrol.

It was easy enough to see where it was coming from, when my eyes got accustomed to the light — easy, and terrifying. Derwent was facing me, leaning against a wooden partition that had somehow remained sound enough for it to take his weight. He had his arms folded and one foot crossed over the other, totally relaxed in his posture, the strain only showing around his eyes. He didn't look at me because his attention was fixed on the person who stood between us, but he lifted his index finger very slightly. *Wait.*

Lydia was tiny in her oversized T-shirt and floor-length skirt, drowning in black. It didn't show the blood that streaked her arms, but blood would be there when the forensics experts examined her clothes. I was more interested in the fact that she was soaking wet, and not with water. Her hair was drenched, droplets oozing from the ends. In one hand she held the petrol can, loosely so it dangled down by her side. In the other hand there was a pink plastic lighter, held tightly in her fist, which was shaking. I couldn't see if she had her thumb on the wheel, ready to strike the light. I couldn't see how much danger she was in. Enough, I thought, edging sideways to avoid standing with the light behind me and sending a telltale shadow across the dirty floor. More than enough.

"You don't want to do anything stupid, do you? It's been a tough day already. You want to go and have a shower. Get cleaned up." He was speaking in a low, soothing voice that was almost hypnotic, and what he was saying was far less important than the tone. All he got in response was a muffled sob that was barely a noise.

"What can we get for you? What would

make you feel better?"

An infinitesimal shake of her head. Her teeth were chattering, a low-level rattle that I could hear over the flutter and coo of the birds in the rafters. I had never seen her in short sleeves before, and the scarring on her arms was wicked. Years of work had gone into making the marks, and they ranged in color from pearly white to an angry red that had to be recent. The blood that smeared her skin was streaked and patchy because of the petrol, but I was fairly sure that she herself wasn't bleeding, and I was fairly sure whose blood it was too.

I moved forward a step, and then another. Derwent kept up the soothing babble, raising the volume very slightly to cover the sound of my progress. I had my eyes fixed on her right hand. I couldn't decide what to do. If I tried to grab her and her thumb was on the wheel, the shock might make her strike a flame by accident as her hand clenched. If she dropped the lighter, it could still spark, and a spark was all it would take. It was petrol vapor that ignited, I recalled, not the liquid; she was surrounded in a cloud of it and I would be well within range if it went up. And it was seriously unstable. You weren't even supposed to use a mobile phone at a petrol pump, not that anyone paid attention to that particular rule. How often had a mobile phone generate a spark when it was used?

Not often, in my experience. Mine was on, in my pocket. Derwent's too.

I didn't want to burn.

I stepped a little closer, testing the floor with my toe before I risked putting my weight on it. The floor was wooden boards, pitted with holes and dry as dust. The whole place would go up in a heartbeat if she did. Old straw. Old wood. A breeze through the open door funneling air up to the damaged roof, making a natural chimney for a flame that would burn until there was no fuel left at all, until there was nothing but ash. They would find our bones, though. It was surprisingly hard to burn human bodies until they disintegrated.

The petrol can slipped out of her hand and clattered on the floor, something that surprised her as much as me. Derwent started forward instinctively then stopped with his hands up as she lifted her clenched fist in warning.

"Lydia, it's all right. I know you got a fright, but it was just the can."

"It was empty." The first words I had heard her say so far, and her voice was dead.

"Give me the lighter, Lydia. You don't need it. That's not the way to go." He took another step toward her.

"Stay where you are." She pointed a shaking finger at him. "Don't come close to me."

"It's all right."

"It's *not* all right. It's *never* going to be all right." She had sounded like a teenager on the phone that morning, giggling about her plans for the day, but now she sounded like a child. Her voice was high-pitched and mournful and somehow distant, as if she had gone to a different place already, somewhere that we couldn't reach her.

If I stretched out my hand, I could touch her arm.

I didn't know what to do.

"Tell us what happened this morning," Derwent commanded.

A sob and she shook her head over and over, sending a fine spray of petrol over me. I shuddered a little, not liking it, wanting to tear off my top and wipe my skin. It was the worst way to die, I'd heard. Painful beyond belief, and that was if you died quickly. People died weeks later, sometimes, after unimaginable agony. People lived with terrible scarring. I tried not to think about it. She was just holding the lighter in her fist, and loosely. She had dropped the can. She was weak. I was quick and strong, and I had the advantage of surprise.

I looked at Derwent, and saw him change his stance a little, ready to move. I looked at Lydia's hand again. I was almost sure it would be all right.

Almost.

I don't know if I could have done it if I

hadn't heard sounds from outside, heard the cavalry turning up at the wrong bloody moment. If they crashed in, she would turn around and see me, and she would be angry. Angry enough to burn? I didn't want to test it out.

I grabbed her wrist like I was pinning down a poisonous snake and held on for dear life, trying to peel her fingers away from the lighter with the other hand. A second later Derwent's arms were around hers, pinning them to her sides so she couldn't fight me off. Her hand tightened around the lighter instinctively but it was small, and slippery, and as we struggled it slid out of her grasp and on to the floor. I kicked at it without thinking and sent it skittering away into the shadows by the door.

"Careful," Derwent said sharply. "Don't do that again."

"Sorry. I was just trying to get it away."

"It could have exploded when it fell on the floor, and then you kick it? Christ." This was all over the top of Lydia's head; the girl was limp in Derwent's arms. She was crying hard, her body shaking with each sob that tore out of her.

"It's all right. It's going to be all right." Derwent smoothed her hair with a hand he had got free somehow.

"It's not. You don't know what I've done."

"We know, Lydia. We were in the house."

"And so was I." Her father had a particularly resonant voice — years of practice at being heard in large rooms — and he delivered his line like a Shakespearean actor giving his all to his very last performance. "What are you doing, Lydia? What were you trying to do?"

"Daddy?" She had twisted in Derwent's arms to see him. He was standing beside Godley and Liv, with Dornton behind them, all with matching expressions of shock on their faces. I couldn't think about how we looked. Terrified, probably. There was no color at all in Derwent's cheeks.

"Let's not worry about that now." Godley put his hand on Kennford's arm. "Let's think about that later. The first thing is Lydia's safety."

"The first thing is to find out what happened, surely." He looked back at his daughter. "Why did you do it, Lydia? What was the reason? You must have had a reason."

She was crying again. She turned her face into Derwent's neck and stayed there, her head on his shoulder, as if she was too weak to hold it up. He held on to her hair, shushing her. To Kennford, he said, "Drop it. Now's not the time. We'll find out later."

"I want to comfort her." Kennford stepped forward. "She's my daughter."

"And you've never behaved like her father," Derwent hissed. He was still gripping her tightly, but it was to support her, not restrain her.

"I'm still her father, for all that. She's my daughter, whatever she's done." Kennford sounded like he was on the edge of hysteria. "I love her. I might not have been the best at showing it, but I do love her. For all her faults, she's all I've got left, and I'm not going to abandon her now."

"What did you say?" Zoe was standing behind the group in the doorway, her eyes wide. She had bags from the supermarket in one hand; her car keys were in the other. "What's happened?"

I went forward, my hand out to her. "Zoe, there's some bad news, I'm afraid."

"What did he say?" She switched her focus to Kennford again. "What was it? Who is all you've got left?"

He gestured in Lydia's direction and Zoe saw her. She put her hand to her mouth. "Oh my God. What are you doing?"

"You should ask her what she's done." Kennford's voice was rough. "Then you'll understand."

"I don't — why —" She looked around at us. "I thought — do I smell *petrol*?"

"Lydia tried to kill herself." Derwent, cutting to the chase as usual. "We stopped her in time."

"You tried to burn yourself?" She glanced down and saw the lighter beside her foot.

"Using this?"

"She's been disarmed." Derwent sounded almost cheerful. "Nothing to worry about. She's safe now." He gave her a little shake. "You're safe now."

"Zoe, I need to tell you what's happened." I put my hand on her arm, which was stiff. "It's Savannah. I'm so sorry."

She wasn't looking at me. She was staring at Lydia. I didn't even know if she'd heard me. I tried again. "Savannah's dead, Zoe."

Lydia twisted in Derwent's arms. "She knows."

I felt the tremor go through Zoe. Shock.

"What do you mean?"

"She was there."

Zoe started to shake her head. "No, Lydia. That's not true." To me, she said, "I don't know why she would lie. Unless she's trying to blame me."

"Blame you? I don't think —"

"What did you do?" Zoe demanded, ignoring me again. "What did you do?"

"You know what." Lydia's face was contorted as the tears began again.

"Do you think you could tell us about it?" I said gently. "Take your time."

Derwent put his hand on her shoulder. "Come on. You'll feel better if you spill the beans."

In the high childish voice she'd used before, Lydia said, "Everything was lovely this morning. We were having fun. Then I was in my room and Zoe came and got me. She said she'd lied to the police because Savannah asked her to. She said Savannah killed Mum and Laura. She told me I had to get revenge for them. I owed it to them. She said Laura would have done it if she'd lived and I'd died."

Zoe took a step toward Lydia and I put my hand out to stop her. I was distracted by Lydia's story but I had enough awareness of what Zoe was doing to notice her bending down. I looked back as she straightened up.

And the lighter wasn't on the floor any-more.

I didn't even think as I stepped forward; I certainly didn't hesitate. I smacked her hand as she lifted it, as hard as I could, hitting it underneath so the lighter flew up, and over her shoulder, and out into the open air. It spun and disappeared into the grass. I heard Derwent swear; I was aware of an exclamation from Philip Kennford and of Ben Dornton going outside to retrieve it.

"What the hell did you think you were going to achieve?" I demanded.

"I wasn't going to do anything." Zoe glared at me. "You overreacted."

"You panicked. You didn't want Lydia to say what she's about to say." I turned back to the girl. "Go on, Lydia. Tell us what happened."

Lydia had closed her eyes tightly, and kept them closed as she went on. I wasn't even sure she'd noticed the interruption.

"She took me into the room and she showed me where to put the knife, but I couldn't do it, so she stuck it in first and then made me do it too. I thought Savannah would wake up, but she didn't. She just died. Zoe went and showered, and got changed, but I just stayed with Savannah. I thought I should have hated her, but I couldn't. She was so nice to me. I couldn't understand how she could have killed them, but I didn't know what else to believe."

Kennford said something under his breath, something I didn't quite hear. His face was sheet-white.

"Then Zoe said I had done the right thing, but no one else would understand and she would get the blame if they knew she'd been here. She said I was to say Savannah confessed everything last night. Then I took the opportunity to kill her today, while she was asleep. And then Zoe hugged me and she left."

"Why did you try to kill yourself?" Derwent asked gently.

"I was scared of going to prison. I was so sad about Savannah too." She covered her face. "I wasn't any better than her once I'd killed her. I'd seen the petrol in the garage, and I knew there was a lighter in the kitchen.

I got it, and then took the petrol and came in here. I was ready to do it, but I wasn't brave enough." The high-pitched voice broke and faltered. "I wanted to be a sacrifice. I wanted to make everything right again. But I couldn't do it."

"This is total rubbish." Zoe's voice was strained and shockingly loud after Lydia's quavering recitation. "You can't possibly believe it. She's murdered her family, she's killed my girlfriend and now she's trying to frame me. Look at her. She's crazy."

I did look at Lydia, whose teeth were chattering. Her hair was tangled around her face and her eyes were wild. I had included her in my list of possible suspects but I'd never truly believed she was capable of murder. Now I wasn't so sure.

"It's time to tell the truth, Lydia." Her father sounded stern. "Not another story."

"I am telling the truth." It lacked conviction, and over her head Derwent's eyes were grim.

Zoe put her hands up to her face. "I don't believe Savannah's gone. How can she be gone?"

"So you weren't there," Godley said. "Lydia's lying."

"Of course I wasn't." She took her hands down and glowered at me again, her eyelashes stuck together with unshed tears. "I didn't know about any of this until I came back. I can't believe you're even willing to consider I might have been involved."

I was still holding on to her arm. "Look, we need to investigate it properly. Examine the evidence."

"It'll show that she killed her and I wasn't there." Zoe was trembling. "This is a nightmare. How could this have happened?"

"Stop *lying,*" Lydia shouted. "Tell them I haven't made any of it up. Tell them!"

Zoe shook her head. "It's a fabrication. It's insane. She's insane. I knew we shouldn't have taken her in." She looked at Philip Kennford pleadingly. "I know she's your daughter but you can't take what she says at face value. She's trying to frame me. She's evil."

"No," Lydia said, her voice raw. "No."

Zoe spread out her hands. "Why would I want to kill Savannah? Why would I even think of it? It doesn't make any sense."

And my phone rang. I caught Liv's eye and she came forward to take my place by Zoe's side as I stepped away. I took two deep breaths of air that was free of petrol vapor once I got out of the barn as I hooked my phone out of my pocket.

"Kerrigan."

"It's Colin Vale." I'd have recognized my colleague's nasal voice straightaway, but he was the sort to introduce himself; I was lucky he hadn't given his rank and badge number too. "Your DNA results from the Kennford

625

case have come back from forensics and we've got a match on the system."

I felt my heart jump. "Go on. Does it come back to Savannah Wentworth?"

"Nope. Hannah Clarke, who would now be . . . let me see . . . aged twenty-six."

"Who?" I shook my head, baffled. "I have no idea who that is."

"She has convictions for shoplifting, theft, that kind of thing. Mainly from a few years ago."

"Is there a description?" I listened as he ran through it. It was from a few years before; it would be out of date now. "Any distinguishing marks? Scars?"

"Upper left arm, there's an inch-long scar in the shape of a teardrop."

"That helps."

"Does it?"

"It might." I hesitated. "Did they confirm this Hannah Clarke is related to Laura Kennford?"

A roll of thunder echoed across the hills, and I almost didn't hear Colin's response.

"Same father, looks like."

"Same father," I repeated. "Christ."

"Is it starting to make sense now?"

"Of a sort." I thanked him and hung up, then retraced my steps to the barn door. Zoe was still standing beside Liv but she had crossed her arms.

"Can I see your upper left arm, please?"

"Why?" She cupped a hand over it.

"I need to see if you have a scar there." I was aware that everyone was listening to our conversation. "I need to know if you're Philip Kennford's daughter."

A confused babble broke out; I was aware of Kennford expostulating, of Zoe laughing hysterically and above it all, Derwent's voice.

"That's fucking twisted, that is. You do realize that would mean she was shagging her sister."

I ignored it all, peeling her fingers off her arm and holding her hand with as much force as I could muster. She was tall, and strong, and she wanted to fight me off, but she must have known she couldn't win.

Halfway down her left bicep there was a pale scar shaped like a teardrop. It was about an inch long. Unmistakable. Undisguisable.

And she stopped laughing.

I cleared my throat.

"Zoe Prowse, also known as Hannah Clarke, I'm arresting you for the murder of Vita Kennford and Laura Kennford, and the murder of Savannah Wentworth. You do not have to say anything but it may harm your defense if you do not mention when questioned something which you later rely on in court. Anything you do say may be given in evidence. Do you understand?"

No answer.

Then again, I hadn't really expected one.

CHAPTER TWENTY-FIVE

"The thing about DNA is that even the thickest juror can understand it."

Zoe stared at the opposite wall of the interview room, her expression stony. It was the same room we'd used to interview Lydia and Seth Carberry, provided by Sussex Police without us needing to do more than ask, and we'd been there for an hour already.

"You can't deny your relationship to Philip Kennford, Zoe. It's there in black and white." I slid the page across the table. "To be honest, I'm not the best at interpreting scientific information, but I won't have to in court. There'll be experts. They can prove your connection to the Kennford family. Or to Philip, anyway."

Nothing.

"Don't you want him to know who you are? Don't you want him to acknowledge you?" I leaned in. "Isn't that what all of this was about?"

A flicker of irritation passed over her face.

"You wanted him to acknowledge you, but you couldn't get a toe in the door."

Derwent had turned a chair around and was straddling it. "We had a word with Vita's sister, Renee. She'd mentioned one of Philip Kennford's illegitimate kids turning up last year, but we didn't know she meant an adult. We assumed she was talking about an infant. It was you, wasn't it?"

"And Vita wouldn't give you the time of day. She just wanted to protect her family and keep you out of their cozy little world." I flipped through my folder of notes on Zoe, hastily pulled together from various official sources. I still couldn't think of her as Hannah, even though it was her real name. "You didn't have what I'd call a privileged childhood, did you? Lots of time in foster care. Lots of trouble with the police, social services. And then your mother died when you were twelve."

The composure wavered for a split second, an unguarded expression on Zoe's face. I knew Derwent had seen it too. It was the first real reaction we had had. A way in, possibly.

"What was it — drugs?" To me, Derwent said, "I bet it was drugs."

"She took an overdose." It was as if Zoe couldn't stop herself from saying it.

"Topped herself?"

"It was an accident."

"She was a druggie, though. Had to have

been for you to be taken off her. Do you know how hard it is to get the courts to take a kid away from a parent?"

"Not hard enough." Zoe glared at Derwent. "She was doing her best."

"Coralie. Pretty name."

"He still couldn't remember her." Zoe sounded bitter, understandably. It was Philip Kennford who had demanded to know Zoe's mother's name back in the barn. I thought it was probably a moment she had dreamed of all her life, but his response fell quite a long way short of what she might have wanted.

"Sorry. Not ringing any bells."

Coralie Clarke had been eighteen when he met her, Zoe told him. She had been pretty — very.

"You slept with her a few times. I don't know how many."

"I'm sorry." He had looked sorry too. "Do you know any more details?"

"Mum wasn't very good with details."

"I just don't recall a Coralie."

Zoe's eyes had been huge, unwavering, fixed on Kennford's face. "She never forgot you."

"I suppose she had you to remind her. I never knew about you."

"She told you. She wrote, twice, and she waited for you on the street when you were coming out of court once. She told you," Zoe repeated.

"None of that happened."

"Would you remember?" I had asked, curious. "You're not very interested in that kind of thing, it seems to me."

"I think I'd remember a child."

"You didn't care about Niele's baby."

"I never had to care about it. It was never going to become a reality. Niele wasn't maternal."

"Nor was my mother." It was the last thing Zoe had said, clamming up while we made the arrangements for her to be transported to the police station. She had stared at Philip Kennford for as long as she could see him, as if she was learning his face. It was the first time she had spoken to him, I reminded myself. And presumably not in the circumstances she had intended.

"It must have been hard for you to see what Philip Kennford's other daughters thought of as a normal life," I said now, hoping she would keep talking. "The things they took for granted."

"Life isn't fair." She said it with a tight smile.

"That wasn't a lesson Laura had learned, was it? She was born to privilege. Money. The best of everything."

Zoe shrugged.

"And Lydia had the same. But she didn't make the most of it, did she? She spoiled it for herself by not eating and hurting herself.

She invented problems for herself."

"Poor Lydia."

"Poor Lydia who according to you is trying to frame you for murdering Savannah." Derwent leaned his head on his folded arms. "You must know that's not going to work."

Zoe looked irritated. "You can believe what you like. I can't make you take my word over hers."

"Why don't you tell us your version?" I checked the time. "You know he's probably at the hospital with Lydia. Sitting by her bed. He's made his choice already."

"He doesn't know what you've done for him. The sacrifices you've made." Derwent shook his head. "I don't have any kids, but I'd love to think someone might care about me some day the way you care about Philip Kennford. You've earned his love. Lydia had every opportunity to impress him and she blew it, time and time again. And yet he's still there with her."

Zoe stared down at her hands, pressing the palms together. "I know what you're trying to do and it's not going to work."

"We're just trying to help. Trying to get you to tell us why you got involved with Philip Kennford's daughters in the first place." I sat back in my chair. *Keep her calm . . .*

"What came first? Meeting Vita or meeting Savannah?"

"Vita," she said reluctantly.

"From what I know of her, she could be quite hard work. Especially if she thought her family were threatened by something."

"By me. By my very existence." She blinked back tears. "I just wanted to say to her, I didn't ask to be born, you know? Same old story — punish me for existing."

"What did you want?"

"To meet him. To get to know him. To have a family." She shrugged. "It was stupid, but I thought he'd be proud of me. I'd gone from having nothing to getting my life on track. I'd worked fucking hard to get somewhere — to make something of myself. I thought he'd admire that. I wasn't asking for money, or much of his time, or anything more than a chance to talk to them."

"And Vita wasn't having it."

"She was a racist bitch," Zoe spat. "She didn't want anyone to know he'd slept with a black woman. She couldn't stand the idea of me being part of her world."

"Did she say that?"

"Not in so many words, I suppose." A single tear slid out of her right eye and she rubbed it away. "I could tell. She said I wouldn't fit in. The girls wouldn't know what to make of me, and nor would her husband."

"Did she offer you money?"

"Some."

"How much?"

"A thousand pounds." Zoe's mouth twisted.

"Not a lot, really. She must have thought I'd be cheap."

"She misjudged you," Derwent said. "Underestimated you. Made you angry."

"I wasn't angry. Not then. I was hurt."

"All right. You were hurt. But you weren't going to give up."

Zoe sighed. "I knew about Savannah. I knew she was his daughter, and a famous model and I wangled an invitation to a London Fashion Week party she was going to."

"Did you plan to start a relationship with her?"

"No." She looked shocked. "Not at all."

"You wanted to get to know her," I said. "Another of your sisters. You could have told her who you were, once you'd got to know her a bit."

She nodded. "That was the idea. I never even thought we could be real friends, but I thought there might be a connection there."

"That was an understatement, wasn't it?" Derwent ran a hand over his face. "I don't know how you could do it, you know. Sleep with her. Your own sister."

The blood rushed into her cheeks. "Don't judge me. It wasn't planned. She made all the running."

"She had a boyfriend," I said quietly. "She dumped him for you. You must have given her the idea her attentions were welcome."

"It wasn't cynical. It wasn't." She looked stubborn. "It happens. Genetic sexual attraction, it's called."

"Incest," Derwent said.

"It's not like that. It happens to people who didn't grow up with their families. They meet as adults and they're alike because they've got the same genes, and there's an emotional bond that feels like love whether they understand they're related or not. It can be mothers and their sons, or fathers and daughters, or siblings, or half siblings, like me and Sav."

"You've read up on it," I observed.

"I didn't know what was happening to me," she said quietly. "I couldn't understand the feelings I had for Savannah. I thought I was sick in the head. I saw a counselor and she explained it."

"Savannah described meeting Zoe as being like finding her soul mate. She said it was like looking in the mirror and seeing Zoe look back," I said to Derwent. "People do fall in love with people who are like them."

"If you say so. I still think it's twisted."

"Your mind is as broad as a cat hair, though." I rolled my eyes at Zoe, inviting her to laugh at Derwent, and managed to get a watery smile. I wanted her to like me. I wanted her to trust me. I wanted her to keep talking. "You know, I should have realized you and Savannah were related. I thought you looked alike the first time I met you.

Both tall. Both like your dad, features-wise. The same shape of hands and ears."

She nodded. "I think if Mum had been white we'd have looked really similar. As it was, Sav had to keep her weight down and I'm more athletic, so that made us look a bit different."

"I hadn't noticed a likeness," Derwent said.

"That's because you were too busy staring at Savannah." She said it without heat, but she wasn't wrong and Derwent didn't try to deny it.

"So you started a relationship," I said. "Was it your idea to keep it a secret?"

"I didn't know what to do. I knew it was burning my boats with my father — he wouldn't want to have anything to do with me if he knew that I knew I was sleeping with my sister. And I didn't want Vita to recognize me and tell the world. So I told Savannah to keep it quiet. We moved down here and stayed out of the public eye. It suited both of us."

"Must have been frustrating, though. You were closer to your father than ever, but you had no way to get to him. If he had been willing to accept Savannah's new girlfriend, I suppose you might have left it at that and formed a relationship with him on that basis. No one would need to know the truth about your identity, and it wasn't all bad, was it? She had money, and good looks, and she thought you were wonderful."

"We fell in love."

"But when you realized that by being her girlfriend you had effectively exiled yourself from your father, and permanently, Savannah was in trouble, wasn't she?"

Zoe stared at me, not answering.

"Once you'd decided to try to get in touch with the twins, you couldn't let her live. She'd have told your father about your relationship. And he was so hostile to the idea of her being with a woman, let alone her half sister, you must have known it would destroy any chance of being part of the family."

"I hadn't planned that it would work out that way. Being with Savannah was never part of the game."

"But there was a game to be played. And that's why you made contact with Laura. How did you find her? Facebook?" Zoe didn't reply but I saw her eyelids flicker; I'd guessed right. "You told her you were her long-lost sister, to see what she'd say, and she thought it was great. Her parents deserved to have their cozy world shaken up, didn't they? You got Laura to trust you and you promised to confront her mother and father, to tell them they were hypocrites and liars and generally do the job that Laura had been trying to do since she became a teenager."

"Have you read her e-mails?"

"We're working on it."

Zoe nodded and sipped from the water in front of her as if she didn't care either way, but I saw the tremor in her hand as she lowered the cup to the table.

"Seth Carberry was Laura's boyfriend. He told us she had messages on her phone from someone who wanted to meet her — someone he assumed was a love rival. It was you, though, wasn't it?"

When she didn't reply, Derwent rocked forward on his chair. "We've got Laura's phone now, you know. Lydia had it all along. We'll trace the messages. You probably used a pay-as-you-go one and I bet it's long gone, but we'll be able to see where you were when you sent them. I'd be surprised if you'd traveled far from home just to text Laura. And the nice thing about the farmhouse is that it's in the middle of nowhere. We'll trace it all back to your door."

She bit her lip.

"In fairness to you, you weren't expecting Laura to be in the house that night. She'd agreed she would be out. But you must have gone prepared to kill Vita. You had a knife." I flipped open the file and took out a photo of Vita's body that had been taken at the morgue. She was naked, her body washed and pale under the light of the flash. Her injuries looked — and were — horrendous. "You told me once you trained as a chef. You must be comfortable around knives, so that would explain your choice of weapon. And you knew you weren't going to get anywhere with Vita when she'd already rejected you once. Vita had to go, didn't she?"

Zoe swallowed. Her freckles were standing out on her skin as if they were painted on, and I wondered if she was going to be sick.

"The thing is, you couldn't kill her in front of Laura. And you couldn't let Laura identify you. And Vita was so obsessed with her children she wouldn't make room for you — just a little bit of room, you weren't asking for much. So killing Laura in front of her was the best revenge you could have had."

"I don't know what you mean." Her voice was husky.

"You cut Laura's throat, but it was a clean kill. Business. Stabbing Vita — that was a pleasure."

The photo sat on the table between us, turned toward Zoe. She hadn't looked at it.

"When Vita ran, she was trying to get to Lydia, to warn her. You didn't realize about the swimming pool in the back garden, and when you went exploring you found your father. Being in the same room as him must have been a shock. Seeing him. You had to knock him out because he might have fought you and won, but there was something half-hearted about it, something indecisive, and it made us think he was a viable suspect. And he thought he had seen Savannah in the mirror, so you did yourself another favor by letting him live."

"You're making this up."

"It's guesswork," I agreed. "But it hangs together. And there is physical evidence too. The bail that was recovered from the scene — it matches ones you use in your jewelry. The soil will match the farm when they test it, won't it? And the DNA on it brought us to you. You were there, Zoe. You were in the house, stepping in blood, walking around."

"It was Savannah."

"That's what you told Lydia so you could persuade her to kill her. But why would Savannah want to kill her stepmother and sister?"

"I can't imagine."

"No, nor can I." I leaned on my hand. "You know, Savannah told me she slept very heavily that night, for hours. If I wanted to buy myself some time, I might drug the person I lived with, like on the night I was going off to commit murder."

"You'll never prove that," Zoe said scathingly. "You'd have had to test her blood straightaway."

"I just don't think you're the sort of person to take a chance on being found out because your girlfriend decides to surprise you while you're supposedly working."

"You gave us an alibi for Savannah, but it was rubbish," Derwent said. "You just needed us to believe you'd been there all night, whatever about her. It suited you that the lack of an oil patch made us suspicious of Savannah."

"Not suspicious enough to stop Lydia from coming to live with you, though. You were determined to have Lydia here."

"Savannah wanted her," Zoe said.

"I think it was your idea for Savannah to ask us to let Lydia stay with you. That's why you came to the interview — that and to find out what we knew about the murders. Savannah was a very useful shield for you to hide behind. You got Lydia away from her aunt's house, where she was safe but unhappy. You gained her trust. You got ready to finish the game, and Seth Carberry turned up. He almost spoiled everything, didn't he? He drew our attention back to the farm, and Lydia, and what had happened before the murders, and we got the phone. And then I called this morning. You must have panicked."

"You're wrong."

"You were lucky with Lydia. She's the sort of person who would take orders from you. She'd admit she was guilty straightaway. You hadn't thought she'd try to kill herself, but that would have suited you even better. As it was, Lydia told us what had really happened and you had to go to plan B, where you pretended she was trying to frame you. You'd been really careful to clean up — both the room and yourself. I'm sure you've disposed of your clothes already. We'll find it hard to tie you to the crime scene, beyond the evidence that you shared the bed with Savannah. You have a good shot at convincing a jury Lydia was lying about what happened today. It would have been better without the forensic links to the Wimbledon crime scene, but a defense barrister would give it a go."

"If we believed you Lydia would go to prison, or a mental institution." Derwent was picking up where I left off, hitting her hard. "And you'd be in the clear."

"You could get to know Philip Kennford. The two of you could grieve together."

"You'd be the only one. His only daughter, even if he didn't know it. You could look after him."

"The two of you could play happy families. Happy ever after," I said softly.

"This is bullshit," Zoe said violently.

"It's convinced me." Derwent nodded to me. "Good work, Maeve."

"Good work," she repeated. "You've made up a load of old shite to get Lydia off the hook because you like her, because everyone cares about poor little Lydia and no one cares about me. It doesn't matter if I go to prison. No one will shed a tear. But we can't let Lydia suffer."

"I think it will bring her much closer to her father," I said to Derwent. "He really seemed moved, didn't he?"

"Like he'd realized what he'd almost lost," Derwent agreed. "But it didn't seem to bother him that we were taking you away in cuffs."

"He had a lot to take in. He'd only just heard I was his daughter."

"He didn't ask where you were going," I said gently.

"He's probably really worried about me now."

"He was more worried about whether Lydia had to be arrested too, the last time I saw him. And he hasn't been in touch since. No messages. He hasn't come to the station to see if you're all right. He's all wrapped up in his real daughter, Lydia, and he's forgotten about you again." I stared at her sadly. "That must sting."

Her lips were drawn back over her teeth. She looked quite insane at that moment, and her voice was unrecognizable when I listened back to the tape. "What more do I have to do to make him notice me? What else could I have done? Why wouldn't he pay attention to me? What more do I have to do?"

Zoe Prowse began to cry.

And just like that, it was all over.

Job done.

CHAPTER TWENTY-SIX

I knocked on the door of Godley's office and waited.

"Maeve. Come in." He looked pleased to see me. "How are things?"

"Derwent and I are just back from the Mags." It had been Zoe's first appearance in court, the day after being charged, and the Magistrates' Court hearings were always a formality to be run through.

"How did it go?"

"No surprises. The first hearing in the Crown Court is next month, and she's tucked up in prison even as we speak."

"That's a nice feeling, isn't it?"

"Yeah. I suppose so." I fiddled with a paper clip that had been lying on the edge of his desk, balanced at the point where a nudge would send it to the floor. "I think she's going to try for diminished responsibility because of her traumatic upbringing."

"That old chestnut."

"We heard a lot about foster care yesterday."

She had talked once she'd recovered from her fit of crying — talked and talked, needing very little prompting. Getting her new story straight, Derwent had said sourly, and I had agreed.

"Had a bad time, did she?"

"Abuse. Violence. Rape. The works." I shuddered. "I can sort of understand how you could come through that and feel you'd been hard done by if you saw your father making a fuss of your siblings when he couldn't even be bothered to remember your mother's name."

"Not everyone who makes it through the system turns into a criminal or a murderer."

"No. Some people stay on the straight and narrow, no matter how tempting the alternative is." I could see by the look on his face that he knew exactly what I meant.

"You did good work, Maeve. You're learning all the time."

"I hope so." I looked at him levelly. "I don't want to make any mistakes. And I don't want to risk my career over someone else's problems."

"No one wants that." He was spinning his pen on his blotter. "I am grateful to you for your help."

"I'm sure you are." I stood up. "But I'd rather not get involved. And you involved me in your business with Skinner."

"No."

"Yes," I insisted. "You thought I wouldn't work out what was going on, but I was already wondering why you wanted to keep Derwent out of the gang case. He assumed it was because of Una Burt, but it was because he'd have spotted you were up to no good."

"There's more to it than you know."

"I know you told Skinner to get rid of his new accomplices and five of them turned up dead a couple of days later. I know you deleted numbers from Niele's phone. I know you were trying to cover yourself and you used me."

"You're making assumptions."

"Maybe so. I can make some more if you like. I can assume you were acting as a go-between for Niele and Skinner, and that's why you needed to clear her phone. You got nervous when she turned up in the Kennford case, even though it was a coincidence that she had been involved with him. Maybe she got in touch with you and asked you to make us go away. Maybe she threatened to tell us she knew you. Whatever happened, you thought it was worth the risk to have them dealt with, and you told Skinner as much."

"Please believe me, it's not about money. It's not anything I could help." He sounded ragged, desperate almost. "I don't want you to think that of me."

"It doesn't matter what I think. It's none of my business."

"It does to me." He drew a square on his notepad and started to shade it. "What are you going to do?"

"Nothing."

"You would be within your rights to raise your suspicions with the DPS."

The Department of Professional Standards were the Met's watchdogs, the ones charged with stamping out corruption and bad behavior — police for the police, in a nutshell — and the thought of reporting Godley to them was not a pleasant one.

"I think you should decide the best course of action and talk to the DPS yourself, if that's what you think is best. I meant what I said, I don't want to be involved anymore." I hesitated. "I still want to work with you, if you're happy to keep me. I still think you're the best around at what you do." I just didn't hero-worship him anymore.

"Of course I'm happy to keep you." He looked pained. "Maeve . . ."

"I'd better go."

He was pale under his tan, his face suddenly gaunt. He looked his age for the first time since I'd known him. "What are you doing now?"

"What I always end up doing. Moving house."

"So soon?"

"It couldn't be soon enough. We're moving on. Cutting our losses. Finding somewhere new to make a home. But together."

"Best of luck."

"Thanks for your time, boss."

"You're welcome." He went over to the window and stared out, his shoulders hunched, a picture of misery. I felt sorry for him, but I felt more sorry that I'd been right.

The first thing I saw when I came out of Godley's office was Derwent with his feet up on my desk, picking his nose and wiping it on the underside of my chair.

"Do you mind?" I picked up his feet and lowered them to the floor.

"Ready to go?"

"No." I picked up my bag. "Yes. But I'm not happy about it."

"I'm helping," he protested.

"You're curious."

"That too." He jumped up. "Will she make me a cup of tea?"

"You won't be staying."

"Come on, Kerrigan. I'll be good."

"You don't know the meaning of the word."

"Being around your mother makes you tense, doesn't it?"

"How can you tell?" My shoulders were already up around my ears. "Come on, for God's sake. If you're driving me, drive. If you're gearing up for some sub-Freudian psychoanalysis bullshit, think again."

He grinned. "You know what I say. When you strike a nerve, that's where you should hit again. Now tell me about your childhood."

It was with some difficulty that I persuaded Derwent to leave once he had helped to carry in the last bag and he didn't go until he had eaten a vast slab of homemade barm brack, and half a loaf of homemade soda bread, and two homemade scones, and had accepted a homemade apple pie for his freezer. His eyes were everywhere, noticing every embarrassing old photograph or memento my mother insisted on keeping in plain view.

"I will never live this down," I hissed to Mum as she refilled the kettle. "Stop *talking* to him."

"But he seems like a nice lad. And he knew Dungannon, imagine. Your cousins live in Dungannon."

"He wouldn't have come across them. He only knew Dungannon because he patrolled it. He was in the army."

"I thought so. You can always tell a soldier's bearing." She carried the full teapot in as if she was carrying an offering; my mother, the Irish Nationalist par excellence, feeding a British soldier (retired). I found it baffling.

Eventually Derwent packed himself into his car and waved goodbye to me, and Rob, and my mother.

"I could be hurt. I thought I was her blue-eyed boy," Rob said out of the corner of his mouth.

"She's a sucker for a job title and she knows DI trumps DS."

"Would she prefer him for you? Really?"

"That would depend."

"On what?"

"On whether you still have prospects in the Met or whether DS is as high as you're going."

"Brutal."

"But clear. Achieve, and keep her on your side. Fail? Eff off."

"Maeve. Language." Mum passed by, her nose in the air.

"Imagine if I'd said 'fuck.' " But I whispered it.

Rob stretched. "Where are we sleeping?"

"*We* aren't sleeping anywhere. Let me show you." I took him upstairs, pointing in through my bedroom door. "This is my bed." I kept walking. "And this is yours." His room was all the way at the other end of the landing.

"Who sleeps here?" Rob asked, pointing to the bedroom between ours.

"Mum and Dad. And she has ears like a bat. And half the floorboards creak."

"Typical. No visits allowed, I take it?"

"What an immoral suggestion. I blush for you." I shook my head. "It's more than my life's worth to attempt it. She'd skin you and slaughter me."

"Oh, well. I'll miss you." He lay down on his bed with his hands under his head.

I sat on the edge of the mattress, pleating the coverlet in my fingers. "Can I ask you something?"

"Go for it."

"Why do you stick around when I keep turning your life upside down?"

"Because I love you."

"I remember you saying," I said, trying to keep my tone nonchalant.

"Well. That, basically."

From the bottom of the stairs, a voice floated up. "It's shepherd's pie for dinner. We'll eat at six."

Rob looked at his watch and groaned. "That's only half an hour. We've only just had tea and cake."

"You're a growing boy." I put my hand on his chest. "I haven't said it back."

"I noticed."

"And minded?"

"Nope." He grinned lazily. "You'll say it at the right time, when you're ready."

"Sure about that?"

"As sure as I am that you'll be in here paying me a visit after lights-out later, mother or no mother."

"Arrogant."

"Always." He tilted his head. "I do love you, you know."

"I know." I stood up and went to the door, then paused. "You know how half the floorboards on the landing creak?"

"Yeah."

"Well, half of them don't."

He started to smile, a smile that matched the one on my face. "Your point is?"

"I know which is which."

"It's no wonder I think you're wonderful."

"I am pretty great," I admitted. "You really are lucky to have me."

"This is what I keep telling you."

I'd moved back in with my parents, yet again. I was doomed to sleep in a separate bed from my boyfriend for the duration, which just made it all the more urgent for us to find somewhere else to live. My stalker was back, and angry. I was seriously worried about my career prospects.

I still wouldn't have changed a thing.

ABOUT THE AUTHOR

Jane Casey was born and raised in Dublin. A graduate of Oxford with a master's of philosophy from Trinity College, she lives in London, where she works as an editor. This is her fourth novel.

The employees of Thorndike Press hope you have enjoyed this Large Print book. All our Thorndike, Wheeler, and Kennebec Large Print titles are designed for easy reading, and all our books are made to last. Other Thorndike Press Large Print books are available at your library, through selected bookstores, or directly from us.

For information about titles, please call:
  (800) 223-1244

or visit our Web site at:
  http://gale.cengage.com/thorndike

To share your comments, please write:
  Publisher
  Thorndike Press
  10 Water St., Suite 310
  Waterville, ME 04901